BEWARE—
THEY'RE SENDING IN THE AUNTS!

"I found Brun and Sirkin," Cecelia informed Heris. "We're all safe." The following pause was eloquent; even over an audio-only link Cecelia could easily imagine Heris searching for a telling phrase.

"You're not *safe*," Heris said finally. "You're square in the midst of a military action. This system is under attack by the Benignity; their ships are in the outer system now, and I need that yacht and its weapons . . . not three useless civilians who were *supposed* to be down on the surface digging in."

Anger flared. "Civilians aren't *always* useless. If you can remember that far back, one of them saved your life on Sirialis."

"True. I'm sorry. It just . . . the question is, what now? I can't get you to safety onplanet . . . if that's safe."

"So quit worrying about it. Do you think I'm worried about dying?"

"I . . . you just got rejuved."

"So I did. It didn't eliminate my eighty-odd years of experience, or make me timid. If I die, I die . . . but in the meantime, why not let me help?"

A chuckle. She could imagine Heris's face. "Lady Cecelia, you are inimitable. Get yourself up to the bridge; someone will find you a place. I'll let the commander know you're coming."

"Good hunting, Heris," Cecelia said. She felt a pleasant tingle of anticipation.

ELIZABETH MOON
WINNING COLORS

BAEN

WINNING COLORS

Copyright © 1995 by Elizabeth Moon

A Baen Books Original

Baen Publishing Enterprises
P.O. Box 1403
Riverdale, NY 10471

ISBN: 0-671-87677-5

Cover art by David Mattingly

First printing, August 1995

Distributed by Simon & Schuster
1230 Avenue of the Americas
New York, NY 10020

Printed in the United States of America

Dedication

This one's for Mary Morell, who introduced me to science fiction in the ninth grade, and then insisted the wonderful (!) stories I wrote in high school were lousy. (She was right.) And for Ellen McLean, who refused to be my friend in the first grade, only to be a better friend later than anyone could ask. And for all the horses, from the horse next door to the little bay mare who presently has her nose in my feed bucket, who enriched my life with everything from (a few) broken bones to the feel of going at speed across country.

✧ Chapter One

Twoville, Sublevel 3, on the planet Patchcock, in the Familias Regnant

Conspirators come in two basic flavors, Ottala thought. The bland vanillas, usually wealthy, who meet in comfortably appointed boardrooms or dining rooms, scenting the air with expensive perfumes, liqueurs, and good food. The more complex chocolates, usually impoverished, who meet in dingy back rooms of failing businesses or scruffy warehouses, where the musty air stinks of dangerous chemicals and unwashed bodies. The vanillas, when they cursed, did so with a sense of risk taken, as if the expletives might pop in their mouths like flimsy balloons and sting their tongues. The chocolates cursed without noticing, the familiar phrases embedded in their speech like nuts in candy, lending texture. The vanillas claimed to loathe violence, resorting to it with reluctance, under the lash of stern morality. The chocolates embraced violence and its tools as familiar and comforting rituals. No wonder, since when the vanillas chose violence, they employed chocolates for it.

Ottala much preferred luxury herself; she considered that a long leisurely soak in perfumed water was the only civilized way to begin the day. She too felt the little shock of surprise when she heard the expletives come out of her own mouth with no immediate punishment. Her skin preferred the sensuous touch of silk; her taste buds rejoiced during elaborate dinners created by talented cooks. But she could not confine her sensuality to the bland end of the spectrum. Vanilla was not enough. In her own mind, she considered her taste for chocolate an expression of unusual sensitivity.

What she tasted at the moment was the sour underbite of processed protein extruded into pseudo-sausages nested in pickled neo-cabbage. She sat on a hard bench, elbow-to-elbow with the rest of Cell 571, munching the supper that preceded the evening's entertainment. Or so she called it; she was aware that her fellow conspirators considered it more important than anything else they did with their lives.

Her friends would not have recognized her. Her normally bronze skin had the pallor associated with the underbellies of cave-dwelling amphibians; her dark eyes were masked with blue contact lenses, which also gave her red-rimmed lids, the better to fit in with the locals. She wore the same dark, ill-cut coveralls and had the same fingertip calluses as the others; she had held a real job on the assembly line—with faked papers, which wasn't that unusual—for the past two months.

It was all a great adventure. She knew things about her family's company that she had never imagined; she would have incomparable tales to tell when she went back topside. Meanwhile, she could eat sour pseudo-sausage, drink cheap wine, use words her parents didn't even know, and find out for herself if the reputation of Finnvardian men was deserved. So far she wasn't sure. . . . Enar had ranked only average on her personal scale, but if Sikar would only look at her . . .

She finished her supper, as the others finished theirs. Odd, how the same custom held at tables high and low—everyone tried to finish at the same time. Across the room, Sikar stood, and silence spread around him. He was the contact from higher up, the man whose respect they all wanted. Even in the baggy dark clothing, he had presence. Ottala couldn't analyze it; she only knew that she felt his intensity as a pressure under her rib cage. She wanted that pressure elsewhere.

As usual, Sikar began speaking without preamble. "We, the young, serve the old," he said. "And the old can live forever now, and they expect us to serve forever. We will grow old and die, but they will not. Is this right?"

"NO!" the room vibrated to that angry response.

"No. It was bad before, when the old rich first set their hands against the gate of death, but a hundred fifty years is not forever. That is why our fathers and grandfathers submitted; they hoped to afford that process for themselves, and it was limited. But now—"

"They live forever," a woman's voice interrupted from behind Sikar. "And we work forever, and our children—"

"Forever." Sikar made the word obscene. "Their children will live forever too; our children will DIE forever." An angry rumble, indistinct, shook the room again. "But there is a chance. Now, while the government is shaken by the king's departure." They had discussed this, night after night, what it meant that the king had resigned. Would it help the cause, or hurt it? Rejuvenants littered both sides of the political scene; almost everyone rich and powerful enough to be a force in the government had been rejuvenated at least once. Apparently the hierarchy had decided: it was a good thing, and now they could act. Ottala pulled her mind back from its contemplation of the aesthetics of Sikar's striking coloring—those fire-blue eyes, the pale skin, the black hair with the silver streak—to listen to his speech.

"But before we act," Sikar said, "we must purify ourselves. We must not allow any taint of the Rejuvenant to corrupt our purpose. Are you sure—*sure*—that none among you harbors a sneaking sympathy with those old leeches?"

"No!" growled the crowd, Ottala among them. Her parents weren't old leeches; they were merely idiot fools. When she had to say these things, she always thought of people she didn't like.

"Are you *sure*?" Sikar asked again. "Because I am not. In other cells, we've found those pretending to be with us, and secretly spying on us for the Rejuvenants—"

"Secretly spying" was exactly the kind of rhetoric that Ottala enjoyed. She curled her tongue around it in her mouth, not realizing until Sikar stood in front of her table what he was leading up to. The tool in his hands, though, clenched the breath in her chest. She recognized it; everyone did, who had ever changed fertility implants. It would locate even unexpired implants, and could be used to remove them. But—no one here had implants. She did.

"Put out your arms, brothers and sisters," Sikar said. "For this is how we found the traitors before—they had implants."

She couldn't move. She wanted to jump and run; she wanted to scream, "You don't understand," and she knew that wouldn't work. Sikar smiled directly into her eyes, just as she'd wanted since she'd first seen him, and the people on either side of her forced her arms out flat on the table. The tool hummed; even though she knew she could not really feel anything, she was sure her implant itched. The skin above it fluoresced, a brilliant blue.

"Perhaps she was a manager's favorite—" said Irena, down the table. She had liked Irena.

"Perhaps she's an owner's daughter," said Sikar. "We'll see." He pressed the tool to her arm; she had no doubt of the next sensation. No anesthetic spray, no numbing at all—the tool's logic ignored her pain and sliced into her arm, retrieving the implant, and pressed the incision closed with biological glue. Her arm throbbed; she was surprised that she hadn't screamed, but she was still too scared. Those holding her tightened their grips. Sikar held up the implant. "You see? And this tool will tell us whose it is."

She had forgotten that, if she'd ever known. Implants carried the original prescription codes; that had something to do with proving malpractice. Sikar touched the implant to a flat plate on the tool's side, and laughed harshly.

"As we suspected. This is no Finnvardian assembly worker. This is a Rejuvenant, child of Rejuvenants, our mortal enemies. This is one who would enslave our children to her pleasure, for all time."

"No—" She got that out in a miserable squeak before Sikar slapped her. It hurt more than she had imagined.

"I hate you!" That was Irena, who had come up behind her and now clouted her head. "You lied to me—you were never my friend—"

"I was—" But no one was listening. Shouts, growls, curses, those hands tight on her arms, and Sikar staring at her with utter contempt.

"Rich girl," he said. "This is not a game."

Before she died, she wanted to revise her earlier opinion, and say that some conspirators tasted of neither vanilla nor chocolate, but of blood. But she could not speak, and no one would have listened if she had.

Castle Rock: the former king's offices

Midafternoon already, and they'd hardly made a dent in the day's work. Lord Thornbuckle leaned back in his chair and stretched. "I could be angry with Kemtre about this, too: because he was an idiot, I have to sit here doing his work."

"You wanted the job." Kevil Mahoney, formerly an independent and successful attorney, had agreed to help his friend in the political crisis left by the king's resignation. "Am I supposed to sympathize? I could be in court, showing off—"

"As if you'd miss it. No, we're doing the right thing, if we can pull it off."

"If? The eminent Lord Thornbuckle has doubts?"

"Your old friend Bunny has doubts. Nothing makes a rabbit nervous like the predator who pretends not to see him. We haven't heard anything from the Benignity; by now, I expected at least one raid."

"Don't stare at that fox too long, my friend: there are wolves in the world too."

"As if I didn't—" He paused, as his deskcomp chimed, and flicked the controls. "Yes?"

"Sorry, milord. An urgent signal from Patchcock. Shall I transfer, or bring it in?"

"Bring it," Bunny said. "And the coffee, if it's ready." He would have that, at least, no matter what the trouble was.

One of the senior clerks—Poisson, he thought the name was—came in with a cube, followed by two juniors with a trolley. Poisson waited until they had left before handing over the cube.

"It's partly encrypted, milord, but I read the part that wasn't. It's the same region on Patchcock where the troubles were before, and apparently a Family heir has gone missing."

Family. Bunny could hear the capital letter that elevated mere genetic relationship to political power—not just a family, but *a* Family, one of the Chairholding Families.

"Ottala Morreline, the second oldest but designated heir of—"

"Oscar and Vitille Morreline, Vorey sept of the Consellines. Right." One of his own daughter's schoolmates. He remembered Bubbles—no, she was calling herself Brun now—talking about her. Brun hadn't liked her; he remembered that much, though he didn't remember why. The Consellines . . . that extended family had over a dozen Chairs in Council; the Vorey sept, though the minor branch, had five. The Morrelines held four of them. "Kidnapped?" he asked.

"Ah . . . no. It seems she had disguised herself as a Finnvardian and infiltrated a workers' group—"

"A Morreline?" The Morrelines had, for the past two centuries at least, chosen to emphasize their darker ancestry. And the video of Ottala that came up when he inserted the cube showed a dark-skinned, dark-haired young woman. A beauty, Bunny noted, remembering now that he had seen her at some social function a year or so before. She had matured, as Brun had, showing more bone structure. But how had this girl imitated a pale, blue-eyed Finnvardian?

"The family located the skinsculptor. She bought a four hundred day depigmentation package, bleached her hair, wore blue contact lenses—"

"Why didn't she get an eye job while she was at it? What if she'd dropped a lens?" That was Kevil Mahoney, cross-examining as usual.

Poisson shrugged. "I couldn't say, sir. When she didn't turn up for her younger brother's *seegrin*, the family popped her emergency cache, and found her last report. She included a vid of herself after she adopted the disguise, and said she planned to involve herself in a workers' organization to see what it felt like."

"Ummm." Bunny watched the cube readout. Ottala's disguised self looked very different, he had to admit—if not quite Finnvardian, at least nothing like the Morreline heir. He wondered if she'd had a temporary bone job too—her face seemed to have changed shape as well as color. According to the readout, she had had no trouble buying false IDs, and getting a job in an assembly factory on Patchcock. But she'd dropped out of sight, without notice to her work supervisor or anyone else, some forty days before her family came looking.

"The problem is, milord, that it's Patchcock. . . ." Bunny looked up.

"Yes?"

"I don't know if you knew . . . *all* about Patchcock."

"Not really. It was a nasty situation, is all I know, and someone in the Regular Space Service messed up in a major way."

"I think perhaps you need to read the background briefs."

That was far more assertive than Poisson's usual approach, and Bunny stared.

"Very well. If you'll—"

"Here they are." A stack of cubes it would take him hours to wade through, all marked with the security code that meant they were encrypted and could be read only with all the room's security systems engaged. Bunny glanced at Kevil, and sighed.

"Don't remind me that I volunteered for this job. I could cheerfully strangle his late majesty." Poisson, he noticed, had the look he had always imagined concealed satisfaction at landing responsibility on someone else.

The Patchcock affair, when they finally got it straight late that night, explained a lot of things . . . many more than were explicated in the cubes, revealing as those were.

"That had to be the stupidest thing Ottala could have done," Kevil said, summing up the latest chapter in the story. "Going undercover in a workers' organization would be risky enough right here in Castle Rock—but on Patchcock! Didn't she know any history?"

"We didn't," Bunny pointed out. "If she thought it was just a military blunder, if she didn't know how her family came to gain control of the investments there—"

"She must be dead, you know," Kevil said. "If she were alive, she'd have refreshed her emergency cache."

"Captive? Held for ransom?"

"No. My criminal experience tells me she's dead. They found her out somehow, stripped her of any information they could pry out, and killed her. Eventually the Morrelines will figure that out too, and then—then we'll have real trouble."

"Yes." Bunny thought about the Morrelines: he knew them in the casual way that all the Chairholders knew each other, but they were not really in his set. They didn't hunt, for one thing. But he had dealt with them more than once in business, and in the Council—they were tough, aggressive, and very sore losers. That this could be a self-description he recognized, but that didn't make the prospect of angry Morrelines any more appealing.

"If we send Fleet back in there, it will only make things worse—"

"If she's dead already—" If she was dead already, why bother? But he had to know what Ottala Morreline had found, even if he couldn't bring her back. He sighed, and stretched his back out. The whole situation he'd inherited—*jumped into*, he reminded himself—felt dangerously mushy. Too many things he didn't know, past and present. Too many ways to make mistakes even if he did know everything. And the image of his daughter Brun intruded—Brun had already involved herself in wild adventures, working her way across Familias space as an ordinary spacer. If Brun heard about this, she would insist on going herself to find out about Ottala. Where could he park her safely?

"At least," Kevil said, stretching in turn, "it'll be a change from this stupid bickering about rejuvenation. Those poor bastards in the mines and factories on Patchcock have more substantial concerns."

Bunny nodded, but his thoughts kept running to Brun. Finally he thought of the one thing he might be able to do; in the morning he would place a call to Heris Serrano.

"I must thank you again, for whatever you said to my daughter," Lord Thornbuckle said. He didn't look much like Bunny in his dark formal suit, in the paneled office. He didn't intend to. "She was, I'm sure, about to do something rash. What she told me afterwards was that she'd planned to run away and join the Regular Space Service anonymously—but I expect it was worse than that."

"No—or at least, that's what she told me." Heris Serrano had been aboard the yacht, supervising the last of its refitting. Her office aboard looked nothing like his; on the wall behind her were only a military-grade chronometer and the framed certificates of her rating. She had a new uniform, not the loud purple Lady Cecelia had once used, but the same competent expression, the same intelligent dark eyes. She paused a moment, but he said nothing. "She outgrew herself in a hurry, on the island."

"I know. And she seems to have inherited ancestral temptations to adventure. You know how she got to Rockhouse Major from Rotterdam?" Heris nodded. "Even the unpleasantness she got into didn't dissuade her. And now she wants to use some of her inheritance to finance a small expedition—a small ship, rather, on which she intends to wander around looking for excitement. Responsibly, she assures me. Nothing wild of the sort she did in her youth." Lord Thornbuckle snorted. "Youth. The girl's barely old enough to consider a Seat in Council, and you'd think she was fifty."

"She did come through safely, sir," Heris ventured. He could tell she was being tactful, wondering if he would understand how important that was. Some people, following every rule of prudence, could hardly travel to the corner and back without breaking an ankle. Brun's luck had to be more than luck, perhaps that unconscious intuitive grasp of situation and character which was more valuable than all the education in the world. But not only the military recognized and used that quality.

"Yes, I know, and I know it means she's inherited—no doubt from the same ancestors—the ability to survive adventure. But I'm not sure I can survive her acquisition of the necessary experience. Not without knowing there's someone with more expertise and more . . . er . . . maturity to help her out of the tight spots she's so determined to get into. Even Thornbuckles have limits to their luck; get Cece to tell you about my great-uncle Virgil."

Heris focussed on the comment that might refer to her. "You were thinking that I might know someone with the right skills to accompany her?"

"I thought you might be that person. Not that alone—" He waved off the protest she opened her mouth to make. "I know, you'll be traveling with Cece. But she said she wanted to do more than make the various horse events, and I wondered if you'd let Brun come along. As an employee, or passenger, or whatever you like. I would of course pay her passage. . . ."

"No, sir," Heris said quickly. "Don't pay her passage; if she's set on adventuring, she might as well earn her own way. She's already proved she could. I assume she has an allowance; let her use that, if she wants."

"Right. Fine. Then you'll take her?"

"I . . . don't know." She had liked Brun well enough, he knew, but clearly she was thinking about the difficulties inherent in mixing a girl like Brun into a crew already facing difficult adjustments. She wouldn't want trouble; she had had enough already. "I'm not sure I'm the right person," she said finally.

Lord Thornbuckle leaned over and touched his desk; he gestured to the row of red lights that came on, and waited for her look of recognition. "Heris, let me tell you something that must remain a secret. A young woman Brun knows—knew—a schoolmate, went off on an adventure, joined a workers' organization over on Patchcock, and got herself killed when she was discovered. Brun doesn't know; we've managed to suppress it. But the girl's family is furious with me. They want me to send the R.S.S. to Patchcock again—"

Heris stared. "That's—not wise, sir." She could easily imagine the carnage; it had been bad enough the first time.

"No, I understand that. I've seen the classified briefings now. The thing is, Brun's the ideal hostage to use against me. Either side might try it. She's too old to send home—she wouldn't stay, and I can't tell her about Ottala. . . . I know she won't be safe, really safe, anywhere, but you might be able to keep her safer than anyone else."

Heris nodded. "All right. I'm willing to have her aboard, if she's willing to come. I'm not about to shanghai her."

"Oh, she's willing. Apparently she made some friends in your crew, didn't she?"

Heris looked puzzled, then her face cleared. "Sirkin, I suppose. At least they went around together for a while, but that was our plan, a way that Brun could pass information about Lady Cecelia to me indirectly. I wouldn't have called it a friendship—Sirkin's lover had just died—but it's something. All right . . . I suppose Brun could have considered it friendship," she said. "I'll list her as unskilled crew, and let them teach her some things, if that's acceptable."

"Good." Lord Thornbuckle smiled at her. "On top of everything else, I'll be glad to have her out of pocket while the political situation is so uncertain."

The country house of Kemtre Lord Altmann, formerly king of the Familias Regnant

"I don't see why you can't understand," Kemtre said, trying not to breathe heavily. "They're your sons as much as mine."

"They're no one's *sons*," his wife said. Although she seemed to lean on the end of the table, elbows on either side of a tray of fancifully carved fruits, that was illusion, a matter of expensive communications equipment synchronizing her image from past breakfasts with her voice from very far away. "Certainly not mine, and not yours either, if you only knew it. They're *clones*, constructs, human only in genome. You were never a father to them; I was never a mother."

He pressed his fingers to his temples, a gesture that had been effective in Council meetings. It had not worked with her for years, and it did not work now, not least because she did not have the visual display on her console turned on . . . he kept hoping to see the telltale red light turn green. He wanted to meet her eyes—her *real* eyes, not those of the construct, and convince her with his sincerity.

"They're all we've got," he said. "They could be our sons, if you'd only—"

"They're grown," she said. "They're not little boys. They're bad copies of Gerel . . . was he the only one you cared about?"

Of course not, he wanted to say. He had said it before, just as they had had this argument before in the weeks since his resignation. At first face-to-face, then down the length of that long dining table, then by the various communications devices required by the increasingly great physical distances between them as she removed herself from his demands.

"Please," he said.

"No." The faint hollow noise of a live connection ended; the construct sat immobile, waiting for his finger to extinguish its imitation of life. He put his thumb down and cursed. She wanted him to give it up, deal with the loss of his sons, get on with whatever life was left him. He couldn't do that, not until he had at least tried to get the clones to cooperate. They were the only sons he had now; he couldn't just give them up.

The Boardroom of the Benignity of the Compassionate Hand

"I don't see any reason to butcher the cash cow," said the Senior Accountant. "Breed her, and we'll have more calves to send to market."

"She's a shy breeder," muttered one of the diplomatic subordinates, who should have kept quiet. It was his last mistake.

When the meeting resumed, several people walked across the damp patch on the carpet as if nothing had happened. It wasn't unusual, and it didn't really reflect on Sasimo, whose protégé had been unwise. Every senior man present had discovered that a first appearance in the Boardroom could unsettle a youngster previously considered promising.

"Still, he had a point," the Chairman said. No one asked who, or what point; those who couldn't figure it out didn't belong there. "The Familias walks like a tart, and talks like a tart, but carries a hatpin in her purse." The hatpin being, as they all knew, the Regular Space Service's unbought fraction, which they knew down to the level of cook's assistants.

After a respectful silence, the Senior Accountant coughed politely and began again. "It is a short hatpin, not long enough to reach the heart of a strong man. A little risk, a prick perhaps, and—better a marriage than a disgrace, eh?"

"Quite so," said the Chairman. "If it is only a flesh wound. Perhaps our admiral would review the situation?"

But indeed, the situation looked good. Not only were so many Fleet personnel on the Compassionate Hand payroll, as it were, but they had been placed into critical positions. Given a good start, with new forward bases increasing the number of jump points they could reach undetected, the Regular Space Service should be immobilized by uncertainty as well as internal problems.

"We start here," the admiral said, pointing out the system on the display. "They're used to neglect from the R.S.S.; Aethar's World raiders took out their stationary defenses last year, and they've been issued nothing to replace them. It's an agricultural world, thinly populated; we'll lose no essential industries if we scorch it lightly."

"Resistance?"

"Negligible. Farmers with hand weapons, even if they scatter and survive the scorch—we can ignore them."

"Principal crop?"

The admiral chuckled, a daring act in that room. "Horses, if you can believe it."

"Horses?"

"And not workhorses. They export sperm and embryos of fancy horses."

The Chairman leaned back, thumbs in his waistcoat pockets. "Show horses . . . I like horses. If they survive the scorch, I'd like a souvenir, Peri." Which meant they had better survive the scorch . . . it was punishment, mild enough, for laughing in the Boardroom.

"Of course," the admiral said, making the best of it.

"My granddaughter, you know," the Chairman said to the others, as if he needed to explain. "She likes pretty horses." He turned back to the admiral. "Be sure to bring one 'Lotta would like. White feet, a long tail, that kind of thing."

"Of course," the admiral said again, tallying in his mind the extra time it would take to scorch selectively, so that the Chairman's granddaughter could have a pretty horse for a souvenir. It shouldn't be too bad, even if their agent betrayed them. He would add another couple of ships to the advance strike force, which would give them the margin for a careful scorch.

"Why not this system?" asked one of the others, pointing. "It has the same advantages."

"Nearly," the admiral admitted. One did not directly contradict one of the Board, not if one wanted to leave the room with breath intact. "But it connects directly to only one jump point, with only three mapped vectors. As well, it's near enough to Guerni space that the Guernesi might take notice. Our chosen target connects directly to two jump points, offering a total of eight mapped vectors, most of them into high-vector points. And of course, its other border is the unstable one with Aethar's World, from which the raiders have come."

"Quite so," said the Chairman. "We have already approved your target, Admiral." That was dismissal, and the admiral saluted, bowed, and left.

When he reached his office, he found that he had been given a final command . . . interesting that the Chairman had not wanted to say that in front of the others. The

Chairman would be honored if the admiral would allow the Chairman's great-nephew, now in command of a heavy cruiser, to be part of this expedition. Unmentioned was the young man's record; neither needed to mention it. The young man had risen more by influence than ability, everyone was sure . . . and yet he wasn't stupid or cowardly. Dangerous to both friends and enemies, the admiral thought. Convinced of his ability; convinced he had not been given a chance because of the relationship . . . that his real successes had been overlooked, along with his mistakes. Perhaps it was true.

The admiral considered. Was this the Chairman's way of letting the younger man hang himself, or his way of sabotaging the admiral, whose own grandson might otherwise have been chosen? He couldn't take both—he could afford only one less experienced captain. Of course he must take the Chairman's choice, but he need not make it easy. He would assume—he would document that assumption—that the Chairman wished to test his kinsman, wished him to prove himself.

He grinned suddenly. Let him be the one to find and bring home a pretty horse for Carlotta.

✧ Chapter Two

Uncertain, Heris thought as she closed her end of the secured comlink, was a mild term for the swiftly unraveling tangle of political yarn that had so recently seemed to be a stable web of interlocking interests. All her life—for many hundreds of Standard years—the Familias Regnant had had its Grand Council, and commerce had passed between its worlds and stations as if no other way existed. She knew of course that other ways did—that Familias space was surrounded by other ways of doing things, from the cold efficiency of the Compassionate Hand to the berserker brigandry of Aethar's World. But aside from those whose business it was to keep the borders safe and enforce the laws, most of the Familias worlds and the people on them had behaved as if nothing but fashion would ever change.

And now it had. With the king's resignation, with Lorenza's flight, the founding families looked at each other with far more suspicion than trust. If the king had poisoned his own sons—or if Lorenza had done it for him—if she had attacked the powerful de Marktos family through Cecelia—then who else might have been her target? Her allies? Those who had used her services through the decades tried to cover their tracks, and others worked to uncover them.

What bothered Heris the most, in all this, was the civilians' innocent assumption that "the Fleet" would never let anything bad happen. She had heard it from one and then another—no need to worry about Centrum Rose; the Fleet will see that they stay in the alliance. No need to worry about the Benignity attacking; the Fleet will protect us. Yet she knew—and Bunny should have known—that the Fleet itself was suspect. Lorenza hadn't been the only rat in the woodpile. Admiral Lepescu and whoever cooperated with him . . .

But she could not solve everything, not all at once. She had other work to do before Cecelia came aboard the yacht.

Her personal stack had a message from Arash Livadhi. Now what, she thought. It had been a long enough day already, and she had hoped Petris would get back in time for some extended dalliance. She called Arash.

"How are things going?" he asked brightly, as if she had initiated the contact.

"Fine with me . . . and you?"

"Oh, very well, very well. It's been an interesting few weeks, of course."

So it had, with rumors of entire squadrons of Fleet in mutiny. With one cryptic message from her grandmother, and a very uncryptic message from the cousin who had always hated her.

"Yes," said Heris, drumming her fingers on her desk. "I had a message that you called," she said finally, when the silence had gone on too long.

"Oh. Yes. That. I just . . . I just wondered if you'd like to have dinner sometime. Tonight maybe? There's a new band at Salieri's."

"Sorry," Heris said, not really sorry at all. "There's ship's business to deal with." Certainly the captain's relationship with the First Engineer was ship's business.

"Oh . . . ah . . . another time? Maybe tomorrow?"

Tone and expression both suggested urgency. What was he up to? Heris opened her mouth to tell him to come clean, then remembered the doubtful security of their link. "I . . . should be free then. Why not? What time?"

"Whatever's best for you . . . maybe mid-second shift?" An odd way of giving a time, for either a civilian or a Fleet officer. Heris nodded at the screen, and hoped she could figure out later what kind of signal he was giving her.

"Mid-second indeed. Meet you there?"

"Why not at the shuttle bay concourse? You shouldn't have to dash halfway across the Station by yourself." Odder and odder. Arash had never minded having his dates use up their own resources. Heris entered the time and place in her desktop calendar and grinned at him.

"It's in my beeper. See you tomorrow."

"Yes . . ." He seemed poised to say more, then sighed and said "Tomorrow, then" instead.

"There's a little problem," Arash Livadhi said. He had been waiting when Heris reached the shuttle docks concourse; he wore his uniform with his old dash and attracted more than one admiring glance. Heris wanted to tell the oglers how futile their efforts were, but knew better. Now he walked beside her as courteously as a knight of legend escorting his lady. It made Heris nervous. "Nothing major, just a bit . . . awkward."

"And awkward problem solving is a civilian specialty? Come on, Arash, you have some of the best finaglers in Fleet on your ship."

"It's not that kind of thing, exactly."

"Well what, exactly?"

"It's something you'd be much better at . . . you know you have a talent—"

She knew when she was being conned. "Arash, I'm hungry, and you've promised me a good meal . . . at least wait until I'm softened up before you start trying to put your hooks in."

"Me?" But that wide-eyed look was meant to be seen through. He grinned at her; it no longer put shivers down her spine, but she had to admit the charm. "Greedy lady . . . and yes, I did agree to feed you. Salieri's is still acceptable?"

"Entirely." Expensive and good food, a combination rarer

than one might suppose. And whatever Arash thought he was getting from her, it would not include anything more than a dinner companion . . . she wondered if he had any idea of her present situation with Petris. Probably not, and better that he live in blissful ignorance.

Salieri's midway through the second shift had a line out to the concourse, but Arash led her past it. "We have reservations," he said. Sure enough, at his murmur the gold-robed flunky at the door let them pass. Heris felt her spirits lift in the scarlet and gold flamboyance of the main foyer, with the sweet strains of the lilting waltz played by a live orchestra in the main dining room. Whatever Arash wanted, this would be fun.

Two hours later, after a lavish meal, he got down to it. "You do owe me a favor, you know," he said.

"True. That and a fat bank account will get you a dinner at Salieri's."

"Hardhearted woman. I suppose even civilian life couldn't soften your head." He didn't sound surprised.

"I'll take that as a compliment, Captain Livadhi. What's your problem?"

"You mentioned my illustrious crew. My . . . er . . . talented finaglers."

Heris felt her eyebrows going up. "So I did. So they are. What else?"

Livadhi leaned closer. "There's someone I need to get off my ship. Quickly. I was hoping—"

"What's he done?" Heris asked.

"It's not so much that," Livadhi said. "More like something he didn't do, and he needs to spend some time out of contact with Fleet Command."

"Or he'll drag you down with him?" Heris suggested, from a long knowledge of Livadhi. She was not surprised to see the sudden sheen of perspiration on his brow, even in the dim light of their alcove.

"Something like that," he admitted. "It's related to the

matter you and I were involved in, but I really don't want to discuss it in detail."

"But you want me to spirit him away for a while, without knowing diddly about him?"

"Not . . . in detail." He gave her a look that had melted several generations of female officers; she simply smiled and shook her head.

"Not without enough detail to keep my head off the block. How do I know that you aren't being pressured to slip an assassin aboard to get rid of Lady Cecelia? Or me?"

"It's nothing like that," he said. In the pause that followed, she could almost see him trying on various stories to see which she might accept. As he opened his mouth, she spoke first.

"The truth, Livadhi." To her satisfaction, he flushed and looked away.

"The truth is . . . it's not like that; it's not an assassin. It's my best communications tech, who's heard what he shouldn't have, and needs a new berth. He's a danger to himself, and to the ship, where he is."

"On my ship," said Heris. "With my friends . . . are you sure no one's put you up to this to land trouble on me?" This time his flush was anger.

"On my honor," he said stiffly. Which meant that much was true; the Livadhis, crooked as corkscrews in some ways, had never directly given the lie while on their honor. She knew that; he knew she knew that.

"All right," she said. "But if he gives me the wrong kind of trouble, he's dead."

"Agreed. Thank you." From the real gratitude in his voice she knew the size of the trouble his man was in. Then what he'd said earlier caught up with her. Communications tech . . . best? That had to be . . .

"Koutsoudas?" she asked, trying to keep her face still. He just grinned at her, and nodded. "Good heavens, Arash, what is the problem?"

"I can't say. Please. He may tell you, if he wants—I don't think it's a good idea, but the situation may change, and I trust his judgment. Just take care of him. If you can."

"Oh, I think we're capable of that. When do you want him back?"

"Not until things settle down. I'll get word to you, shall I?" Then, before she could say anything, he added, "Well, that's all taken care of . . . would you like to dance?" The orchestra had just launched into another waltz. Heris thought about it. Arash had been a good dancing partner in the old days, but in the meantime she'd danced with Petris at the Hunt Ball.

"No, thank you," she said, smiling at the memory. "I had better get back to work. When shall I expect . . . er . . . your package?"

Arash winced. "Efficient as ever. Or have I lost the touch?"

"I don't think so," Heris said. "You just put the touch on me, if you think about it that way, and I do. But my owner isn't thrilled with the number of ex-military crew we have now, and she's going to have kittens—or, in her case, colts—when she finds out about this. I have some preliminary groundwork to do."

"Ah. Well, then, allow me to escort you at least to the concourse."

"Better not." Heris had been thinking. "This was a very public meeting, and I can understand your reasoning. But why let whomever is interested think you might have convinced me of whatever it is you were after?"

"I thought an open quarrel would be too obvious," Livadhi said. "If we were simply courteous—"

Heris grinned at him. "I am always courteous, Commander, as you well know. Even in a quarrel."

"Ouch. Well, then, since I can't persuade you—" He rose politely, with a certain stiffness, and she nodded. An observant waiter came to her chair, and although they walked out together, they were clearly not a couple.

In the anteroom, she said, "I'm sorry, Commander, but things have changed. It's not just being a civilian . . . I have other . . . commitments. I'm sure you'll understand. It's not wise, at times like these . . ."

"But—"

"I can find my way, Commander. Best wishes, of course." Watching eyes could not have missed that cool, formal, and very unfriendly parting.

The newly refurbished yacht *Sweet Delight* lay one final shift cycle in the Spacenhance docks, as Heris Serrano inspected every millimeter of its interior. Forest green carpet soft underfoot . . . she tried not to think of its origin, nor that of the crisp green/blue/white paisley-patterned wall covering in the dining salon. At least the ship didn't *smell* like cockroaches anymore. The galley and pantries, left in gleaming white and steel by Lady Cecelia's command, had no odd odors. In the recreation section, everything looked perfect: the swimming pool with its new screen programs . . . Heris flicked through them to be sure the night sky had been removed. Lady Cecelia didn't want any sudden darkness to remind her of the months of blindness she'd endured. The massage lounger had its new upholstery; the riding simulator had a new saddle and a whole set of new training cubes, including the two most recent Wherrin Trials recordings.

The crew quarters, while not quite as luxurious as the owner's section, had more amenities than crews could expect anywhere else. Heris's own suite reflected a new comfort with her civilian status; she had installed a larger bed, a comfortable upholstered chair, and chosen more colorful appointments. Down in the holds, she checked for any leftover debris from the renovation. She had already found a narrow triangle of wall covering and two odd-shaped bits of carpet.

"Heris!" That had to be Lady Cecelia herself. Heris

grinned and backed out of the number three hold. Cecelia would want to see for herself that every single cockroach cage had been removed.

"Coming," she called. But the quick footsteps didn't wait for her to get back to the owner's territory. Cecelia's rejuvenation had left her with more energy than she could contain; here she was, striding down the corridor at top speed.

"Did you know about this?" Cecelia waved a hardcopy at her; she had bright patches of color on her cheeks and her short red hair seemed to be standing on end.

"What?" Heris couldn't tell what it was, although the blue cover suggested a legal document. Whatever it was had made the owner furious, and Lady Cecelia furious made most people move quickly out of her way. Heris, secure in her status as captain and friend, stood her ground.

"This court decision." The blue-gray eyes bored into hers.

"Court decision? On your competency?" Of course the court would restore full competency to Cecelia; it would be crazy to pretend that this individual was anything but competent.

"No—on the yacht."

For a moment Heris was completely confused. "No—what about it?"

Cecelia bit off each word as if it tasted foul. "The court has decided against the petition of my family to set aside that portion of my will which left you the yacht. Therefore, the yacht belongs to you." Heris stared at her.

"That's . . . ridiculous. You're not comatose; you're competent. That reverses all the bequests—you told me that—"

"Yes . . . it does. It would have, that is, if that idiot Berenice and her fatheaded husband hadn't quarreled with my will and involved the court directly in that instance. Because the matter came under separate adjudication—

don't you love this verbiage?—the court's decision is final, and not reversed by my regaining competence. And the court decided in your favor, thank goodness, or otherwise it would've been Berenice's. It's your yacht."

"That's the stupidest thing I ever heard of." Heris raked a hand through her dark hair. She had not even thought about the bequest or the court's decision since Cecelia had been declared competent. "I can't—what am I supposed to do with a yacht—or you, without one?" She came to the obvious decision. "I won't take it. I'll give it back to you."

"You can't give it back. Not unless you're willing to pay the penalty tax—it's within the legal limit for a bequest, but not a gift."

"Oh . . . dear." She had no idea what that tax would be, but her own affairs were somewhat confused at the moment, thanks to the abrupt changes in the government. She didn't know if she had enough to pay the tax or not.

"It's not so bad," Cecelia said. Now that she'd blown her stack, she had calmed back down, and leaned comfortably against the bulkhead. "I suppose you'll run it as a charter, and I suppose you'll let me charter it."

"Of course, if that's what it takes, but—what a mess." Still, she felt a little jolt of delight at the base of her brain. Her own ship. Not even a Fleet captain owned a ship outright. She fought back unseemly glee with little struggle when she realized the other implications of ownership. Docking fees. Repairs. Crew salaries. All her responsibility now.

Cecelia's expression suggested she had already thought of these things and was enjoying Heris's realization. "Don't worry," she said, after a moment in which Heris was trying to remember the last time the crew had been paid, and how much was due. "I'll pay generously. I'll supply my own staff, cook, gardener. . . ."

"Er . . . just so." And there were bound to be legalities

associated with running a charter, too. Heris had no idea what kind of contractual agreement owners needed with those who hired them. What permits she might need from whatever government bureaus were still grinding out the daily quota of paperwork.

"Kevil Mahoney," Cecelia said, with a wicked grin, as if she really could read minds. "He can tell you where to go for legal advice, if you don't want the same person who argued your case for the bequest."

"Thanks," Heris said. "It would have been so much easier—"

"I know. And I don't blame you for fighting back when my family acted like such idiots. It's not your fault, though I was mad enough to grind you into powder too. Just when I'd gotten her back to a decent look, instead of that lavender and teal abomination. Berenice will pay for this." She glowered. "I've filed suit against them, and I intend to make up every fee they cost me."

"I'm sorry," Heris said again, this time for the trouble between Cecelia and her family. "It's just that I thought if I had the ship, I could help you."

"And you did. And don't lie to me, Heris Serrano. I may be rejuvenated, but I didn't lose eighty years of experience. One second after you were appalled, you were delighted. You've always wanted your own ship."

Heris felt herself flushing. "Yes. I did. And I tried to fight it down."

"Don't." Her employer—still her employer, even though the terms would be different now—gave her a wicked grin. She had found Lady Cecelia de Marktos to be formidable enough as an unrejuvenant . . . clearly, that had been the mellow form. "Nobody knows what the government's going to do, now; Bunny seems to be running things with the same bureaucrats—except for poor Piercy. I don't myself think it was Piercy's fault, but everyone's afraid he was in it with Lorenza."

Surprising tolerance from someone who had been Lorenza's helpless victim, for someone planning to sue her family . . . family that had, however ineptly, tried to protect her interests. This was no time to argue, though. Heris looked away, and spotted another bit of scrap from the renovation.

"I don't hate Piercy," Cecelia said. "I don't even hate Lorenza, although if she stood in front of me I would kill her without a second thought, as I would kill anyone that vile. I do hate to think of her running around loose somewhere."

"I don't think she is," Heris said, glad to change the subject from the yacht. "A few of my crew—" Oblo, Meharry, Petris, and Sirkin, though she didn't intend to mention names where anyone might have left a sensor. "—had a bone to pick with the individual who gave the orders that led to Yrilan's death. The . . . er . . . remaining biological contaminants were salted into her quarters. In the ensuing investigation, it was discovered that she had a very efficient lethal chamber built into her counseling booths—"

"I didn't hear about this—"

"Station Security didn't allow it to be newsed. They thought it would cause panic, and they were probably right. Just the discovery of that many illicit biologicals could panic Station dwellers. Anyway, they also found items the lady could not account for, which apparently match with jewels known to the insurance databases as Lorenza's."

"And you found out because—?"

"I found out because I have the best damn datatech in or out of Fleet, milady, and that's all I'll say here and now."

"Ah. Then suppose you come to my suite—if you still consider it my suite—and we'll decide where your ship is headed, and whether I want to tag along."

Cecelia's furniture had been reinstalled, and they settled into her study. Cecelia looked around nodding. "I do like the effect of that striped brocade with the green carpet," she said finally. "Although I'm not sure about the solarium yet."

"I thought you were going to restock it with miniatures," Heris said.

"I was—but I keep thinking that I could go back to riding—" She meant competition, Heris understood, just as she herself would have meant "the Fleet" if she'd said "return to space."

"I like the ferns," Heris said, watching the miniature waterfall in the solarium; she preferred falling water to any sort of fake wildlife.

"One thing I will insist on, if you're to have me for a passenger, is a crew no more than half ex-military." Cecelia leaned back in her chair, with an expression that made it clear she meant what she'd said.

Heris bit back the first thing she could have said, took a deep breath, and asked, "Why?" Skoterin, probably, but surely Cecelia ought to realize that Skoterin had been more than balanced by that crew of civilian layabouts and incompetents she'd had before. This didn't surprise her, but she'd hoped Cecelia would be less blunt about it.

"Not just Skoterin," Cecelia said, as if she'd read Heris's mind. "I know you can argue that my original civilian crew was just as full of lethal mistakes. Of course not all ex-military are crooks or traitors, nor are all civilians honest and hardworking. But what bothered me was your inability to see past the distinction yourself. You had had superb performance from that girl Sirkin all through the earlier trouble; you had been so happy with her. And you were willing to believe that she went bad when even I, isolated as I then was, could spot sabotage."

Heris nodded slowly. "You're right; I did make a mistake—"

"Not *a* mistake, my dear: a whole series of them. You misjudged her not once but repeatedly. That's my point.

You have a pattern, understandable but indefensible, of believing that the military is more loyal, more honorable, than most civilians. You even told me that Sirkin was 'as good as Fleet' more than once. And your inability to see past that pattern nearly got us all killed." She grinned, as if to take the sting out of it. It didn't work. "I'm doing this for your own good, Heris—as one of my early riding instructors used to say when making us post without stirrups by the hour. You have chosen to live in a civilian world; you must learn how to trust those of us who can be trusted, and recognize deceit even in former shipmates."

"And you think the way to do this is to hire civilians." That came out flat, with an edge of sarcasm. She didn't like that "chose to live in a civilian world." If there'd been any other way . . .

"I think the way to do it is to admit what went wrong and work on correcting it. Isn't that what you would do if an admiral pointed out a characteristic error?"

Heris wanted to say that Cecelia was no admiral, but she had to admit the logic of Cecelia's argument. She had mistaken the cause of Sirkin's problem; she had not even looked for sabotage, not seriously. "I don't want to fire any of our present crew," she began, crossing mental fingers as she told herself that Koutsoudas, not yet aboard, still counted as "present crew."

"No need. Just hire civilians for a while. Like Brun." Heris almost glared. Had she set this up with Bunny, as much to force a civilian crew on Heris as to help Brun? Cecelia smiled at her. "I'm sure you can find others, perhaps not as good as Sirkin, but good enough. Think of recruits, if you must, rather than the trained people you had. Surely there were good and bad recruits."

"Oh yes." Heris chuckled in spite of herself, remembering a miserable tour as an officer in charge of basic training. She had hated it, and she hadn't been very good at it. Of course there had been bad recruits—Zitler, for instance, who had come into the Fleet convinced that he could make a fortune manufacturing illicit drugs aboard ship. Or the skinny girl from some mining colony who had gotten all the way through medical screening without anyone noticing she had parasites.

"There you are, then," Cecelia said. "It's just a matter of overcoming your biases."

"Yes, ma'am," said Heris, with enough emphasis that Cecelia should know when to quit. She hoped. It was unnerving to see all those years of experience in the bright eyes across from her. She began to understand why Cecelia had been reluctant to have rejuv treatments before.

"I don't see why it makes the least difference," Ronnie said, into Raffaele's dark hair. "I didn't go along with my family; you know that. I'm the one who got Aunt Cecelia out of that nursing home. Why should your parents take it out on me?"

"They're not taking it out on you," Raffaele said. "They're pulling their investments out of your parents' operations, and they don't think that's a good time to discuss marriage settlements."

"But will they come around later?" He didn't want later; he wanted right this minute. But with Raffaele, pressure wouldn't work.

"I don't know, Ron. They're seriously annoyed with your parents, and they don't see your prospects improving any time soon. They think you'll be under a cloud politically—"

"Hang politics!" Ronnie said. "I have enough; you have enough; we could go off somewhere and just live—"

"But you have a Seat in Council now—"

"As long as that lasts," Ronnie said under his breath. While daily life seemed to be unchanged, the political structure had shifted back and forth dramatically in the past few weeks.

"They don't want trouble between us because you're voting your family stock, and your Seat, and they're voting against you. And don't say it wouldn't cause trouble, because look how angry you are now."

Unfair. He wasn't angry because they'd voted against him in Council; he was angry because they didn't want Raffa to marry him because he might be upset later if they voted against him. That was too complicated; he fell back on the obvious. "I love you, Raffa," Ronnie said.

"I know. And I love you. But we are both wound up in our families and their rivalries, and I can't see either of us pulling something dramatic and stagey." With her hair in a neat braid behind, and a tailored soft tunic over the blouse and slacks, she looked entirely too rational.

"Brun did," Ronnie said. He could imagine himself running off with Raffa . . . he thought . . . but then again he wanted to have his usual credit line, his usual communications links. . . .

"Brun is a law unto herself," Raffa said. "Even as a fluffhead, she was, and now—we aren't like Brun, either of us. We were born to be respectable."

"We did have one adventure," Ronnie said, almost wistfully. He didn't like thinking of most of their time on the island, but finding Raffa and being comforted . . . *that* he could live with.

"And we'll have each other later, or we won't, and we'll survive either way. Be reasonable, Ronnie: you got your aunt out of the building, but it was Brun who thought up the hot air balloon. Neither of us could have been that crazy."

True, but he wanted to be crazy enough to live with Raffa the rest of his life, starting this moment. He started to say he'd wait for her forever, but he knew she might not. And he might not either, really. "I don't want to leave you," he said fiercely. "I don't want to lose you."

"Nor I." For a moment she clung to him with all the

passion he desired, then she pushed herself away and was gone, her light footsteps barely audible on the carpeted hall.

"Damn!" Ronnie wanted to kick the wall, as he would have before the island. He really hated it when she was right. Then he thought who might be able to help. If only he could make her understand how important it was.

Cecelia looked up from her desk to see her nephew standing in the doorway. "Ronnie—I'm delighted to see you. I'd hoped you'd come before we left."

He didn't answer, just gave her a sickly smile.

"What? I already thanked you for getting me out of that place—and if you don't think I mean it, just take a look at your stock accounts."

"It's not that, Aunt Cecelia—and I wish you hadn't done that, really."

The boy didn't want money? That was new; that was unbelievable. She looked more closely. The wavy chestnut hair looked dull; he had lavender smudges under his hazel eyes, and a skin tone that would have made her think "hangover" if he hadn't been so obviously sober and miserable.

"What, then?" she asked, without much sympathy. She'd fixed him once; he was supposed to stay fixed; she couldn't provide deadly danger every time he needed pepping up.

He slouched into her room as if his backbone were overcooked asparagus, and slumped into one of her favorite leather chairs. "It's Raffaele," he said.

Of course. Young love. She'd been glad he wasn't still involved with Brun, since that young lady was in no mood for romance, but she'd approved of Raffa. Moreover, she'd thought the girl had more sense than to jilt Ronnie. He wasn't bad, and Raffa was just the sort of girl to keep him in line.

"What did you do?" she asked. It must have been

something he did; perhaps he'd had another fling with theatrical personalities.

"Nothing," Ronnie said. His tone held all the bitterness of disillusioned youth. "But my parents did plenty, and her parents told her to break it off."

"Because of—"

"Because of you." He shook his head to stop the protest already halfway out her mouth. "I know—you've got every right to be angry with them—" She had more than a right, she had very viable suits in progress. "But the thing is, Raffa's parents don't want the families involved right now."

"I'm not angry with *you*," Cecelia said. "They shouldn't blame you if I don't."

"She says they do."

"And you're sure it's not that she's found someone else?"

"Yes. I'm sure. She said . . . she said she loves me. But— she won't cross them."

"Idiot." Cecelia opened her mouth to say more, and then realized the other implications, the ones Ronnie hadn't yet seen. Her suits imperiled the holdings of Ronnie's parents—his guarantees of future income—and might imperil any financial settlements made in the course of betrothal, exchange of assets being the normal complement to marriage. And Raffa, the levelheaded Raffa that she considered strong-minded enough to keep Ronnie in check, would not tangle her family in any such trouble either. It all made perfectly good sense, and Cecelia found herself doubly angry that the good sense could not be denied.

"She's not, really," Ronnie said. "She's just loyal, that's all." Greedy, thought Cecelia. Carrying prudence to a ridiculous degree—the girl had money enough of her own; she was of age, she could make her own decisions. As Ronnie went on making Raffa's arguments, as a true lover would, Cecelia found herself countering them, in the courtroom behind her eyes. Ronnie's final declaration caught her off balance; she'd been imagining herself as the judge, looming over Raffa as incompetent counsel. "So," he was saying, "I thought if I could do something to prove myself . . . and maybe you would let me come along. . . ."

"No!" Cecelia said, even before her mind caught up with what he had actually said. Then more mildly: "No, Ronnie, though you are my favorite nephew and I owe you my life. This is not the place for you."

"But I thought if Raffa's parents knew I was with you, it would change their minds—"

"No, dear." The *dear* slipped out and shocked her. She never called any of her relatives *dear*; had the Guernesi done something to her mind during rejuvenation? The memory of those lawsuits reassured her: she hadn't softened. Not really. "It won't work because you'd still be seen as a boy with a patron. You need them to see you as a man, an independent man with his own property, his own assets." He looked at her as if he had never thought of that. Perhaps he hadn't. He was, after all, some sixty years younger.

"Then what can I do?" he asked. Cecelia wished for a moment she had been a more conventional aunt. He would not have consulted a more conventional aunt; he would have found someone outrageous, someone who had never been married, or wanted to be, and she could have clucked from the sidelines. She felt like clucking now. Grow up, she wanted to say. Just do something, she wanted to say. But there he was, born charming and even more so with this new and genuine worry upon him. She wanted to smack him, and she wanted to cuddle him, and neither would do any good.

When in doubt, call in the experts. "You might go talk to Captain Serrano," she said. She didn't expect him to agree, but his face lit up.

"Great idea," he said. "Thanks—I will." And he bounced up, suddenly vibrant and eager again. She watched him stride out, with the spring in his step and the sparkle in his eye, and wondered at herself. Rejuvenation was supposed to rejuvenate everything; she had herself made the usual jokes about those of her friends who suddenly acquired young companions. But Ronnie did nothing for her, and she knew it wasn't because he was her nephew. She just didn't feel like it.

"Not that I was ever ridden by that torment much," she muttered, as she ran over the shopping lists on her deskcomp again. She had been too busy, and too aware of the power such a passion would have over her schedule, if nothing else.

Heris saw not the spoiled brat she'd once despised but the handsome, bright young man who had become what she thought of as officer material. "Aunt Cecelia said you might be able to help me," he said.

"If I can, of course," she said, wondering if this was Cecelia's obscure vengeance for Arash's favor.

"It's about Raffaele," he began, and outlined his problem.

Heris recognized the implications as Cecelia had, but unlike her saw no reason not to tell Ronnie about them. She still thought of him as "young officer material," which put her in the teaching role. She led him through the relevant financial bits, and watched his dismay growing.

"But—but Raffa isn't that greedy," Ronnie said at the end.

"I don't know that I'd call it greedy." Heris steepled her hands. "But you're both Registered Embryos, remember? Smart, educated, trained from birth to consider the welfare of the family as a whole. I don't think it has anything to do with wanting more things than you could give her; I think it has to do with conflicting loyalties."

"But if she loves—"

Hormones, thought Heris. "Ronnie, think: would you have married that opera singer?"

She could see "What opera singer?" forming on his forehead, until his memory caught up. "Oh—her. No, of course not. She was nothing like Raffa."

"Why not? You were besotted with her at the time, I gather. Loved her, didn't you?"

"Oh, but that was—it was different. She'd never have done for a wife."

"And why? Was she personally disgusting in some way? Lacking manners? Stupid?"

"No . . . no, it wasn't anything like that. But—she wouldn't have been a good match . . . for the family. . . ." Finally, he was catching on.

"Whether you really loved her or not—you can imagine someone you did really love, that wouldn't be right because it would hurt the family. Right?"

"Right." Now he sounded glum and sulky.

"Ronnie, this isn't an age in which anyone gives much for romantic love. If it happens that you fall for someone of the right class, at the right time, then fine. But most people don't. Petris and I served on the same ships and never allowed ourselves to notice that we loved each other: it would have been bad for the ship. Grown-ups have values outside their own skins."

"And you're saying I'm not a grown-up yet?"

"No. You are—you've grown a lot in the time I've known you, and frankly you've surprised me. But this last lingering bit of adolescence is hanging on, right where it usually does."

He gave a rueful laugh. "I suppose you think I'm silly."

"Not at all. Nor do I think your situation with Raffa will last forever, especially not if you set out to change it."

"How?"

Heris was tempted to say, You're a grown-up; you figure it out, but she had never seen Ronnie as a master of strategy. Brave, yes. Bright enough in limited circumstances, yes. But not a strategist. "Two things. You either need to change the overall situation so that your parents' quarrel with your aunt no longer imperils your inheritance and your parents' political and economic allies, or you need to change your situation in relation to your parents. Ideally, both."

"Both! That's impossible." Ronnie began to stride around the small office, exactly like a nervous colt in a small box stall. Heris expected him to bump his nose into a wall and rear at any moment. "I can't make Aunt Cecelia change her mind; nobody's *ever* made Aunt Cecelia change her mind. And I can't make my parents be someone else. Not unless I repudiate them and change my name or something. How will disinheriting myself help convince Raffa?"

Just as she'd thought, no strategic sense at all. "Ronnie, look at what you've told me you want. You want to marry Raffa, but I assume this means you also want a long, happy, profitable life and you don't want to harm either her family or yours."

"Well . . . yes."

"You also want the best for your Aunt Cecelia, don't you?"

"Yes, but I can't do all that at once."

"Not if you don't look at it. You know my background; well, a consistent mistake I've seen commanders make is defining the mission too narrowly. Did you ever study the Patchcock Incursion in the Royals?"

"Uh . . . yes. It got kind of complicated. . . ."

"It was complicated from the beginning, and an oversimplified mission statement made it worse. Military commanders like to see neat, tidy problems . . . well, I suppose everyone does. The dog is howling: shoot the dog. The contract colonists are rioting: shoot the colonists. The contract corporation reneged on its contract to provide medical services: shoot the corporation CEO. The Council told Fleet Command they wanted no more rioting on Patchcock. They *didn't* tell Fleet Command that a two-month interruption in shipments of ore would bankrupt

Gleisco Metals, with cascading effects through its parent corporation into half a dozen Chairholders. They didn't tell Fleet that a two-month interruption in ore shipments would mean cutting off the food supply not only to Patchcock but also to Derrien and Slidell. They didn't tell Fleet that Gleisco Metals had refused to provide services agreed on, and then altered the contracts to reflect that. So Fleet went in to sit on some malcontents, and ended up responsible for the deaths by starvation of several thousand people, the deaths by direct action of thousands more, and—if you care to look at it that way, which the then king did, the suicides of eighteen members of high-ranking families, including five of the six Chairholders most closely connected to Gleisco. The other one was murdered by his own sister."

"I didn't know all that," Ronnie said. He looked very uncomfortable. "They told us it as an example of a commander losing control of troops in a battlefield situation."

"Hushed it up," Heris said. "I thought they might have done it, even after the trials at the time." She grinned, without humor. Her family had been involved in that one, too. "My point is that if you want something to happen, you must specify that something with great care and as much completeness as possible. Then, and only then, can you devise a strategy to accomplish what you really want— all of it—and not some little bit that turns out to be meaningless when everything else falls apart."

He didn't answer at once, a good sign. When the silence had become uncomfortably long (for Heris had chores to do) she tried to divert him to another topic.

"What are they going to do with the Royal Aerospace Service, now that the king has abdicated?" she asked.

"Hmm? Oh . . . I don't know. I'm not—I was told I was not required to report, which really meant they didn't want me. That's one reason I thought I'd do better with Aunt Cecelia, staying out of trouble."

That didn't sound good. The rich young men who made up the officer corps of the Royal Aerospace Service might cause trouble in a lump while on duty, but would surely cause trouble if suddenly turned out, idle and feckless, into the streets of the capital. Someone wasn't thinking clearly, not for the first time.

"That's good for you," she said crisply. "You are free to do something else, something that will convince Raffaele's parents that you are a mature, responsible, independent young man. Ideal husband material."

"But what?" he asked. What indeed? Then it came to her.

"Go talk to Lord Thornbuckle," she said. "I'm sure he can find a mission for you. Don't tell him about Raffa—just ask what you can do to help."

When he'd left, she put her head in her hands for a moment. She wanted to get away before someone else had a crisis for her to deal with. If only Cecelia would quit fuming about her family, they could leave for somewhere—anywhere—and be out of reach of everyone's family problems.

✧ Chapter Three

"What is it, another little problem?" Cecelia was scowling into a viewscreen. "Bad hocks," she muttered, before Heris said anything.

"Where?"

"This excuse for a hunter stallion—look at it!" Heris came around the end of the desk and looked at the shiny black horse on the viewscreen. It trotted back and forth, looking sound enough to her. Cecelia froze the picture, and pointed. "Here—this is the problem. Those hocks should be much bigger—"

"It's the feet that always look too small to me," Heris said. No use trying to get Cecelia's mind shifted to the crew until she'd worked her way through the horse business. "Why are the hocks too small?"

The answer took longer than Heris had expected, because Cecelia insisted on bringing up video files on a dozen or so horses, as well as an animated skeletal model. And when Heris dismissed it, at the end, with "I see—just like ankles, as you said—ankles sprain more often than knees or hips," Cecelia threw up her hands.

"You are ridiculous! It's the same joint, but it's not the same stresses. I give up. What was it you came about?"

Heris had hoped to soothe Cecelia, but since that hadn't worked, she tried for a bland, quick summary of her reasons for wanting a quick departure. "Arash Livadhi, who saved our skins as you recall, has asked me a favor; he wants me to transport one of his crew, who needs to be . . . er . . . out of touch for a while."

"Why?"

"He didn't say, exactly. It has something to do with the mess we were all in, and something the person overheard. He's a communications tech."

Cecelia scowled at her. "Is this a way of sneaking in another ex-military crewmember?"

"No." Heris didn't explain further; it wouldn't help.

"I don't like it," Cecelia said.

"Arash's medical teams saved Sirkin's life," Heris pointed out. "And yours. We owe him, both of us. He got us back here, past potential enemies, in time for the Grand Council."

Cecelia's expression didn't soften. Inspiration hit. "You don't have to consider this person a crewmember, if you wish. Since it's technically my ship, consider him my guest."

"You—!" Cecelia's face went white, then red in patches, then she burst into laughter. "You *stinker*! I almost wish I'd known you when you were all military. You must have been—"

"Difficult," Heris said demurely. "Difficult is what they called it."

"Brilliant on occasion, I've no doubt. If you were my age, I'd thrash you, but considering—I'll just put some interesting problems in your next riding lesson."

It was Heris's turn to stare. "You can't mean that—you think I'm going on with riding?"

"It would exercise something besides your ingenuity," Cecelia said. "And you never know when physical fitness will come in handy. You and Petris, for instance—"

Heris felt the heat in her face. She and Petris indeed. She struggled for something, anything, to say, and blurted it out before her internal editor had a chance at it. "We have other ways of maintaining physical fitness. . . ."

"I'll bet you have," Cecelia said, and smirked. Heris glared.

"Other than *that*." But she had to chuckle; she had done

it to herself. "I don't know why I thought you'd mellow after rejuvenation."

"I don't either," Cecelia said. "And I didn't. Mellow was never my virtue. But we've had even honors on this one; I won't say any more about that man's crewman, whatever he is."

"Thank you," Heris said. "May I ask why you were looking at that stallion whose hocks you didn't like?"

"Rotterdam," Cecelia said. "Those people did a lot for me; they're old friends, of course, but . . . I want to do something for them. Of course I can share the bloodstock I have there—but I've been doing that for years. What I'm looking for is some outcross lines that will broaden their base, that they couldn't possibly afford on their own."

"Is that all the planet does, raise horses?"

"Almost." Cecelia touched her screen, and brought up a graphic montage. "It's a combination of climate, terrain, and the accidents of discovery and development. Horses are useful in a variety of ways in colonization: self-replicating farm power, for instance. Pack animals in difficult terrain. Personal transportation. But they're displaced if industrialization provides alternatives. So usually you have poor planets with horses—workhorses—and room to breed but no recreational bloodstock. Then you have industrial planets with a demand for recreational horses, but those horses squeezed into less and less land. Rotterdam was settled as an agricultural world, complete with draft horses. But its climate is far better suited to permanent pasturage than grain farming. Someone apparently obtained some bloodstock semen and began breeding recreational horses. . . ."

"How did they market them?" Heris asked. Horses, she remembered, shipped badly aboard spacecraft.

"With great difficulty. But somehow they got a colt nominated for a famous stakes race, and got him there alive and capable of running. More than capable. That was Buccinator—it was one of his descendants that I rode at Bunny's. I bought into his syndicate as a young woman—"

This made no sense to Heris, but the general plan did. "So you're going to find additional semen or whatever for your friends on Rotterdam. . . ."

"Right. I've got a dozen cubes to review—ordered them from bloodstock agents—and then we'll go take a look. So far most of Rotterdam's produce is semen and embryos. It's too far off the main shipways, and very rarely can a group get together to haul mature animals someplace. When I first set up my stud there, I'd planned to work on that . . . but things changed. . . . Anyway, if they have the quality, the money will follow. And provide transport."

"Have you decided where to go first?"

"Wherrin Horse Trials. I've missed two of them—no reason to miss this time. I should pick up more ideas there, breeders not yet with bloodstock agents, that sort of thing."

"I'd like to leave as soon as Koutsoudas is aboard," Heris said. "He's not the only problem—I know you talked to your nephew—and you know that Lord Thornbuckle has asked me to take on Brun."

"I'm willing," Cecelia said. "The lawyers can handle my suit just as well without me. Better perhaps. They say I interfere. . . . I didn't know it would affect Ronnie and Raffaele."

Heris thought of saying what she thought about the lawsuit, but considering her own family relations she decided against it. She was hardly one to preach reconciliation with relatives.

Brigdis Sirkin hated being back on Rockhouse Major. Over on Minor, she had been able to pretend that they weren't in the same system where Amalie died. Here, every shop window, every bar, every slideway and bounce tube reminded her of Amalie. Here she had died, and into this station's recycler her physical cells had gone, to become the elements of something else . . . even this meal. She shoved it away, disgusted suddenly by the rich aroma of stew and bread.

"What's wrong, hon?" Meharry leaned across the crowded table. "Got a bug or something?"

She didn't want to answer. Meharry and the others had been so careful of her since the shooting, so sorry they'd believed a former shipmate and condemned her. They had organized that revenge on Amalie's counselor in hopes of cheering her up; they had enjoyed it a lot more than she did. She was tired of it, tired of having to be kind in return. What she really wanted, she thought, was to be somewhere else, with someone else, someone who wasn't part of the original mess. A face flickered in her memory a moment, the rich girl who had been Lady Cecelia's friend and pretended to be hers as well.

She scolded herself into a deeper depression. Probably she wouldn't see Brun again. Why would a girl like that want to be around her? It was silly to keep looking at the presents Brun had bought, as part of their pretense of courtship.

"Hi, there!" Sirkin looked up, startled. Meharry scowled, and Oblo grunted. Brun in the flesh, clearly excited and happy, in a soft blue silk jumpsuit that must have cost a fortune and brought out the blue of her eyes. Brun squeezed in next to Sirkin, with a chair she snagged from the next table. "We have to talk," she said.

Sirkin felt her face going hot. There was no need for this; that other game was long over.

"And how did you find our humble eatery?" Meharry asked, with a bite to her voice.

Brun smiled, smugly. "I asked where the *Sweet Delight*'s crew usually ate. Since I'm now in the crew—"

"You're not!" Oblo stared at her wide-eyed, then shook his head. "I wonder what the captain's thinking of."

"My father," Brun said, and reached for a hunk of bread.

"He thinks I need seasoning before I'm turned loose on an unsuspecting universe, and he thinks Captain Serrano is the right person to provide it. And you, of course." She grinned around the table. The others all stared at Brun, and Sirkin hoped no one would notice how fast her own pulse was beating. She didn't know yet if she was happy about this or not, but she couldn't be indifferent.

"I hope you're ready to go aboard and start working," Meharry said. "Captain's told us to be ready to ship out at a half-shift notice."

"Fine with me," Brun said. "I've already put my stuff aboard."

"It's called 'duffel,' " Meharry said.

"Duffel." Brun smiled at her, blue eyes wide. "Are you really angry, or just pretending? Because I'm not really an idiot—I actually have some ship time."

"On what?" Oblo said quickly, hushing Meharry. Brun's grin widened.

"On a shit-shoveler," she said. "Caring for critters."

Oblo snorted. "That's not ship time . . . that's just work. Proves you can work, but—we'll see about you and the ship."

Sirkin watched the others watching Brun, and wondered. She felt less alone now, less the one being watched. And Brun still gave her a good feeling, as if they might really be friends.

Esteban Koutsoudas arrived at the shipline in a plain gray jumpsuit with a *Sweet Delight* arm patch already on it. That didn't surprise Heris. What did surprise her, a little, was that he'd made it here alive if Livadhi was right about how much danger he was in. Surely it would have been easier to take him on the station than on her ship. If not—she didn't want to think about that.

"Esteban Koutsoudas, sir," the man said. He carried an ordinary kitbag slung over his shoulder, and a couple of handcarries. She would have passed him in the concourse without a second thought—just another traveler, neither rich nor broke, with an intelligent but unremarkable face. Until he smiled, when his eyebrows went up in peaks.

"Glad to have you aboard," Heris said, though she still wasn't sure of that. "Mr. Petris will show you your quarters," Heris said, by way of taking up a moment of time.

"Commander Livadhi sent you this," Koutsoudas said, handing over a datacube. "And he said I was to assist you any way you liked."

Right. Turn a superb longscan communications tech loose on her equipment . . . could she trust this man? Yet she lusted for his expertise; she had suspected for years that Koutsoudas was the secret of Livadhi's success in more than one engagement.

"When you've stowed your gear," she said, "Mr. Petris will introduce you to the crew. Then we'll see." She left a message for Lady Cecelia, who had gone off to talk to her lawyers again. Heris could believe they wanted her out of touch, at least for a while. She had been angry with her own family—she still was, if she thought about it—but it had never occurred to her to sue them. The rich are different, she reminded herself, as she notified Traffic Control that she would need a place in the outbound stack.

Maneuvering in and out of Rockhouse Major had begun to seem routine; Heris found her mind wandering even as she recited the checklist and spoke to the captain of the tug that snared the yacht's bustle. They were leaving behind the problems of the new government, Cecelia's family, Ronnie's romantic problems, and whatever had been chasing Koutsoudas. Ahead—ahead, the frivolity of horse trials, though she dared not call it frivolity to Lady Cecelia.

Her ownership of the yacht had begun to sink past surface knowledge . . . having to pay the docking fees and the tug fees out of her own account certainly made an impression. True, Lady Cecelia had prepaid the charter fee to the Wherrin Trials, but still—Heris hoped she understood how to calculate what to charge.

They had an uneventful system transit, and the jump transition went smoothly as well. Day by day, Sirkin seemed brighter; she and Brun hung around together when they were off-shift. Heris hoped this would last, at least through the voyage. She didn't want to have to deal with young passions unrequited, not with her own relationship going through a difficult period. She and Petris still found it awkward to get together aboard the ship; the intellectual knowledge that their situation was now different could not quite eradicate the habit of years.

She had expected Koutsoudas to be an unsettling presence, but oddly enough, he turned out to be very incurious about his shipmates. Did he already know (or think he knew) everything, or did he not care? Heris found it difficult to believe he didn't care. Was he focussed only on the mechanical, on ship identities? Unlikely: she knew from rumor that he carried with him an analysis of opposing commanders. Perhaps he was here not to be kept out of someone's eye, but to keep her under someone else's. No, that was paranoia. She hoped. She wished her paranoia button had a "half on" setting, just in case.

Brun scowled over the maintenance manual for ship circuitry. "I wasn't fond of ohms and volts two years ago, and they aren't any friendlier now."

Sirkin looked up from her own reading, a year's worth of *Current Issues in Navigation* on cube. "You didn't realize you'd have to learn what you were doing?"

"I didn't on that shit-shoveler. Just put the output into the intake with a tool that's been around since humans had domestic animals."

"This is different." Sirkin prodded Brun with her toe.

"Captain Serrano wants her crew to be cross-trained and above-average in skills."

"I know, I know." Brun punched up the background reference again. "It's just that electricity has never made sense to me. I keep wanting to know *why* it does what it does, and all my instructors insisted I should memorize it and not worry about the theory." She entered the values she needed for the problem set. "And these names! How far back in the dark ages was it when they named these things? Volt, ohm, ampere: might as well be biff, baff, boff, for all the sense it makes."

Sirkin opened her mouth to lecture Brun, then saw that the screen had lit with the colored flashes meant to cheer on the successful student. "You got them all correct," she said.

"Of course." Brun didn't look up; she was entering her solutions to the next series of problems. "I'm not stupid; I just don't like this stuff."

Sirkin watched the angle of jaw, the cheekbone, the droop of eyelid as Brun looked down at the reference. She had heard Amalie complain so often about her classwork, but Amalie had had real trouble with it. She had not imagined that someone who could race through the material would still dislike it, and say so.

"You're good at it," she said, feeling her way. "So why don't you like it?"

Brun looked up as if startled, and gave Sirkin a sober look that quickly turned to a mischievous grin. "I'm good at lots of things I don't like," she said. "I was bred to be good at things; that's part of being a Registered Embryo."

"But how do you know what to do? What speciality to pursue?" Sirkin remembered clearly the aptitude tests she'd had, year after year, that had aimed her at her present career with more and more precision.

Brun turned completely around, and set down her stylus. "I never thought about it," she said frankly. "No one expects

us to specialize, unless we have an overwhelming talent."
That seemed incredible to Sirkin, and her expression must
have shown that, for Brun wrinkled her own nose and
went on. "There's general stuff we all have to know:
economics, and management, and whatever is done by
our family interests. You know."

"No." Sirkin didn't know, and she had a vague feeling
of irritation. She had never wondered much about the
children of the very rich, how they were educated, what
they did. But this sounded too flabby, too shapeless, to
be worth anything. "I don't see how you can expect to
learn anything useful if you study only generalities."

"We don't." Brun, she saw, had picked up that irritation,
and chose not to reflect it. "We have a lot of specifics,
too—things we'll need—"

"Which fork," Sirkin interrupted. Brun waved that away.

"Trivial. Children learn that by the time they start school,
just from eating at tables with a range of flatware. No,
there's a lot of background information, on our own families
and the other Chairholders. Some of it we pick up, but a
lot has to be learnt, formally. To vote my shares intelligently,
for instance, I have to know that certain families will not
invest in any phase of pork production on religious
grounds."

"Shares of what?" Sirkin asked, forgetting her pique in
genuine interest.

"Family companies. You know, the things our family
invests in, products and processes . . ." Sirkin shook her
head. "Do you know how investment works?"

"Not . . . exactly." Not at all, really. She had started her
own savings account in the Navigators' Guild; she knew
vaguely that they "invested" in something to keep that
private bank going, but she had no idea how or what.

The process, when Brun finally got it across to her, she
found appalling. She had thought that money—some real
substance—sat in the Navigators' Guild vaults. She had

thought that some real substance lay behind the ubiquitous credit cubes and credit slips which she used in everyday transactions.

"Not anymore," Brun said cheerfully. "It's all a tissue of lies, really, but it works, and that's all that matters." That didn't sound right, but Sirkin was past asking questions. "It's whether people believe the credit cubes are any good that matters, and they define 'good' by the exchange rate."

"I'm lost," Sirkin said.

"No, you're not." Brun squirmed into the nest of pillows at one end of the bunk and began waving those long arms. "Look—what's the smallest unit of money in the Familias?"

"A fee." At least she knew that much. In rural districts, on more backward planets, you could still find vending machines that took fees, little disks of metal with designs stamped into them.

"And what can you buy with a fee?"

"It depends," Sirkin said. Not much anywhere, she knew that, but something that cost ten fees in one town might cost fifteen somewhere else. She said that; she did not add that already she was beginning to believe in the worth of Brun's education, however unusual.

"Exactly. So a fee is worth what someone will give you for it. The same with all our monetary units."

"But that's not the same as saying they're no good if someone says so. . . ."

"Brig, think a moment. Suppose we're on a station somewhere: I run a restaurant, and you want a meal. You hand me your credit cube . . . why would I take that in exchange? I have to believe that with the credits I take off your cube, I can buy things I want or need—like the food I'm going to cook to make your meal."

"But of course you can—"

"As long as we all agree on the same lies, yes. But if we don't—if I suspect you'll eat the food, but the grocer won't accept credit for the raw foods—"

"What else could they want?" It made no sense; everyone used credit cubes, and only a stupid person would refuse them.

"Something of hard value . . . you know, barter. Surely you had friends you traded around with? You know, you liked her scarf and she liked an earring you had, and you just traded."

"Well, of course, but that's not like buying it—"

"It is, really. Look—you might have seen her scarf, and said 'What'll you take for that?' and it wasn't a close friend, so she wouldn't give it to you, and you'd pay a few fees. And then a week later, she spotted your earring, and bought it from you. Only difference is, if you have the things there, you can just trade. . . ."

"Seems more honest, that way," Sirkin said.

"As long as you know how to judge the value of everything—but it wouldn't work overall. I mean, an employer can't keep a warehouse full of everything every employee might like, and let you rummage for a day's worth of goods."

"I see that," Sirkin said. "But I still think money has to be real somehow. Solid. Stored someplace. They talk in the news about depositories as if they had something in them."

"They do, but it's mostly to keep counterfeiters from running down the value—" Brun stopped, aware that she was only confusing things. "Sorry. Look—this is sort of my field. For all of the Chairholders, I mean. I've explained it badly; I should have started slower."

"I'm not stupid." Sirkin turned away.

"No, and that's not what I meant." Brun waited, but Sirkin said nothing. She sighed, and went on. "Look, if you're determined to be angry, I can't stop you. Lots of people hate the rich. That's understandable. We go bouncing around having fun, and even when we are working it doesn't look like what you do."

"That's not it," Sirkin said, still looking away.

"Are you sure? If not, what is it?"

"It's—not that you have more money. That you can buy things." Sirkin was looking down at her hands now, her fingers moving as if on a control board. "It's that you seem to live in a different universe. Larger. You're so smart, in everything. You've had all this education, in everything. Maybe I know more about navigation, and ten days ago I knew more about this electronic system . . . but you learn so *fast*. I always thought I was smart—I *was* smart; I had perfect scores. And you come waltzing in and learn it without trying, it seems like." Her head dropped lower. "I feel like . . . like you're going to read me, learn me, as fast as you have everything else, and then I'll be just a bit of experience that enriches your life." Sirkin tried to copy Brun's accent. " 'Oh, yes, I had a woman lover once; she was a nice girl but rather limited.' That's what's bothering me. I don't want to be your adventure with gender orientation."

"Oh."

"Which is what Meharry says you're doing," Sirkin said, getting it all out in a rush. "She says you're an R.E., and R.E.s are all made hetero, because your families want you to marry—"

"Meharry was supposed to be playing a role," Brun said savagely, slamming her fist into one of the pillows. She didn't want to be talking about this now, and especially not after Meharry had taken the high ground. "And besides she's wrong."

"About what, Registered Embryos in general, or you in particular?"

Brun waited a long moment, gathering her thoughts. "When I was in that cave, I realized that I didn't want to be anyone's designated blonde. So I understand that you don't want to be my fling with sexual experimentation, a sort of bauble on the necklace of my life story. But that's not how I've seen it, Sirkin. I admired you, and the way

Captain Serrano talked about you . . . if it hadn't been for you, they wouldn't have come after us in time. Then we met, and . . . and I liked it."

"But do you love men or women?"

Brun stirred uneasily. "I don't know. I like both—to have as friends, I mean. I never really thought about it, because it didn't matter a lot. Until now."

"How can you not think about it!" More accusation than question. "You have to think about it."

"I didn't." She had assumed, growing up in her family, knowing she was a Registered Embryo, that she would eventually marry and have children, most if not all of them also Registered Embryos. Being an R.E. determined your destiny; only the freelofs could choose. But on Sirkin's face was an angry look that didn't want to hear about complications. She had to try, anyway. "You know about genetic engineering—"

"Of course. What does that have to do with—oh."

"I am a Registered Embryo, Brig. You knew that before Meharry said it; I told you early on. She's right—at least, I thought it meant I wouldn't love women, just because . . . because it's so expensive."

"Expensive?" Sirkin's brow wrinkled. "Loving women?"

"No, being an R.E. They're tough enough to produce with well-mapped sets—and we're fourth generation R.E., so all our stuff's on file except any new mutations. Because of that, we're all set to be heteros—so the work that goes into each of us will be available for the next generation."

"There's always A.I." Sirkin said. Brun realized she didn't know how Registered Embryos were made. Most people didn't.

"A.I. is already part of it," she said. "Harvesting of ova and sperm, in vitro fertilization and then splicing . . ."

"Then what does it matter what orientation the Registered Embryos have?" Sirkin asked. "If the whole reproductive bit is handled outside?"

"Prudence," Brun said. "In the . . ." she hesitated, trying to think of a polite way to say "important families." There wasn't, so she plunged on to the second level of reasoning she'd been told about years before. "If things go wrong— if something happened to the Registered Embryo program, the families would still need children. We'd have to provide them the . . . er . . . old way. And they'd want us to want to. At least, not to want *not* to."

"Oh." Sirkin reflected on that a moment. "So it's to protect the family against the loss of childbearing capacity if the medical infrastructure fails?"

"Right." Brun frowned. "My mother said that even then the orientation of women wasn't critical—in some cultures, women can be forced to bear children no matter what their wishes—but our culture thought that was unethical. Although it seems odd, that they would consider it ethical to determine our orientation so that it wouldn't be overruled later. But formal bioethics always seemed full of loopholes to me, anyway."

"I still think you have to know what you love, though."

Brun threw up her hands. "I love *lots* of things, Brig. I'm that sort . . . I'm sorry, but that's the truth. That's what got me into that fast crowd at school, really. I want to try everything, do everything, be everything. Logically, that's not possible, but . . . it would be such *fun*."

"And fun is what matters?"

Brun winced. "Not all that matters, no. But—I'm trying to be honest with you, Brig, so please try to understand. I don't think it's being rich that did this. I think some people are like me, rich or not, R.E. or not. When we were trying to think how to get Lady Cecelia out of that horrible place, *I'm* the one who thought of the hot air balloon. And one reason it worked was that it was so utterly ridiculous. Impossible. Crazy. I loved that about it—the very outrageousness of it. New things—different things—they draw me. I asked Dad—I thought maybe the R.E. process had fouled up with me—and he said they'd asked for an extra dollop of some set of multi-named neurochemicals that produce my sort of person. They'd opted for conservative intelligence with the older ones; he said they wanted a little sparkle in me."

"I think we are too different," Sirkin said. "Maybe it's your genes, and maybe it's your background, but we aren't enough alike—"

"Not for a permanent sexual relationship, no. But I don't see why we can't enjoy each other now and be lifetime friends. I like you; I admire you. Doesn't that help?"

"Yes. I just wish—"

"You need a long-term lover. I understand that. And if you want Meharry instead of me—"

"No!"

"I thought you liked her. She's angry enough at me that I thought you two had some kind of—"

"We don't have any kind of anything," Sirkin said. "I mean, I like her, as a sort of big sister, but like any big sister she tries to run my life too much. And she's hard."

"That's being ex-military, probably."

"I still don't like it. She makes me feel like a fluffy helpless kitten, and I don't like feeling helpless."

"But fluffy?" Brun cocked an eyebrow at her.

"Well . . . I have to admit I've enjoyed shopping with you. I was brought up to be practical, of course. But it's—it's kind of fun to dress up."

"So . . . even if you think fun isn't enough—even if you think I'm just a spoiled rich brat with more money than sense—you could have fun sometimes."

"With you, you mean," Sirkin said. It wasn't fair, the way Brun could coil an argument into a trap. "You think I should just relax and enjoy you, and forget the future?"

"Forget it? Never. But right now you can't go hunting a better partner; I understand that you'll want to, when you leave this ship. If you choose, we can be friends—I'd really like that, because I like you, and the friendship can last beyond this voyage. Lovers? Again, that's up to you. I don't want to hurt you, though I may have already—" Brun frowned, thinking about it. "I'd like to help you, if I knew how."

Sirkin looked at her, at the body she now realized had been carefully engineered for health and beauty and even sexuality, at the mind behind the eyes which had also been engineered for intelligence and whatever the genetic specialists meant by "sparkle." She couldn't help admiring Brun; she suspected that that, too, had been built in, as ineradicable as the choice of height and coloring. In one way it seemed weak to admire, to love, someone engineered to be admirable and lovable—it gave her the queasy feeling that she was being manipulated by the genetic engineers. Yet Brun had been the material of their manipulations; she was even less free than Sirkin. She couldn't help being who she was, any more than Sirkin could help being attracted.

"I would like to be friends," she said, after a long pause. "I don't know if it will work, in the long run, but—I do like you, and it's fun having another young woman to talk to. But not more than friends. I could fall for you, Brun, and if there's no chance for permanence, I don't want to risk it."

"Fair enough," Brun said. A faint flush reddened her face, then faded. "Now—if we can go back a bit—I'd like some help with the navigation sets our beloved captain sent down for me."

"You're going to end up better at navigation than I am," Sirkin grumbled.

"Not so. I'll pass the test, that's all. Didn't you ever know anyone who could pass tests but flunked real life?" The tension of the past conversation shattered, and Sirkin found herself laughing, not quite in control, but content to be so.

✧ Chapter Four

Heris could not define the concern she felt. Cecelia looked healthy, strong, and sane; she spent several hours a day on her riding simulator, but that was normal for Cecelia. Now she didn't need the massage lounger after each ride; she showed no stiffness or soreness. Her appetite was good, her spirits high—so Heris told herself. What was wrong? Was it her own imagination, perhaps her own envy of someone with so much privilege getting even more?

At dinner that very night, Cecelia brought that up herself. "It's indecent, in a way . . . to be so lucky. I try to tell myself it's fair payment for the hell Lorenza put me through, but that's a lie. I've had such good luck nearly all my life, and for the year I lost have been given back forty—not a bad bargain."

Heris wondered how much she believed that. "Would you go through it again for another forty years?"

"No." It came out reflexively; her face stiffened. "It's not the same; it couldn't be. I didn't know how long—or that it would end this way—" Her breath came short.

"I'm sorry," Heris said. "That was a tactless question; of course no one would choose that year. I guess I thought you were making too light of it—"

"Too light! No . . . I don't think so. I'm trying not to let it rule the rest of my life . . . put it behind me." The tension in her shoulders suggested that it still weighed on her.

"Does it bother you that you're not competing?" Heris asked.

"Of course not!" It came almost too quickly, with a flush

57

and fade of color on Cecelia's cheeks. "It's been thirty years; it would be ridiculous."

"Still—"

"No. I just want to see it. I might—someday—think about going back."

Zenebra's orbital station carried an astonishing amount of traffic for an agricultural world. Heris had had to wait two days for a docking assignment, and had eased the yacht in among many others. On the station itself she found the kind of expensive shops she remembered from Rockhouse Major. Cecelia had called ahead, purchasing tickets for the Senior Trials, all venues. Heris saw the prices posted in the orbital station's brochure, and winced. She hadn't realized it could cost as much to watch other people ride horses as to own them. Or so she assumed. She also hadn't realized that Cecelia expected her to come along— that she had bought two sets of tickets. Heris didn't quite groan.

On the shuttle ride down to the planet she heard nothing but horse talk. At least Cecelia's coaching had given her the vocabulary to understand most of what she heard. Stifles and hocks, quarter-cracks and navicular, stocking up and cooling down, all made sense now . . . what it didn't make, she thought to herself, was interesting conversation. The talk about particular riders and trainers made no sense at all—she didn't know why, for instance, "riding with Falkhome" was said with such scorn, or "another Maalinson" seemed to be a compliment. But any notion that Cecelia had no equal in fixation on horses quickly disappeared— the universe, or at least that shuttle, was full of people with equally one-track minds.

Zenebra's shuttle port had a huge bronze-and-stained-glass sculpture of a horse taking a fence in its lobby. The groundcars had horse motifs painted on the side. Along the road to the hotel, a grassy strip served as an exercise area for the horses—all sizes, all colors—that pranced along it. The hotel itself, jammed with enthusiasts, buzzed with the same colorful slang. Heris began to feel that she'd fallen into very strange company indeed—these people were far more intense than the foxhunters at Bunny's.

Heris had by this time seen dozens of cubes of the Wherrin Horse Trials, both complete versions of the years Cecelia had competed, and extracts of the years since. She recognized the view from the hotel room window—the famous double ditch of Senior Course A, and the hedge beyond. Although modeled on the famous traditional venues of Old Earth, the trials had made use of the peculiarities of Zenebra's terrain, climate, and vegetation. One advantage of laying out courses on planets during colonization was the sheer space available. At Wherrin, the Senior Division alone had four separate permanent courses, which made it possible to rotate them as needed for recovery of the turf, or for the weather conditions at the time of the Trials.

Up close, the Wherrin Trials Fields looked more like the holocubes than real land with real obstacles. Bright green grass plushy underfoot, bright paint on the viewing stands, the course markers, some of the fences. Clumps of green trees. Bright blue sky, beds of brilliant pink and yellow flowers. Heris blinked at all the brilliance, reminding herself that Zenebra's sun provided more light than the original Terran sun, and waited for Cecelia to get back from wherever she'd run off to. They had agreed to meet at this refreshment stand for a break, and Cecelia was late. Then Heris saw her, hurrying through the crowds.

"Heris—you'll never guess!" Cecelia was flushed. She looked happy, but with a faint touch of embarrassment. Heris couldn't guess, and said so. "I've got a ride," Cecelia went on. Heris fumbled through her list of meanings . . . a ride back to the hotel? A ride to her chosen observation spot on the course? "A *ride*," Cecelia said. "Corry Manion, who was going to ride Ari D'amerosia's young mare, got hurt in a flitter crash last night. A mild concussion, they said, but they won't put him in the regen tanks for at least forty-eight hours, and by then it will be too late. Ari was telling me all this and then she *asked* me—I didn't say a word, Heris, I promise—she *asked* me if I would consider riding for her. I know I said I didn't mean to compete again, but—"

"But you want to," Heris said. From the cubes alone, and from her brief experience of foxhunting, she had had a vague notion that way herself, but one look at the real obstacles had changed her mind. "Of course you do. Can I help?"

"You don't think I'm crazy?" Cecelia asked. "An old woman?"

Heris did think she was crazy; she thought they were all crazy, but Cecelia was no worse than the others. "You aren't an old woman anymore," Heris said. "You've been working out on the simulator. You've got a lifetime of skills and new strength—and it's your neck."

"Come on, then," Cecelia said. "I'll get you an ID tag so you can come in with me—you have to see this mare."

Heris didn't have to see the mare; she had only to see the look on Cecelia's face, and remember that less than a year ago Cecelia had been flat in bed, paralyzed and blind.

As with the foxhunting, more went on behind the scenes than Heris would have guessed from the entertainment cubes she'd seen. The Trials organization had its own security procedures; Heris and Cecelia both needed ID tags, and Cecelia had to have the complete array of numbers that she would wear during competition. Cecelia spent half an hour at the tailor's getting measurements taken for her competition clothes.

"I have all this somewhere, probably in a trunk back

on Rotterdam," Cecelia said. "Maybe even somewhere in the yacht, though we didn't move everything back aboard. I don't remember, really, because it had been so long since I needed it."

"Why so many changes of clothes?" Heris asked. She had wondered about that even with the foxhunters. Why not simply design comfortable riding clothes that would work, and then wear them for all occasions?

"Tradition," Cecelia said, wrinkling her nose. "And I'd like to know what a shad is, so I'd know why this looks anything like its belly." She gestured at her image in the mirror; Heris shook her head. "Yet that's what this kind of jacket is called."

Heris followed her from the tailor's to the saddler's, where Cecelia picked out various straps that looked, to Heris, like all the others. "Reins are just reins, aren't they?" she said finally, when Cecelia had been shifting from one to another pair for what seemed like hours. Cecelia grimaced.

"Not when you're coming down a drop in the rain," she said. "And by the way, see if somebody can dig my saddles out of storage and put them on the next shuttle. I'd rather not break in a new saddle on course." Heris found a public combooth and relayed the request; Brun promised to bring the saddles herself if Heris would give permission to leave the ship.

"Fine," Heris said, and anticipated her next request. "And why not bring Sirkin down, too? She's probably never seen anything like this."

Finally they arrived at one of the long stable rows. Ari D'amerosia had four horses in the trials, two in the Senior Trials and one each in Training and Intermediate. Grooms in light blue shirts bustled about, carrying buckets and tack, pushing barrows of straw, bales of hay, sacks of feed. Ari herself, a tall woman with thick gray-streaked hair, was bent over inspecting a horse's hoof when Cecelia came up with Heris.

"Tim, we're going to need the vet again. Cold soak until the vet comes— Oh, hi Cece. Have your rider's registration yet?"

"Yes—and this is Heris, who's hunted with the Greens at Bunny's." Nothing at all, Heris noted wryly, about her main occupation as a ship's captain.

"Ah—then you can ride. Ever event?" The woman straightened up and offered a hand hastily wiped on her jeans. She was a head taller than Cecelia.

"No," Heris said. "I came to riding a bit late for that."

"It's never too late," Ari said, with the enthusiasm of one who would convert any handy victim. "Start with something easy—you'd love it."

"Not this year," Heris said. "I'm just here to help Cecelia."

"Next year," Ari said, and without waiting for an answer turned to Cecelia. "Now. I've had the groom warm her up for you—we've got two hours in the dressage complex, ring fifteen. Get to know her, feel her out—she may buck a few times, she usually does."

"Where can I change?" Cecelia asked.

"Might as well use her stall—your friend—Heris?—can hang on to your other stuff until we clear out Corry's locker."

Cecelia ducked into the stall and reappeared in breeches, boots, and pullover; Heris took the clothes she'd been wearing, rolled them into Cecelia's duffel, and felt uncomfortably like a lady's maid. She followed Cecelia down the long row of stalls and utility areas, past grooms washing horses, walking horses, feeding and mucking out, around the end of the stable rows to the exercise rings.

"The great thing about Wherrin," Cecelia said, "is there's no shortage of space. You don't have to make do with a few practice rings, a single warmup ring . . ." So it appeared. A vast field, broken into a long row of dressage rings separated by ten-meter alleys, and another long row of larger rings with two or three jumps each. Everywhere horses and riders and trainers.

At the far end, Heris saw the number fifteen. A bright bay mare strode around the outside, ridden by a groom in the light blue shirt of Ari's stable. Cecelia showed her competitor's pass, and the groom hopped down to give her a leg up. Heris stood back. She thought the horse looked different from those Cecelia usually praised, but she couldn't define the difference. Taller? Thinner? In the next ring, a stocky chestnut was clearly shorter and thicker, but looked lumpish to her.

She didn't understand most of what Cecelia was doing, that first session. That it would lead to a dressage test the day after next, yes, but not how Cecelia's choice of gait and pattern aimed at that goal. Cecelia's expression gave her no clue, and her comments and questions to the groom, and then Ari, didn't clear things up. Heris felt uncomfortable, not only because of the hot sun. If anyone had asked her, she thought it was a silly thing to do in the first place, trying to get horses over those obstacles. And for Cecelia, at her age, when she hadn't done it for thirty years—and on a horse she didn't know—it was worse than silly. But no one asked her, and she kept her opinion to herself, through the few hours of training that Cecelia had before the event began.

When Brun and Sirkin arrived with Cecelia's saddle (which looked just like all the other saddles, to Heris's eye), she noticed that Sirkin reacted as she did, while Brun clearly belonged with the equestrian-enthused. Before the day was out, Brun had convinced Ari to let her work with the horses—for no pay, of course. Sirkin, having been stepped on by the first horse led past her, had even less enthusiasm than Heris.

Early in the morning two days later, Heris found herself perched on a hard seat in the viewing stands of the dressage arena. Cecelia, already dressed for her own appearance, sat with her at first to explain the routine. A big gray, paired with a rider who had won the Wherrin twice before, moved smoothly through the test. Cecelia explained why the judges nitpicked; Heris thought it was silly to worry about one loop of a serpentine being flatter than another. It seemed an archaic concern, like continuing to practice drill formations never used in real military actions.

Then Cecelia left, to warm up her own mount. Heris worried. She still couldn't reconcile the old Cecelia, well into her eighties, with the vigorous woman who seemed a few years younger than herself. She kept expecting that appearance to crack, as if it were only a shell over the old one.

She was thoroughly bored by the time Cecelia appeared. All the horses did exactly the same thing—or tried to. Some made obvious mistakes—obvious to the crowd, that is, whose sighs and mutters let Heris know that something had gone wrong. One went into a fit of bucking, which was at least exciting, if disastrous to its score. But most simply went around and around, trot and canter, slower or faster, until Heris fought back one yawn after another.

Cecelia and the bay mare did the same, not as badly as some and not as well as the best. Heris tried to be interested, but she really couldn't tell how the judges scored any of it; the numbers posted afterwards meant nothing to her. She climbed out of the stands after Cecelia's round, sure her backside would have been happier somewhere else.

To her surprise, Cecelia said hardly anything, shrugging off Heris's attempt at compliments with a brusque "That's over with—now for tomorrow." Tomorrow being the cross-country phase, Heris knew, with four sections that tested the horse's endurance, speed, and jumping ability. "That's the fun part," Cecelia said. Heris had more than doubts, but at least she wouldn't have to sit through all of it. She could watch on monitors, or walk from one obstacle to another.

❖   ❖   ❖

Heris watched the start on the monitor, trying not to listen to the announcer's babble. He had already said too much, she thought, about Cecelia being the oldest rider in the event, on the youngest horse. Cecelia had the mare gathered up in a coil, ready to explode, and when the starter waved, she sent the mare out at a powerful canter. The first fence, invariably described as inviting, didn't look it to Heris: the egg cases of the native saurids glittered bronze in the sun and their narrow ends, pointed up, looked too much like missiles on a rack.

"We used to use the whole eggs," someone said in her ear; she glanced around and saw that it was another of Ari's people. "But someone crashed into them one year, and the stench was so bad none of the other horses would go near the fence. Ruined the scoring, completely upset everyone. Now they have to weight the bottoms of them, but at least there's no stink."

Cecelia and the mare were safely over the first fence, and Heris decided to walk across the course to the water complex. Cecelia had said it would be a good place to watch.

Cecelia grinned into the wind. The mare had calmed down on the steeplechase, where she could run freely, and she met all the fences squarely, with the attitude of a horse that knows it can jump. Of course, most horses would jump on the steeplechase course, with its open grassy terrain and its clearly defined fences. The problems would come in the cross-country phase. During roads and tracks, Cecelia tried to feel out how the mare felt about different surfaces, about dark patches of shade and reflections from water. The mare didn't like sudden changes in light, but she would go on if supported by the rider. She paid no heed to the loose dog that suddenly yapped at her heels—a good omen because the crowds in the event course often had dogs, and at least one always got loose.

On the big course, Cecelia continued to feel her way into the mare's reflexes. So far, she was amazed at how easy it all seemed. Her own reflexes had come back as if the thirty years since her last big season had never been. They had cleared that first easy fence. The second fence was another straightforward, well-defined obstacle, made of the intertwined trunks of a stickass thicket. The mare flowed over it.

Now the course ran toward the ridge for which it was named, the grade gentle up to a scary but jumpable set of rails over a big ditch. The mare looked at the ditch, but jumped without real hesitation when Cecelia sat tight. Next came the Saurus Steps, a staircase arrangement that required the horse to bounce up a series of ledges, then take one stride and jump a drop fence. Here Cecelia thought the mare was going to run out of impulsion on the last bounce, and legged her hard into the stride at the top. The mare stretched and almost crashed the fence, but caught herself and landed without falling.

My mistake, Cecelia thought. Too much pushing, too much delight in being here again. But there was no time to reride it in her head; she was already entering the switchbacks that led to the ridgetop, with trappy obstacles at each turn. Two of them required a trot approach; the others could be cantered if the horse didn't pull too badly. The mare pulled like a tractor, fighting the down transitions, snaking her head. On the second trot fence, the mare charged straight ahead past the fence and ran out past the flag.

"Settle down," Cecelia said, as much to herself as to the mare. She was still pushing too hard, abusing the fragile, two-day relationship. The mare switched her tail and backed up, kicking out finally before Cecelia got her lined up for the jump. She jumped willingly once aimed straight at the fence, and didn't charge the next fence. "Finesse," Cecelia muttered. "It's easier if you don't fight the course."

Or the rider, but it wouldn't help to tell the horse that. She had to convey that with her body, all the mare would understand.

Now they were on the ridge, headed back to the east, roughly parallel to the early part of the course but higher. Here the obstacles were built to take advantage of natural stone formations. Horses had to jump into depressions, leap back up and over the ridgeline, twisting and turning, changing leads and stride length between each obstacle.

Cecelia had always enjoyed this demanding part of the course. On a good day, it had a compelling, syncopated rhythm, very satisfying to mind and body. On a bad day it was a bone-jarring, breath-eating nightmare of near catastrophe. This mare continued her headstrong, stiff-sided refusal to bend left, but Cecelia kept her on course, regaining her own confidence with every successful jump. Perhaps she was out of practice, but—she hauled the mare around a stone pillar and got her lined up for the next— she could still handle a difficult horse on a difficult course. She felt more alive than she had in years. She knew the tapes would show a wide grin on her face.

The most dangerous part of the course lay downhill to the water complex. From above it could look all too inviting, a long sweep of green to the tiny red-and-white decorations at the water's edge, tempting horse and rider alike to set off down the slope at full speed. But on the way down were two punishing obstacles, a drop fence and a large bank with a ditch below. Cecelia had seen many a rider come to grief here; she had done it herself. She took a firm hold of the mare, and eased her over the drop fence.

Below it, the mare picked up speed. She wanted to charge at the bank, fly off the top. Cecelia wrestled her down to a rough trot, paused briefly at the top and thought she had the mare ready for the slide and jump below. Suddenly the mare swung sideways on the steep slope, reared, plunged, and fell, rolling over into the ditch. Cecelia flung herself off on the upslope side as the mare went down.

"You idiot," she said, without heat. She meant both of them. This finished the round as far as scores went. Completion was the best she could hope for now, and one more refusal would eliminate them. She knew this debacle would be featured on the annual cube; she could imagine the commentator's remarks about her age. At least she hadn't been wearing a camera herself.

The mare lay upside down for a moment, legs thrashing, then heaved herself over and up, clambering out of the muck with more power than grace. She seemed unhurt as Cecelia led her away from the course and checked her legs. Cecelia looked at the saddle, now well-greased with mud, and accepted a leg up into the slippery mess with the resignation of experience. The mare was sound; the best thing to do was keep going and finish the course.

If she could. The water complex was next, offering a serious challenge even to riders with dry saddles and steerable horses. Cecelia decided on the straight route, mostly because the mare's mistakes had all been steering problems. With that in mind, she eased the mare around the one sharp turn on the approach, and legged her at the first fence. The mare jumped clean, sailing into the water with the enthusiasm of youth and a tremendous splash. She cantered gaily through the stream, leapt out the far side, and over the bounce, as if she'd been doing it all her life.

On the far side of the water complex, the course made a circuit of a large open area, with obstacles spaced along it, rewarding horses that liked to gallop on. Here the mare had no problems, attacking one jump after another with undiminished verve. Cecelia put the problems behind her and enjoyed the ride. This was what she loved; this was what she had dreamed of, in those months of blind paralysis. The warm, live, powerful body beneath her, the thudding hooves, the wind in her face, the vivid colors, the way her body moved with the horse, pumping her own breath in and out. Even the sharp bite of fear that made the successful jumps individual spurts of relief and delight.

At the finish, the mare galloped through the posts with her ears still forward and her legs intact. Cecelia felt that if she'd had mobile ears, hers would have been forward too.

"Sorry about the problems," she said to Ari, when she dismounted. "I think I was too rough with her on the stairsteps, and that's why she fought with me later." She didn't really want to talk about it; Ari, after a few perfunctory questions, seemed to realize that and led the mare away. Cecelia wanted to be alone to savor the feelings, the joy that thrust so deep it hurt. She was back where she belonged; she could still do it. Common sense be damned; she didn't have to give it up yet.

Heris, familiar with the cubes of Cecelia's great rides of the past, couldn't help thinking that this had been a disaster. The horse had refused one fence; the horse had fallen upside down in a ditch, and Cecelia was lucky not to have been squashed underneath. Mud from the fall caked Cecelia's breeches.

"Not too shabby," was Cecelia's comment on her own ride. "The mare and I needed more time together." She caught sight of herself in the mirror. "Whoosh! What a mess. I've got to get cleaned up. An old friend asked me to dinner."

"But tomorrow—"

"Tomorrow's just the jumping, and she's going to be a pain to truck around that course. We'll probably have a few rails down. But it's worth it—I can't tell you how much fun it's been." Fun. Heris opened her mouth and shut it again. Her memory reminded her that she had once thought fox hunting was stupid, and had found it fun herself. Maybe this was fun, if you were good enough. She wasn't, and she told herself she never intended to be.

The next morning, Heris was back in the stands, this time with a cushion she'd brought. Since competitors rode in reverse order of standings, Cecelia's show jumping round came early. Most of the horses with more faults had not completed the course and would not be jumping. Heris watched the mare shift and stamp as Cecelia checked the girth and mounted. The horse showed no signs of the previous day's efforts; her bright bay coat gleamed, clean of the mud from the ditch.

The jump course required not only jumping ability but a level of steering that this mare hadn't attained. Heris could see that Cecelia was trying to give the mare the easiest route through the maze, with sweeping turns that set her up at a good distance from the next obstacle. The mare resisted, trying to cut the round corners and charge at any fence that caught her eye. That she went over the fences in the right order seemed a minor miracle; the large one was that she didn't fall or crack Cecelia's head against either of the large trees in the ring. She still had two fences down, one of them in a scatter of rails that made Heris wince—she could almost feel the bruises on her own shins.

By the end of the day's performances, Heris understood a bit more about the sport, but she had no intention of risking her own neck that way. People who craved that much danger should be firefighters, or some other job that accomplished something worthwhile to balance the danger. Cecelia was flushed and happy, eager to talk now about today's winner (someone she'd known as a junior competitor) and the number of Rejuvenants competing. Of the five top placings, three were Rejuvenants.

"Does that mean you'll go back to competition—if other Rejuvenants are doing it?"

"I might," Cecelia said. "I'm not sure. Pedar—my friend that I went out with last night—wants to talk to me about

Rejuvenant politics." She made a face, then grinned. "I'll listen to him—but I can't think of myself as a person whose interests have changed just because I'm going to live longer."

"Perhaps not," Heris said. "But if three of the top five riders are Rejuvenants, where does that leave the youngsters just starting? Experience counts." She was sure Cecelia would compete again; she was far too happy to give it up. She couldn't help wondering what that would mean for her and the *Sweet Delight*.

"And some Rejuvenants don't place," Cecelia said, laughing. "I certainly didn't." But she looked thoughtful.

Cecelia had recognized the face but at first had not known whether this was Pedar himself, a son, or a grandson. The long, bony, dark-skinned face looked all of thirty. Had Pedar taken rejuvenation? How many times? He wore a full-sleeved white shirt with lace at the collar over tight gray trousers . . . he had always, she recalled, favored a romantic image. He had been the first man she knew to wear earrings . . . though now he wore three small platinum ones, in place of the great gold pirate hoop of his flamboyant youth.

"My dear Cecelia," he said, holding her hand a long moment. "You look . . . lovely."

"I look fortyish," Cecelia said, with some asperity. "And I was never lovely."

"You were, but you didn't like to hear it," he said. "And yes, I'm Pedar himself." He tilted his head; his rings flashed in his ear. "I notice you aren't wearing any—are you trying to pass?"

"Pass?" Now she was completely bewildered.

"As your apparent age, I meant. Perhaps you are planning to compete seriously again, and—"

Rage tore through her. "I am *not* trying to be anything but myself. I never did."

"Sorry," he said. "I seem to have hit a sore point. It's just that you aren't wearing any earrings—"

"I don't follow fads in jewelry," Cecelia said, biting each word off. "I prefer quality." She glared, but he didn't flinch. Of course, he hadn't flinched much when they were both in their twenties and she'd glared at him. Now, he shook his head, and chuckled. She had always liked his chuckle; for some reason it made her feel safe.

"Forgive me," he said. "I should not laugh, but it is so like you to be unaware of the code. You're right, Cecelia: you never paid attention to fads, or tried to be anything but what you are. Let me explain." Without waiting for her reaction, he went on. "Those of us who've experienced the Ramhoff-Inikin rejuvenation process several times found that we were confusing some of the people we'd always known. Even within the family we might be taken for our own descendants. We didn't want to wear large signs saying 'I am Pedar Orrigiemos, the original,' or anything like that. We wanted some discreet signal, and—" he touched the rings in his left ear, "—this is what we use."

"Earrings?" Cecelia asked. It seemed a silly choice. She tried to remember how many earrings she'd seen lately, and whether Lorenza had worn them.

Pedar laughed. "They aren't just earrings. The first serial rejuvenations were all done under special license, with very close monitoring. They wore implanted platinum/ceramic disks encoded with all the necessary medical information, from their baseline data to the dosages. Someone—I forget who—objected to the disk, and asked if it could be made more decorative. Next thing you know—rings. Now we use them to indicate how many rejuvenations we've had, which is a clue—though not really precise—to our full age."

"But why would you want to?" Cecelia said, intrigued in spite of herself. "I can see what you mean about families— although there's no young woman in mine who resembles me that closely. But surely they could learn—"

"Oh, I suppose so. It's handy in business, though, when associates know that the youngish man with the three earrings is the CEO, while the one with the single earring is his son, merely a division vice-president."

"Ross never sneaks in another earring?" asked Cecelia, remembering Ross very well. She had never liked him.

"Not while I'm in the same system," Pedar said. "I suppose he could, but then he'd have to sustain conversations with any of my friends—and he couldn't. Which brings up the other issue, perhaps the main one. Haven't you discovered yet how boring the young are?"

"I have not," said Cecelia. She was in no mood to agree with Pedar about anything.

"You will." His face twisted into the wry expression she had once found so fascinating. "Having a young body is one thing—I like it, and I'm sure you do too. No more aches and pains, no more flab and stiffness. Vivid tastes and smells, a digestive tract with renewed ability to cope with all the culinary delights of a hundred worlds. You can ride a competitive course again, if you want. But—will you want to?"

"I just did," Cecelia pointed out.

"True, but that was—survival euphoria, perhaps, after your ordeal. Will you continue to compete?" When she didn't answer immediately, he went on. "The physical sensations you enjoyed, those are strong again, just as I swim in big surf, which I always loved. You will always ride, perhaps. But you may not always want to compete. One reason is the constant contact with the young. There's nothing *wrong* with the young—they will grow up to be old—but you have already solved the problems they find so distressing. Just as, when you were originally forty, you found adolescents boring—and don't tell me you didn't, because I remember what you said about Ross when he was in school."

That was Ross, Cecelia thought to herself. Ross had

been boring because all he thought about was Ross. Although, come to think of it, that description fit most of the adolescents she'd known. Certainly Ronnie had been like that.

"Take your average forty-year-old," Pedar said. Cecelia immediately thought of Heris. Heris wasn't average, but she didn't like average anyway. "Your average forty-something is worrying about a personal relationship, and if not rejuved, is having concerns about the first signs of physical aging." Well, that was true. She could not have missed the tension between Heris and Petris, and both of them were making a fetish out of using the gym. "More than half the things you know directly, they know only by hearsay—from their education, which includes only what educators think is important. Nothing of the little things that you and I remember effortlessly. Remember the craze for sinopods?"

Cecelia laughed. She hadn't thought about that for years, a fashion so peculiar it had penetrated even her horse-focussed mind. She had had a sinopod herself, a red and yellow one.

Pedar nodded at her expression. "You see? If sinopods are mentioned anywhere outside obscure biology texts, it's in some terminally boring treatise on the economic impact of fads for biologicals on the ecology of frontier worlds. You and I—the others our age, with our background—we remember the sinopods themselves, and even if we can't explain the attraction, we remember the ones we had."

"I wonder whatever happened to them?" she asked; she remembered that she had even named her sinopod, though she couldn't recall the name. Pedar laughed outright.

"Cecelia, you have a genius for getting off the subject. If you really care about sinopods, look it up. My point is that people in the same generation share experiences—know things—that others cannot know directly. Long ago, people who wanted to pretend they weren't aging tried mingling with those younger—hoping the youth would rub off, I suppose. We don't have to do that. We can have the best of youth—the healthy bodies—and the best of age—the experience."

"So you wear rings in your ears." She hated to admit it—she would *not* admit it aloud—but Pedar made sense. She remembered her exasperation with Heris as far back as that insane adventure on the island. To waffle around like that, about whether or not she loved Petris—she herself would not have been so baffled, and she had straightened the younger woman out. Heris had been wrong again about Sirkin, and again her own age and experience told. But Heris wasn't boring. Ronnie, maybe.

"A ring like this—" Pedar tapped his rings, "simply tells us—those who have had multiple rejuvenations— that you have had one, and how many. We choose to stabilize at different ages, so you have to do a little calculation. The commercial version gives about twenty years per treatment, so if you combine the appearance and the number of rings, you can come close to the actual age." He grinned again, a challenging grin this time. "Or, you can wear no ring and simply pretend to be forty. Talk to other forties, live among them, and become like them. . . ."

"No," Cecelia said firmly. "I have no intention of pretending to be younger than I am. That's why I never wanted rejuvenation in the first place."

"Then wear the ring," Pedar said. "It will save you a lot of trouble."

Restlessness, too much energy . . . was it all because she hadn't had the chance to confront Lorenza directly? She had confronted Berenice directly enough, and that hadn't satisfied her.

Something bothered her about Pedar's advice, about

Pedar's complacency. She had deliberately refused to think about the implications of rejuvenation. It complicated things; she wanted to go on with her life and not worry about it. But his attitude suggested that this wouldn't work, that others would always be assessing her, looking for correspondence or conflict between her visible age and her real self.

Exactly why she hadn't wanted to do it. Better than being blind or having to use optical implants, certainly. She wanted to be healthy, whole, able to do what she wanted to do. But she didn't want to waste her time wondering if she was confusing people or what they thought.

And he implied a whole subculture of rejuvenated oldsters, a subculture she hadn't even noticed. How many serial Rejuvenants were there? She began to wonder, began to think of looking for the telltale rings.

They weren't always in ears, but once she looked, they were on more people than she had expected. Discreet blue-and-silver enamel rings on fingers, in ears, in noses, occasionally in jewelry but most often attached to the body. She began to suspect that where they were worn signaled something else Pedar hadn't told her. Certainly when she saw couples wearing them, they were usually in the same site. She wondered if anyone outside the Rejuvenant subculture had caught on, if some of the rings were faked. She had had no idea so many people had been rejuvenated at all, let alone more than once.

Cecelia pulled out her medical file from the Guerni Republic, something she'd stashed in the yacht's safe without another glance. Sure enough, a little blue-and-silver ring slid out of the packet, and the attached card explained that it contained the medical coding necessary for a rejuvenation technician to correct any imbalance. Odd. Why not just implant a record strip, as was done all the time for people with investigational diseases?

She sat frowning, rolling the ring from one hand to

another. Did she want to identify herself to others as one of the subculture? She wished she knew more about it. She disliked even that much concern . . . and yet . . . she couldn't deny that Pedar was right about the callowness of the young.

◇ Chapter Five

Heris left Cecelia onplanet and went back up to the yacht where, she hoped, she could have ten consecutive minutes in which no one mentioned horses or anything connected with them. She found Sirkin making the same complaint to the rest of the crew about Brun. She herself had had to remind Brun firmly that she was a crewmember, not a rich girl on vacation, and order her back to the ship.

"All she talks about is horses. And she knows a lot of other things, but from the minute she unpacked Lady Cecelia's saddle, everything else went out of her mind."

"Everything?" Meharry asked.

Sirkin reddened. "Well . . . you know what I mean."

Heris cleared her throat and they all straightened. "Any messages?" she asked.

"Yes, Captain." Meharry could be formal when she chose. "All disclaimed urgency when we offered to transfer them down to your hotel, but you do have a stack."

"I'll get back to work then. I have no idea how long Lady Cecelia will stay—the Trials are over, but she's meeting old friends. However, we should be prepared to depart in a day or so." She glanced around. "Where is Brun?"

"Probably watching Trials cubes," Sirkin said. "Again." Everyone laughed, including Heris.

"How's the installation coming?" She had finally decided to let Koutsoudas install his pet equipment on their own scans, with Oblo to ensure that nothing went wrong.

"It's done, Captain." Koutsoudas looked at Oblo, and

Oblo looked back; Heris recognized the expression from years in the Fleet.

"And just what have you gentlemen been up to with it? Looking into the yachts of the rich and famous?"

"Something like that," Oblo said, scratching his head. "But nothing too . . . damaging. They all seem to be down on the planet playing with horses."

In her office, she found most of the messages to be routine queries, including some from travel agents who wondered when she would be free for bookings. She hadn't thought of having any client but Lady Cecelia—but if Cecelia stayed here too long, she'd have to find another charter. And that meant hiring service staff as well . . . she felt her shoulders tensing. She hated the thought of dealing with service staff; she was a commander, not a . . . whatever you called it.

She had gone through the messages in order of time, the usual way, so the one headed "Serrano Family: request meeting" came last. It had arrived days ago, but she saw by the comments that whoever it was had refused several offers to forward the message. She stared at it, breathing carefully: in, out. Which of her many relatives could it be? And why? Only one way to find out; she posted a message to the station address and waited for the response. It came almost at once: request for meeting, and a suggested location, the dock outside the yacht's access tube.

The dark compact form in uniform looked vaguely familiar. Heris paused, suddenly wary. Upright, as only the military youth were, and ensign's insignia. Who? Then the young man turned and met her eyes; she felt that look as a blow to the gut. "Barin!"

"Captain Serrano." His formality steadied her. Her own distant cousin, and he gave her her title.

"What is it?" she asked then. "Would you prefer to talk in my quarters?"

"If—if you don't mind." He waited for her answer in that contained, measured posture she knew so well. He would wait for a day if she chose to make him.

"Come along, then." She led the way; her neck itched with his gaze on it. She felt vulnerable, as she had not for a long time. He could kill her easily, be gone before anyone knew . . . no, that was ridiculous. Why would he?

They passed no one, and neither of them spoke. When they reached her quarters, she preceded him through the door, and went around behind her desk. "Have a seat," she offered, but he stood before her desk like any junior officer called before her. His eyes, after one quick flicker around the room, settled on her face. She waited, wondering if she must prompt him with a question, but he spoke before her patience ran out.

"I came to offer you formal apologies on behalf of the family," he said, stopping there as if he had run into a wall.

"You?" Her mind raced. Formal apology? If they had wanted to apologize, if this were genuine, they'd have sent someone more senior. Not one of the admirals Serrano, of course, but someone her former rank or above.

Barin flushed at her tone. "Captain Serrano, I admit I—perhaps I overstated my authority." That had the phrasing learned in the classroom.

"Go on," she said. In her voice she heard authority and wariness mingled.

He did not answer at once, and she let her gaze sharpen. What had he done, gone AWOL? But his answer, when it came, seemed just possible. "My grandmother—your aunt, Admiral Vida Serrano—asked me to find you. With apologies: no one more senior could be spared, under the circumstances."

"The circumstances being?" All her old instincts had come alert.

"The unsettled state of things in the Familias, that is. All leaves canceled, all active-duty personnel called in—"

"I know what all leaves canceled means," Heris said, dryly. "But I also know they released all the Royal junior officers and dispersed the onplanet regiment on Rockhouse—"

"Things have . . . changed," Barin said. "Glenis and I were the only ones old enough, that didn't have other assignments. She went up-axis and I went down—they weren't sure where and when we'd catch up with you, you see."

"But the point is . . . apology? And for what?" As if she didn't know; as if her heart didn't burn with it.

"For not backing you when you were under investigation," Barin said. In his young voice, it sounded innocent enough; she wondered if he understood what had happened, if his elders had explained it to him. "I was told to say that your aunt the Admiral Serrano was not informed until too late of the situation you were in, and would certainly have given you assistance had she known."

Her aunt the admiral. It was just possible that she had not known, until after Heris's resignation, if no one had thought to inform her. But she should have been told. She was then the most distant high-ranking family member, but not the only one. Other admirals Serrano had been closer, must have known about it. Why hadn't one of them done something?

Barin went on then, as if he had been reading her thoughts. "I—I didn't know any of this before, sir. Ma'am."

That bobble made Heris grin before she thought. "I wouldn't expect you would have," she said.

"I mean, the admiral said there was some kind of trouble in the family, something she hadn't anticipated. Not whatever it was with you, but—"

Heris felt her brows rising. "You mean you don't know what happened to me? Whatever's happened to the grapevine? It's been long enough I'd expect it to be all over every prep school with a single Fleet brat in it."

He flushed. "There've been rumors—"

"I would hope so. What's a lifetime of experience for, if not to make rumors fly? Let me straighten out a few things for you, young man." She paused, thinking how best to put it. Honesty first, and tact second, but without bitterness if she could manage it. "What happened was that I accomplished my assigned mission, but not in the way I'd been told to do it. My way saved lives, but it made an admiral look stupid—Lepescu, if you ever heard of him."

"Uh . . . no, I haven't."

"Bloodthirsty bastard," Heris said. "He liked wasting troops. I killed him—"

"What!" He looked as if the sky had just fallen; she almost laughed. Had she ever been that innocently certain that everyone followed the rules, that hierarchies never tumbled?

"Not *then*. Sorry; I got out of sequence. Let's see. He was furious that I had not won the battle his way, and swore he'd get revenge. There was a Board of Inquiry, of course. Evidence had . . . disappeared." She didn't really want to tell him how; it was too complicated, and involved too many names he might know. "I was offered immunity for my crew if I would resign my commission," she went on. "Otherwise, courts-martial for all. Considering Lepescu's position—the Rules of Engagement—and the fact that no one from the family spoke for me, I decided to resign and save my crew."

He stared at her; clearly he hadn't heard this before. "But—but why didn't—?"

"I don't know why someone didn't do something. Let me finish." More bite got through than she intended; he flinched. It wasn't his fault, she reminded herself, and tried to breathe slowly. "What I didn't know was that after I resigned, after I was gone from his sector, Lepescu charged my crew. Most were convicted of serious breaches of regulation and were dispersed to various Fleet prisons. Some—" The old rage blanked her vision for a moment and she had to force another deep breath to continue. "Some he took to a private hunting reserve and hunted."

"Hunted . . . you mean . . . like animals?"

"Precisely. With friends of his who liked the same thing." She didn't mention the prince; his death had earned her silence.

"How did you . . . how did you find out?" That had not been the first question he thought of; she answered what she thought it had been.

"I killed him when I found him, which was—luckily for me—in the process of that hunting trip, when his guilt was not in question. My crew—the survivors—were rehabilitated and given the choice of remaining in Fleet or taking a settlement and going civilian. Some of them are here, with me."

"Couldn't you have gone back?" He looked puzzled.

"Of course. But—" Heris wondered how much to explain to this young man—this mere child, as he seemed to her. Could he understand that it wasn't merely pique? She'd already explained more than he was likely to absorb. He knew no world but Fleet; he could imagine no other choice than returning to it. "So," she said, changing direction. "That's what my side of the trouble was like. Now—what did the admiral want me to know?"

He looked confused a moment, then got back to it. "She didn't explain much, really. She wanted you to know she hadn't known about your trouble in time, and I think she blames some of the others in the family." As well she might. "Uh . . . your parents among them . . ."

"It's not my problem now," Heris said crisply. She wasn't about to discuss her parents with him.

"No . . . but she'd like to talk to you, the next time you're anywhere near."

Which was likely to be a long time from now. "Did she give you an itinerary?" Already her mind had moved beyond

this to how she was going to ease this young relation off
the ship and on his way.

"Yes—here." He fished in his pocket and came up with
a small datacube. "It's compressed format—she sent an
adapter in case you don't have a reader with the right
interface."

"Thanks," Heris said. She wasn't going to tell him that
she had a couple of experts who could strip the data out
of virtually any storage device. Whatever her aunt the
admiral was up to, she would keep her own secrets.

Someone tapped at the door. Barin looked around, and
Heris called, "Come on in."

Brun opened the door. "Captain, the new installations
are ready for inspection."

"Thank you; I'll be along shortly." Heris repressed a
grin. Brun definitely had the right touch, timing and tone
both impeccable. Brun nodded and withdrew.

"I'll—I'll be going," Barin said, with a hint of nervousness.

"Yes—I'm sorry, but I do have some ship work under
way. Tell you what—why not have dinner with me this
evening? You can bring me up-to-date on your sibs and
cousins."

"Do you really—? Grandmother said not to waste your
time. Just give you the message, and the cube, and get
out of your way."

Heris laughed. "She must think I've grown to be quite
an ogre," she said. *That* Admiral Serrano would know how
ogres were grown. Perversely, Heris was now determined
to be cordial to the youngster. "Are you scheduled out of
here?"

"No—not yet."

"Fine—then you can meet me at the Captains Guild
for dinner. They use a screwball clock setting here—five
shifts in the day and five hours in each shift, and it starts
at what we'd call mainday or first shift. So make it third
and one."

"Yes, sir." This time he didn't change it to the civilian usage.

"I'll guide you out." He could find his own way on such a tiny ship, but she wouldn't let even a relative wander around unescorted.

The cube contained substantially more than the admiral's itinerary for the next year or so. Heris had suspected it would when she turned it over to Meharry.

"Video, audio, and an almighty big chunk of encrypted stuff. Does your family have its own code scheme?"

"More than one," Heris said. "I suppose she wonders if I kept the key."

"I should have known," Meharry said sourly. "You great families—"

"As if you didn't have something of the same sort," Heris retorted. "What I'm really concerned about is any kind of ghost or vampire, or even an owl." Anything that might compromise their own information systems.

Meharry shook her head. "No hooters at all, and nothing that my spook catchers notice. Want me to let Esteban have a look?"

"No." That came out with more force than Heris intended, and she calmed herself. "No, I trust your judgment on this. Let's see if my key works on the encrypted stuff."

She didn't bother to explain the key. As with the rendezvous protocols cooked up by young officers and elaborated over the years to an intricate but precise interpersonal code, family encryption keys were combinations of predictable and unpredictable private data. Events important to the family as a whole, to individuals within it, might form part of the key, along with informal rules for making changes. Heris didn't so much have a key, as a procedure for finding the key, a procedure which functioned as part of the key.

Video came up. "She looks like you on a bad day," Meharry blurted. Then, "Sorry, Captain."

"It's our classic bone structure," Heris murmured. "Plus thirty or forty years—I forget how old she'd be by now. Anyway she's taller." Her aunt the admiral had silver hair now, even more striking against her dark face. She still had the Algestin accent, as she identified herself and suggested that Heris watch the rest in private.

"How'd she know I was here?" asked Meharry suspiciously. "Is this going to have a compulsion component in it?"

"I doubt that. Family matters, mostly. Stay, if you want; I'm not sensitive to dirty laundry at the moment."

"No thanks. I don't want more than one Serrano mad at me." Meharry stalked out, very much like a cat twitching its tail after being sprinkled with water. Heris didn't laugh.

Instead, she started the datastream again. Her aunt the admiral . . . someone she had dreamed about being, as a girl. Someone she had hoped to impress, as a young officer. Someone she had thought of as a mentor, and even a friend.

Someone who had not come to her rescue when she needed it desperately.

Now that dark face with the silver aureole wasted no time in apology. "Heris: I trust that you will hear me out, no matter how bitter you are. This is critical material, and it may be my only chance to brief you. I am still not sure who kept me from finding out about your trouble, and at the moment that's no longer a priority item. The future of the Familias Regnant and the Regular Space Service is—"

A full hour later, Heris sat back and drew a long breath. In the same organized, concise way that had earned her an admiral's stars two years ahead of anyone else in her cohort, her aunt had laid out what she knew of the factional disputes within the Regular Space Service, and where the present political stress might rupture the Fleet. She had been given her aunt's best guess on which family members to trust, which senior officers to trust, where certain fragrant bones were buried . . . assuming that she could trust her aunt.

The memory of the last moments of the cube came back full force. Admirals apologized rarely; her aunt had once explained, at a family party when Heris was still a student and her own stars were years in the future, that that was because they planned ahead and had no need to. But the good ones could and did, her aunt had said, when they must. She had believed her aunt was a good admiral . . . her aunt, who had apologized for her own and the family's betrayal.

"I love you, Heris," her aunt had said at the last. "I hope you believe that, if nothing else. With the trouble coming . . . I want you to know that I consider you one of the best Serranos of your generation. And one of the best young officers we had, too."

It would take a long time to digest everything in the cube. If it was true . . . but she felt that it was true. It felt right, and she'd always had good intuitions about that. And if true, then she thought she understood some things Livadhi had not told her.

The sooner they were off this station the better. Deep space was going to be a lot safer for everyone for a while.

The Captains Guild dining room on Zenebra Station had the usual quiet, respectable atmosphere, not quite as stultifying as the Senior Officers' Club at a sector headquarters, but almost. Two tables away, a merchant captain in the uniform of a major line dined alone, without looking up; across the room, a quiet group of officers from another line chatted while waiting to be served.

Barin had recoiled from the menu's prices at first. "I'm treating you," Heris said. "Have something you like."

"It's all so . . . fancy."

"Not really. Only a step up from any ordinary restaurant

on dockside. You've been eating Academy chow too long.
If you want to see fancy, you should see Lady Cecelia's
tables. I couldn't believe it when I first went to work for
her. She thinks every meal should be a work of art."

He wavered, uncertain. Heris took a guess, from his
eye movements, and ordered for him, waving away his
objections. "Maybe it *is* just curiosity, but if you don't like
it you can always get yourself a basic cube of processed
goo afterwards."

"But Lassaferan snailfish?"

"You wanted it; I could tell. You might like it; I do."

He relaxed, bit by bit, as he worked his way into the food
with youthful appetite. Heris asked no questions, letting
him tell her what he would about himself. Jerd and Gesta's
oldest son, normal Fleet childhood—which meant in and
out of service creches. Academy prep school: he had
graduated fifth in his class there. Academy: he had been
second to a brilliant daughter of an admiral, who'd been
killed in her first assignment when a glitch in a powerplant
readout turned out to be a real problem in the powerplant,
not the readout. Heris wondered about that, after her aunt's
report. *Top Fleet officers are losing too many of their
children—the best ones—in accidents in the first two years
out of the Academy.* Of course those were the dangerous
years. Youngsters full of book knowledge, eager to prove
themselves—they got into trouble. So had she. But someone
had been there to get her out, and if her aunt was right,
there were fewer rescues these days.

This boy, though—he was bright enough, and good
enough. She liked the way he described his first tour, as
ensign on a cruiser. He didn't reveal anything he shouldn't—
even though she was a family member and former Fleet
officer—and yet he didn't appear to be holding back.

"Communications," she mused, when he ran down. "You
know, when I was commissioned, we didn't have FTL
communications except from planetary platforms. I was

on *Boarhound* when they mounted the first shipboard ansible, and at first it was only one-way, from the planet to us. That was still pretty exciting. Then they worked out how to get enough power for transmission."

"It's still not unlimited," he said, and flushed.

"No, I know that." She didn't tell him how. He didn't know about Koutsoudas and didn't need to. "But someday I expect they'll figure out ways to give us realtime communication in all situations. Something in jumpspace would be a real help." An understatement. A way to communicate in and out of jumpspace would radically change space warfare. "But that's beside the point—you're going back to see the admiral?"

"Yes, sir. Ma'am."

Heris chuckled. "Either will do. Tell her from me that I don't entirely understand, but I have heard what she's saying. Can you do that?"

"Of course, sir."

"Good. And tell her—tell her I love her."

He flushed again, but nodded. Heris was almost glad to see that embarrassment; an honest young man would be embarrassed to repeat such a message, but he would do it. Coming from him directly, it would have the effect she wanted.

She looked at the chronometer on the wall. "Sorry to leave you, but I've work scheduled. If there's anything I can do to assist, feel free to call on me." He pushed back his chair, with a last glance at a dessert guaranteed to cause heart failure in anyone over twenty, but Heris waved him down. "No—finish that, don't waste it. I'll take care of everything on the way out. Give my regards to family." Meaning everyone but the aunt admiral; he could interpret that how he liked. But, polite to the end, he stood until Heris had left the dining room. She hoped he would sit back down and finish that dessert. He had earned it.

❖ ❖ ❖

The next day, Cecelia arrived without warning. "I had to take a standby seat on the shuttle," she explained. "People are leaving in droves, of course." Heris had noticed that; half the ships docked when they arrived had already left. "But I wanted to talk to you."

"Here, or en route to your next destination?" Heris asked. "If you want to leave, I need to file with the Stationmaster."

"Here for now. I might even go back down once more, to talk to Ari." Cecelia paused, and gave Heris a sharp look. "What's happened? Did you and Petris have a fight? You look upset about something."

"It's not Petris," Heris said, annoyed to feel the heat rising in her face. "It's my family . . . they sent someone to talk to me."

"About time." Cecelia kicked off her boots and wiggled her toes luxuriously. "Ahhh. I was standing in line for two hours. Standing in line is a lot worse than walking."

"Agreed," Heris said. She hoped Cecelia would stay on another topic, but that was too much to expect.

"Your family sent someone," she said. "I hope whoever it was crawled on his or her belly and licked your toes."

"Cecelia!" Despite herself, Heris couldn't help laughing. "What a disgusting thought! No, it was a very nice young man, just out of the Academy, my aunt admiral's grandson."

"Apologetic," Cecelia said.

"In a way. Not personally, but on behalf of. And she sent a datacube herself. It's just—I'm still not sure I understand."

"I know I don't understand. Why didn't she help you?"

"She says she didn't know in time. She wants to talk to me about it, if it's convenient."

"And you?"

"I want to think it over," Heris said.

"Heris, I want to ask you something."

"Of course." Heris seemed relaxed and alert at once, no tension in her face.

"Do I seem different since my rejuvenation? I don't mean the obvious . . . something else."

Heris took a sip of coffee before answering. "The obvious—your body, your hair color. I'm not sure about the rest. A young person is supposed to have more energy, so I presume that along with a younger body, a healthier body, you have more intrinsic energy. Is that right?"

"Yes, but that's not exactly—"

"No . . . I'm feeling my way. You are different, in behavior as well as body, but I'm not sure which caused which. You were never . . . ah . . . passive." Cecelia snorted at that attempt to be tactful. Heris grinned at her. "Look, even as an old lady, you were energetic, feisty, and stubborn. Now your body's younger, and you're even more energetic, feisty, and stubborn. High-tempered. But I didn't know you when you were this age the first time around, so I can't say if you're changed."

That was the crux of it, right there. Heris hadn't been born when she had been forty. What she was right now wasn't really forty—it was eighty-seven in a forty-year-old mask. "I'm not really forty, Heris," she said, trying not to sound as frustrated and annoyed as she was. "I have all the experience of the next forty-seven years. All of it. What I need to know is whether the treatment changed me—the person I am—and sent me off on a new course."

"Mmm. I would say that it had to. The course of a life without rejuvenation, for someone your age—you were preparing to detach, to relinquish your grip on life itself—"

"Not *yet*!" Cecelia said. "I was only eighty-four; I'd have had another twenty years—"

"But you'd given up competitive riding; you'd gradually reduced your social contacts. All signs that you accepted, however reluctantly, the evidence of age. You expected to enjoy your remaining years, but you weren't pushing toward anything new."

"True, I suppose." She didn't like to hear that analysis, but she could not deny the evidence.

"Now you've been put back, physically at least, to your most productive period. You have twenty to thirty years of vigorous activity before you begin the decline again—unless you renew the process. That has to change your course—you could not fail to act differently now than three years ago."

"I had a visitor, that man—"

"Yes." Heris's voice chilled; clearly she didn't like Pedar.

"He's a multiple Rejuvenant. He thinks I should . . . identify myself with them."

"Who?"

"Those who have rejuvenated with the new procedures; those who expect to renew their rejuvenations. They have adopted customs for identification, for interaction. Given the age of the procedure itself, most of those who have used it are my age or younger."

"I thought it had been around for eighty years or so," Heris said.

"It has. But remember that it competed at first with the old procedure, which had proven its safety." Heris couldn't remember, of course. She herself just remembered a discussion of the new procedure, then far more expensive than the standard. By the time she was thirty, it had gained some ground. But it was incompatible with the earlier procedure. No one who had the Stochaster could then have the Ramhoff-Inikin. Lorenza had been one of the first to test—illegally, at the time—the safety of repeated rejuvenation with the new procedure. Cecelia had been nearly fifty when the laws forbidding serial rejuvenation were changed. She explained this, aware of the gaps in her own knowledge. She had been so sure she wouldn't choose rejuvenation that she had ignored most of the arguments about it.

"There's always been age stratification," Heris said slowly.

"Particularly those who have attained prestige or power—the older they are, the more they hold. But if there's a sizable group now which is . . . immortal . . ." Cecelia could tell from the pause that the word bothered her. "I see the potential for more rigid stratification, even alienation."

"That's what bothers me," Cecelia said. "I've always been rich; I've always known that my life wasn't anything like the average. I've enjoyed my wealth, but felt that it was fair because I was going to die someday and someone else would have everything I had owned. True, most of it would go to other rich people—my family—but I wasn't trying to hang on to it. From what Pedar said, I'd suspect that others are. Lorenza certainly was. And I feel my own ambition stirring, along with the changes in my body. I won the All-Union championship before; I could do it again."

"How many times?" Heris asked.

"I don't know. I never tired of it when I could still do it; the feel of riding a great course is like nothing else. Mind and body together—stupid riders, no matter how athletic, don't survive, and clumsy smart ones don't either. Yet, in the field I care most about, the prizes are limited. I've won Wherrin, I've won Scatlin, I've won Patchcock—"

"Patchcock!" Heris stared at her. Cecelia had not wanted her train of thought interrupted, and glared back.

"Yes, Patchcock. It's not the equestrian center Wherrin is; it's uglier, for one thing. Not really an ag world. But they have a circuit of five or six major events, in the uplands, and—"

"Patchcock is politically unstable," Heris said.

"That's since my time," Cecelia said, and shrugged. She had not been back since winning the Patchcock Circuit Trophy twice in a row and then losing to Roddy Carnover, the fall that broke her leg in several places. That had been . . . had been over forty years before. She took a breath and went on.

"My point is, I've achieved all the goals that attract event riders in the Familias. I could compete in the Guerni Republic, I suppose, or even beyond, though the travel times get to be fierce. But why? Suppose I did win the All-Union title forty years in a row—and then rejuved again and won it forty times more. I can't see that, even though I love riding and want to keep doing it."

"And this Pedar—"

"My goals," Cecelia said, "have always been limited. I did learn to manage my own investments, after my parents died, but only so that I had plenty of money to pursue my real interest—the horses. I didn't really care about gaining power in those organizations, running them— there's not time, you see. And horse people have always had more contact with other social strata . . . you can't compete with horses unless you're active in the stable as well. Not mucking out all the stalls, no—again, there's no time—but you aren't likely to be stupidly contemptuous of those who do. Horses are natural levelers, and not only when they dump you in the mud."

"But equestrians have always been rich. . . ." Heris said.

"Yes, and no. The really good ones from poor families get corporate sponsorship, just as really good singers and dancers and actors get sponsorship. While those of us who do it think of riding as recreational, its position in the economy is actually entertainment . . . the recreation of the audience, not the participant. So there's been access for the equestrian with less talent." Cecelia frowned, remembering that she had told Heris about her own misuse of power and money against a talented junior. Best get that over with. . . . "Of course there are abuses. I did it myself, as you know. But in general, there are openings."

"Don't you think the other Rejuvenants will get as tired of chasing their prizes as you say you will become of chasing eventing titles?"

"I'm not sure—I'm afraid not. By the nature of the

system, an equestrian's goals are limited. But someone whose joy is gaining economic or political power . . . what will stop him?"

"I . . . see."

"Lorenza, for instance. Where would she have stopped? Had her ambition any limits? And the more benign Rejuvenant, someone like Pedar—" Though, even to herself, she had trouble with that label. Pedar benign? Better than Ross, but still.

"If the ambition has no natural saturation, then the split between generations gets worse. I see your point. The logical answer is expansion, opening new opportunities. . . ."

"And the Familias Regnant has never been an expansive system," Cecelia said.

"No, but we both know who is." Heris looked worried enough now. "Just how long do you suppose the Benignity has had this process? And did they think of the implications back at the first?"

"It's like training," Cecelia said. Heris looked confused. "The inexperienced or incompetent trainer attempts to control everything through the horse. The good trainer controls *herself.*"

"That sounds like something Admiral Feiruss used to say," Heris said. "You can't control anyone else until you can control yourself—"

"Not only until, but only by means of," Cecelia said, glad to have found common ground at last. "It is your control of your own body that allows you to give the signals needed, and notice if they're understood. The bad rider flounders around, blaming the horse that 'isn't paying attention' when he's given so many signals that the horse is confused."

"I've had instructors like that," Heris said with a grin. "I remember one—always yelling at us to pay attention to him, then telling us to concentrate on something else, then yelling again—I couldn't tell if it was more important to watch him or the demonstration."

"What I'm afraid of, with this group Pedar talks of, is that they'll try to control everything else before themselves." Cecelia wasn't going to let Heris wander off on side roads of memory. "I don't want to be around people like that."

It had been easy to say that, but in real life—in practical terms—she wondered what difference it might make. Cecelia clipped the blue and silver ring to her ear and grimaced into the mirror. It felt like the first time she had worn a competition number, all those decades ago: she was declaring herself part of something she didn't understand. Although she had a much better idea of what competitive riders were like than she had of her fellow Rejuvenants. She didn't know what kind of reception she would get—if anyone else would notice.

"Ah . . . Lady Cecelia." The bank officer's gaze had snagged briefly on the ring; she noticed that he had two, one in each ear. "And how may we assist you today?"

"I'm going to be traveling to agricultural research worlds, picking up equine samples for my breeding farm on Rotterdam," Cecelia said. "I may be out of touch for extended periods, and I wanted to be sure that there were no problems with my line of credit."

"I wouldn't expect any," the man said. "So far the political situation has had no effect on commerce; certainly our institution is stable—"

"I wasn't doubting it. Only my travel advisors pointed out that some of the worlds I want to visit are served only by ansible, for anything beyond a system transfer."

"Ah . . . do you have a list of these worlds?"

"Yes—" Cecelia handed it over. "Ordinarily, I could deal with an agency that specializes in equine genetics, but I'm looking for something I can't really define. I'll know it when I see it—"

"Yes . . ." He didn't sound interested; he probably wasn't. Then he looked up. "I think the best thing would be a batch dump to the local systems' registered financial institutions. That way, they'd have your references when you arrived, and your line of credit would be established at both ends. Can you estimate your needs?"

Cecelia had that information as well, and he fed it into his desktop. "We're leaving Zenebra shortly," she said, as she waited. "Can you give me an estimate of clearance times?"

"Unless your yacht is faster than anything I ever heard of, your local approvals will all be waiting days before you arrive, milady. And—may I say it's good to see you back in competition. I hope you find the right mount for next year's trials."

The assumptions took her breath away, but she merely nodded her thanks and returned to the ship. The ring in her ear felt huge, heavy with responsibilities she didn't want.

✧ Chapter Six

Castle Rock

Ronnie knew perfectly well he'd been dismissed. His aunt wouldn't listen to him; Heris Serrano, while she might have had good advice, wouldn't help him directly. And Raffa wouldn't answer his calls. He went to George, and poured out his troubles. George's solution, which would have been adequate a year before, now seemed childish.

"I don't *want* to make Raffa jealous," he said. "I don't care about singers, or dancers, or . . . or anything else."

"Then take the bold captain's advice and go do something brave and wonderful, and impress Raffa. She'll come around." That in the confident voice of a young man whose heart had never been shaken.

"It's easy for you," muttered Ronnie. George was perilously near to odiousness again. As far as he was concerned, he had been plucked from life's tree to lie sodden in the gutter, a dead leaf.

"Tell you what," George said. "I'll go with you. It *is* dull, with no more Royals to play games, with no regimental ditties for dancing. Let's go explain to Bunny and my father how useful we can be, if they'll just give us the appropriate errand for two handsome, talented, brave young men."

"You're ridiculous," Ronnie said, but his heart lifted a little, a dead leaf still, but one that might blow where the wind sent it. He let George make the call, and the appointment.

"And don't tell your parents," George said after he had named the day and hour. "It's all their fault, remember, and you're furious with them."

He wasn't, really. It wasn't their fault; they had tried, and Aunt Cecelia had simply gone off like fireworks. But he understood George's point. It was hard enough to have them lurking around trying to cheer him up about Raffa; if they knew he was about to go do something, they'd hover even more.

Ronnie let George explain that they both felt they could be of use to the new government—that they had unique talents which should be exploited. He halfway expected Lord Thornbuckle and George's father to laugh at them and send them away. But instead, they exchanged significant looks.

"You're serious," Lord Thornbuckle said. "You would be willing to go anywhere and do anything?"

"Well . . ." George looked at Ronnie. "Perhaps not *quite* anything. I mean, if you had in mind sweeping streets in some benighted mining village, I'd rather not. Be a waste of our abilities, anyway."

"And you see your abilities as?"

"Discreet, loyal young gentlemen of the world, able to take care of themselves, strong, healthy, the usual. Intelligent enough, ingenious—" That did get a laugh, from George's father.

"Ingenious, yes. That's how you nearly got yourself killed, wasn't it? But we might have something suitable for two young wastrels, at that."

"It's fairly complicated," Lord Thornbuckle said. "And it's extremely confidential. If you were still on active service, we could not possibly share this with you." That sounded serious enough. Ronnie tried for an expression of intelligent interest. To his surprise, Lord Thornbuckle started by talking about rejuvenation.

"Most people now use the Ramhoff-Inikin method, which allows serial rejuvenations—"

"Up to how many?" George asked.

"I don't know," Lord Thornbuckle said. "Anyway, the pharmaceuticals used in this process are manufactured in the Guerni Republic, or under their license in a few other places. Most are imported from the Guernesi, simply because of their known quality. They developed the process; they know it best. And, of course, it was originally illegal in the Familias, so people had to go there to have it done."

"Why was it illegal?" George asked.

"It's a long story that doesn't concern you," Lord Thornbuckle said. "It's not illegal now, but most of our supply still comes that way. Now. You know that Lorenza was involved in the distribution of illicit pharmaceuticals, right?"

"Like what happened to George and the prince," Ronnie said, nodding.

"Yes. And others—some we know, and some we suspect. Lady Cecelia's medical reports suggest that some of these drugs are very similar to variants of the rejuvenation drugs. We are concerned that our supply of Ramhoff-Inikin drugs might be adulterated at some point between the manufacturer and the user. The Guernesi ship by commercial carrier, and something Heris Serrano said made us wonder about the security of those shipments. If the Compassionate Hand wanted to cause us real trouble, adulterating those drugs—perhaps contaminating them with mind-altering components—would be a good start."

"So," Kevil Mahoney said, before George could interrupt, "it would be very useful to us if you could take a sample of these drugs back to the Guerni Republic and have them analyzed. Are they still what we paid for? If not, what would be the effects of using them in the rejuvenation procedure?

What symptoms should we look for in multiple Rejuvenants that suggest a misuse of the drugs?"

"You want us to go—with some drug samples?" George sounded insulted.

"It would be helpful, yes. And the data we've collected so far. We'd been wondering whom we could trust to hand-carry these things; it's not something we want to risk to ordinary shipping."

"You've got perfect cover," Mahoney pointed out. "Young men, rich and fun-loving, the sort who would ordinarily be running off to distant places for the fun of it. Everyone knows Ronnie and Raffaele Forrester-Saenz broke up; everyone suspects the reasons. What's more natural than fleeing from the constraints of home? Especially since your aunt had been there, and you might have legitimate questions about her medical treatment."

"I might?" Ronnie felt humiliated enough to hear older men discussing his lack-of-love life.

"Of course. She came back and sued your parents; you might be questioning whether her rejuvenation—which did not involve suspect drugs, since it was done there—had influenced her mind, or whether the original attack did."

"Oh."

"How are we going to keep the samples from being stolen?" asked George. They had adjourned to George's suite at his father's house, where they could be reasonably sure they were free of intrusive recorders.

"Why would they be? If no one knows we're carrying them—"

"But if someone suspects—"

"Look—you heard what they said. I've got the perfect excuse for going to the Guerni Republic. My aunt was rejuvenated there, and her doctors asked for clarification of the records—"

"They won't let you look at her records!"

"How do you know? They have different laws—maybe their laws don't say anything about medical confidentiality. Besides, I can ask—they don't have to answer."

"I suppose that makes sense." George reached out and took a handful of tawny grapes. "These are good—I wish we were traveling with your Aunt Cecelia. I've never forgotten the food her gardeners and cooks put on the table."

"Which brings up how we will travel. It will be too obvious if we take a private yacht."

"We're going *commercial*?"

"Yes, and not even a major line. Your father suggested a mixed-cargo vessel."

George wrinkled his nose. "Blast him. He's afraid we'll get into trouble on a big passenger liner. He should know better by now."

Ronnie shrugged. "Well, unless you want to pop for the ticket yourself, we haven't much choice." His parents, faced with a lawsuit from his aunt, were busily divesting themselves of assets, trying to lessen the blow. That meant his usual generous credit line had been pared down, if not to the bone at least well beneath its usual cushion.

"No. My father says this is no time for us to show off our wealth, and I'm not in the Royals anymore, so I don't need that size allowance. I think he's trying to get me to go *do* something with my life. You know?"

"I know." Ronnie stared at the wall, took a deep breath, and intoned, "It's time you made something of yourself young man, and when I was your age I had already—that speech."

"He doesn't say it like that, but he's hinting. At least he's not pushing me to take classes at the University."

"Brun had fun on a mixed-cargo ship," Ronnie said. "We should be able to survive."

❖   ❖   ❖

Survival won out over fun, when they discovered that
there were no—absolute zero—eligible girls on the *Sekkor
Vil*. No eligible anythings, in fact; the other passengers
were bored middle-aged middle managers on business
trips. Once they discovered that Ronnie and George were
Chairholders' sons, and not active in any corporation, they
went back to their handcomps and ignored them. Ronnie
spent hours with the Guernesi language tapes, because it
was better than listening to George complain about the
way the cards fell when they tried to play a hand.

Finally they arrived in the Guerni Republic and
transferred to a local line for the run to Music. At last
there were other passengers, not only Guernesi, and not
all over forty. Ronnie had no trouble enacting the rich
young man, and although he missed Raffa, he had to admit
that evenings spent dancing in the passenger lounge were
more restorative than those spent lying in the bunk wishing
she were there.

On Music, they delivered their samples, and the
datacubes, to the pharmaceutical industry's combined
quality control laboratory. "We'll have the preliminary
results in a day or so," the director said. "But you'll want
more precise tests, if anything shows up. If these were
not manufactured here, for instance, I presume you would
like some idea where else they might have been made."

"Well . . . yes." Ronnie hadn't known that was possible.

"You're not a chemist or pharmacist," the man said. It
wasn't a question at all.

"No," he said. He hated to admit he was nothing but
an ignorant errand boy, but that was the truth.

"I understood that you had the . . . er . . . confidence
of your new prime minister or whatever you call him."
That with a doubtful look, as if he might have fabricated
the whole thing.

"Yes . . . that is, he's a good friend of our family."

"Mmm. Well . . . we'll be in touch. If you'll just give

me your local address." Clearly a dismissal. Ronnie looked at George and shrugged. Whatever the man thought, they *were* the Familias in this matter, and when he viewed the cube he would probably feel differently about it. In the meantime, they had a world to explore.

Naturally, they spent that evening discovering the many ways in which young people of the city amused themselves. "Let's not stay too long anywhere," George said, as he watched two stunning women stroll out of the bar they were just entering.

"Mmm. No." Ronnie, with Raffa at the back of his mind, was more interested in music. He had chosen this bar not quite at random, from the music drifting out when the door opened. "Come on, George—we still haven't eaten yet."

"That's not what I meant," George said, but he settled at the table Ronnie chose, and punched up the table's menu. "Ah—I'm hungry too, and they have an illustrated menu. Makes up for their incomprehensible language." George, having declined to "waste any time" with the Guernesi language tapes, was finding it difficult without his usual audience for repartee. Ronnie, who had known he had no aptitude for language learning, now had a serviceable set of travelers' phrases, although he suspected his accent was atrocious. Ronnie leaned back and looked at the musicians clumped on a tiny stage. He saw two instruments new to him, one with strings and one that he guessed was a woodwind. His gaze drifted toward the bar itself . . . and he grabbed George's arm.

"George—look over there. Who's that remind you of?"

"Who—good lord, it is. Gerel. But he's dead—your aunt said he died on her yacht."

"Well, *that's* not dead. If it's not Gerel, it must be a clone. Do you suppose the Guernesi did it?" Through Ronnie's mind ran all the grisly possibilities he'd ever heard of, mostly from wild adventure yarns. Clones developed from the cells of dead men, raised to seek vengeance on murderers and the like.

"It hasn't been that long—I thought they took years to grow." George, clearly, was thinking of the same stories.

"We'd better find out," said Ronnie. "Suppose Aunt Cecelia was wrong? Someone ought to know." Memory tugged at him with that phrase. Who'd said that, with disastrous results? He watched the prince—or his clone—take a long swallow of something in a tankard. It had to be the prince. That way of holding his head, the way his shoulders moved when he drank—it couldn't be anyone else.

"Wait for me," he said. "I've got to check this out." Without hearing whatever George tried to say, he moved closer, his awareness narrowing to the young man at the bar as if he were a hunter stalking prey. When he was close enough, he cleared his throat; the young man looked around, the very picture of slightly bored courtesy.

"Excuse me," Ronnie said. "I believe we met—you're Gerel—"

"You're mistaken," the young man said, interrupting. "My name is Gerald Andres Smith, but we've never met." His eyes had betrayed him, with a moment of fear now shuttered in caution.

"Ah," said Ronnie, who had no idea what to say next. This close, the young man looked exactly like the prince, but a prince not as stupefied as he had been in the last few years. Even the little scar on the temple, from the time he'd fallen against a goalpost playing soccer. "I'm . . . sorry to bother you," Ronnie went on. "But you remind me very much of someone I grew up with. Extraordinary resemblance."

"I'm sorry," the young man said, with what appeared to be genuine sorrow. "But I think we need not continue this conversation. Under the circumstances."

"But—" Ronnie felt a little nudge under his pocket and

glanced down. Something glinted there, something his mind recognized, refused, and recognized again.

"I'm sorry," the young man said again. "But I'm not going back."

"But I didn't mean—" Ronnie got that out as fast as he could. The young man's eyes, Gerel's eyes, met his.

"Whatever you meant, it's trouble for me. I don't want trouble. I want to live here, and be left alone. My treatments are almost finished."

"Ronnie—what's wrong?" That was George, finally aware that Ronnie was in trouble. But he was in danger too. Ronnie couldn't think what to do or say. Then he glanced beyond George, and saw another prince—or clone—or whatever they were.

"We need to go outside," said the one whose weapon nudged his ribs. "Don't we?"

Anti-terrorism lectures had instructed Ronnie that going with an abductor made things worse—resist in place, he'd been told. But the lectures hadn't told him about the sudden hollow feeling under his breastbone, or the way his knees would tremble, when he thought about the weapon pressed to his side. And he was sure this was Gerel, whom he'd known all his life. Gerel might want to have their postponed duel at last, but he was honorable . . . wasn't he?

"Are you planning to kill us outside?" he asked, just to be sure.

"I very much hope not," the young man said. "But it's imperative that we talk without witnesses, and I don't intend to argue with you."

Much more decision than Gerel had shown in years, but Ronnie felt vaguely comforted. "All right," he said. "Don't hurt George. He went through enough last time."

The young man's mouth twitched. "I know. But we can't talk about it here. Come on."

George, who had been stopped from an outburst by the same surprise as Ronnie, said plaintively, "But who *are* you?"

The two identical young men gave each other quick, amused glances. "Gerald Smith," they said in unison.

Herded between the two Geralds, Ronnie and George found themselves moving along a crowded street, then into a less crowded one, and finally into a tiny tavern opening on a square with a fountain.

"I didn't know there were places like this here," George said, looking around. It was empty except for an aproned woman behind the bar, and the four of them. "Until now, the Guernesi have been entirely too practical for my taste—everything modern and convenient." Ronnie wondered if his unconcerned tone fooled the Geralds—it didn't fool him.

"This is modern and convenient," one Gerald said. "The Guernesi simply have a different style of modern and convenient. They like small gathering places that cater to particular clients."

"Like clones?" George said, as if determined to make a point of it.

"Clones aren't illegal in the Guerni Republic," the same Gerald said. "In fact, clone work groups are common, even preferred for some occupations."

"Like abducting people?" George said. Ronnie wanted to throttle him—hadn't he learned his lesson on the island? Did he still think he was invincible?

"The odious George," said the other Gerald, almost affectionately. "You haven't changed a bit."

"You are the prince's clones," Ronnie said. He hardly believed it, even now. They looked steadily back at him, then sighed in unison. It was eerie.

"Yes," one of them said. "We are. Illegally created, in the Familias Regnant, to be the prince's doubles when necessary. No one was supposed to know about us, except the necessary few." The other one snorted, a knowing snort, and Ronnie looked at him.

"A secret kept by a couple of doctors, implant-tape

technicians, the odd crown minister, the king's immediate family, and who knows what other oddments can hardly be called a secret."

"Did Gerel know about you?" asked Ronnie.

"Oh, yes. He thought it was some kind of game. He wished we could all be together like brothers—he missed his brothers a lot, I think—but of course that was impossible. The only times we were together, in that sense, was when we underwent the matching programming."

"Which is?" George asked.

"Conditioning tapes shared among us, so that we all knew what the public persona was supposed to know, and anything of Gerel's that they felt we needed. Cosmetic alterations to match appearance, following any trauma." The clones touched the matching scars that had convinced Ronnie they had to be Gerel himself. "And no, that didn't hurt. They were humane, our controllers, if you look at it that way."

"I don't think I do," said George. "It doesn't seem fair—"

They both shrugged. "No one chooses a birth," the one on the left said. "It was a better life than many. Privilege, wealth, an endless party in a way. You know that."

"Yes." Ronnie found it hard to remember clearly how he had thought two years ago—it was embarrassing, really—but he knew he, like the prince, had assumed limitless privilege, boundless wealth, and constant entertainment were his birthright.

"I owe you an apology, really," said the one on the right.

"For threatening me?"

"No . . . for causing trouble between you and the prince. The quarrel was really my fault," the clone said. He traced designs on the tabletop with the condensation from his beer mug. "Gerel Prime had lost interest in that singer months before, but I hadn't. Her voice—I don't know what you did in your time with her, but I was learning opera, you see. She thought it was touching that the prince really cared about music. I prolonged the relationship, so it overlapped with yours. You were jealous, I think—and she certainly found you a better bed partner than I, who cared only for her voice."

"If you'll excuse my mentioning it," George said, "you seem to be . . . er . . . brighter than the prince was toward the end."

"We're clones, but we're not the same person he was. We can't be. Identical twins—bionatural clones—were like that too. Each an individual person, even if outsiders couldn't tell them apart. We have similarities built into the genome, but we're not determined. I happen to love old-fashioned opera; the prince himself had an ear for music, but preferred instrumental."

"And that's *that* Gerald," the other said. "I too have the inborn ear for music, but my preference is far more popular; since I've been here I've discovered *casanegra*, which they tell me is descended from an entirely different Old Terran tradition than opera."

Ronnie glanced from one to the other. "I can't deal with this Gerald A. and Gerald B.," he said. "If you don't help me out, I swear I'll give you nicknames, both rude."

"You forget," the clone said, "that we're armed and dangerous."

"So shoot me," Ronnie said. "But I'm not going to struggle with it." The clones looked at each other, and finally nodded.

The one on the left spoke first. "I'm Andres and he's Borhes. Borhes and opera; Andres and casanegra, if you can keep that straight."

"I don't see why, if you're clones, you're not identical mentally as well," George said. "What's the use if you're not?"

"Identity is more than genes," Andres said. "I didn't understand it all myself, until the medical experts here explained it as they tried to figure out which of us was which. I always knew who *I* was, even when others got us confused. And Bor knew, and . . . and the others, whatever names they might have chosen, if they'd had the chance. And Gerel I suppose."

"When he wasn't so confused he didn't know day from night," Borhes put in. "And in case you wondered, apparently we never got the full dose of the drugs used on Gerel. They tell us we're normal. But even though we're identical at the genetic level, developmentally there are always minute differences in brain structure resulting from exactly which neurons connect with which in what order."

"But why didn't you tell Captain Serrano which was which when she came to take the prince for medical treatment? Or at least explain once you were here? It might have saved—"

"I don't see why we should care," Andres said. "They had us made for their own selfish reasons—yes, we enjoyed a life that was mostly pleasurable, but we had no freedom. Why should we risk anything to help them?"

"I suppose I thought you were a gentleman," said George. Andres laughed unkindly.

"Gentlemen? Clones? I suppose in the historical sense we are, if you think it's all in the blood, but otherwise absolutely not. Not if you mean some ridiculous code of behavior—"

"Which, after all, our Prime didn't adhere to, as you know very well." Borhes grinned at Ronnie. "I don't know what Gerel would have been if he hadn't been drugged, but on the whole he was as little bound by notions of duty as anyone I ever knew. You at your worst were a paragon of dedication beside him."

George flushed, and turned to Ronnie. "I thought your aunt said they were nice young men."

"She also said she was sure that the one who was killed was Gerel himself. A fool, but a noble fool." Ronnie took another direction. "Look—you remember Captain Serrano."

The clones exchanged glances. Andres finally answered. "Of course. An . . . unusual person, we thought."

Undoubtedly. Ronnie wondered if she'd treated them to any of the special methods she'd used on him. "What did you think of her?"

Again the quick exchange of glances; this time Borhes spoke. "Well . . . unusual, as Andres said. Intelligent, perhaps a bit stuffy the way Fleet officers often are."

"And my Aunt Cecelia? I know she talked to all of you."

Borhes looked thoughtful. "She's your aunt? I didn't realize that. She's the one who told the king our Prime was not normal, wasn't she?"

"Yes." Ronnie said no more. They seemed willing enough to rattle on; let them rattle.

"I liked her," Borhes said. It sounded real. "She told us we shouldn't go back; she told us we could make a better life here."

"And she was right," Andres said. "The Guernesi have given us limited citizenship—we can get full rights in five years if we're employed and have a clean legal record. Clones are not only legal, but valued. We'd be crazy to go back."

"I wouldn't ask you to go back," Ronnie said. Had they thought he might? Had that been the core of their resistance? "My aunt would skin me if I did." They grinned at him. "But in your position you might have heard things—things we need to know now, that might help us hold the alliances together. That's what I'd like to ask you about."

Borhes shook his head. "We're a lot safer if we don't know anything—if we did know, did remember, and told you, then the next person who wanted to know mightn't be so friendly. Surely you can see that."

He could. He could imagine a whole series of people who would think the clones must certainly know . . . some of them very rough indeed.

"But we wouldn't have to tell anyone where we got the information," George said.

The clones merely looked at him. Of course that wasn't enough. Of course they wouldn't trust that. Would they trust anything?

The clones' apartment, when they reached it, was a decent-sized three-rooms-with-bath in an area they said housed many students. Ronnie had tried to convince himself to bolt on the way there—surely the clones wouldn't *really* kill them. If nothing else it would interfere with their citizenship application. But the Gerel who had thrown himself on the gas grenade on Sirialis was dead, from another gallant act: these were only clones, who had already made it clear their ethics did not match Gerel's.

"We'll think of something," Andres said that first night. "We would prefer not to kill you; we're not experienced at this sort of thing and we might botch disposing of your bodies. That way you'd cause us even more trouble. Maybe we can get hold of some drugs to alter your memories or something. In the meantime—" In the meantime meant uncomfortable positions, tethered back to back.

The next morning, Borhes raided their pockets. "Sorry," he said. "But we don't have enough money to feed you and us, and I presume you're hungry."

"We are expected back at the Institute," George said.

"Thanks for reminding us," Andres said, grinning. "I think you need to send a message saying you went somewhere and won't be back for a few decads, at least. Let's see . . . what might two wealthy young men do on this planet besides hang around here? Bor, pick up a travel cube, why don't you?"

With the threat of imminent death, Ronnie found he was quite willing to contact the hotel and explain that they had decided on a tour—no, hold their luggage, they were going horse-packing and would have to buy the survival gear they needed closer to the trailhead. George grimaced when Ronnie got through. "I don't know why you wouldn't go for that cruise," he said. "If anyone asks, Andres, they'll know it wasn't us. Ronnie and me riding horses in the mountains?"

"The cruise ship has constant contact with the shore; it would be easy enough to transfer a query. We inquired, and this tour company offers a real wilderness experience. No comsets at all." Andres smiled. "No one from the Familias is going to try—if they call the hotel, they'll be told you're out of the city, touring. It costs too much, and takes too long, to have a realtime conversation."

Over the next few days, George kept after the clones whenever he was awake, pointing out repeatedly that they had no plan, that they couldn't hold prisoners in an apartment forever, that someone would eventually find out.

"We could kill you," Andres said finally, in a temper. "At least we wouldn't have to listen to you, even in prison."

"You don't want to kill us," George said. "You know that; you've said that. What you want is decent anonymity, right?"

"Of course."

"Then get plastic surgery." The clones looked at each other, then back at George.

"We like being clones; we're used to it."

"Fine. I'm not asking you to change that . . . but get enough change so that you don't look like Gerel to any casual tourist from the Familias who might happen into a taverna and see you. You can kill us, of course, and you may be right that my father wouldn't be able to find you or extradite you, but if Familias visitors start dying off, the Guernesi are going to notice."

"And you already told us they have a very efficient law-enforcement system," Ronnie added.

The clones looked at each other again. "We're used to looking like this," Borhes said.

"You're also used to being mistaken for Gerel," George said. "But you don't like it. Just a little change—enough that the Familias crown prince isn't the first person that pops into mind when you're seen. Then you could be a normal clone pair here, and no one would ever know."

"Except you two," Andres said.

"And my Aunt Cecelia, and Captain Serrano," Ronnie said. "They haven't spread it around—why do you think we would?"

Andres laughed unpleasantly. "Ronnie—I know you too well. Remember the Royals?"

Ronnie felt himself flushing. "I was a silly young ass then."

"And you are suddenly a wise old graybeard?"

"No. But if I couldn't be discreet, I'd never have gotten my aunt out of that nursing home."

"She didn't tell us that." Were they interested, or just pretending? It didn't matter; Ronnie was more than willing to keep talking if it gave him a chance to live longer.

He spun the tale out, emphasizing everyone's role: George spreading the rumors about a "drop-in" party at the facility that had created the confusion, Brun with her hot air balloon modified with unobtrusive steering apparatus, and the scramble to get his aunt into it. He hadn't told even George all the details, his mingled terror and disgust as he unhooked Cecelia from her medical monitors and dressed her.

"And what did you do then?" asked Andres when he had gotten as far, in the story, as leaving the parking lot at the facility.

"Went home, got out my parasail, and joined our crowd for a party at the beach." The police had found him there sometime after midnight, with witnesses to say he'd been there since late afternoon. And the facility staff had checked him out as he left there, alone. "They knew she hadn't walked off by herself, and they suspected that she'd been—

abducted was the word they used—during the Festival, when so many balloons were around. But they couldn't prove anything against me. I kept expecting the attendant who had set up the tape loop to accuse me, but he disappeared. They claimed they had no tape records of any of the patients for that day—that something had happened to them—and Mother threatened to sue them for negligence. I was afraid if she did they'd search harder and find them. Perhaps the attendant ran off with them when he realized Cecelia was gone and his job was forfeit."

"And you didn't confide in anyone?"

"No. It was too dangerous. George knew or suspected that I had something to do with it, but all he'd been told beforehand was to spread those rumors. I knew Brun was going to take Cecelia out in the balloon, but not where— I could guess it was to her family's private shuttle, but from there—I didn't know."

"You would claim this proves your ability to keep secrets?"

"Well . . . yes. Doesn't it?"

"Not really. You just told us, presumably because you're scared. What if someone scared you about us?"

Ronnie sagged, and glanced at George hoping he had a bright idea. But George had gone to sleep, to snore in the irregular, creative way that made sleeping in the same room with him so impossible.

✧ Chapter Seven

"Raffaele . . ." Her mother's expression hovered between anxiety and annoyance. Raffa blinked. Her mind had drifted again, and the direction it had drifted did no one any good, and would infuriate her mother if she knew.

"Yes?" she asked, trying for a more mature boredom.

"You're thinking about that boy," her mother said. It was entirely unfair that mothers could, breaking all physical laws, practice telepathy.

"He's not a boy," Raffa said, in a counterattack she knew was useless.

"You agreed—" her mother began. Raffa pushed away the untouched breakfast which had no doubt given her mother the evidence needed, and stared out the long windows at the formal garden with its glittering statuary. *The Lady of Willful Mien* gazing scornfully past *The Sorrowful Suitor*. *Boy with Serpent* (she had hidden childish treasures in the serpent's coils) in the midst of the herbs with snake in their names—a silly conceit, Raffa thought now. The group *Musicians* in the shade of the one informal tree (since no one could prune a weeping cassawood into a formal shape) and the line of bronze *Dancers* frolicking down the sunlit stone path toward the unheard music. She pulled her mind back from the memory that led straight from a child fondling the dancers' bronze skirts, to the feel of Ronnie's hand on her arm.

"I agreed to break the engagement. I agreed not to marry him secretly. I did not agree never to think of him again. It would have been a ridiculous agreement."

"Well." Her mother looked pointedly at the congealed remains of an omelet, and then at Raffa. "It will do no good to starve yourself."

"Hardly," Raffa said. She lifted her arms, demonstrating the snug fit of the velvet tunic that had been loose several weeks before.

"Still." Parents never quit, Raffa thought. She wondered if she would have the energy for that when she was a parent herself. Assuming she became one. She supposed she would. Eventually. If Ronnie came back, and his parents quit quarreling with her parents, and so on. In the meantime, she was supposed to look busy and happy. Busy she could manage. She stood up, while her mother still groped for the next opening, and forced a smile.

"I've got to get to the board meeting. Remember that Aunt Marta asked me to keep an eye on her subsidiaries for her?"

"You don't have to go in every day, Raffaele—"

"But I'm learning," Raffa said. That was true. She had known vaguely what sorts of holdings her family had, had understood that whenever certain products changed hands, money flowed into the family coffers, but she had paid far more attention to what she spent her allowance on, than where it came from. "It's actually kind of interesting."

"I should hope so." Delphina Kore had managed her own inherited corporations for years; of course she thought it was interesting. "I just meant—you have plenty of time to learn."

"You used to say, 'when I was your age, I was running DeLinster Elements singlehanded—'" Raffa reminded her.

"Yes, but that was before—when everyone knew rejuv was a one-time thing. Now you have plenty of time—as much as you want."

And parents would live forever, the most effective glass ceiling of all. She would have rejuv herself, when the time came, but she didn't look forward to a long, long lifetime of being the good daughter.

"We might get tired of running things," her mother said, surprising her. Had she been that obvious? Her mother chuckled. "You'll have your turn, and it won't be as far ahead as you fear."

She didn't argue. She rarely argued. She thought about it, calmly and thoroughly, as she did most things.

Brun had wanted to be an adventurer. At least that's what she'd said. Raffa wondered. All those years as a practical joker, a fluffhead party girl . . . had she really changed? Raffa remembered the island adventure well enough. She had been scared; she had killed someone; she had nearly died. She had done well enough, when you looked at the evidence—no panic, effective action— but she wouldn't have chosen that way to maturity, if what she had now was maturity. She had always been the quiet one of the bunch, the one who got the drunks to bed, the injured to the clinic, the doors relocked, and the evidence hidden. She had imagined herself moving happily into an ordinary adult life—ordinary *rich* adult life, she reminded herself. She liked privilege and comfort; she had no overwhelming desire to test herself.

Now . . . Raffa looked at the serious face in the mirror and wondered why she was bothering. Brun, yes—not only her wildness, but her family's flair, if that's what you wanted to call it. Her own family had had no flair, not for generations. Steady hard work, her parents had always told her, made its own luck. Do it right and you won't have to do it over. Think ahead and you won't need good luck.

But Ronnie. Logic had nothing to do with that. She had argued with herself, but her mind had argued back: he was eligible on all counts except that right now his parents and her parents were on opposite sides, politically and economically. Otherwise—they were both R.E., they were both rich, they had grown up together. AND she loved him.

Word had spread that she and Ronnie were no longer an item. She suspected her mother, but it was not something they could discuss, not now. With the Royal Aerospace Service on something like permanent leave, there were more rich young men lounging around, lining the walls at social events, than she had ever known. Cas Burkburnet, who danced superbly and whose parents had something to do with the management of Arkwright Mining. Vo Pellin, a great lumbering bear who could hardly dance at all, but made everyone laugh. Anhera Vaslin and his brothers, all darkly handsome and eager to find wives to take back home. She knew better than that; Chokny Sulet had been a reluctant annexation to the Familias, and the women who went home with its young men were never seen offplanet again.

She had all the dancing, dining, and partying that she could absorb. If she had been a storycube heroine, it would have defined social success. And like a storycube heroine, she felt stifled by it all. She scolded herself for being selfish and silly, for remembering the feel of Ronnie's head in her lap—his cold, muddy, unconscious head in her lap—when she was dancing with Cas. She had expected to hear about Ronnie from George Mahoney, who gossiped freely about everyone, no matter which side of a political divide you or they were on, but George had disappeared from social functions at the same time as Ronnie. No one seemed to know where they were, and Raffa couldn't ask pointed questions without brows being raised and word getting back to her mother.

She was delighted, therefore, to get a call from George's father Kevil, who asked her to meet with him and Lord Thornbuckle. She had not been in the Council complex since the king's resignation. But she had grown up hearing about Kevil and Bunny, contemporaries of her parents, long before she had realized that they were important people. Now, as they settled her in a comfortable leather chair and offered her something to drink, she felt an odd combination of maturity and childishness. She was being admitted to adult councils in a way that made her feel even younger than she was.

"Ronnie and George went on a mission for us," Lord Thornbuckle said, after she had accepted coffee and refused thinly sliced nutbread. Raffa clenched her hand on the saucer and set it down before it shook and rattled the cup. Ronnie and George? They had sent those two out together?

"We thought they'd help each other," Kevil Mahoney said. Raffa held her tongue. No use arguing with a lawyer of that class. "It may have been a mistake," he admitted, after a short silence.

"We thought of asking another of their friends—someone from the Royal Aerospace Service—but things are rather . . . delicate at the moment."

"Delicate?"

The two men looked at each other. Raffa felt like screaming, but didn't. What good would it do?

"They've disappeared," Lord Thornbuckle said. "And we don't know whom we can trust, in the old administration. We don't know if the reason they've disappeared has something to do with their mission, with something else entirely, or with communications failures. There've been problems recently, as I'm sure you're aware."

Everyone was. The interruption of commercial transfers, even for so brief a period, had panicked the public.

"At the moment, we're dealing with a crisis—more than one, in fact, though you don't need to know all of them. We can't go. We need the information we sent them to get, and we need to know what happened to them. If we send more young men, especially those who've been in the military, it will be noticed in the wrong way."

"You want me to go." Neither of them met her eyes at

first. Raffa felt her temper rising. This was ridiculous; they didn't live back on Old Earth, in prehistoric times. "You want me to find Ronnie or George, and you think whoever's up to mischief will believe I'm chasing after Ronnie because of romance."

"That was the idea," said Lord Thornbuckle.

"It's ridiculous," Raffa said. She let herself glare at him. "It's out of a storycube or something. Lovesick girl goes haring after handsome young man in need of rescue. What do you want me to do, wear a silver bodysuit and carry some impressive-looking weapon?" Even as she said it, she realized she would look stunning in a silver bodysuit, and she imagined herself carrying one of the rifles from the island. No. It was still ridiculous.

"People do," Kevil Mahoney said, peering at his fingertips as if they had microprint on them. "People *do* do ridiculous illogical things. Even for love."

Raffa felt herself going red. "Not me," she said. "I'm the sensible one." It sounded priggish, said like that in this quiet room. She opened her mouth to tell Lord Thornbuckle about the times she'd saved Brun from official retribution, and shut it again. That was the past, and didn't matter. "Where?" she asked, surprising herself.

"The Guerni Republic," Lord Thornbuckle said. "Some planet called Music."

"It would be," Raffa said. She felt trapped, on the one hand, and on the other there was a suspiciously happy flutter in her chest. Trapped? No . . . out from under Mother at last, and with a good cause. She was not going out there to be silly with Ronnie, of course not, but . . . "I'll go," she said, as ungraciously as possible, but also quickly. Before she thought about it. Because, underneath it all, she wanted to go. She wanted a chance to get away from her mother, away from everyone, and think. And she wanted to see Ronnie alone, very far away, and make up her own mind.

❖   ❖   ❖

Traveling alone on a major liner was not an adventure, she told herself firmly. It was nothing like Brun's mad dash across space, working in the depths of livestock freighters and what all. She didn't want that, anyway. She ate exquisitely prepared meals in the first-class dining room, worked out in the first-class gymnasium, flirted appropriately with the younger stewards, and pushed away the occasional desire to measure herself against Brun.

She pored over the tourist information on the Guerni Republic. Her Aunt Marta's holdings included small interests in several Guernesi corporations, inherited through marriage a couple of generations back. Raffa was surprised to find that one of them had its corporate headquarters on Music—handy, but odd. She'd thought it manufactured something used in agriculture—and Lord Thornbuckle had said that planet specialized in medicine. But the headquarters were on the tourist cube as "an example of post-modern business architecture, vaguely reminiscent of the Jal-Oplin style favored in the Cartlandt System two millennia ago." The visual showed an elaborate fountain surrounded by vast staircases that seemed to exist just to create interesting shadows.

Raffa peered at it several ways, and gave up. It didn't really matter what it looked like. She could reasonably visit, as the near relative of a stockholder from the Familias. She composed a short message, and put it in the mail queue. Then she called up the language tutor for another session of Guernesi. She had always enjoyed learning new languages, and Guernesi seemed fairly close to one she'd studied before, the "native" language of Casopayne.

Raffa settled into her rooms at the hotel her travel agent had recommended. She found the Guernesi accent captivating rather than confusing, and her shipboard study had made her comfortable with many routine phrases.

She had no idea where Ronnie and George would be staying, but it shouldn't be too hard to find out. The Travelers' Directory listed visitors by homeworld.

The Familias Regnant section had more names than she had expected—and for a moment she let herself wonder what Venezia Glendower-Morreline se Vahtigos was doing there; that redoubtable old lady should have been driving her numerous family crazy at the annual plastic arts festival on Goucault, where she insisted on exhibiting her own creations. Raffa had been at school with one of her nieces, who had had to display a particularly hideous vase and a mask that looked like dripping wax in order to pacify the family artiste. She hadn't thought about Ottala Morreline for a couple of years, at least—she'd wondered at the time if living with her aunt's artwork had warped her mind. But never mind—where was Ronnie?

She found his name, finally, listed as "traveling" rather than at a fixed address. Communications could be left with the Travelers' Directory, the listing said. Great. Ronnie and George had run off somewhere for a little unauthorized fun, and she had no idea when they'd be back. She felt angry, and was annoyed with herself. They didn't know she was coming; it wasn't deliberate. Perhaps a good meal would help. She called up the hotel directory, and decided on the smallest of the dining rooms, described as "quiet, intimate, and refined, yet casual."

The Guernesi definition of quiet, intimate, refined, and casual had tables set into mirrored alcoves. Each alcove was divided from the main room by an arch of greenery from which graceful sprays of fragrant orchids swayed. Once ensconced in her alcove, Raffa discovered that the mirrors reflected only the greenery and the delicate curves of the chandelier . . . not the diners. She glanced casually into other alcoves, just to check—and wondered briefly how the mirrors worked.

She had worked her way through most of her meal, when

someone passed in a flamboyant trail of scarlet ruffles that caught her eye. A tall, black-haired woman whose walk expressed absolute confidence in her ability to attract attention. The red dress left the elegant line of her back to no one's imagination, and a drip of diamonds down her spine only emphasized its perfection. Two men in formal dress followed her, one tall, with a mane of red hair, and the other short and stout. Raffa leaned forward, excited despite herself. It had to be Madame Maran, who had toured in the Familias Regnant, though she lived here. Raffa fiddled with the table controls, cut off the sound damping for her alcove so that she could hear the open center of the room.

"Madame—" she heard someone—probably the waiter—say.

Then "Esarah, I *still* think—" and the privacy screen of the other alcove covered the rest. No matter. She had seen the famous diva hardly an arm's length away. She would check the entertainment listings. Perhaps there would be a performance while she was here. She hoped it would be *Gertrude and Lida*, but she would happily listen to Maran sing a grocery list.

She glanced around the tables she could see. And there he was.

The last person she had expected to see was the Familias' former king, but there he sat, spooning up the cold fish soup as if he were at home back on Castle Rock. Raffa blinked and looked down at her own meal. It couldn't be the king. Former king. Former chair of the Grand Council. Wherever he was, he wouldn't be here in the Guerni Republic. Rumor had it that his wife had moved out after his resignation, and returned to her family's estates. Everyone had said he was "helping with administrative matters."

She blinked, but the shape of his face, his way of holding the spoon, did not change. He paused, pressed his hands to his temples a moment, in a gesture she had known from childhood. It had to be the king. It could not be the king.

She lingered over dessert, sneaking furtive glances at the man now placidly working his way through some kind of meat wrapped in pastry. It still looked like the king. Her parents' age, or a little older, but that was hard to tell after a rejuv or so. He held himself like someone used to being served. Anyone would, who stayed in this hotel, and ate in this dining room. He ate quickly, neatly, and refused dessert with a gesture. When he rose, and turned to leave, Raffa looked down, wondered why she didn't smile and greet him.

It was the king. It could not be the king. She would go to bed and think about it tomorrow.

The next morning, the Directory reported no response from Ronnie or George. Raffa delivered the samples Lord Thornbuckle had given her to the Neurosciences Institute. Then she took a tour of the city's botanic gardens, and discovered that the orchids in the hotel dining room were only one of 5,492 species cultivated on Music. The guide explained more about orchids than anyone on the tour wanted to know, and seemed to think tourists were responsible for the unwanted information. "And *how* many species have been adapted for the production of neuroactive chemicals?" the guide said at the end. No one could answer, and the guide pouted. Raffa looked at the available tours for that afternoon, and decided to work on her Guernesi language cubes.

Traveling alone with the intent to have no adventures continued to be more boring than Raffa had expected. After three days of sensible sightseeing and language practice, with no word from Ronnie and George, she was ready for a change. She was used to having someone to keep out of trouble, which also meant someone to talk to. She had seen the ex-king, and she had no one to tell. Her growing facility with the Guernesi language allowed her to make small talk with hotel employees and tour guides, but she missed the late-night discussions of the day's events. Even her mother, she thought, would be preferable to this empty room with its bland blue, gray, and beige color scheme. It didn't make her feel rested and sleepy; it made her feel like going out to find some color and excitement.

Color and excitement, as the tourist brochures made clear, could be found in the Old City, which was actually newer than the New City, but had been rebuilt to look older. Raffa had found this sort of reasoning on other planets, where war or economic clearances had suggested the profitability of nostalgia. She headed for the Old City, after a discussion with the concierge, who agreed that it was safe at this early hour of the evening.

The New City became the Old City at a dramatic arch. Beyond, the street itself narrowed, but expanded in irregular bays to each side, marked off by changes in paving, colorful plants in decorative tubs, and even the occasional row of formally clipped trees.

Most of the color and excitement aimed at tourists involved displays of Guernesi dancing to music from antique instruments. Raffa wandered into several courtyards, where male dancers in full-sleeved shirts, tight trousers, and boots whirled and stamped, and the musicians plucked the strings of melon-bellied wooden instruments. But this wasn't what she had in mind, she realized. She didn't want to be one of the young women tourists ogling the dancers. Nor did she want to join the tourists in other courtyards ogling buxom female dancers in low-cut blouses and ruffles. From somewhere down the street, a curl of brass slid through the pervasive strumming and lured her on. She almost recognized the melody, but with the competition of clattering boots and the occasional ritual shout "Hey-YA" she couldn't put a name to it.

It came, she discovered, from an open door, not a courtyard. Inside, tables crowded around a low stage. By

then the music was over—or interrupted, because she saw
the horn player, trumpet tucked under his arm, leaning
over to talk to another musician with an instrument she
recognized, a violin, on his lap. Two more string players
were stretching as they chatted.

"Dama?" When she smiled and nodded, the waiter led
her to a table halfway between stage and wall.

She set her elbows on the table and peered at the napkin
which, besides suggesting in four languages that the
appropriate tip was twenty percent, gave the name of the
players. If her Guernesi was sufficient, they were the "Blithe
Grasshoppers." Tati Velikos on the "tromp" which had to
be trumpet. Sorel Velikos, Kaskar Basconi, Ouranda
Basconi, Luriesa Sola. She amused herself during their
break by trying to figure out who was who.

The musicians readied themselves again, and Raffa
blinked at them. If Tati was the trumpeter, then Sorel must
be a twin brother: he looked identical, tall, lean, and dark-
haired. And the two Basconis—she assumed the other pair
of twins, the women, were the Basconis. They were dark
too, though not quite as tall and decidedly bosomy. She
had thought Kaskar was a male name . . . Kaskar Aldozina
had been one of the historical figures in Guernesi history,
and she remembered that the pronoun reference had been
male.

She glanced around, suddenly uncomfortable for no
reason she could define, and it hit her. At least half those
watching came in pairs, triplets, quads—all identical.
Another Velikos (she was sure) reached over to hand the
musicians some music. Most of the identicals were pairs—
twins?—but a few tables away four identical blonde women
chatted with three identical blonde men—and when Raffa
took a second look, she realized that the men and women
were, but for differences in hairstyle, dress, and cleavage,
identical with each other. Seven faces alike; she shivered.
These must be clones. She had heard of them, but never

seen them. They were illegal in the Familias space, she knew that much.

The string players began, a sprightly lilting melody Raffa did not know. She looked at them more closely. Were they all clones? They didn't look as much alike as the seven blondes, but there was a family resemblance, even in the fifth player. Raffa tried to tell herself that it was just a matter of different customs; there was nothing *wrong* with clones, and she wasn't in danger or anything. And she liked the music . . . it flirted from violin to cello, tripped into the bass, and then the trumpet plucked it away and flung it out across the room, past all the talk and clink of dishes.

When the music ended, knotted into a tight pattern of chords that left no opening for more variation, Raffa found herself wondering where clone designers found their patterns. That man she had been so sure was the ex-king, for instance . . . could that have been a clone, perhaps? Surely a neighboring government wouldn't make clones of its neighbors' political leaders . . . or would it? Speculation bothered her; she didn't want to wonder about that or anything else.

She had an appointment at the corporate headquarters of Atot Viel the next day. In real life, the arrangement of fountain and stairways made sense; the structure was built into a slope, and the stairs offered open air communication from level to level. Raffa noted that without pausing, and followed the markers set alight by the button that had come with her appointment notice.

The young woman who met her at the reception area seemed to find Raffa's presence entirely understandable. She said, "We'll take you on the usual tour, and then you tell me what else you'd like to see. Your aunt's never visited us herself, but we understood that was for health reasons—"

Raffa, unprepared for that opening, said the first

conventional thing that came into her head. "I'm so sorry;
I wouldn't know."

"Of course, you can't tell us. We've established no need
to know. But if it *is* health, you might want to investigate
the medical facilities. Recently one of your prominent
citizens benefited from the expertise of the Neurosciences
Institute; I'm sure they'd give you references."

"Lady Cecelia," said Raffa, automatically.

"Oh, you know her? Good. We really do welcome
stockholder participation, you see, and if your aunt could
travel, we would very much enjoy the benefit of her
expertise."

Raffa wondered. Aunt Marta's expertise, as far as she
had known, consisted of an instinctive grasp of what to
sell and what to buy. She never involved herself with
management, preferring to live in relaxed comfort, pursuing
her hobbies. As for health, she always seemed hale enough
to go for month-long camping trips in the mountains behind
her main residence. An early experience of Aunt Marta
and Lady Cecelia's had convinced Raffa that old ladies
were anything but dull and passive, a hope she clung to
when surrounded by the senior set at Castle Rock.

Now she followed the young woman along gleaming
corridors, wishing she had the foggiest notions what
questions to ask. By the time she'd had the usual tour,
and collected an armful of glossy brochures, she was ready
to quit for the day.

"But you'll come again, I hope," her guide said. "Your
aunt's is one of the few licensed facilities using our process."
Raffa still wasn't sure what process, but she knew she would
have to find out. It would keep her mind off Ronnie.

She had not seen the man who resembled the king for
days; she had not forgotten him, but he was no longer
part of her anticipation. But the next morning, he appeared
again, striding along the carpeted corridor toward the lobby

with the firm stride of someone who knows where he's going. Raffa put down the storycube she had just picked up, and watched him. He paused by the concierge's desk, then headed for the doors. Inexplicably, Raffa felt drawn to follow.

"Later," she said to the clerk, and darted through the gift-shop door. The man had already disappeared through the front doors; Raffa stretched her legs and followed. There he was, outside, chatting with the doorman, waiting for a car, no doubt. One of the sleek electric cabs pulled up, and he got in. Raffa waited until it began to move, then went out to the street. The cab moved smoothly away.

"You can't keep us here forever," George said. "Eventually someone will come looking, and you'll have accomplished just what you want to avoid. People who are likely to know you by sight on your trail."

The clone on guard looked at him, an unfriendly stare. "It won't help you."

"But why are you angry with us?" George persisted.

"Remember the commissioning banquet?" the clone asked. George flushed.

"Surely you don't hold that against me—I thought you were him—the prince, I mean."

"I know who you mean," the clone said. "Why does that matter? You were willing to do that—"

"Everyone gets drunk at the commissioning banquet," George said, glancing at Ronnie for support. Ronnie lay back on the bed, eyes shut, but George was sure he wasn't asleep. He couldn't possibly sleep so much. "And after— and the pranks are all traditional—"

"Are you going to try to convince me you drew my name—excuse me, *his* name—from a hat?" The clone made a display of cleaning his fingernails with the stiletto. Overdramatic, George thought; the bathroom had modern facilities. Then he thought about lying; how could the clone know the name he had really drawn?

"No . . ." he said at last, choosing honesty for no reason he could name. "I drew someone else's, but—I thought I had a grudge."

"Have you ever been glued into your underwear?" The tone was light, but the menace of that blade needed no threatening voice.

"As a matter of fact, yes," George said. "At camp one summer, when I was twelve. Ronnie and I both."

"They were trying to toughen us up, they said," Ronnie said, without opening his eyes. "They'd found out that I liked the wrong kind of music—that I even *played* music." He opened his eyes, and a slow grin spread across his face. "They glued us back to back; we must've looked really silly. Took video cubes, the whole thing. The counselors finally trashed the cubes, after they'd watched them and snickered for a day or so. George and I spent the time in the infirmary, growing new skin."

"Oh." The clone seemed taken aback. "I—we weren't active then."

"That's why I diluted the mix," George said. "You weren't nearly as stuck as I was."

"What did you do to them?" the clone asked, seeming to be truly interested.

"Nothing . . . really." Ronnie had closed his eyes again. George admired the tone he achieved and waited. Let Ronnie tell it. "There was another boy, not even an R.E., but smarter than all of us put together. He could bypass the read-only safety locks on entertainment cubes."

"You trashed their cubes?"

"Not just that. We replaced their music with . . . other things." Ronnie heaved a satisfied sigh. "Remember, George, how mad that cousin of mine was, Stavi Bellinveau?"

"Yes. And Buttons, too—it was before his stuffy stage," he said to the clone. "He wasn't at all stuffy at fourteen."

"I blame myself," Ronnie said, putting a hand over his heart. "I think it was having to spend the next three weeks listening to an endless loop of all the *Pomp and Circumstance* marches. I should have put at least one waltz on that cube."

The clone glared. "If you're trying to make it clear that you and George share a life I never knew except secondhand, you've succeeded. It doesn't make me like you better."

"No . . . I can see that. But it's not our fault you're what you are. If we'd known, we might have made things easier for you, or harder . . . depends. We were all kids, with kids' idiocies. Rich kids . . . we could be idiots longer than some. It wasn't until my aunt's new yacht captain straightened me out that I began to grow up."

"Heris Serrano," the clone said.

"Yes. You met her—you understand."

✧ Chapter Eight

Aboard the *Sweet Delight*

Lady Cecelia had debated for several days where to go first after Zenebra. Heris left her to it. She had spent enough time thinking about horses. Now, as the yacht worked its way out of the crowded traffic patterns of Zenebra's system, she concentrated on the crew's training. Koutsoudas worried her, especially in light of her aunt's message. No one but Livadhi knew what he could really accomplish with two bent pins and a discarded chip. An undetectable hyperlight tightbeam comlink, for instance. Cecelia's concern that she could not see clearly where Fleet personnel were concerned warred in her mind with her aunt's trust in her judgment. She would like to believe her aunt, but if she did that, she might as well believe her aunt on everything. Her mind shied away from the implications like a green horse from a spooky fence . . . and that image brought her back to Cecelia.

Inspection. It was more than time for an inspection. Heris checked the set of her uniform before she headed down the passage to crew quarters. As she would have anticipated, the ex-military crew kept their quarters tidy, almost bare of personal identity. The programmable displays that other crew left showing tropical reefs, mountain valleys, or other scenery had been blanked.

Heris continued into the working areas of the ship. The new inspection stickers—real ones, not fakes—made bright patches on the gleaming bulkheads. She checked every readout, every telltale, the routine soothing her mind. Even the memories of violence on the ship—here Iklind had died, from hydrogen sulfide poisoning, and down this passage his distant relative Skoterin had nearly killed Brig Sirkin and Lady Cecelia. Redecoration had removed any trace of corrosive gases, of blood. The memory of faces and bodies that floated along with her were no different from those that haunted any captain's days.

In the 'ponics sections, she found Brun replanting trays, a dirty job that always fell to the lowest-level mole.

"What are you growing this round?" she asked.

Brun grinned. "Halobeets," she said. "I hadn't realized how much sulfur uptake ship 'ponics need."

"There's a ship rhyme about it," Heris said. "Eat it, excrete it, then halobeet it. And it's always confused me that we call the sulfur-sucking beets halobeets . . . you'd think they sopped up the halocarbons, but they don't. How are you getting along with Lady Cecelia's gardener?" Lady Cecelia's gardener produced the ship's fresh vegetables. Ship's crew produced only the vegetation needed to normalize the atmosphere. Brun wrinkled her muddy nose.

"I think he worries that I'll steal his methods for Dad's staff. You know I'm supposed to check the oxygen/carbon dioxide levels on his compartments, but he hovers over me as if I were after industrial secrets."

"Are you telling me you're never tempted to sneak a tomato?" Heris asked.

"Well . . . perhaps." Brun's wide grin was hardly contrite.

Heris left Brun to the tedious work, and continued her inspection. She was not surprised to find Arkady Ginese on his own tour of inspection, checking the weapons controls interlocks. The yacht had once had spacious storage bays, far larger than it needed for the transportation of a single passenger. Now those bays were stuffed with weaponry and its supporting control and guidance systems, with the jamming and other countermeasures that Heris hoped would serve as well as shields if someone were shooting back. They had not had the volume to mount both effective weapons and strong shields; Heris hoped she'd made the right choice.

"All's well, Captain," Ginese said. "I did want to ask you—Koutsoudas says there's a new wrinkle in ECM that we could probably rig onto what we have, if you wanted." *If you really trust Koutsoudas* hung in his words.

Heris thought a moment. "Do you understand it? Does it make sense to you?"

"Yes—it's a reasonable extension of the technology. I don't see why it wouldn't work."

"And how do you feel about Koutsoudas?"

Ginese looked around. "Well—"

"Of course he may have ears everywhere—the better to hear the truth, Arkady. He's smart—he has to know we don't completely trust someone from Livadhi. How do you feel?"

"I—like him more than I thought I would. He's like all scan techs, clever and sneaky. But he doesn't give me that bad feeling . . . then again, I missed Skoterin."

"So did we all," Heris said. "But I think all our sensitivities are flapping in the breeze now. Let's go on and make that change—send my desk a complete description, and I'll file it. If anything comes up—"

"Of course, Captain." Ginese looked happier, and Heris went on to complete her inspection.

By the time she reached the bridge again, Lady Cecelia had sent a message—she had chosen their destination, a planet called Xavier. Sirkin already had the charts up on display for Heris, with a recommended course.

"Looks good so far," Heris said. "I'll want to check—some of those intermediate jump points may have restriction codes on them—"

"Yes, ma'am, they do," Sirkin said. "Four of them are heavy traffic; we'd have to file here before we jump for clearance through them. Xavier itself is in the frontier zone; we have to file with the R.S.S., a letter of intent. I've done a preliminary file, in case—and there's an alternate course that doesn't use any restricted jump points, though it will add sixteen days."

Sixteen additional days times the daily requirements for food, water, oxygen . . . Heris ran the numbers in her mind before checking them on computer. "We can do it, but it's already a long trip, especially counting the long insystem drop at Xavier. You're right, Sirkin, that short course is the best. What's the maximum flux transit you've plotted?" That, too, was within acceptable limits; Heris reminded herself again that Sirkin had not made the mistakes she'd been blamed for. On her own she had always done superb work.

"Fine—complete that application for the restricted jump points, file the letter of intent as agricultural products purchase, wholesale, and tell me when you anticipate we'll start the sequence. Good work." It was, too. Most navigators would still be setting up a single course.

"Thank you, ma'am." Sirkin might have been her old self, the bright, vibrant girl Heris had first met, but there was still the wariness of old injuries in her eyes. That was maturity, Heris told herself, and nothing to regret. Nobody stayed as young as Sirkin had been and lived to grow old.

Xavier, when they arrived at its orbital station, looked like the uncrowded agricultural world it was. Its main export was genetic variability for large domestic animals too inbred in other populations. A variety of habitats and temperature ranges allowed relatively easy culture of equids, bovids, and less common domestics for many purposes. Cecelia had been there before; she knew most of the horse breeders, and planned to spend several weeks with those most likely to have what she wanted.

"Captain Serrano . . . could I speak to you on a secure

line, please?" That request got through; Heris had been
wondering how long exactly Cecelia meant to stay, and
what the daily docking charges would run to. Some of
these outworld stations tried to squeeze every visitor,
because they had so few.

"Of course," she said. She wondered what was wrong;
they hadn't popped a hatch yet.

"I'm the Stationmaster," the face on the screen said.
Heris hadn't doubted it, but she nodded politely.

"I've been authorized to ask this . . . and if it's an offense,
please excuse me . . . but are you related to the . . . er . . .
Fleet Serranos?"

That again. Heris hoped her reaction didn't show. "Yes,
I am," she said. "In fact, I was Fleet myself."

"That's what we hoped," the Stationmaster said. "Lady
Cecelia said—but I had to make sure."

"Why?" Heris asked. The Stationmaster seemed the sort
to pussyfoot around the point for hours, and she didn't
want to wait for it.

"We really need your help, Captain Serrano. Your
expertise, if you will. I've been authorized to invite you
to a briefing, with our Senior Captain Vassilos, who
commands the planetary defense."

Heris felt a prickle run down her backbone. "Planetary
defense? Is there a . . . problem?" She would have
Koutsoudas for lunch if they had dropped into a shooting
war without his noticing.

"Not now, Captain. At the moment. But if you would
come, if you would consider helping . . . just advice, I mean;
you don't have a warship, we know that." He sounded more
desperate than he should if they were in no imminent
danger. Heris paused, considering her answer. Behind her,
she heard a stir, and glanced around. Cecelia.

"I told them you'd be glad to help," Cecelia said, as if
she had the right to dispose of Heris's time and effort.
Heris glared at her, then turned back to the screen.

"I'll attend a briefing," she said. "At this point, without knowing what you want—my responsibilities to my ship must, you understand, take precedence."

"Oh, of course. If you'll—when you're ready, there will be a shuttle at your disposal. I'll just tell Captain Vassilos." And he cut the link. Heris turned back to Cecelia.

"Just what did you think you were doing?"

She didn't understand or she wouldn't. "I didn't see any harm in it. They asked about your name; I told them you were ex-Fleet; they started babbling about some kind of problem and needing expert guidance. You don't mind, do you?"

Mind was not the right word. Heris took a deep steadying breath, and told herself that she did, after all, care about the security of the outer worlds . . . and that clouting one's charter across the room was no way to run a chartered yacht.

On the shuttle down, she read through the scanty briefing material she'd been handed, and tried to explain to Cecelia why she should stick to horses and leave defense to the military.

"I know that," Cecelia said, unrepentant. "That's why I said you should take care of it, whatever it is. I know it's your specialty—"

"Used to be my specialty," said Heris between clenched teeth. "You were the one who pointed out so firmly that I am a civilian now."

"I know." For an instant, Cecelia's expression might even have been contrite, or as close as that arrogant bony face ever came. They rode the rest of the way in unrestful silence.

The little military band in its bright uniforms, buttons and ornaments glittering, played some jaunty march which Heris could have sworn she knew. Across the sunburnt grass, the music practically strutted, as if the notes themselves were proud.

"It's—charming," said Cecelia beside her. Under the clear blue sky of Xavier, her cheeks were flushed, more with excitement than sunburn.

"It's ridiculous," muttered Heris. "If this is their protection—"

"But it's so . . . it makes me feel good."

"That's what it's for, but feeling good because you've got a decent bandmaster won't save your life if you don't have some armament, and I don't see anything here that could take care of a good-sized riot."

"Maybe they don't have riots," Cecelia said. She sounded cross.

"Then they've had no practice, as well as having no armament," Heris said. She knew she was cross. Damn Livadhi and his specialist. Damn her family name, which at the moment was pure embarrassment. Without that, she'd have been comfortably ensconced in the yacht, while Cecelia visited horse farms. Instead, her fame had preceded her, and produced a fervent appeal for help—help which Cecelia had generously offered, on her behalf.

The band switched from one tune to another, this one even more bouncy than the last. Her toes wanted to tap; her whole body wanted to march along a road with a band of brave and loyal friends. A double crash of cymbals and drums, and the music stopped, leaving its ghost in her ears. Trumpets blew a little fanfare, and someone left the group to approach them.

"Lady Cecelia . . . Captain Serrano . . ." He wore a uniform that had been tailored for a slimmer man; it bunched and pulled around the spare tire fifteen years had given him. "I'm Senior Captain Vassilos. Thank you for your willingness to help."

"You're very welcome," Cecelia said. Heris nodded, silently, and waited to see what would come next.

"I presume you'd like to know more about the problem?"

"Quite," said Heris, before Cecelia could say anything.

"If you'll come this way, then." He led them to a brightly polished groundcar with a big boxy rear end and a little open cab for the driver. Heris had never seen anything like it. She and Cecelia and Senior Captain Vassilos sat in back on tufted velvet; the compartment would have held four or five more in comfort.

"We've had trouble from the Compassionate Hand from time to time—as you know, milady—" He turned to Cecelia, who nodded. "But we don't believe these are the same people. For one thing, the survivors report nothing like the discipline we associate with Compassionate Hand raids. For another, the entry vectors are all wrong. I know: the Black Scratch could be using a roundabout jump sequence. But they'd almost have to trail past an R.S.S. picket line that way, and Fleet keeps telling us there's nothing in the records. Any of them. Of course, they think we're overreacting—at least, that's the message I've had from them. They're stretched thin on this frontier—"

"On all," Heris said. And would be thinner yet, if the government fell. She hoped fervently that Lord Thornbuckle would cobble something together before that happened.

"We used to get a patrol ship in here at least yearly; that kept the vermin away. But in the past eight years or so, it's been less than that, and in the past two years we haven't had a patrol closer than Margate." Margate, two stars away. That wouldn't help. "Frankly, I don't know why the Compassionate Hand hasn't been at us again."

Heris thought they had, but were being circumspect just in case the lack of patrol activity was a trap. Instead of mentioning that, she asked, "Has anyone ever gotten an ID on the raiders?"

"Here." He loaded the cube reader and began pointing to items in the display. "Last time, they knocked out the scanners and the records at the orbital station, but a farmer down here in the south happened to catch a bit—his oldest daughter's crazy for space and handbuilt a scanner of her own. But it was at the extreme of her range, and we don't know how valid the data are."

"We'll have—our expert—look at it, if you don't mind." Heris just caught herself from saying Koutsoudas's name.

"No, that's fine. If you can make anything of it, so much the better."

They had better make something of it. After a look at the files, Heris realized that a farmer's brat's homemade scanner had the only possible data of any importance.

"What sort of defense do you have?" She thought she knew, but better to ask and be sure.

"Well, it's always been Fleet policy that planets didn't need their own heavy ships, as you know." Heris nodded. It was always easier to keep the peace if the peaceful weren't too well armed. "We had two Desmoiselle class escorts forty years ago, but one of them was badly damaged in a Compassionate Hand raid and we cannibalized her to get parts for the other." Heris winced. The Desmoiselle class had been obsolete for decades; it mounted no more weaponry than the yacht, and handled worse. Designed initially to protect commercial haulers from incompetent piracy in the crowded conditions of the Cleonic moons, it had been someone's poor choice for a situation like this.

"And your remaining ship?"

"Well . . . it's not really operational, and we haven't the expertise locally to fix it. Nor the money to send it somewhere." He flushed. "I know that must sound like we want to be sitting ducks, but it's not really that. We keep *Grogon* hanging around with her weapons lit up, hoping to scare off trouble, but the pirates have figured out she has neither legs nor teeth."

"What's the problem?"

"She was underpowered to start with, and she needs her tubes relined, at a minimum. She makes only seventy percent of the acceleration she had when she came, but there's no shipyard nearer than Grand Junction or Tay-Fal. And the cost—"

"Let's see if my engineers can suggest something," Heris said, making a note on her compad. She had to have something as backup, if it were only a shuttle with a single missile tube and a lot of electronic fakery. If this *Grogon* could move in space at all, it was better than nothing. "Anything else?"

"We *did* have a fixed orbital battery, but they got that on the last raid. Then one of the shuttles—" There were only three, as Heris already knew. "We took two of the phase cannons off the other escort—"

Heris blinked. They had mounted *phase cannon* in a shuttle? "Have you ever fired them?" she asked.

"Not yet. But we think it will work."

"I think perhaps my engineers should take a look." Quickly. Before anyone tried it and tore the shuttle apart.

"Of course, Captain Serrano." The man beamed as if she were conferring a great favor. "Does this mean you'll take the commission?"

"Let me confer with my . . . er . . . staff," Heris said. "And if you have any engineering specs on those vessels—?"

"Right away, Captain," he said.

Koutsoudas received the scan cassette with a curl of his lip that made Heris want to smack him. Oblo, she saw, had a sulky look. Fine. Let Oblo work it off on Koutsoudas.

An hour later, Koutsoudas called her with no sneer at all in his voice. "Good data, Captain. The kid knew what she was doing, whoever she is. Recruit her."

Heris had already asked. Regret edged her voice: "Can't, I'm afraid. She died a year back, of some local disease. So what do you have?" She didn't mention the younger sister she'd been told about, who seemed to have similar talents. Time enough for that later.

"Aethar's World, but I think the ship ID's falsified. It'll

be Aethar's World, just from the flavor of it, but not that number. It's in the commercial sequence, probably midsize trader . . . too bad that girl didn't build a wide-band detector as well."

"I'll ask," Heris said. "Maybe she did. But only one ship?"

"So far. I'll let you know."

Heris put in a call to Petris, who had gone to take a look at the cannon-loaded shuttle.

"Just got here," he said. "But you were right. They assumed that only the mass mattered. They've got them bolted into the frame—the unreinforced frame—with homemade ports cut in the hull plates." He sounded less contemptuous than she expected as he went on. "Quite a job, really—they put some thought into it. Pity they didn't know more about phase cannon. To make this thing operational, we'll have to dismount them, reinforce, and remount. At best, that's five weeks of work with the equipment available—"

"Downside or orbital?" Heris asked.

"Downside—they've no orbital facilities at all. Anyway, that'd give you a slow shuttle that could fire a couple of bolts every five minutes or so. Not worth it, unless we're desperate."

"That will depend on how bad the old escort is."

All along Heris had wondered who crewed the two escorts. When she swam aboard the remaining Desmoiselle, she found out. Anyone who wanted, it seemed. Oldsters retired from space, youngsters desperate to get above atmosphere, balancing a complete lack of proper training with intimate knowledge of their single ship.

"*Grogon's* not a bad ship," its elderly captain told her. "She takes a bit of easing along, that's all. . . ." Petris raised his brows but said nothing; he'd explain later. Heris could see for herself most of its problems.

Back with Captain Vassilos, Heris showed him the recommendations of her engineering staff. "Can you tell me why you think the raider's due?"

"It's more a guess than anything else," he said. "It's come twice before in our springtime, and now it's late spring. It feels like the right time."

Heris had heard worse reasons. "Those phase cannon in the shuttle can't be used as they are—and five weeks of downtime, if your planet-side yards can do the work, still give you only a very minimal weapons platform. If you have the resources to start that work, go ahead, but don't count on it to do much. I do have another suggestion. . . ."

"It's a little thing, whatever it is." Esteban Koutsoudas and Meharry bent over the displays. "Let me just tinker a bit here—ahhh." He signalled Meharry with one stubby finger. "That cube I had—put it in here—" Another screen came alive with numbers that scrolled so rapidly Heris couldn't see anything but lines. Then it froze, with one line highlighted.

"Hull constructed at Yaeger, registered with Aethar's World as a medium trader . . . but Aethar's traders are everyone else's raiders."

That much any of her own crew could have gotten, but Koutsoudas wasn't through. The screen wavered and steadied on a new display: the other ship's design details, shown in three-dimensional display. Colored tags marked deviations from the listed criteria. Where *Sweet Delight*'s other detectors merely showed blots of warning red for weapons on active status, this one showed the placement and support systems for weapons not otherwise detected as live.

"Where'd you get this stuff?" Meharry asked, her voice expressing her lust for that equipment.

"You know how it is," Koutsoudas said without taking his eyes off the display. "A bit of this, a bit of that. It's not exactly standard, so I can't mount it in any Fleet craft—"

"But you can't *get* that resolution that far away," Meharry said. "Thermal distortion alone—"

"You need an almighty big database," Koutsoudas said. He sounded almost apologetic, as he tweaked the display again and an enlarged view of the distant vessel's portside weapons appeared, with little numbered comments. "I've been sort of . . . collecting this . . . for a long time." He tapped the cube reader. "Had to design new storage algorithms too. And the transforms for the functions that do the actual work . . ."

"Magic," Meharry said. Koutsoudas grinned at her.

"That's it. Got to have my secrets, don't I? If I teach you everything, who's going to care about my neck?"

"Nobody cares about your neck now, Esteban. Other parts of you—"

"Are off limits," he said. "Besides, that ship's no good."

"Can you tell what it's getting?" Heris asked.

"It won't have us now," Koutsoudas said confidently. "Not with the last batch of little doodads Oblo and Meharry and I installed. We're in no danger, and we can sit here and read their mail if we want to."

"Not and let them run amok in this system," Heris said. "Not if we can stop them, that is."

"Oh, we can stop them." Koutsoudas pointed to his display. "Their weapons look impressive on scan—or will, when they go active and light up the station's warning system. But this is old tech, slow and stupid stuff. Good for scaring the average civilian, though I'll bet they never take on any of the big commercial carriers. And when they refitted that hull with new engines, they made a big mistake." He brought up a highlighted schematic, and Heris saw it herself. They'd wanted more performance, and they'd mounted more powerful drives . . . but without reinforcing the hull or mounts. If they used those engines flat out, they'd collapse either hull or mount. Even worse, they could do structural damage by combining a lower drive setting with missile firing.

"I'd bet they never have fired many shots in anger," Heris

said. "At least, not while under any significant acceleration. That's a beginner's mistake." If only she had a real Fleet warship, she'd simply chase them into their own fireball.

"With any luck, they won't live long enough to learn better," Meharry said.

"Not luck," Koutsoudas said. "Skill. Knowledge."

Heris wasn't sure if that was an attempt to flatter her, or to brag about his own ability. "How long before you can strip the rest you want off them?"

"Twelve to fourteen standard hours, Captain," he said. "With the captain's permission, I'll put one of the juniors on scan, and plan to be on the bridge in four hours for a check, and then in ten hours—"

"Of course," Heris said. "We'll use the Fleet scheduling for this. Firsts, give me your interim schedules, and make sure you are offshift enough for real rest before then."

Koutsoudas smiled. "I didn't know if we'd have the crew for that—"

"Not quite, but better than they have, I expect. As long as we don't let them get past us—or get the first shot—we'll do very well."

After she had the schedules for the next twelve standard hours, Heris went to see Cecelia.

"I don't know how that man does what he does, but we're damn lucky Livadhi wanted me to run off with him. With my people, I'd have a lot less margin to play with."

"So we're going to fight again?" Cecelia looked as if she were trying to project eagerness. But she would be remembering that other battle, in which she was trapped in her aged and disabled body, unable even to speak clearly. She had to be scared.

"Yes, we'll fight—but it won't be anything like the time before. They won't have detected us—and they're unlikely to do so until we blow them away." She used Cecelia's desk display to diagram what they intended to do.

"It's not very sporting, is it?" Cecelia asked.

"It's not 'sporting' at all. It's not a game," Heris said. "Lepescu made that mistake; I don't. This is a band of ruffians who have terrorized this system repeatedly, and I'm going to destroy them. True, their homeworld may send more—I can't help that. But if Koutsoudas is right, Aethar's World may have more to worry about than a missing allied pirate. These people will have months— maybe years—of peace and a chance to develop their own effective defense. So yes, I'm going to destroy them with the least possible risk to us."

"How can you be sure they're the right ones? What if you're about to blow up an innocent ship?" She didn't sound really worried about it, but Heris considered the question seriously.

"By the time we do it, we'll know what brand of dental cleanser they use," she said. "Right now we know they are running with a falsified ID beacon—which doesn't necessarily mean criminal intent; we had one. But they've also got a whopping load of armament. And they're from Aethar's World, which is always suspicious. About the only time those barbarians leave home, it's to cause trouble for someone. They fit the profile of the trouble your friends have been having. . . ."

With the enemy ship only a light-second away, Koutsoudas continued to pour out a torrent of information about it. "Not only Aethar's World, but one of the Brotherhood chiefs. Svenik the Bold, I think—certainly he had this particular ship a while back, and this sort of raid is his specialty."

"I'm surprised he's lasted this long with that hull/engine combination," Petris said.

"So am I," Koutsoudas said. "But he hasn't been up against anything that made him redline it. Yet." He grinned at Heris. "I know you want to do this the quick way, Captain, but I wish we could push him to it."

"Not worth it," Heris said. "I know—it would be fun,

but none of our friends can match our scan capability, and if we made a mistake—or he got lucky—"

"He's gone hot," Arkady Ginese, on weapons, did not look up for anyone else's conversations.

"It's not us," Koutsoudas said. "He isn't side-scanning—that's just preparation for hitting the station. He should be transmitting his demands—yes—there it goes—"

"Go ahead, Mr. Ginese," said Heris, feeling that familiar sensation in her belly. Plan, plan, and plan again, but at the moment, there was always one cold thrust of fear. Arkady and Meharry both touched their boards, and their own displays lit. Now, if the raider were looking, they could be seen. The weapons boards flickered through the preparatory displays, then steadied on green, with the red row at the top showing all the weapons ready. It had definitely been worth it to get that fast-warm capability, though it cost half again as much. Or would have, if Ginese and Meharry hadn't done the conversion themselves.

They had the raider now, though he didn't know it and might not before he died. They had calculated their ideal moment to attack, but from here on, the conclusion wasn't really in doubt.

"Screens warm," Heris said. Their puny screens wouldn't deflect much, but better a little protection than none. Second by second they closed.

"Second scan," Koutsoudas said suddenly. "Jump insertion, low velocity. Preliminary says it's a medium-size cargo hull; weapons minimal."

It had always been a possibility, that the raider would have a companion. Or rival.

"Koutsoudas on the new one; Meharry, you take main scan on the raider. Ginese?"

"Any time, Captain."

"It's hours out," Koutsoudas said. "And it's not in any hurry. Could be tramp cargo—I'm just getting the beacon ID—but the timing's suspicious."

"That's why we have backup. Meharry, give me a replay of the raider's transmission to the station." The station, as agreed, had rebroadcast that narrowbeam transmission in omni, which allowed the *Sweet Delight* to pick it up— and enter it in the log, for evidence. It was about what she'd expected, the wording varying only slightly from the previous raids. Koutsoudas glanced up briefly.

"That's Svenik the Bold. I recognize his voice; it was one of our voice-screen samples on file. Want a verification?" Heris nodded. He reached over to Meharry's board, and flicked a switch on the module he'd added.

"Transmit our authorization," Heris said. Koutsoudas grinned, and hit another switch.

Half a light-second; the raiders should be startled to receive a transmission from a source they hadn't spotted, giving them official notification that they were unwanted and about to be fired upon. The question was, what would they do next?

"There's *Grogon*," said Ginese. "Right on time." The old escort had been given a special set of electronics and now lit up the scans as if she were studded with more armament than the yacht. Positioned as she was, on the far side of the intruder's path, she limited its possible maneuvers. He would have to assume a coordinated attack plan.

"Now," Heris said to Ginese. He ran his thumb down the firing controls, and the green telltales flicked to red, the red ready lights to yellow. The *Sweet Delight* shuddered at launch, even though the missiles were shoved out of the tubes at low velocity, to light outside. Red to orange to yellow to green, as the weapons reloaded automatically, and the red row at the top reappeared.

Meanwhile, Ginese and Meharry tracked the launches. "Five—eight—all lit," Meharry reported. Half a light-second still left over 90,000 miles between the two vessels, though that distance was closing as the raider approached.

Certainly it was enough time for them to maneuver. But which way? They should be worrying about the old escort; they should be wondering what other weapons she would launch.

"Koutsoudas?" Heris watched the back of his head. "What's our friend up to?"

"Dumping vee. With the lag, still a safe distance out. Very interesting ID, Captain."

"Yes?"

"In the FR registry as an independent hauler, crew-owned. But I've got a flag on her in the Fleet database for suspicious activities, and a personal flag . . . she's been in the same system, but remote, during raids by Aethar's World pirates and by the Jenniky gang." He cleared his throat. "My guess is she's either a spotter or a paymaster. Maybe both. Not in her own right, of course, but for someone else. My guess there is the Black Scratch; she claims to trade with Xolheim and Fiduc, and you know the Benignity has a strong presence there."

"Agreed. Keep an eye on her, then. Arkady?"

"Nothing—there. They've launched at us, and kicked up another ten gees acceleration. It's within our pattern, and I could stop their salvo with my bare hands, just about. Old stuff."

"A rock in the head will kill you just as dead," Heris quoted; Ginese laughed.

"Yes, Captain, but Aethar's prefers bang to finesse . . . look at my scans." Already the *Sweet Delight*'s elegant ECM had confused the enemy missiles; Heris would need to order no evasive maneuvers at all. She worried more about the old escort, with her novice crew and her faked signatures. If they fired anything much at her . . . but the raider seemed intent on getting away.

"A lot of screaming on their bridge," Meharry said. "I can't understand their ugly language, but it's loud."

"Let me—" Koutsoudas switched back to that channel,

and then grinned. "Svenik cussing out his scan tech for not seeing us first . . . someone's left the main speaker open; the station should be getting all this too. Handy for court, if we ever want to pursue it." If there was any court to pursue it in, Heris thought.

The *Sweet Delight*'s missiles carried guidance systems normally found only in military weaponry. Whatever ECM the pirate vessel had didn't affect them; on Koutsoudas's enhanced scans, the missiles closed inexorably. Heris wondered if Svenik's ship had shields of any quality, or if he'd try to outrun them. She almost hoped he would; if he redlined his ship and blew it himself, it wouldn't be her fault. That was thinking like a civilian, though.

"Got him." Koutsoudas, who had seen the inevitable an instant before any of the rest. The pirate ship and the missiles merged, and exploded.

"Easiest kill I ever saw," Oblo said, as if affronted.

"I don't trust it," Heris said. "What's that other doing?"

"It'll be a while before they get it on their scans," Koutsoudas said. "They're still dumping . . . ask me again in a couple of minutes."

"Just tell me, 'Steban," Heris said. She felt itchy all over; like Oblo, she was almost irritated that it had been that easy. It felt unreal, like a training exercise. Something picked at her memory. The raider had been there before—that same raider—destroying things but doing less damage than such raiders could. So they'd expected the raider, and they'd gotten the raider . . . and all this time the second ship hung out there and watched. "Weapons off," she said abruptly. Meharry gave her a startled look, but shut her board down. " 'Steban, signal *Grogon* on tightbeam—shutdown, as dark as possible."

"You want me to put us back in hiding?"

"Not until there's a natural obstacle between us and that other ship. I think we just did something stupid."

"Stupid?" Meharry stared at her.

"We expected an Aethar's World raider, and that's what we got. The same raider. Why?"

"Because the Bloodhorde are stupid," Meharry said impatiently. "They do things like that."

"For a profit, yes. For honor, if you can figure out what they mean by it. But here—look, we were told they've had raiders several times, but they didn't actually blow the station—"

"They wanted to milk the cow, not kill it," Oblo said. But he had a worried look on his scarred face.

"The Bloodhorde always figure there's another cow down the road," Heris said. "I thought maybe—this is so far from their usual range—they were just skimming on the way home from something else. But suppose they weren't. And suppose they weren't on their own business."

"The Black Scratch," Koutsoudas said, without looking away from his scans. "Hired 'em, maybe, or offered Svenik backing against Kjellak—that might do it. Send him in on feints at irregular intervals, see what happens. Likely Svenik didn't know he had a trailer."

"Right. And nothing much happens once, twice, and then we show up out of nowhere, and sparkle all over their scans with stuff no civilian vessel could have. Blow Svenik without a scratch on us—no contest—" Heris paused, wishing she had the faintest idea where the nearest Fleet communications node was.

"He's boosting," Koutsoudas said. "Must have just caught the fight, and he's not wasting time. Wonder why he doesn't just jump? He's far enough from anything massive. . . ."

"Anything we know about," Heris said. She felt little cold prickles down her back. "No, most likely he wants to see what we'll do. If he can get us into a chase. Let's pretend we don't see him. Suck all you can, but don't react."

"And we're not going back on the stealth gear because you hope they'll think we popped out from behind a rock?" Meharry's tone expressed her doubts.

"I think they'll wonder. We're small, and it's a messy system—it wouldn't take a big rock to hide us. If we went back in the sack now, they'd know for sure there was a ship with that capacity."

The distant ship vanished into FTL six hours later; Heris trusted Koutsoudas's scans enough to return to the orbital station then and confer with the Xavierans. They were, she thought, entirely too jubilant, and in no mood for warnings.

✧ Chapter Nine

"We want to honor you," Senior Captain Vassilos kept saying when she tried to get her point across.

"There's nothing to honor, yet," Heris said for the tenth time. "You may well have worse trouble coming."

"You must understand, Captain Serrano, that this is the first time in years that we have been able to resist successfully. I shouldn't say *we*, since you did it. But we must celebrate this victory—it will put heart in the troops."

"They mean it," muttered Cecelia from the corner of the office. "Remember that band? That's how they are—you must let them celebrate."

"Very well," Heris said, with as much grace as she could muster. "But I'm still worried—I would very much like to have a serious discussion—"

"Of course! Of course, Captain Serrano. The General Secretary wants to meet you—the entire government wishes to thank you. After the parade—" Heris tried not to let her eyes roll up at this. Cecelia, out of pickup range, was grinning at her wickedly. "And just a few speeches, nothing really fancy—" She could imagine.

As it happened, she couldn't have imagined.

"Aren't you glad I taught you to ride?" Cecelia asked. She sat the stocky white horse with the flowing mane as if she'd grown out of its back. After the first block, Heris had had enough of the rhythmic bouncing trot of her matching white horse. So it was in time to the music—so her legs hurt. She knew she didn't look as good as Cecelia.

She was sure her uniform jacket over riding breeches looked particularly silly. Hard to believe that real soldiers had once ridden into battle.

"I'm glad this is a small city," Heris said. "I bounce too much."

"Open your joints and relax," Cecelia said. "This is fun."

Fun for someone who had been born with callused thighs, maybe. Fun for someone who had ridden in front of crowds much of her adult life. Heris would rather have celebrated victory by floating for a few hours in some body of warm water. But duty was duty.

By the time they arrived at the site of the celebration, Heris wondered if she'd ever get off the horse without help. Cecelia wasn't sympathetic.

"I told you to spend more hours on the simulator," she said.

"I had other things to do," Heris said. It wasn't an excuse she'd have accepted from anyone else, but she still couldn't see that riding horses was a necessary skill for a ship captain.

"Captain——?" That was a young man in the colorful uniform of the Civil Guard. Heris sighed, and managed to dismount without either groaning or kicking him in the head. She was going to be more than sore for a few days. Cecelia, already down, looked eager and happy. Heris moved over to stand beside her. She had no idea what this world would consider an appropriate celebration, certainly not what might come after a parade on horseback.

The same little band she had first seen on the wide plain of the spaceport (she recognized the conductor's exuberant moustache) struck up another of those jaunty marches. Despite herself, she felt a prickle of excitement run up her spine.

"Up here, Captain," said her escort. Up here was atop a stone platform that resembled every reviewing stand she had ever seen except its being solid stone instead of slightly quivery metal and plastic. Rows of chairs, each with a bright blue cushion on it—that was different—and a little railing painted brilliant white. Behind the chairs, the flags of Armitage, Xavier, Roualt, and the Familias Regnant swung gently in the light breeze. In front of them, the wide field where the parade was coming apart into its constituent elements. Some of them reformed into obvious military units, and some (the children on ponies) milled around until the Civil Guard shooed them away.

Heris sat where she was bidden, and found herself looking down on the heads of the band. Directly beneath her the coiled shape of some kind of horn gleamed in the sun, and it produced substantial deep blats from its great bell. In front of that row were the horns held up and facing outward, and in front of them the little dark and silver cylinders . . . she wished she knew more about musical instruments. The required music appreciation classes long ago had left a residue of tangled facts: some things had strings, and some had tubes you blew through or tubes with holes in them you blew across. Which left that thing on the end there: it looked like an inflated pillow with sticks coming out. Whatever it was, it made a sound she had never heard before, as if something alive were being strangled inside.

As she watched, its player stepped smartly out in front of the band, revolved in place, and faced the reviewing stand. Now she could hear the discordant squeals and gurgles clearly; the rest of the band had stopped in mid-phrase (if music had phrases) to allow it a solo turn.

"Our top piper," her escort said. Heris smiled politely. At least now she had a label for it. Piper.

"You'll see the massed pipes, too," he said, as if that were a treat in store. A mass of these squealers? Heris thought longingly of earplugs. She looked beyond the band. Now the near side of the field was almost empty, and a crowd had formed on the far side. A couple of dogs ran in circles, chasing each other. "I'm sorry for the delay," her escort murmured. "We wanted to get everyone here—"

"Quite all right," Cecelia said, before Heris could think past the piper's screeches to what she might politely say.

"But here they are—" A horse-drawn vehicle rolled across the field, to distant cheers from the crowd. One of the dogs fled; the other ran yapping after the horses, who ignored this familiar accompaniment. So did the elegant spotted dog sitting upright beside the driver.

"The General Secretary, the Mayor and Council," her escort said. "I hope it accords with your etiquette; in ours, the greater honor goes to the one who arrives first." He stood, and Heris took the hint. The little band began something that made her want to sway from foot to foot— not a march, but almost a waltz. The General Secretary, resplendent in a long cape edged with silver braid, bowed to the reviewing stand. Heris had no idea what was required; Cecelia, she noticed, stood still. The Mayor's cape had bright red braid; the Council, in various bright-colored outfits, all glittering with braid, buttons, or other adornment, descended one by one from the carriage and bowed before climbing the steps. When the last was seated, the solo piper let out a resounding screech. Heris was delighted to see that the horses hitched to the vehicle flattened their ears and tried to shy. The driver lifted the reins and they exploded into a fast trot.

No one on the platform said a word; if they had, no one could have heard it, Heris was sure. With a final tweedle and squeal, the piper spun around, and the little band snapped to attention, and marched away. Now what?

Now the General Secretary, it seemed, had something to say. Long experience of political speeches had Heris ready for long-winded platitudes.

"We're here to honor our old friend Lady Cecelia, and our new heroes," the General Secretary. "You saw Captain Serrano in the parade; we now consider her a friend of the same status as Lady Cecelia." The General Secretary turned to Heris. "Please accept this as a token of our esteem," he said. "Wear it when you visit us, if you will." It was a small silver button, stamped with the design of a leaping horse.

"Thank you," Heris said. Before she could finish with the requisite reminder that she had done nothing of herself, but only with the help of others, the General Secretary was interrupting.

"And now, let's show our visitors and friends the pride of our people." And he sat down abruptly, leaving Heris no choice but to do the same.

Heris blinked. Short, and not particularly graceful— not at all what she expected. But it wasn't her place to expect. Now at the far end of the field, a thin sound like the strangling of dozens of geese . . . "The massed pipes," her escort confirmed. Suddenly they were in motion, and with them an array of drums.

"I'm . . . not familiar with the instrument," Heris said, hoping for a diversion. Her escort beamed.

"Not that many worlds have preserved them," he said with evident pride. She could understand that; suppression seemed more reasonable than preservation. "Here we have not only preserved, but developed, the four main varieties of pipe that survived the Great Dispersal. For marching bands, we prefer the purely acoustic, though there is an amplified variety with a portable powerpack."

"They seem quite loud enough," Heris said.

"Oh, but they were battlefield instruments at one time. We find them very effective in riot control."

She could imagine that. An amplified piper—or, worse, a mass of amplified pipers—could send the average rioter into acoustic shock. Most security services had acoustic weapons, but none that looked or sounded like this.

Cecelia leaned past the escort between them. "Isn't it thrilling? I've always loved pipes."

Heris was saved the necessity of answering by the pipes themselves, now close enough to make a wall of sound. The pipers marched with a characteristic strut, the drums thundered behind them, and despite herself her toes began to move in rhythm inside her shoes. The pipes when playing a quick melody sounded much more musical, she thought, dancing from note to note above the rattling drums. Behind this group marched what must be, she realized, the entire planetary militia, each unit in its own colors. Each, as it passed the reviewing stand turned heads sharply, and shouted out its origin (so her escort explained). She had no idea where "Onslow" and "Pedigrate" were, but the pride certainly showed. Far to their right, the massed pipes wheeled and marched back, this time nearer the crowd.

To Heris's relief, they returned through the town in the gleaming cars of their first visit. She had not looked forward to climbing back on a horse.

"I could get addicted to this," Cecelia said. They had the closed compartment to themselves. Her cheeks had reddened with the unaccustomed sun, but her eyes were bright. A few rose petals clung incongruously to her red hair, and one lay for a moment on her shoulder until the errant breeze lifted it off.

"Addicted to what, riding in parades?" Heris asked.

"That and . . . being the conquering hero. Knowing I did something really worthwhile."

Heris refrained from pointing out that Cecelia herself hadn't done that much. She'd volunteered her—well, their—yacht and crew, but she herself had not fired a weapon. Still, she had been in danger with them. And in all honesty, Heris herself had enjoyed the cheering crowds, even the roses and ribbons. "This is the easy part," she said.

"I know," Cecelia said. "But then I always did like victory

celebrations. I never thought I'd have another one—not like the old days."

"Didn't you get any satisfaction out of your return to Rockhouse?" Heris asked.

For the first time, Cecelia looked ready to answer that. "Not really. The king resigned—I had no chance to talk to him first. And Lorenza—she escaped. Even if she died— and I agree she must have—she escaped *me*. I wanted to slap her smug face myself. Then I found out the yacht wasn't mine anymore—I couldn't even take off on my own—"

"But we did—"

"Yes . . . we did. Out of your courtesy; it was no longer my *right*." Cecelia sighed. "I'm sorry, Heris. It must sound silly to you. But all the way back from the Guerni Republic, I fantasized such a gorgeous, impressive homecoming— storming in and confounding everyone. The feeling we've had today—that's what I had in mind. Bands playing, flags waving, my family all in a heap of contrition. Admissions of guilt, begging of forgiveness. Instead—with the king's resignation, everything seemed to fall apart. My affairs didn't matter that much compared to the change in government; I wasn't a hero after all. Very annoying, actually, especially when Berenice had the nerve to say that if I was going to get rejuvenation, I should have spent a little more and gotten some remodelling—"

"What!" Heris had not heard this before.

"Oh, yes. After all, I didn't have to live the same selfish life as before, and if I'd bother to try, I could look quite nice and perhaps marry—I swear, Heris, it was at that moment I decided to sue them for their idiocy. Before that I had been annoyed, but that did it. Not a scrap of remorse for the hell she'd put me through in that damned nursing home, but the same old superior attitude about my looks and my duty to the family. I'll show her duty, I thought."

Heris had wondered more than once why Cecelia was so determined to sue the family; now she was caught between sympathy and laughter. "It wasn't very tactful of her," she said, trying for middle ground.

"She never was tactful," Cecelia said. "No small child is—one reason I don't like small children—but she was remarkable even for a child. She told me once 'You may be famous, but I'm pretty, and you never will be.' It was true, of course, but it hurt anyway."

"So that's why you've sued them?"

"Yes . . . mostly. I suppose. They keep thinking I'm nothing—handy to do their chores, when they wanted Ronnie off Rockhouse for a year, handy for loans when they want to expand their holdings, handy for a joke whenever they want to feel elegant and so on . . . and I just got tired of it."

Heris said, "It's Tommy this and Tommy that and Tommy take a walk. . . ."

"What?"

"I thought perhaps you might know Kipling. One of his poems that will live as long as military organizations, because that's how the military's always treated. Despised until needed, then cozened into things—blamed for whatever goes wrong, and praised—when it gets praise—for the wrong things."

"Exactly. Though I suppose my life hasn't been that bad, really." Heris watched the flicker of amusement in Cecelia's eyes. Just when she'd given up, the woman would show that wry self-assessment, that ability to keep things in balance. They rode another few blocks in companionable silence. Then Cecelia shifted to face Heris directly. "What's worrying you? You were as tense as on the island today, and it wasn't all saddle sores."

"We're celebrating too early," Heris said. "There's something wrong with that raid—we won too easily, and we may have made things worse by winning. I'm half-expecting

Koutsoudas to call and say there's an entire fleet of enemy ships coming in."

"That's ridiculous," Cecelia said. "Here? What are they going to steal, horses and cattle and antelopes and sheep? And what enemy?"

"There are mining colonies on the gas giants' moons," Heris said.

"Piddly," Cecelia said. "They're hardly two decades old, and just now beginning to break even. Nothing unusual, and most of it will be processed in this system, developing an industrial base to allow bulk mining later."

"A slow payback on the investment," Heris said, just to make a comment. To her surprise, Cecelia looked startled.

"You're right—it hadn't occurred to me, but—I wonder if that's going to be an effect of Rejuvenant political influence?"

"What?" Heris was still trying to think why some enemy would make Xavier a target. As Cecelia had said, horses and cattle weren't usually of great interest to aggressive political entities. Shipyards, manufacturing centers, things like that.

"Well . . . Rejuvenants can afford the years to develop slow-growth industries—things that would have been marginal at best for non-rejuvenated individuals. Projects that families can carry out only if they convince successive generations to support them."

"Mmm." Heris filed that away to think about later. At the moment, she was more interested in what had really happened with the raid, and what she could say to the Xavieran government. Such as it was.

Once at the party, the General Secretary bowed over her hand and murmured, "I understand you are worried and need to talk. Give us an hour or so, eh? And then we'll find you. People just want to say thanks." Unlike Senior Captain Vassilos, who had seemed almost theatrical in his military posture, the General Secretary looked like an amiable bear. Graying brown hair, bright brown eyes . . . Heris had not really looked at him before, but now she liked what she saw. She smiled, nodded, and let herself be passed on down the reception line.

Beyond the line, her faithful escort showed her to a comfortable, softly padded seat. A waiter appeared with a tray of drinks, and another with a tray of finger foods. Heris chose a sunset-colored juice, and found it tangy and refreshing; the crisp shapes on the plate at her side turned out to be bite-sized pastries filled with meat or cheese. None of the people who came up to her seemed to think she looked funny, and after a while she quit thinking about the riding boots and breeches. Especially when she saw half a dozen others wearing them.

"Heris—these are the Carmody sisters," Cecelia said, appearing at her side with three rangy women as tall as herself. "They own one of the breeding farms I'll be visiting."

"Cecelia says you ride," said the youngest of the sisters— or the one who looked youngest—Heris suddenly noticed a blue-and-silver ring like Cecelia's, only higher on the woman's left ear. Then it sank in—another horse enthusiast.

"Only a little," Heris said. "In the parade, for instance."

"But she said you rode to hounds," the woman said. "Tell me—does Bunny still have that fierce trainer—what was his name?" Heris couldn't believe it. Did they know anything but horses? Did they think this reception was about horses?

"Yes, he does, and you're supposed to be thanking Heris for knocking off that raider," said Cecelia. Heris felt her irritation subsiding.

"Well, of course. But Davin said all that, I thought. Now that it's over—"

"I'm really not an expert on horses," Heris said, as gently as she could manage. "Lady Cecelia has very kindly tutored me, but I'm already out of my depth."

"Oh. Well . . . Cecelia, suppose you give us some idea what you're looking for?" Heris would have laughed if she hadn't been trapped by her stiffening body into a corner that soon filled with all the horsey set on Xavier . . . breeders, mostly, whom Cecelia introduced. Most of them just managed to remember why Heris was being honored before they launched into anecdotes about horses, arguments about breeding strategies and training methods, and plain unmistakable brags. By the time the General Secretary's assistant came to suggest that she might like to meet with him and a few others in the library, she was feeling very grumpy indeed.

"If I understood Captain Vassilos correctly, you believe there were more ships in the system, observing your battle with the raider. If that is so, can you explain why it bothered you? I may as well mention that none of our scan technicians found a trace of such a ship, even when they went back over the recorded scans."

Heris chose her words carefully. "Sir, let me take the last point first. Your scan techs are working with civilian-level scans, and old ones at that. We happen to have more up-to-date scans on the yacht, which means that we can see farther and detect smaller disturbances."

"You have military-grade equipment?" asked Vassilos.

"I . . . prefer not to specify the equipment we have," Heris said. "Not to impugn the integrity of anyone in this room, but—it may be that our ability to detect trouble at a range where trouble believes itself undetectable will save lives."

"I see." The General Secretary went back to his first point. "And you believe there were other ships in the system, observing . . . how many ships?"

"We detected one," Heris said. The General Secretary nodded; he had caught the implication. "It may, of course, have been an innocent vessel with a very cautious captain . . .

but its arrival, its response to the battle, and its departure, suggest something else. My scan tech has been working on the data we got; there is some indication that the ship has a history of traversing systems just as raids are going on. A paymaster, perhaps."

"But who would be doing that? Even when they trashed our orbital station, they got little for it—we couldn't figure out then what they really wanted."

"To see if the Fleet would come clean house, I suspect," Heris said. "When you got so little response from Fleet, they came back—as much to test that hypothesis as anything else."

"But why? We have no great wealth—we are not on the direct route to anywhere else, as I'm sure you noticed."

"To be honest, I have not yet had time for a serious consideration of what may lie behind what we saw. But I am sure that another ship observed our handling of the raider, and that it was there precisely to observe your defensive capability. That suggests some plan for an attack. From whom, or why, I cannot say at this point." She suspected, but she did not want to commit herself yet.

"What should we do?"

"Send an urgent message to Fleet, of course. I'm sure you're aware that things are . . . unsettled . . . in places. They have other problems. Still, we can draft a report that should elicit some response. Even sending such a report may help out; I would expect those watching your situation to know of such a request. They would probably delay any action until they ascertained whether Fleet responded in force." Or they would attack all the faster. If they were nearly ready. Heris wished she had more knowledge, and less intuitive sense of time ticking away.

"You were not . . . sent here? As a sort of . . . representative of Fleet?"

"No," Heris said, making it very firm. From the tone, they wanted her to be a covert presence; they wanted the reassurance that Fleet had not forgotten them. Remote worlds often felt neglected, and some were. "I am not now in the Regular Space Service. I'm a civilian, hired by Lady Cecelia to take her where she wishes . . . in this case, here, to look for bloodstock."

"I thought it was her yacht," someone down the table said. A third secretary to the defense council, Heris remembered.

"It was, but through a legal tangle when she was in a coma last year, it became mine. She will probably tell you the whole thing if you ask her." Heris didn't want to; she realized that someone who wanted to see her arrival with the *Sweet Delight* as more than providential could find other reasons for the change of ownership.

"As long as you *are* here," the General Secretary said, "could we beg your assistance, your advice? I quite understand that you are not, as you say, now in Fleet . . . but you have more experience in these matters than anyone else here. If you could suggest how we should think about this menace you spoke of, or how we could prepare to meet it . . ."

Prepare to die, she could have said honestly enough. With one cranky old escort, underpowered and lightly armed, with no bulk transport to get its population away to someplace safe, Xavier would be no more a match for a serious invasion than the raider had been for *Sweet Delight*. But for all their bright, perky music, their colorful impractical uniforms, their screeching massed pipes—yes, and even the number of horse enthusiasts—Heris liked these people. She liked the careful way a farmer's daughter had documented the raider's characteristics with her homemade scan equipment. The stubborn determination to resist and keep resisting that had led them to mount phase cannon in an atmospheric shuttle. The surprising competence of the old escort's crew . . . even the length of the General Secretary's speech at the parade ground . . . all went into the equation.

"While we're here," she said finally, into the silence, "I will be glad to give you what advice I can. But whether it does any good—that I can't know."

"Of course not. And we will show our gratitude by taking your first advice, to send word to the Regular arm of Fleet—" He reddened. "Sorry—I mean to Fleet Sector HQ."

"I'll get back up to my ship, and see what we've got in our records," Heris said. "Lady Cecelia brought her things down—she plans to visit various breeders here. So, if you can tell me about the next shuttle—"

"You won't stay the night?"

"No—to be honest, I'll be more comfortable up there, in direct contact with our scan techs."

"Quite so. Then if it's agreeable, we'll plan to confer with you on the station in the next few days. And there'll be a shuttle ready—when, Captain Vassilos?"

"Three hours," Vassilos said. "It's fuelling now."

"Thank you," Heris said. She started to stand up, and winced. "Lady Cecelia's right," she said. "I really should practice more on her simulator."

"Never mind," the General Secretary said. "It's not your equestrian expertise we need now."

"All the better, since I haven't any," said Heris; they all laughed.

Back aboard *Sweet Delight*, she called up the data they had gathered and came up with the answers—or answers that made sense. The Xavierans considered themselves remote, far from any population or power center. They were remote from the center of any political entity, but not so remote from frontiers. After all, she had had to file a letter of intent with the R.S.S. to visit Xavier, because it was in a frontier zone.

"Location, location, location," she reminded herself. The Familias Regnant had grown by accretion, expanding along trade routes through unclaimed space, until it bumped into resistance. The neat "spheres of influence" predicted by earlier planners existed only for small political units. Larger entities looked more like multidimensional models of complex organic molecules. Although this meant a larger "surface" to protect for the volume included, the advantage of an outlying lobe that included vital jump points more than compensated for the extra defensive exposure.

Castle Rock, with its massive stations Rockhouse Major and Minor, lay more or less at the center of Familias Regnant space—at least in three major axes. But those axes were not equal. The longest dimension was five or six times the shortest, including two fat tentacles or pseudopods extending toward Compassionate Hand territory. The interface between the Familias and its neighbors resembled that of an enzyme and its protein companion: star by star, the competing entities had fit themselves together in a way that increased the defensive difficulties by making the contact surface vast. Most of the time, this surface was merely a potential one: in spaces far too large to garrison, contact existed only sporadically, and along the usual mapped routes of travel.

Heris knew from experience that the ability to visualize the spatial interactions required both innate talent and practice. The visual representation she took to the next meeting with the General Secretary and his staff was far simpler than the one she and Petris and Koutsoudas would use. Even so, the General Secretary had trouble with it.

"What's this little skinny thing out here?" he asked.

"Us." Heris grinned at his shocked expression. "I know—you thought we were closer to the interior because Xavier is a short jump from Byerly and Neugarten and Shiva. But they're all strung out along one jump route, with an even smaller twig for Neverfall." She pointed. "There's Rockhouse. And there's Rotterdam—" Rotterdam, on its own slender twig, three jump points from Xavier because of the need to go around the saddle-shaped Compassionate Hand intrusion.

As the General Secretary stared at the color-coded visual, Heris added the icons that were Koutsoudas's best guess for the locations of Fleet and Compassionate Hand warships. The Compassionate Hand maintained major bases in the saddle between the lobes where Xavier and Rotterdam lay. Logical—so did the R.S.S. When this survey had been taken, they had had two battle groups at Partis, and one at Vashnagul.

Heris explained what that meant, trying to keep it simple. "The Compassionate Hand intends its battle groups to be more than just space fighters. Each battle group deploys units capable of invading and occupying fixed positions such as space stations and satellite defense systems. On a sparsely settled planet without good defenses, such teams could even take control of the entire world. More commonly, they would 'scorch' the population from space— blow the population centers, perhaps with tactical nukes. Then they'd land their own construction teams and equipment."

"They'd just—kill everyone, for no reason?"

"From their point of view, there's a reason. They don't care about people they don't need, and if they've chosen Xavier for a forward base, they won't want to waste time converting your population."

"And they might choose us because—"

"Because of the jump point access Xavier provides. Although the direct route in is straightforward, there are more alternatives from here than from Rotterdam. It's still tricky—look—" Heris pointed out the difficulties the Compassionate Hand would face. "The point of coming through here is surprise, so if they lose surprise here they've expended effort for no gain. That means they'll try to interrupt communications as soon as—even before—they attack. Do you have daily ansible traffic?"

"No . . . in fact, the charges are high enough that we usually store and batch it. Once a week at most."

"So no one outside would notice if you didn't send a batch for a week or so."

"That's right—oh. I see. Then I suppose they could fabricate a message—"

"If they needed to. My point being, Xavier is most valuable in the early stages of a war, then its value drops until they can get their defenses up, when it becomes valuable again simply because it denies those jump points to Fleet."

"And our strategy?"

"Tell Fleet what we think, and keep telling them until they listen—and don't let ourselves be surprised by an invasion force we weren't expecting." And hope that the enemy had not already intercepted their messages. But Heris kept that grim thought to herself.

✧ Chapter Ten

On the planet Music

Raffa wandered around the street market, but caught no sight of the king, or clone, or whoever that had been. She couldn't see far anyway, past the colorful awnings and dwarf flowering trees, the little clusters of booths strung with banners. Finally, when her stomach informed her it was lunchtime, she followed her nose to a booth where a deft-fingered man wrapped spirals of meat and bread dough on sticks, and grilled them. Next to that booth, another sold fruit punches; Raffa picked something called omberri, which she had never had before.

She chose a bench under one of the nonflowering trees—she had noticed the bees humming among flowers—and worked her way down the meat and bread spirals. Her omberri punch had tartness enough to be refreshing on this warm day, without puckering her mouth. When she was through, she sat a few minutes with her legs stretched, watching the crowds of noontime shoppers. She had seen several booths she'd like to visit—shell jewelry, ribbon weaving worked into striking belts and vests—along with displays of native crafts that didn't interest her. Even some pottery as ghastly as that made by Ottala Morreline's crazy aunt.

Now that she'd lost track of the king, and had no idea where Ronnie and George were, she might as well spend the afternoon shopping. With that cheering thought, she worked her way through the booths, back to the one with the shell jewelry.

Then she saw the young man with the familiar way of carrying his head. It couldn't be. Raffa ducked among the people, working her way closer. From behind, he still looked familiar. She edged her way around a booth to get a side view, and caught sight of his profile just an instant before he turned and looked her way. It *was*. Raffa opened her mouth to call out, just as he focussed on her and paled. He spun on his heel and darted away.

Raffa, startled, didn't move until someone touched her arm and pointed out that she was blocking the whole aisle. "Sorry," she said, still feeling blank. It had to be the prince. It had to be Gerel, who was supposed to be dead, and he was afraid to see her.

In one flash she saw the whole pattern of deceit. Gerel wasn't dead; the man she had seen *was* the king, and he had come here to meet Gerel. King and prince . . . the phrase "government in exile" came to mind from her history studies. Lord Thornbuckle and Kevil Mahoney only *thought* they'd defeated the king—he was planning an insurrection.

Which meant that Ronnie and George, if they were still alive, were in mortal danger. Her skin tingled; she felt as preternaturally alert as she had that first night on the island. Did they know? Or were they about to walk into a conspiracy?

She set off slowly in the direction Gerel had fled. She didn't expect to find him—she didn't even want to find him—but she wanted to see what that part of the city was like.

Behind the street market, the streets resumed their normal, sedate appearance. Raffa noted that she was now on Bedrich, just crossing Cole. This was a residential area, five-story apartments lining both sides of the street, each with its own distinct facade. She saw a woman with three identical children in blue smocks . . . tried not to let herself think "clone." They were children—and when they grinned up at her with identical sticky smiles, she couldn't help grinning back. A yellow and white cat leapt off a window ledge in front of her, paraded to the curb with its tail in the air, and then sat to lick its paws.

This would get her nowhere but farther from the hotel. Gerel had been scared; he wouldn't come back to see if she was in the neighborhood. Raffa slowed at the next street and glanced at the sign. Hari . . . and her tourist handcomp told her she would find nothing scenic if she kept going the same way. Just sore legs on the way back. She glanced around, and finally shrugged to herself. She might as well go back to the hotel, see if any messages had come in from the Institute about the pharmaceutical samples she'd turned in.

"These were not manufactured here. They were manufactured in modern equipment, using a process similar to, but not identical to, the one we developed. I can show you—here—" Raffa stared at the squiggly lines, and wished she had paid more attention to chemistry. "They've used an alternate synthetic route which we don't like because it produces more waste. In addition, the isotope fractions suggest that the raw materials came from a source we don't use. Although we do have one old sample that parallels it—from a mine in your territory. Do you know the Patchcock system?"

Raffa shook her head. "Not except for that mess when there was a war or something." She realized that didn't sound very intelligent, but after all she hadn't been old enough to pay much attention.

"Well, before that we used to import a little from one of the planets there, and we still have reference samples. It's not definitive, by any means, but the Patchcock system could be a source of the raw materials. I do know that there's a sizeable pharmaceutical industry on Patchcock itself. The Morrelines, I believe, are major investors."

Raffa wondered if those were the same Morrelines whose daughter Ottala had been such a pain at school. She and Brun had never liked Ottala that much—well, to be honest, at all—but she supposed she could look Ottala up when she got back to Familias space. "And the drugs themselves? Are they complying with your standards?"

"Aside from the fact that they're breaking the licensing agreement by using an alternate process, those in the first sample submitted do meet our standards. The second sample, however, is subtly different. Do you read chromatographs?"

"No . . . I'm sorry."

"Never mind. I'll give you the complete analysis and references, of course . . . it's important for your neurologists to have this, and understand the effects. In essence, the changes in the ring structures—the substitutions—are going to affect the quality of the rejuvenation, and this degradation will accumulate with repeated rejuvenations. It's not as bad as the old method, and it should be reversible, but if your specialists have noticed some deterioration in memory and cognitive ability in some patients, this may explain it."

"I know there's concern," Raffa said, without specifying whose concern.

"Frankly, I'm not surprised. It's possible that this is merely sloppy quality control in manufacturing—if for instance the reaction in the fourteenth step is poisoned, it's possible for that ring substitution to occur. But you must also consider industrial sabotage. Either a deliberate intent to adulterate the drugs to manipulate someone, or deliberate carelessness with the intent to maximize profits. Especially with the alternate process being used, it would be expensive to maintain the kind of quality we demand; the biologicals used to clean up the unreacted substrate can be difficult to extract."

This was all gobbledygook to Raffa, except the part about sabotage and profit margins . . . she could see possibilities either way, and so, she was sure, could Lord Thornbuckle.

"I think this is too important to depend on one messenger," she said. She dug out the authorization card Lord Thornbuckle had given her. "Here's the account number—"

Kemtre Lord Altmann, the former king of the Familias Regnant, limped slightly. His legs ached. He had walked more kilometers in the past week than in the year before. The Neurosciences Institute had refused to give him his sons' address, had said they would not violate the privacy of their patients. When he tried to insist that he was their father, he had rights, they pointed out that under his law the clones had no legal identity at all.

"Here, they are eligible for full citizenship. The biological relationship is irrelevant, especially for clones derived not from division in the embryo but from tissue culture of an older individual. To the extent that these persons have a parent, it is the donor individual—their prime, as they called him."

"But I was his father, too," the king protested.

"And how many biological children did you father?"

"Three boys," the king said.

"And what happened to them?" He could tell by the tone of the question that the interviewer already knew the answers.

"They're dead," he said, after a pause.

"All three. Somehow that doesn't recommend you as a father."

He wanted to say *It's not my fault*, but he knew the other man thought it was.

"What we will do," the man said, "is send word to the young men that you are here, and want to contact them. It is then their decision whether or not to seek you out."

"But—but that's not fair," the king said. "What am I supposed to do if they won't see me?"

"Go back to the Familias," the man said, as if it were obvious.

"I can't do that. I really want—I must see them. If I can only talk to them, I'm sure I can make them understand."

The other man's frown told him he had gone too far. "I rather doubt that—you haven't convinced me. We will do as I said—tell them you are here, and let them decide. They are adults under our law; they've applied for full citizenship. They have the legal right to decide for themselves . . . and I should warn you that you have no legal right to harass them."

He could hardly harass them when he couldn't find them. He knew their alias, at least the one they had been given, and he had started with the Smiths in the city directory. The name was not so common here as in the Familias, but it was common enough. He had met Smiths who were bakers, who were attorneys, who worked in the city's utility repair division, who were midwives and machinists. At least half of them were clones; he learned quickly not to explain his search. None would help him, not even to eliminate their clonesibs from the pattern. At this rate, it would take him years to find all the Smiths on this single planet.

"It's not just your girlfriend," Borhes said. "There's some strange man looking for Smiths. Claims to be the king." He took a gulp of his drink. "I didn't dare get close enough to find out. If he saw me—"

"You should have changed your name," George said helpfully. "At least you know that the Neurosciences people are keeping your secret."

"There are lots of Smiths," Borhes said. "And we didn't really think anyone would come looking for us."

"Surprise," murmured George. Ronnie cocked an eye at him. Was George going to be odious again? Here? It was a bad time, he thought, eyeing the tension in every line of the clones' bodies.

"Shut *up*," said Andres. "I didn't like you before, and I don't like your idea of jokes."

"We're even," George said. "I don't like your idea of hospitality. This is silly, you know. Holding us like this doesn't accomplish anything you want. You need new identities, so your father—sorry, Gerel's father—doesn't find you. You need to be free to move around; you need friends who will steer the king away from you, warn you when he's near, all that. Instead, you have tied yourself down, and us up; you're isolated, you don't have friends—"

"I said, shut up!" Andres hit George, then looked at Borhes for his reaction. Borhes shrugged; Andres looked away.

"You could go on and kill us," George said, undeterred by the blow that reddened his face. Ronnie felt a sneaking sympathy with Andres. "—But that wouldn't help, either. You'd have to get rid of two fairly large, heavy corpses. Someone might see you, and although the Guernesi have been cooperative so far, I suspect that murdering us would strain their sympathy. It would certainly upset Raffaele, and since you don't know her as well as I do, I warn you that she is likely to stick on Ronnie's trail until she finds him, dead or alive."

Ronnie felt himself blushing. "George, shut up!" he said. "You're not helping."

"Neither are you," George said. "We've tried being nice. We've tried being polite, helpful, entertaining, amusing . . . and they're still being idiots. Probably enough of that stupidity drug still in their systems—"

"It is not!" Borhes, this time, loomed over George with his hand raised.

In a tone of sweet reason that would have enraged angels, George persisted. "So I thought perhaps a bit of aggravation might make them wake up and think. If they can. Or listen to wiser minds, if they can't."

"We are not stupid!" That was both clones together, almost shouting.

"Right. Raise your voices. Yell and scream, and someone may call the police or whatever the Guernesi call them."

"The Gard," Borhes said, but more softly.

"Whatever. Listen, Borhes, this has gone on long enough. Raffa saw you—she's going to start thinking and doing, a very dangerous combination. She probably thinks you're Gerel, and if she knows the king's here, she's going to think it's a conspiracy to regain the throne—"

"What? That's crazy!"

"No crazier than what you've done. It's what any person would think, believing that Gerel, who's supposed to be dead, and the king, are in the same place. She's going to put that alongside our disappearance, and think we're either dead or being held by the king and Gerel—or their supporters."

"I haven't seen her again," Borhes said. George shrugged as well as he could.

"She's not stupid, Bor. She can recognize danger when she sees it. And she can act. So the smartest thing for you to do is enlist us as allies—let us run some interference for you."

"As if we could trust you!" Andres and Borhes exchanged glances and glared at their captives.

"It's probably hard for clones to trust anyone outside the clone cluster," George said. "Especially with the life you had. But someday you'll have to, and you know us better than anyone else so far."

"So what do you suggest?"

"What I said before. Get new identities. Simple disguises to start with, maybe, but probably plastic surgery or biosculpts later. Change your names legally. I'm sure the Neurosciences people will help."

"But—we can't go out until—"

"Oh, come now! This isn't an adventure cube thriller. Wait until dark. Take a private cab. Call the Institute from here and make arrangements." The clones looked at each other but said nothing. Ronnie held his breath. Would this work? "Or," George began, and Ronnie wanted to smack him. Why couldn't he be still a little longer? "Or, you could let one of us out to arrange disguises, transportation, even check at the Institute and make sure the king isn't hanging around the front door. Find the back door."

The clones laughed. "I don't think so," Andres said. "The other—perhaps you're right; it does make sense to disguise ourselves and take other names. One of our therapists at the Institute did suggest that, but it seemed unnecessary then."

"One thing to consider," George said. "The king may not be the only one who wants to find you. If someone did want to set up a contender for a future throne, your tissues would be helpful. With or without your cooperation."

"Well, we certainly can't trust *you*," Andres said. Then he pulled Borhes to the far side of the room, where they whispered in rapid Guernesi.

The outside felt large and dangerous; Ronnie was surprised to find himself flinching away from the bustling crowd on the sidewalk. He had loathed that small cramped room while he was in it, but now it seemed a safe haven. He understood why the clones were reluctant to go back out.

When he came to the street market, he half-hoped to see Raffa there. He bought himself a fruit pastry with the last coin in his pocket and ate it as he walked. No one seemed to notice him; no Raffa appeared, nor did the king. He wondered if Raffa had come across the king—he hoped not. That would really confuse things.

At a public combooth, he stripped his messages at the Travelers' Directory. Eleven from Raffa, all with a reply code. He punched it in, and listened to a series of unmelodious buzzes and hisses, until a message came on: "Please leave a message," followed by the three bleeps the Guernesi used to signal readiness to record.

Ronnie cleared his throat and tried to sound casual. "Hi, Raffa—it's Ronnie. What are you doing here? Did your parents change their mind about the engagement? I'll call again later." He hoped he would. He hoped anyone intercepting that message would hear only a young man in love. He hoped she was all right.

Some dim memory of spy adventure stories suggested that he shouldn't use the same booth for all the calls he planned to make. He walked across the street to another one, and called the Neurosciences Institute. The clones had told him which extension to ask for. The name they'd given him was out to lunch, though. He could leave a message or call later, he was told. He chose to call back. In the meantime, he could find out if the king was using his own name.

Raffa threw her packages on the table, and started to stretch out for a nap—then saw the blinking light on the comconsole. A message? Could it possibly be Ronnie and George? Her heart pounded; she took a breath and told herself to be calm. When she flicked REPLAY and heard Ronnie's voice, her vision dimmed for a moment and her heart pounded. The message was almost over by the time her vision cleared . . . and the idiot hadn't left a reply code. Rage replaced whatever strong emotion had just swept her—she didn't stop to think about it. The comconsole could capture the calling number and display its location; she looked at that, at the time the message had been left, and forgot about the nap.

She was two blocks away when it occurred to her that this might not be a wise move. Perhaps Ronnie hadn't left a reply code because there were problems. Perhaps— she kept walking. Perhaps if she was quick enough, he would still be there.

The booth he'd called from, on the corner of Osip and Dixha, contained a thin woman and three active preschoolers, clearly a triad. Raffa looked around, ignoring the crafts, the food booths, and spotted another cluster of combooths on the far side of the market.

And there he was. Unharmed. Angled away from her, talking—his free arm moved, gesturing—and she was suddenly angry enough to wring that handsome neck. She strode across the market, ignoring everything, until she was right behind him. She could hear nothing—the Guernesi combooths had enviable privacy shields—but he had not blanked the booth visually. Raffa moved around until she could see his face . . . she wanted to see his face very badly, especially when he caught sight of her.

He turned paper white and grabbed at the booth rail. His lips shaped her name, then he held up a hand. He glanced away briefly, as if something said to him required a change in attention, then ended the connection and shot out of the booth as if kicked. "Raffa! How did you—I mean—Raffa!"

She had been prepared to give him a stony glare and a crisp demand for information, but his hug was more frantic than possessive. And it felt good.

"I was so worried," she said, feeling her anger leak away, to be replaced by first relief than a wave of pure physical passion. Her legs felt odd; the ground seemed very far away. "I was afraid you were in trouble—you'll never guess what I've seen."

"Oh?" He was looking past her now, scanning the crowd as if he expected someone.

"Where's George?" Raffa asked. "We need to warn him— did you know the ex-king was here?"

"Uh . . ."

"And the prince. Gerel, who was supposed to be dead? He's not. I saw him. I think the king is in league with his son to take over the government again."

"The king is not in league with his son. Gerel is dead."

"But I saw him—and he recognized me and took off—"

"That wasn't Gerel." He was still looking beyond her, as if he expected to see someone he recognized.

"It was. I'm not blind, Ronnie—don't think you can treat me like a little idiot." She wanted to grab his chin and make him look at her, but a lifetime of prudence prevented her.

"You're not blind, but that wasn't Gerel." Now he looked at her, but not with the look she wanted. "Think, Raffa— what have you seen since you've been here?"

"Clones," Raffa said. "Gerel's clone? Has the king come here to get another son, take over the government?"

"Not with them—him—" Ronnie smacked himself on the forehead. "Blast it . . . I've already screwed up. No, it's not the king, or not exactly. The clones are from before, when Gerel was still alive. They doubled for him."

"But that's—" Illegal, she started to say, but with so much illegality going on, why not?

"And they don't want to have anything to do with the Familias now," Ronnie said. "They want to get on with their lives, here in a place where clones are normal, where they can be full citizens."

"You've seen—you've *talked* to them. Is that where you've been?"

"Raffa, I can't talk about it now. We have to get them some help, before the king finds them. I was just talking to the Neurosciences Institute; they'll help them get new identities, but we have to help them get there without the king noticing. The Institute says he's made a pest of himself, and they suspect he's having the place watched." He was scanning the crowd again; she could feel the tension in his arm.

"Let's go, then. Take me to them."

"I can't do that!"

"Why not? You don't think I'm going to let you walk back into trouble, do you? So that I can sit here and worry? Forget that." She realized that she had clenched her hand on his arm; her voice had risen, and a few people were glancing their way. She let go and turned away, furious again.

"Raffa, I—I don't want to take chances." With you, he meant.

"And did I survive on the island just as well as you, or not?"

"You did, but—"

"But you're afraid for me now. Who do you think will hurt me? Gerel's clones?"

"They're not quite . . . stable."

"No, but I presume they've had a good upbringing." She gave him another long look, noticing the shadows under his eyes, the tight-drawn skin. "You look hungry—who's been feeding you?"

"They have—but they had to use our money too, and it's been short."

"Well, then. That's my cue." Raffa took his hand again and led him into the market. "I'll be the traditional lady, the loaf bringer. Buttered toast does more than music to soothe the savage beast." She was aware of butchering several traditional quotes, but in the meantime—she led Ronnie from one booth to another, loading his arms with sacks of pastries, loaves of bread, a fat round cheese, and a sausage of indecent length and girth. "Fruit," she muttered then, and carried away a sack of bright gold pebbly-skinned fruits and a basket of dark purple berries. Ronnie quit arguing after she stuck a cheese-filled pastry in his mouth, and when she asked he led her away, to the far side of the market.

"Along this street," he said finally. "You know you're risking a lot."

"Not my sanity, though," Raffa said. "And that was about to disappear right along with you. This is much better. Besides, I have news about your original mission."

"You do?"

"Yes, but I won't tell you until we're there. So hurry up."

Ronnie led her up the narrow stairs, half-hoping the clones would be out, and George would let them in. Instead, Borhes opened the door. His eyes widened. "You promised!" he muttered. "I thought we could trust *you*." Then he recognized the sacks for what they were. He swallowed.

"She found me," Ronnie said. "I swear it—and she bought the food. You'd better let us in."

If Borhes had had any other thought, Raffa made sure he didn't act on it; she pushed her way through the door with her nose on Ronnie's back. George, still tied up, looked around and his eyes lighted.

"Raffa!"

She ignored him for the moment, but gave both clones a long look that brought a flush to their cheeks. "Well, gentlemen. Ronnie tells me you aren't Gerel, either one of you. I presume you have names: may I know them?"

"I'm Andres; he's Borhes." Andres seemed shaken; Ronnie felt an unexpected pang of sympathy. He would not have seen Raffa on the island; he probably thought of her as a frivoler, like the old Bubbles.

"I thought you might like something fresh to eat," Raffa said, and began unpacking the food. When Borhes reached for a pastry, she stopped him with a glance. "Untie George," she said.

"Good for you, Raffa," said George, gleefully.

"Shut up, George," she said, in much the same tone. "I expect you were being odious again. It's not the time." George got up, when Borhes had freed him, and came to the table stiffly, rubbing his wrists.

"Are you going to let us eat?" he asked.

"Yes," Raffa said. "In the faint hope that hunger is what's been dimming your collective wits." Whatever protests they might have made were lost in the descent on the food. Raffa nibbled a few of the purple berries while she watched the food disappear. When the rate of disappearance slowed, she tapped the table with the knife Borhes had used on the sausage. They looked up with the guilty expressions of little boys who have hogged the birthday cake.

"Sorry, Raffa," George said. "We were just so hungry—"

"I'm not complaining about that," she said. "But it's time to start thinking again." When she paused, they said nothing, jaws still chomping busily. Raffa sighed. "All right. Ronnie told me that the Institute is quite willing to help you acquire new identities, but the former king has been badgering them, and they think he may be having the Institute watched."

"And these two—and now you—know about us," Andres said, picking his teeth inelegantly.

Raffa ignored the rudeness. "We're no threat, sir— Andres or Borhes or whichever you are. Ronnie and I have nothing more in mind than living in peace as far from our families as we can get." Ronnie sat up straight; he hadn't realized that she had made up her mind on that as well. "Even George, I'm sure, has better things to do than make your lives miserable."

"Many better things," George said, in the tone of earnestness with which the salesman assures you the item in question is worth twice its price, and only the serious illness of his grandmother allows him to consider such a sacrifice as the present sale.

"Shut up, George," said Raffa again, this time with no sting in it. "So we can help you get to the Institute—and once inside, you know the king can't bother you. He has no authority here."

"But what about the—" Ronnie began; he stopped short as Raffa's glance landed on him like a brick on the head.

"Once we've helped these gentlemen," Raffa said, "then we can discuss the matters you and I still have to discuss."

"It sounds to me as if you'd settled them all," said Andres

without sarcasm, as if he were describing the movements of an alien creature.

"Within the limits possible, yes." Raffa made no apologies. "Now, about getting you safely to the Institute—what sort of hours did they mention, Ronnie?"

"They said any time, and I thought in the dark—"

"Would be the obvious time to pick. Have another pastry. May I suggest lunchtime? Few fugitives choose midday to move around, and the king likes his meals. He wanders around in both morning and afternoon—and goes out in the evenings—but at lunch he's sitting in the hotel, eating. And—as soon as possible. Tomorrow, for instance. If he has people looking for two copies of Gerel, we'll give them something else—a group of young people, none of them exactly like Gerel. Surely you two can do simple disguises?"

"Of course," said Borhes. He looked at Andres. "It might work."

"It will," said Raffa. "Tomorrow, late morning—I'll come here alone. Be ready." She got up to leave, and then laid a sheaf of the local currency on the table. "And here—be sure to eat a good supper."

Late the next morning, Raffa found four alert young men, eyeing each other with some suspicion but no open hostility. Two of them looked like brothers, but not clones. Something had changed in their hair color, the bones of their faces, their way of moving. She didn't stop to analyze it. "Come on," she said. "The king's back in the hotel—I waited to leave until he'd gone into the dining room. Ronnie, George—put your stuff in these packsacks."

"Shouldn't we be less . . . conspicuous?" Andres asked. He was eyeing her cherry-colored tunic, and the sheaf of bright flowers she carried, along with a basket of pastries.

"We can't really be inconspicuous," Raffa said. "What we can be is conspicuously something other than they expect. Students . . . whatever. Anything but two scared

clones. If you'll just chatter along like normal people—
or eat . . ."

They trooped downstairs as casually as if they were going
to a party. George started an anecdote that had nothing
to do with anything; Ronnie munched a cheese pastry,
and the clones looked a bit dazed.

"I don't see why you didn't bring a private car," Borhes
said, under cover of George's story about the girl who had
painted her brother's feet purple.

"That would have been conspicuous," Raffa said. "How
often do hire-cars come to this neighborhood? Come on—
just through the market." The market, bustling with the
lunchtime crowd, all more interested in food and drink
than a girl with a bunch of flowers and her four companions.
At the transit stop, a loose clump of people waited, most
of them eating. Raffa had begun to relax when someone
called to her.

"Raffaele Forrester-Saenz!" Raffa jumped as if she'd
been poked with a pin, then tried to pretend nothing had
happened. All four young men had gone rigid; the clones
looked as if they might faint. "Raffaele!" came the voice,
louder yet. Through the noise of her heart beating, Raffa
could now tell that it was an old lady's quavery disapproval—
certainly not the king. She turned around, and found herself
face-to-face with Ottala's aunt.

"Yes?" she said, as casually as she could while impaled
on that indignant gaze. Ottala's aunt, draped in shades of
mauve, with a knitted purple cap adorned with droopy
knitted flowers in pink and beige . . . Raffa had to struggle
not to burst out laughing.

"Don't pretend you don't know me," Ottala's aunt said.
"You were at school with my niece Ottala. You ought to
be ashamed of yourself! Your parents will hear about this!"

"About what?" Raffa said. Beside her, Ronnie's arm
twitched, but he and the other young men were steadfastly
not looking that direction.

"Running off to carouse in foreign parts with a young man! And not just one of them!" Ottala's aunt shook a ring-covered finger under Raffa's nose. "Everyone knows your family doesn't want you to marry Ronald Carruthers, and here you are—" Her head shot forward, like a turtle's from its shell, as she peered at the back of four young male heads. "You needn't hide, young man. I saw you across the market, laughing and chatting as if you had nothing better to do. And who are the others, if you please?" Ronnie sighed and turned around; the others still pretended not to hear.

None of your business was what Raffa wanted to say to the question, but practicality as well as manners prevented her. Old ladies like this didn't quit bothering you just because you were rude; they had dealt with more rudeness already than the average youth could think up. Raffa tried to think if anything would help, and glanced past Ottala's aunt to the person behind her. He was pushing a barrow, and on the barrow were . . . pottery pieces of incredible ugliness. Half-melted graceless shapes in colors that made her stomach turn. Recognition and counterattack came together.

"Those pots," she began. Ottala's aunt turned one of the colors on them, an ugly puce.

"You wouldn't understand," she began. "They aren't just pots, they're . . ."

"I understood that you yourself were quite an artist in pottery," Raffa said, with emphasis. "You gave some to Ottala; she had them at school. I noticed, when I was in the market the other day, how much the local wares resembled them. Perhaps—"

"Great artists derive inspiration from many sources," Ottala's aunt muttered. Her dark little eyes peered up at Raffa.

"And lesser artists plagiarize," Raffa said, with no softening. "Sometimes those who aren't artists simply—"

Ottala's aunt held up her hand, and Raffa stopped. "All right. I—I couldn't make enough pots on my own—my family kept asking for more, and more, and more. Finally I got someone to make a few for me—and then a few more—"

"But why such ugly ones?" Raffa said, shocking herself. Ottala's aunt shook her head, as if she hadn't heard right, and then smiled sadly.

"I kept hoping they'd quit asking—you know, if I made them uglier and uglier." After a pause, she went on. "I really can't explain how everyone in the family has such bad taste—it seems the worse the product, the more they want."

"Why didn't you just tell them you were tired of making pots?"

"My dear, you aren't old enough to understand." The old lady leaned forward, confiding. "Someday, when you're grown, and you're enjoying things, your relatives will start complaining. 'You never finish anything you start,' they'll say. 'You pick up one hobby after another—you're just wasting time and money with all these enthusiasms.' 'You should stick to one thing and learn to do it really well.'" Ottala's aunt sniffed. "It doesn't matter what it is. I expect that Ronald's aunt, Cecelia de Marktos, heard the same thing about her horses."

"That's true," Ronnie put in. "It's one reason Aunt Cecelia's so angry with my parents; they kept telling her that her riding was just a hobby, and not worth all the time she put into it."

"You see?" Ottala's aunt looked triumphant. "I think my family wanted to make sure I stuck to pottery, and that's why they kept asking for more. And to be honest, my dear, I did want to quit. They were right."

"Still . . ." began Raffa, who wanted to get the conversation back to the covert negotiation she had started. "About these pots . . . and Ronnie . . ."

"Oh, all right," Ottala's aunt huffed. "I won't tell on you, if you don't tell on me. But I still think young girls have no business running around in foreign lands with *four young men.* One was quite enough for me, in my young days." As the tram came in, and Raffa moved to board it with the others, Ottala's aunt called, "And don't think I don't recognize young George Mahoney there, with his ears the color of ripe plums. . . ."

The rest of the trip to the Institute passed without incident.

◇ Chapter Eleven

"We have more troubles than getting the clones to safety," Raffa said, when they met again. Ronnie and George, fresh from showers, in clean clothes, had their usual glossy surface. "Some of the rejuvenation drugs have been adulterated, and none of the samples we brought—yours or mine—were manufactured here."

"None?"

"None. They did an isotopic analysis, and in their database—which they admit isn't all-inclusive—there's a match with Patchcock." Ronnie and George looked at each other, startled, over her head. "What?"

"Nothing," they both said in the tone of voice that means Something.

"Tell me." Raffa was not about to take any more nonsense.

"Ottala Morreline disappeared on Patchcock. I don't know any more; I'm not supposed to know that much, but I always could read upside down and backwards." George smirked. Raffa could have smacked him, but she wouldn't let herself be distracted.

"Is that why Lord Thornbuckle sent Brun off with Captain Serrano?"

"Maybe. Probably. Just in case someone's out to get the daughters of wealthy families."

"And they sent me *here*." Raffa was seriously annoyed with Lord Thornbuckle and her own parents, but on mutually exclusive grounds. She didn't like being thought incompetent enough to need to be sent away, and she didn't like being thought negligible enough to be sent from Castle

Rock to the Guerni Republic alone. If anyone had wanted to harm her, she'd have been unprotected.

Ronnie seemed to have read her thoughts. "You're trustworthy, Raffa—you wouldn't get into trouble. Brun would poke her nose into every stinging nettle she could find. Ottala was the same. . . ."

"She was not," Raffa said. "Ottala was a mean-minded snitch. Brun got into mischief for the fun of it; Ottala poked into things to get other people in trouble."

"I'll never understand the way women pick at each other," George said in his most sanctimonious tone.

"You would if you'd been in school with Ottala," Raffa said. "She nearly got Brun expelled. Besides, I've heard you talk about your schoolmates."

"It's different. None of us were the sweet flower of young womanhood—OUCH!" George recoiled and glared at her. "You hit me."

"And will again if you don't behave," said Raffa. She winked at Ronnie. "Be odious to someone else for a change."

"It's odd about Patchcock," Ronnie said. "It keeps showing up in all this—Captain Serrano told me about the Patchcock Incursion, and Ottala disappeared—"

"That can't be connected," George said. "Those riots were years ago—we were infants or something."

"And now this, about the drugs. It ought to make sense some way, and it doesn't." Ronnie frowned. "It would be great if we could wrap the whole thing up for them. Go to Patchcock, find out what happened to Ottala, find out if the Morrelines are adulterating the drugs on purpose, or just chasing profits. They might not even understand what could go wrong."

"I don't think we can," Raffa said. "We need to take this evidence back to Lord Thornbuckle first, and—"

"He needs it, I agree. But we can't add anything to it. None of us are chemists; we don't understand this stuff."

He patted the hardcopy. "If we sent it—by several routes, to be sure it got through—that should be enough."

"Certainly Ottala's friends are more likely to figure out where she's hiding than someone who doesn't even know her," George said. "Not that we're friends, exactly—even I thought she was an awful prig sometimes."

"Besides, we have a flair for it," Ronnie said. "Look at what we accomplished here. It could have been a very sticky situation indeed, even dangerous, but we all came out of it with what we needed to know and no damage done."

Raffa had her doubts about that. Those two unhappy young clones would have more trouble than they thought adjusting to life as independents. Their new faces— whatever they were—would not change their natures. A fragment of poetry her Aunt Marta quoted swam into her mind. "No thing, neither cunning fox nor roaring lion, can change the nature born in its blood," she said.

George looked startled, but Ronnie grinned at her. "Exactly. You and I—and George of course—are good at this sort of thing. Besides, think what will happen if we go back home. We'll all be wrapped away in protective familial swaddlings. Whereas, if we solve the whole rejuvenation problem for them—well, the drug part anyway—they'll have to recognize that we really are adults, and let us make our own decisions."

"I don't know, Ronnie," George said. "Raffa's not enthusiastic about this, and if it's dangerous . . . she shouldn't go, perhaps. She can explain to Lord Thornbuckle what we're up to, in case we need backup or something." In his tone, Raffa heard *She's not Brun.* And he thought Ottala was priggish; did he think the same of her?

"Don't be ridiculous," she heard herself saying. "If you'll remember, I did quite well on the island. Just because I can be prudent doesn't mean I'm timid."

The com chimed; Raffa, who was nearest, answered it.

"Dama—a Venezia Glendower-Morreline se Vahtigos wishes to speak with you."

"Oh—of course." Raffa held up her hand for silence, then said, "It's Ottala's Aunt Venezia again." Ronnie and George nodded, and settled back into their chairs with the clear intention of letting Raffa deal with it.

"Raffaele—" That was Venezia. "My dear, it just occurred to me—there's something you could do to help me."

"Yes?" Raffa was not about to commit herself.

"It's Ottala. You were her friend in school, I know." Raffa tried to stop that train of thought.

"Not a close friend, really."

"Well, I remember your name." In auntian logic, that seemed to be enough. "I'm worried about her," Venezia went on. "She missed her brother's *seegrin*, and her parents keep telling me not to worry, that she's a wild girl still under the influence of schoolmates such as yourself, my dear, and that blonde girl—Bubbles or whatever her name was. Do you know where she is?"

"No," said Raffa, leaning heavily on her minimal knowledge of sophistry. She didn't know where Ottala was, even though George had seen something which reported that Ottala had gone missing on Patchcock. Perhaps George had misread it, or the report was wrong, or she wasn't still there.

"I *thought* she told me she was going to visit Patchcock, such a silly idea because there's nothing to see, but her parents insist that I misunderstood, that I must have had my head in the kiln. Of course they don't know that I don't do that anymore, and I couldn't explain—" She paused. Raffa could think of nothing to say; she had to clench her teeth to keep her jaw from dropping open. "I wanted to go look for her," Venezia went on, "but they made it quite clear that I was not welcome to do so. Silly, really, because I own enough stock in the company that I should be able to do what I want. I had to help Oscar and Bertie out a while back, and they repaid me in shares. Not that I care, you understand, but . . . anyway, whatever they say, I think that's where she went and she should have come back by now. I thought that you—that perhaps you, having gone off with a young man, might know if that's what happened to Ottala. Because if it is what happened, then I could tell the family and they'd quit worrying."

Raffa found her attention caught by details that bobbed past in the torrent of words . . . that connected with other details from the earlier conversation. Suddenly the somewhat scatty aunt who created—or faked creating—the ugliest pottery *objets d'art* she had ever seen began to look like someone else—like the investor, perhaps even the major stockholder, who was being kept away from the business while nefarious activities went on. What if Ottala had suspected as much?

"If I could just come up and talk to you," Venezia said. "A bright young girl like you . . . and with a young man like Ronald Carruthers, you couldn't come to any harm."

"Harm?" Raffa managed to say past the whirling in her brain.

"Could I? We could have tea, or—" The thought of tea with Venezia made for a quick decision.

"Not tea," Raffa said firmly. "Why don't you just come up and we'll chat."

"Wonderful," said Venezia, and before Raffa could mention that she had other visitors as well, the connection blanked. Quickly, in breathless phrases, she told the other two what she had heard.

"And so, if *she* wants us to go to Patchcock, it gives us the perfect excuse."

"To be thrown out by her family," Ronnie said glumly. "I suppose she's going to tag along, too, just for decency's sake."

He was interrupted by a tap on the door. Venezia, looking more auntlike than ever, floated in on ripples of sheer lavender that seemed to drape her from head to heel. Scarves competed for space on her shoulders, and strips of lace fluttered in her wake.

"Ah, my dear Raffaele. So like your dear Aunt Marta. She used to wear just that color—"

"You know Aunt Marta?" Raffaele asked, only slightly startled.

"Long ago," Venezia said. "She was more serious—she even took a doctorate in synthetic chemistry, did you know that?" Raffa hadn't; while she digested this surprising fact about her favorite aunt, Venezia looked around. "Ronald—George—where are the other two?" Ronnie's attempt at a smile froze into position. Raffa leapt in.

"Other two—oh, the young men at the tram stop? Just some boys Ronnie and George met in a bar one night."

"Locals?" asked Venezia, but without waiting for an answer she launched into her plan. "I'm glad they're not here, dear, because I would not wish to discuss family business in front of strangers. I know I can trust all of you." She favored them all with a bright little smile that made Raffa's teeth ache. "Have you explained about Ottala?"

"Not . . . really. I thought you—" With that, Venezia interrupted to go over the whole thing again, this time with additional commentary on Ottala's scholastic record, the errors in judgment that had made it necessary for Bertie and Oscar to ask for her financial assistance, her opinion of men in general and her family in particular . . . on and on, until Raffa felt that she would doze off in sheer self-defense.

"And what you would like us to do—" she said, in one of the rare brief pauses for breath.

"Oh. Well. What I'd like you to do is go to Patchcock and find Ottala. If, as I suspect, she's living some kind of adolescent fantasy of being a hero of the working masses or something, let me know that she's safe. I'm quite willing

to pay your expenses—" She slowed here, eyeing George
in particular as if his expenses might well run over budget.

"We couldn't possibly ask that of you," Raffa said, with
all the charm she could muster. "Besides, suppose your
family noticed something. We all have ample allowances;
it's really no problem." Ronnie stirred; she ignored that.
If they were going to be partners for life, he would have
to learn to use her resources as she intended to use his.

"I insist," said Venezia, with a touch of color to her cheeks.
"At least the tickets there."

"All right," Raffa said. "But we must make our own
reservations. In case your family is hiding something from
you, it will be easier if they don't make the connection."

Passenger service to the Patchcock system routed
through Vardiel and Sostos. Vardiel, Raffa remembered,
was the ancient seat of the Morrelines. Ronnie, poring
over the display in his copy of *The Investor's Guide to
Familias Regnant Territories* (a guidecube purchased in
the Guerni Republic), commented that it was a roundabout
approach. "I'll bet they don't ship freight that way," he
said. "If this is accurate, there are two near jump points,
with easy vectors to Brot, Vesli, Tambour. And Tambour's
a direct to Rockhouse."

"Morrelines like control," George said. "But why not?
It's their investment base." He glanced around their cabin
and shrugged elaborately. Raffa glared. If they were being
monitored, his glance and shrug would look as stagey to
anyone else as it did to her. They had agreed not to discuss
their plans once on board the ship to Patchcock. The system
itself, yes, since none of them had been there.

The other passengers were all on business transfers, older
men and women whose conversation was full of technical
detail. Raffa strained her ears and memory to interpret
them, but the veneer of chemical knowledge she'd picked
up on Music didn't help her penetrate the dense thickets

of jargon. They had dropped into the Patchcock system before any of the other passengers spoke to the young people.

"Are you in Bioset or Synthesis?" an older woman asked Raffa in the lounge. Raffa noticed that the nearest group of older people paused in their conversation.

"Neither," Raffa said. "I don't even know what they are. I'm just a tourist, really."

"Ah." A little pause, during which Raffa could almost see the cascades of decision points in the other's mind. Then, "You're with a Family?"

Though the words were polite, Raffa heard the faint sneer that meant "rich, spoiled, idle." But that was the most harmless hypothesis, so she didn't react. "Yes," she said. "My aunt's trying to get me involved in business, and I told her I needed to travel more. I'm hoping to visit some of the pharmaceutical facilities here."

"Here? Where did you hear about them?"

Raffa tried for the offhand tone that would disarm suspicion. "I went to school with Ottala—Ottala Morreline."

"Were you planning to visit her?"

"Is she here?" Raffa raised her brows. "I thought she lived on Vardiel—at least when she was in school we visited there—"

"No—I mean, yes, she still lives with her family, the last I heard. I just wondered why you were *here.*"

"Well, Ottala bragged about the facilities—my aunt, you see, has investments in pharmaceuticals, so I told her I'd like to see these—and others—"

"A good excuse for traveling, then?"

Raffa smiled, and leaned closer, confiding. "Yes . . . and you see, my family doesn't approve of . . . of Ronnie. This way they think I'm traveling on business for Aunt Marta; Ronnie and I met a long way from the capital."

"And the other young man?"

"Ronnie's friend George. Well, of course I know George,

too. But everyone knows Ronnie and George travel together, so it's less obvious that I—you know."

The older woman smiled. "I think it's incredible that you Family people go through all these maneuvers . . . why not just take your shares and go live with the boy, if that's what you want?"

"I couldn't do that," Raffa said. "It's just not—not done." She had never thought of it. The idea sat in her mind staring back at her; she forced herself to ignore it.

The Guernesi tourist cube had an account of the Patchcock Incursion (under "investors' warnings: possible political instability") far more extensive than what Raffa remembered vaguely from school. Ronnie read the section and nodded. "Captain Serrano told me about that. I wonder how the Guernesi found out about the terms of the Gleisco contract?"

"They said they'd bought raw materials from the Patchcock system," Raffa said. "They probably had agents of their own poking around."

"I suppose—in the aftermath of the incursion—it would've been easier to start manufacturing the drugs here—retooling the lines wouldn't be as obvious if they needed complete rebuilding anyway."

"How are we going to approach this?"

"Didn't you hear what I told those people in the lounge? My Aunt Marta has pharmaceutical investments; she's asked me to gather background . . . she *has*," Raffa said, as the two looked at her in disbelief. "I was in the Guerni Republic, and heard about Patchcock . . . that's all I have to say. We'll see where it goes from there."

"Something's going on," George said. He had finally seen Raffa's point about the way Venezia's family treated her. "I'm just not sure Ottala's aunt is as stupid as she pretends to be."

"I don't think she's stupid at all," Raffa said. "But she

may be baffled by the family. And if they're manufacturing illegal pharmaceuticals, perhaps they're even drugging her."

"If they could do that, they could get their shares back—"

"Wait—" George looked excited suddenly. "It's—it's all about the rejuvenation process. And the legal changes— what do you want to bet that Ottala's aunt hasn't had the new one? Maybe none at all, but if she did, it was the Stochaster."

"How do you figure that?"

"Because it changed the inheritance laws, and it's going to change the laws about cognitive competence. The ones that caused your aunt so much trouble, Ronnie."

"Huh?" Ronnie looked confused. "I don't see how the kind of rejuvenation someone has matters that much."

"Weren't you listening to them at all? Because the Stochaster procedure couldn't be repeated—but people kept trying it and going bonkers. First they made it illegal to do repeats, and then they changed the laws so that a crazy senior couldn't tie up a family's assets forever."

"Yes, but now it's not illegal. The new procedures—"

"Can now be legally repeated, yes. And we have laws about how competency affects inheritance, but no laws dealing with indefinitely extended lives. Think, Ronnie. Suppose your father, or mine, lives . . . well, hundreds of years, if not forever. Those of our class who've been expecting to inherit a tidy living will wait . . . having our own rejuvenations . . . until they finally die."

"But nobody's going to live that long," Ronnie said, frowning.

"Are you sure? I'm not. The oldest serial Rejuvenants are now in their nineties—the oldest people now alive used the Stochaster, which they can't repeat. In the next decade or so, the balance will shift, until all the Rejuvenants are repeats. Maybe the first generation of them will be content with only a few rejuvenations . . . but someone's going to want to live a lot longer. Will your father give up his position in the family business just because he hits eighty, or a hundred, or a hundred and twenty? I doubt it. And the law is set up to test competency, not age."

"But—but no one is . . ." Raffa's voice trailed off.

"And if the Morrelines think they have a corner on the process, they're not going to want a nosy old aunt—whom they cannot control, because she can't rejuv anyway—poking around in their business backyard."

"Even if they're manufacturing the drugs illegally," Raffa said, "does this mean they're adulterating them? I don't see that it follows. . . ."

"Perhaps not," said George. "But if you wanted to control a good bit more than one end of the pharmaceutical industry, wouldn't you be tempted to slip a few attitude adjustments into the mix? Lorenza certainly did."

"We are going to be very careful on Patchcock," Raffa said slowly. "Very, *very* careful."

Patchcock would never qualify as one of the beauties of empire, Raffa thought as she watched the dull gray-green brush slide past the windows of the commuter train from the shuttle port. Vagaries of geology and terraforming had resulted in low-relief landmasses and a monotonous climate. Irrigation freshened the vast fields of staple grains and root crops that fed the planet's work force, but beyond the fields—whose bright greens and yellows seemed almost garish—the vegetation consisted of many varieties of thorny scrub between three and six meters high. When the wind blew, which it usually did, the sky hazed with grit; when it rained, erosion scoured the thin, loose soil into twisting arroyos. The train racketed across a bridge over one of these, and Raffa noticed a pile of construction waste that looked as if someone had thought of damming the dry watercourse. It hadn't worked; a deeper channel cut around one end of the pile.

Twoville, almost as dull as its name, was a low-built

compact city on the coast itself. Raffa had arranged rooms at the one real hotel. Ronnie and George would share a room in a hostel for transient workers. They were in the car behind her, carefully separate.

When she reached the hotel address, she was startled to find herself facing a small one-story cube with a single solid door. Had someone made a mistake?

Inside, she realized she was at the top of a well, looking down into the hotel. Across the gap, a waterfall poured over a tiled edge to fall . . . she felt dizzy when she looked over the edge.

"It takes most newcomers that way," said a voice behind her. She looked around to see a respectable-looking older man in business clothes. "Especially if they didn't know anything about how Patchcock was built. Bet you thought this was a mighty small hotel."

"Yes." Raffa tried to get her breath back.

"Patchcock's mostly underground," the man said. "There's not much scenery topside, or a climate to brag about, and fierce storms off the ocean. Everything's dug in, just shafts and warehouses on the surface."

"But aren't you too close to the ocean? Doesn't it seep in?"

"Flood would be more like it, except that there's a Tiegman field generator holding a barrier on it."

This meant little to Raffa, who had no idea what a Tiegman field generator was. She did have a clear memory of the perpetually damp sublevels in a seaside resort, resulting from percolation of seawater through porous soil. Patchcock soil certainly looked porous. She wished the building had windows to the outside—she wanted to know exactly how far below the water they would be.

Her nervousness must have shown, for the man went on. "It's quite safe, I assure you. The Tiegman field is absolutely impermeable, and the field shape has been designed to enclose all the sublevels—"

"It must take a lot of energy," Raffa said.

"Not once it's on. Starting it up, now . . . that took half a Patchcock year, and every bit of power they could find. But it's stable once it's on and locked."

"Excuse me, madam." That was the doorman, with her luggage on a trolley. "Would you prefer to glide down, or take the lift?"

"The lift," Raffa said. It would have comforting walls and doors. The hotel registration desk also seemed ordinary, as long as she could pretend it was on ground level, and the great open shaft with the waterfall went that far up in the air.

Her rooms opened onto a private terrace lush with flowering plants. Between the thick vines and bushes, she caught glimpses of what looked like distant green meadows under a twilight sky. Concealed lights produced the illusion of sunlight, shifting with the hours, on her terrace. If not for the EVACUATION PROCEDURES display on the reverse of the door, with the critical data highlighted in red, she'd never have suspected that she was twenty-seven meters below mean sea level, far out of sight of Patchcock's real sky and sun.

It was perfectly dry, with no smell of the sea. She felt the carpet surreptitiously; no hint of dampness. It didn't really make her feel safe. That it was dry now didn't mean it would stay dry. She looked around at her small domain. A bedroom and sitting room, both opening onto the terrace, and a large bathroom with every variety of plumbing she'd encountered before. Handsome furniture, fresh flowers, a cooler stocked with a dozen or so bottles and cans . . . she recognized only a few of the brands. Amazing what money could do . . . she would not have guessed that Patchcock had such amenities. Then she noticed the table lamp.

Puce and turquoise, with an uneven streak of mustard yellow down one side, as ugly as any of Venezia's pots.

Raffa eyed it suspiciously. It might have been a pot once. So might the bedside lamp, garish pink splotched with a funguslike pattern of blue-gray. Above the cooler hung a decorative object that reminded her of the mask on Ottala's wall at school. When she looked at the terrace plantings more carefully, the graceful ferns and brilliant flowers were rooted in odd-shaped pots of astounding ugliness.

So—was this what happened to Venezia's output? Were the ceramics her family claimed to prize stuck away in the obscurity of Patchcock? She wondered how many other places in Twoville had been given the dubious honor of showing off Ottala's aunt's presumed talent.

She flicked on the comconsole. Again the emergency procedures, this time requiring her to thumb-sign an affidavit that she had read and understood them. She glanced over to the open closet, making sure that a p-suit hung there, as advertised. Then a string of advertisements for local tour guides and recreational facilities. None looked inviting. ("See the unique sea life on Patchcock's nearest barrier reef," one offered, but the unique sea life in the display was all small and dull-colored. She had not come all this way to see odd-shaped beige and gray blobs no bigger than her hand.)

What she needed was a business directory. There: on the menu after the obligatory tourist advertisements. The list of businesses by type. Vertical integration seemed to be the guiding philosophy here, of industry as well as architecture. Her experience in her aunt's affairs helped her recognize the components of a complete pharmaceutical industry . . . raw materials used to manufacture unit and bulk packaging, labelling, and all the rest, the manufacturing stages for everything from intravenous solution containers to the foam that cushioned the final shipping containers. By the time she called the numbers she thought most likely, she felt she would understand whatever they might say.

"You're who?" the voice said. Raffa repeated what she had begun to think of as pedigree and show experience: her family name, her sept, her aunt's authorization to act as her agent. She rather hoped Aunt Marta didn't ever know how far her authorization had been stretched.

"I went to school with Ottala Morreline," Raffa added. Surely it couldn't hurt to claim (honestly) acquaintance with a daughter of the CEO of the company that owned Patchcock.

"You *what?*" This time the voice fairly squeaked. Raffa frowned. While she doubted that Ottala's friends visited here frequently, surely being a friend wouldn't create that level of upset.

"We went to school together," Raffa said. "The Campbell Academy." Silly name, really—neither its founders nor anyone else involved had been named Campbell; apparently someone a century or so back had simply liked the name Campbell.

"Ah . . . I see. Well, I suppose—there's a tour we give visiting . . . er . . . executives. You'd have to present your credentials—"

"I suppose," Raffa said, with ill-concealed sarcasm, "you're often annoyed by people impersonating Ottala's school friends."

"Pharmaceuticals," Raffa said, trying to sound vague and ignorant to the bright young man assigned as her tour guide. She had met him in the corporate branch office, where she noticed a large, ungainly, ceramic piece in purples and oranges in the reception area, and a small one full of desk accessories on the receptionist's desk. Now they were descending into the bowels of a factory, and even here, in odd corners, she'd noticed signs of Venezia's work. She still thought of it as that, even though she suspected that everything here came from Venezia's sources in the Guerni Republic. "But there's lots of kinds, aren't there?" That

sounded really stupid; she wasn't surprised that her guide
gave her a sharp look. "I mean," she said, trying to make
up for it, "I know there's antibiotics, antivirals, neuroleptics,
contraceptives, but the other companies my aunt invested
in usually stick to one or two chemical classes. Vertical
integration, she says, is very important, from the substrate
to the finished product. So 'pharmaceuticals' seemed
vague."

"I can't discuss specific processes, you understand," her
guide said.

"Of course. But in general?"

"Er . . ." He paused, then spouted a long string of
chemical syllables that Raffa suspected were faked. She
caught "indole" and "pyrimadine" and "something-
something-ergic-acid" but none of it sounded like the quick
course she'd had from the Guernesi.

"I see," she said, allowing herself to sound as confused
as she felt. "I guess that's what I'll tell Aunt Marta, though
I never heard of that before."

"Your aunt's planning to invest?" he asked, as if surprised.

"Didn't they tell you, from the head office?" she asked.
"I explained—that's why they sent me on this tour."

"But this is a family business. The Morrelines—"

"Apparently some family member's died, and she thought
of picking up anything that might be on the market—"
Raffa stopped; her guide's face had gone paper white.

"Died? Who died?"

Raffa shrugged. "I don't know." Especially since she'd
made it up. The Morrelines were a large family; surely
someone had died recently. "Probably a distant cousin or
something," she said. "Aunt Marta didn't say. She just sent
me here to look into things." That with a bright smile that
was supposed to disarm suspicion. But her guide looked
away, tension in every line of face and neck.

✧ Chapter Twelve

Sweet Delight, **Xavier System**

The more Heris worked with the local government, the more she knew about local resources, the more threatening the situation appeared. The mining colonies, most of them concentrated on the second largest satellite of the larger gas giant, Zalbod, had no defenses at all. Rockhounds, miners who worked the smaller chunks of debris, used little two-to-six person pods for transportation; nothing could be mounted on them which would affect a ship with shields. There was one antiquated ore-hauler, large enough to mount both screens and weapons if they had had screens and weapons to mount, or if it had had enough powerplant to do more than crawl slowly from one orbital base to another.

"We have to hope someone's listening back at Sector HQ," Heris said. She could hope it, but she also knew, from experience, how civilian reports of trouble could end up at the bottom of someone's stack. She didn't have the current override codes that might have bumped their report up.

"Where's Lady Cecelia?" Petris asked.

"At another horse farm, of course. I have no idea how it can take so long to pick out what she wants—particularly since there are genetic surgeons who specialize in equine design—she told me that. But now she's visiting somebody she calls 'Marcia and Poots,' which sounds faintly obscene. She says she expects to be there several weeks, and I'm not to worry. Then she sent all these pictures—" Heris flicked through them on the display. "They're just horses. Here we are in real danger, and she's worrying about whether this one's hocks are wiggly. I love the woman, but really!"

"Captain—" That was Koutsoudas, from the bridge. Heris leapt up.

"Coming now," she said.

When she arrived, all the ex-military crew were clustered there, around Koutsoudas's screen. They moved over so that she could see.

"It's ours," Koutsoudas said. He didn't have to; Heris recognized the drive signature herself; she had commanded just such a cruiser. "And . . . another . . ." That, too, was familiar; although cruisers patrolled alone, this would not be a routine patrol. She expected three, cruiser and two patrol ships, and the final signature appeared even as she thought it. A ragged shift out of jump, or appropriate caution, depending on how much trouble the commander had expected to find.

"Find out who's commanding, when you can," Heris said. "I'll let the Xavierans know—" She turned to her own board, and tapped in the code. They'd be relieved to know that the Fleet had finally listened, that help had arrived, that their survival didn't depend on one armed yacht and its ex-military captain. And if they weren't relieved enough, she herself was . . . those had been anxious days, wondering who would get here first. She knew her limits, even after roses and bagpipe parades.

"Captain, it's Commander Garrivay." Koutsoudas's expression, which Heris was learning to read, gave some signal she couldn't yet decode. She tried to remember a Garrivay, and couldn't dredge up anything but the vague impression of the name on a promotion list years back.

"Which Garrivay?" Maybe the first name would mean something.

"Dekan Garrivay . . . Captain Livadhi had . . . uh . . . served on the same ship with him when they were both jigs. Sir." Heris gave Koutsoudas a long stare, intended to remind him that she was now his captain, and this was no time to withhold loyalty. Koutsoudas sighed. "Right, Captain Serrano. Dekan Garrivay, in the opinion of Captain Livadhi, would require divine intervention to achieve the moral stature of a child rapist."

"Even for Arash, that's strong," Heris said. More importantly, while Arash had colorful opinions of many officers, he didn't usually—to her knowledge—share them with his enlisted crew.

"It wasn't just that once, either; Captain Livadhi didn't say much about the details of that cruise, but Garrivay was in the same battle group we were during that mess on Patchcock. Sonovabitch blew the second reactor station *after* the cease-fire, and it was only because the rebels came back with heavy stuff that he got away with it. Nobody noticed because they knocked out the command ship, and they had the scores—"

"But you had your own pet scans?" This was something that hadn't made it into the briefings.

"Yes—I did, and Captain Livadhi wanted to make something of it, but the scan data were tricky . . . I'd just figured out how to—to boost the definition, and it was nonstandard. And he wasn't commanding then, of course; he wasn't sure how his captain would take it."

"I don't suppose you know where Garrivay has been stationed lately?" Heris watched the incoming scan data, but let her mind roll fantasy dice . . . the probability of a bad captain being in command of a strike group here, at such a time, the probability that she, and Koutsoudas, would be here to notice. . . . "Livadhi suspected this, didn't he?" she asked, before Koutsoudas had answered the first question. She didn't look at him, but made a private bet on whether he would answer, and if so in what order.

"He thought something would blow, yes." Koutsoudas wasn't looking at her, either; out of her peripheral vision she saw his profile, intent on the displays in front of him. "It's true that I was in some danger; my modifications of scan technology had become a bit too famous. But he said you were the lightning rod, and you'd need some help—unobtrusive help. I don't think he thought Garrivay, in particular. Garrivay *was* attached to Third Ward, Inner Systems." Third Ward, Inner, where Lepescu had been for eight years before taking over the combat position that had cost Heris her commission.

Heris had the prickling feeling all down her back that usually preceded battle. "I am a lightning rod?"

"Serranos in general, he said, and you in particular. Your aunt the admiral told him—"

"My *aunt!*" Now the prickling sensation shifted to anger, pure and white-hot. "What was she talking to Arash for—DAMMIT!" Her vision blurred a moment, then she felt the long habit of control settling back into her mind like a rider on a fractious horse. She glanced around the bridge; none of her crew were staring. They knew better. Koutsoudas met her eye for a moment, as if checking to see if she was about to hit him, then looked away. "Never mind," Heris said, to no one in particular. "I never have been able to predict Aunt Vida. Sorry, 'Steban. If you have any aunts, you'll understand."

"My Aunt Estrellita," Koutsoudas said promptly. "Actually a great-aunt, on my mother's side. She's not in Fleet, or she'd drive me crazy . . . every time I'm home on leave, she's promoting an alliance with yet another second or third cousin twice removed. She runs the whole family, except for my cousin Juil, who's just as pigheaded as she is."

Heris wondered if he really had an aunt like that, or if he just made her up on the spot. It didn't really matter. What did matter was that someone—Livadhi, or her aunt, or both—had expected her to be in trouble, and had provided Koutsoudas, presumably to help her out—or get rid of her, a dark thought intruded. She shoved it back; no time to worry about that. Instead, she could worry about the choice of Garrivay for such duty as this.

Her worry translated into a discreet request to be included in the invitation to senior administrative personnel to meet the new military commander of Xavier's defense. That amounted to a reception and meeting to follow, on the orbital station. Heris, who had met all but Garrivay before, mingled easily and worked her way to the back of the group as she heard the unmistakable click of approaching boots.

A large man introduced himself to the General Secretary as Commodore Garrivay, commanding a battle group. Heris did not let her eyebrows rise at that but wondered why he was trying to impress. True, commodore was the correct term for someone commanding a battle group, but a battle group was defined as a formation comprising at least two heavy cruisers. Commonly, battle groups had two heavy cruisers, a light cruiser, and three to five patrol ships. One cruiser and a couple of patrol ships could be a battle group only if you'd just lost the others in combat.

Garrivay had a strong-boned face well padded with flesh; if he had been a horse (she grinned to herself for picking up Cecelia's habits of thought) he would have been considered to show a coarse, coldblood influence. She noticed that his gaze locked on the person to whom he spoke, a fervent intensity that, in other people, she had found to accompany both the ability and willingness to lie convincingly.

Still, his first questions to the General Secretary were reasonable, as he asked for clarification of the message that had brought him, and the raider's attack. He listened to the somewhat rambling report the General Secretary's aïde gave—Heris winced at some of the inaccuracies which Garrivay patiently dissected—and then commended the Xavierans on their successful response.

"Captain Serrano helped us out when the raider attacked," the General Secretary said. Heris wished he'd left her out of it.

"Serrano . . ." Garrivay seemed to consider, then his eyes narrowed. "*Heris* Serrano?"

"Yes, that's the name."

"You *were* lucky." The emphasis could be taken either way; Heris waited to see how he would shade it. He still did not look at her, as if he had not noticed her among the others. "I never had the honor of serving in the same organization with Captain Serrano, but I believe she had a . . . er . . . distinguished record." Again, an emphasis that might be taken more than one way; the pause suggested that another adjective had come to mind before "distinguished." His gaze raked the assembly and snagged only briefly on hers before passing on. So he did recognize her. And had no intention of acknowledging her at this meeting.

"She blew that raider neatly enough." A challenging tone from someone who recognized the ambiguity of Garrivay's . . . Heris didn't recognize the voice and dared not peer down the room.

"I daresay," Garrivay said carelessly. "From what you've said, a cobbled-up mismatch of weaponry and hull . . . not much threat, really, though I understand your being anxious for the station. Even a gap-toothed wolf can bite."

Heris blinked. They weren't going to like that, neither the words nor the tone, not after the previous raids they'd suffered. And where had he heard about the raider's design flaws? She didn't think her crew had gossiped about that among the stationers—though she'd ask, before making the obvious connection. Sure enough, the General Secretary had puffed up like a rooster.

"I hardly think a raider capable of blowing our main station out of the sky could be called a gap-toothed wolf, Commodore." He glanced around for support, and got it in the expressions of the others. "Those raiders have been at us for a decade, during which no one from the R.S.S. has seen fit—"

"But it didn't blow your station, did it? Not this time, nor any other. So why do you think it could? Because Captain . . . er . . . Serrano told you so?"

She could feel the stubbornness as if it were a visible pall hanging smoglike over their heads. Surely Garrivay knew how they'd react. Why would he want them to react like this, stiffening into dislike of him? With a war looming, he should be doing what he could to rally the civilians behind him. Perhaps he was one of those officers who thought civilians were all fools, good only for providing the money to keep the Fleet going. Perhaps he assumed that if he dismissed their fear of the raider, they would then believe him when he told them something else was a threat. Whatever his intent, she knew it was a mistake.

When the meeting broke up, he made a point of coming to her side.

"Well, Captain Serrano . . . I never had the pleasure of meeting you before." This close, the strong face with its bright green eyes had a raffish charm. His skin was a shade lighter than her own; his hair, clipped short, might have been any shade of brown. "My misfortune, I must say. Of course I heard—your family has branches everywhere, it seems."

Heris decided there was no advantage to be gained by pretense. "Isn't calling one cruiser and two patrols a battle group a bit much?" His eyes widened a moment, then narrowed as he grinned, squeezing the light from their green until they looked almost black.

"Surely you don't feel an obligation to explain," he began.

Heris said nothing. "I thought it would reassure the locals," he went on. "Convince them they weren't forgotten. There's not likely to be anything much here—certainly nothing to justify a *real* battle group—and if this satisfies them—"

Heris shrugged as if she didn't care, and glanced around the compartment. "I merely commented. If there were veterans here, for instance . . . they might say something."

"Barring you, I don't expect to find any veterans. Xavier apparently sent few recruits to Fleet, and those old enough to retire chose more populous worlds. Not that I blame them."

"It's not a bad place," Heris said, more to draw him out than in serious argument. She found it more than interesting that he had bothered to check on Xavier's recruitment to Fleet, and where its veterans went.

"You think not?" Garrivay's mobile face drew itself into a knot of distaste. "I hate ag worlds, myself. Dirty, backward, half of them free-birthers whose discontented spawn scrabble for a way offplanet and clog the ranks of unskilled labor hanging around spaceports. I like to eat as much as anyone, but we could subsist quite well without them."

His venom surprised her; she wondered what had given him a dislike for ag worlds. Had he come from one? "It has strategic importance, at least," she said.

"If the Black Scratch is crazy enough to attack through here, I'm not going to be able to stop them," Garrivay said. "Surely you don't think they will? It would be a very inefficient approach—"

"There's the Spinner jump point," Heris said. She had trouble keeping the edge out of her voice; he was treating her as if she were a combination of crazy and crony.

"That!" He waved his hand. "Fleet's got a couple of battle groups on the other side—the Black Scratch can't take it, and they must know that."

Heris opened her mouth to protest this obvious idiocy

and stopped. Why reveal herself? "I suppose," she said, and added, as if without thought, "They used to have just a single cruiser—"

He relaxed a little; she recognized the shift in his facial muscles. "Ah . . . no wonder you worried. Of course you wouldn't know the current dispositions." That had a half-heard question mark on it, which she ignored.

"So you're just here to show the flag, as it were?"

"Something like that. Perhaps snag another raider." He grinned at her. He had a good grin, one she might have liked if she hadn't known all the rest. "By the way, I didn't mean to slight your accomplishment in there. Going after a raider—even a shoddy thing like that—with a rich lady's yacht took guts. And you couldn't know how incompetent the raider was until afterwards. . . ." Again, the hint of a question. Heris smiled blandly.

"No . . . to tell you the truth, I was more than half expecting to be blown away myself. The only advantage of being small is that you're hard to detect in the first place, and hard to hit in the second."

"Lucky for you the raider had no decent weaponry. Did he get off even one shot?"

"A couple," Heris said, sticking to the facts that would have been reported by the distant watcher. "But inaccurate—as you say, he had no decent weaponry. He just looked dangerous."

"And these poor sods have been paying tribute to that sort of trash. Well, I can take care of *that*. Tell me, how long do you plan to be in the system?"

"I don't know." Heris frowned as if it bothered her. "Lady Cecelia is visiting bloodstock farms; I think she expects to find the perfect horse genes somewhere and go back into eventing."

"And you have to hang around until your owner is through? Lucky you. It's almost like being back in Fleet, isn't it?" He didn't wait for her to answer. "Hanging around waiting on someone else's bright ideas. Of course, your owner's a Rejuvenant . . . *she* has plenty of time."

Interesting. He didn't know she owned the ship herself. It wouldn't have been big news, not with everything else going on, but he might have picked it out of the datanet if he'd looked for it. Would she, in his place? Of course. On the other hand, never assume the enemy is stupid . . . perhaps he was just sounding her out. "I suppose so . . . but so are many admirals, aren't they?"

"True enough." He sighed. "I don't suppose you could lend me your onboard weaponry . . . beef up this old clunker they've got here, use it as a decoy or something . . . ?"

"Sorry," Heris said, not sorry at all. "It's not much, and you'd have to take the hull apart to get it out anyway—you can't imagine what it took to get it installed in the first place. Anyway, since Lady Cecelia paid for it, I suppose it's really hers. Of course you could confiscate the whole ship, if it's really an emergency. . . ."

"Oh no, nothing like that. Although if your employer is nervous, I would advise you to get her out of here."

"I'll speak to her," Heris said. That pleased him; his eyelid flickered. He wanted her gone; he wanted her weapons gone. What was he up to? She itched to get back to Koutsoudas and his scans; she was ready to throw roses all over her aunt admiral and even Arash Livadhi. With any luck—and Koutsoudas made his own—he would have the probes in place and she would soon have an ear in this fellow's private counsels.

"There's never been a suspicion of treason," Koutsoudas said when she told him about the conversation. "Overzealousness, misinterpretation of orders allowing him more leeway . . . but nothing to harm the Familias."

"Adding to the mess at Patchcock harmed the Familias," Heris said. "There's more than one way to cause trouble."

"I . . . hadn't thought of that." Koutsoudas looked taken

aback; Heris grinned to herself. She had begun to wonder if the man was a genius at everything.

"We're one of the logical places for the Benignity to strike. You're sure there was a watcher out there when we took that raider—" Something that had bothered her while talking to Garrivay now surfaced. "And he called them the Black Scratch."

Koutsoudas's eyebrows went up. "So? Everybody knows that nickname."

"Everybody knows it, but . . . think, 'Steban. Did you ever hear Arash use it during a briefing? I know I never did. It's slang, and this may be war."

"Now that you mention it . . . no. Commander Livadhi always said the Benignity, or the Compassionate Hand." And Koutsoudas, for the first time, referred to Livadhi by his rank, not his position as captain. Interesting.

"You think he's turned," Petris said. It was not a question.

"I think . . . yes. I do. And I have no proof, and no one to tell . . . not within any range that would help."

"Does he know what you think?"

"No. He shouldn't. I played stupid for all I was worth. Accepted his judgment that the raider was almost harmless—" Ginese growled something incomprehensible at that, and Heris let herself chuckle. "Oh yes, he did. He knew about the mismatched drive/hull fit, too, which none of us told him."

"That counts," Koutsoudas said. "He couldn't have found out about that any other way—unless it was in your report to Sector HQ."

"No, it wasn't. They had no need, and I supposed—I suppose I was looking for something like this. If this is what I think." She didn't want to think that. "It all boils down to data," Heris said. "His . . . ours . . . if any of it's trustworthy. How much of it's compromised. If he knows who you are, what you are, then we're in even worse trouble."

❖   ❖   ❖

Heris was working her way through routine reports when Koutsoudas called her to the bridge again.

"Captain, you must hear this—it's what Garrivay and his senior officers have said—"

Heris touched the control. Amazing sound quality; she still wished she knew how Koutsoudas did what he did. Garrivay, sounding as pompous among his own people as with her. She was glad to know she hadn't been given special treatment. It will work, he was saying. That Serrano bitch doesn't know anything; she's negligible. One of the others questioned that—a Serrano negligible? Garrivay laughed in a tone that made Heris want to smash all his teeth down his fleshy throat. As they talked on, their plan appeared much as she had expected. The Benignity ships would arrive to find a blown station and helpless planet. Garrivay would exit to another place to do much the same thing. Where else? Rotterdam . . . *Rotterdam*. Cecelia's friends, that lovely place she had wanted to revisit . . .

"Not likely," she muttered. Koutsoudas started, and she realized she had put into that all the frustration and anger she felt at the whole situation. She looked at the others. "We have to stop them."

"Stop them! What—Garrivay, or the invasion?"

"Both, ideally. Garrivay first, of course."

"How?" That was Meharry, blunt as always. "We couldn't breach his shields if we put everything we have into his flanks sitting next to him in dock."

"Actually we might," Ginese said, looking thoughtful. "Of course, his return would vaporize us *and* the station."

"There's nothing in this system that can take Garrivay's ships," Heris said. "Except wits."

"Wits?" Now it was Koutsoudas who gave her a startled glance. "You're planning to trick him out of his ships? How—at the gambling table, perhaps?"

"No. I'm not going to gamble with his notions of honor.

We will have to capture his ships, and since frontal assault won't do, it will take wits."

"You're planning to walk onto his ships and just take over?" Meharry asked. "Just say 'Please, Commodore, I think you're a traitor, and I'm taking over'?"

"Something like that," Heris said with a grin.

"And you expect him to agree?"

"I expect him to die," Heris said. A silence fell, as her crew digested that. She went on. "He's not going to surrender and risk court-martial—neither he nor his fellow captains. The only way to get those ships is by *coup de main*—and then great good luck and the Serrano name."

"I was going to mention," said Meharry, "that most crews don't take kindly to someone murdering the captain and taking over."

"You do realize the legal side of what you're doing?" Petris gave her a dark, slanted glance.

"Yes. I'm proposing treasonous piracy, if you look at it that way, and some people will. A civilian stealing not one but three R.S.S. combat vessels in what will be time of war."

"You won't get all three," Ginese said. "One, maybe. Two if you're very lucky. Not all three."

"That may be. I will certainly try to get all three, because if I don't, I may have to destroy one." She had faced that, in her mind. She could not leave a ship loose in this system committed to helping the Benignity invasion.

"If you're wrong about any of it," Petris said, "you'll have no alternatives. If the Benignity doesn't invade through here, if Garrivay is just a detestable bully, but not a traitor, if you're not able to get the ships—"

"Then I'm dead," Heris said. "I've thought of that. It means you're dead as well, which is bothersome—"

"Oh, it's not that, Captain," Meharry said. "I wouldn't miss this for anything, and it's a novel way to die, after all. Trying to steal one of our own ships for a good cause. More fun than jumping that yacht out of nearspace."

"If you try it and aren't killed," Petris said, "you'll be an outlaw . . . you can't stay in Familias space."

Heris stared at him; he did not look down. "Petris, if you think I can't do it, say so. If you think I shouldn't do it—if you think I'm working with bad data or logic, say so. But trust that I can do elementary risk analysis, will you?"

He didn't smile. "I know you can. But I also know how much you want to set foot on a cruiser bridge again. Have you factored that into your analysis?"

"Yes." Despite herself, her voice tightened. She forced herself to take a long breath. "Petris, I do miss—have missed—that command. You're right about that, and it is a factor. But I'm not about to risk our lives, and the lives of everyone in this system, crews and landborn alike, to satisfy my whims. There's something I haven't shared with you." Before anyone could comment, she flicked on the cube reader; she had already selected the passage.

Her Aunt Vida's face, an older version of her own Serrano features, stared out at them. She spoke. "I have complete confidence in your judgment," her aunt said. "In any difficulty. You may depend upon my support for any action you find necessary to preserve the honor and safety of the Familias Regnant in these troubled times."

"I don't think my aunt admiral anticipated pirating Fleet warships," Heris said. "But it gives me a shred of legitimacy, and I intend to weave that into something more than a tissue of lies."

"How?" Petris asked bluntly. "Not that I don't believe you, and not that I'm opposed, but—how?"

In the pause that followed, while Heris was trying to work out why Petris was being so antagonistic, Oblo spoke. "What it really is, Captain, is that we never had a chance to be this close while you were planning before. We enjoyed the result, but we never got to see the process."

Petris grinned. "All right, Oblo. You're partly right. It

still seems impossible to me that she's going to take over three warships all by herself—well, we'll help, but it's not much. The peashooters we have on this thing wouldn't hurt those ships, and they'd blow us away before we could get a shot off anyway. There's no way to sneak aboard, and even if we could, I don't see how the four of us could seize control of the ship against resistance. She can't just stroll over and say 'By the way, Garrivay, I'll be the new captain as of today.' " He made the last a singsong parody of the traditional chanty.

The delay had given Heris time to come up with the outline of a plan. "Like this," she said. "You're half right, Petris. We're going to walk in peacefully, invited guests—"

"They'll scan us for weapons—" Ginese warned.

Heris grinned. "What is the most dangerous weapon in the universe?" A blank pause, then they all grinned, and repeated the gesture with which generations of basic instructors had taunted their recruits. "That's right. What's between your ears can't be scanned . . . and you're all exceptional unarmed fighters."

"So we stroll in for afternoon tea, or whatever—" Meharry prompted.

"Properly meek and mild, yes." Heris batted her eyelashes, and they broke into snorts of laughter.

"Begging the captain's pardon, but if you did that at me, I'd think you were having a seizure." Oblo, of course.

"And then we jump Garrivay and kill him? It's going to take all of us, and no one's going to notice?"

"Petris, for a bloodthirsty pirate, you're being ridiculously cautious. No, we're going to walk into as many of the traitors as we can find gathered with Garrivay—Koutsoudas's ongoing sound tap will help us there—and kill all of them. You notice that they like to gather and gab—Koutsoudas has them on three separate occasions already. I'd like to take out all three ship captains, but I doubt we'll find them *all* together. Four or five traitorous officers, though, will reduce the resistance we face. Admiral Serrano's reputation will do the rest. Or not, as the case may be."

"Everyone knows you're not in Fleet anymore," Meharry said.

"Yes . . . officially. But suppose the whole thing was a feint—suppose I'm on special assignment." They stared at her, this time shocked into silence.

"You're . . . not . . . really, are you?" asked Ginese finally.

"See?" Heris grinned at them. "If *you* can think that, even for a moment—after what we've been through—then it can work."

"But seriously—you didn't resign because your aunt—" Ginese continued to stare at her with an expression blank of all emotion.

"No! I resigned—stupidly, I now admit—for the reasons I told you, and without hearing a word from my sainted aunt. But if she *had* intended something like this, no one would know. It is plausible—just—with the Serrano reputation. And it's our chance. A slim one, but a chance."

"I've seen fatter chances die of starvation," Petris said, but his tone approved. He sighed, then stretched. "One thing about it, Heris . . . Captain . . . it's never dull shipping with Serranos." She ignored that.

"So now for the details. It's tricky enough, so we'll have rehearsals—and hope we're not still rehearsing when the Benignity arrives."

✧ Chapter Thirteen

Xavier, Fairhollow Farm

Cecelia felt a certain tension as she entered the stable office. Nothing she could put her finger on—dear Marcia smiling so amiably, and Poots with an even more foolish grin. Slangsby, the head groom, with no grin at all but something twinkling in the depth of his little blue eyes. Were they upset, perhaps, because she had visited two other breeding farms before coming here? They hadn't been that sensitive in years past.

"Such a fortunate escape," Marcia said. "We've heard all about it."

Now what did that mean? Lorenza's attack, or something else entirely? "I'm surprised such a minor matter stayed on the news this far out," Cecelia said. "With the king's resignation—"

"As if you didn't have something to do with that!" Poots sounded almost annoyed with her. Cecelia blinked, assessing the undercurrents.

"I think perhaps my influence was considerably exaggerated," she said. "Of course, I was at the Grand Council meeting, but—"

"Never mind, then." Marcia's smile vanished, replaced by her more usual expression, which had always reminded Cecelia of one of those toys with a spring-controlled lid that snapped tight. "If you don't want to trust your oldest, dearest friends—"

So that was it. Plain jealousy, and feeling left out. None

of the honest replies that sprang quickly to mind would work, because, though true, they were insulting. Marcia and Poots were so far from being old and dear friends that they made the phrase ridiculous. Yes, they were rich, in the same class as those who played with the titles of vanished aristocracies. Yes, they considered themselves the equal of anyone. But half of that was the fraternity of horsemen, who allow no rank but that earned in the saddle. She had known them for years, ridden with them, bought and sold horses in the same markets . . . friends? No. Cecelia tried to think of something placating, but Marcia was already in spate again.

"I suppose you're upset that we didn't come at once to help you," she said. Cecelia had not thought of that, and now resented the suggestion that she might have held such a foolish hope. "I'm sure we *would* have," Marcia said, "except that we didn't even find out for months and months, and by then it seemed—and it was foaling time anyway—and it would have taken us months to get there, because as you know we don't have a private yacht. . . ." The explanation, like most explanations, simply dug a deeper and muckier hole in the claimed relationship. If they could "know all about it" so soon after the king's resignation, then they should have known about her collapse that soon too. Foaling season was a weak excuse; no one would have expected them to load up a ship full of pregnant mares, and it had been years since Marcia attended foalings herself. As for "don't have a private yacht," that was, strictly, true. Their *Fortune's Darling* was well out of the yacht class, and might have served as the flagship of a small shipping company.

Cecelia reminded herself that she had not expected help from them, and wasn't (despite the clumsy excuses) upset that they hadn't provided it. "Never mind," she said, trying to drag the conversation back to her reason for being there. "All I'm really interested in is your bloodstock. Mac said you still had some of that Singularity sperm available?"

"What are you doing, restocking the royal—excuse me, formerly royal—stables for yourself?"

That was too much. Cecelia felt her neck get hot, and didn't really care what her face looked like. "Not at all," she said with icy restraint. "I am trying to do a favor for some friends who saved my life and assisted my recovery. Since you are, as you say, old and dear friends—" The accent she put on "friends" would have sliced through a ship's hull plating. "—I had hoped to purchase both sperm and time-locked embryos from you. However, it seems that other suppliers might be more convenient."

Marcia turned red; Poots, as usual, looked as if he might cry. Slangsby now had the grin the others had discarded.

"I didn't—you don't have to take it that way—"

"What way?" Cecelia considered herself a reasonable person, and she could put no friendly interpretation on Marcia's words. But, as a reasonable person, she would let Marcia try to wriggle out of this. It might even be interesting, in a purely zoological way, to watch the wriggling.

Marcia tried a giggle that cracked in midstream. "Cecelia, my dear, you take everything so seriously. I was just teasing. Honestly, my dear, that rejuvenation seems to have affected your temper." But the oyster-gray eyes were wary, watchful, entirely unlike the frank tone of the voice.

Cecelia let her eyebrows rise of themselves. "Really?"

"All right; I'm sorry." Marcia didn't sound sorry; she sounded very grumpy indeed. "If you want Singularity genes, we've got 'em. Sperm and embryos both. I suppose you're thinking of the Buccinator line you favored so?"

Buccinator, Cecelia thought to herself, had only been the most prepotent sire of the past three decades for performance horses. Minimal tweaking of the frozen sperm gave breeders options for speed on the flat or substance for jumping; Buccinator had been almost a sport, but his genome had enough variety for that. But Marcia had refused to jump on that fad, as she'd called it, and out here in the boonies she had produced, after decades of work, one horse not more than fifteen percent worse than Buccinator. Singularity's sperm would offer genetic diversity, but she intended to have top equine geneticists do some editing before she turned it over to her friends.

"Perhaps," she said, "you'd be kind enough to show me what you've got available. I'd like to see the breeding stock, then the ones in training, then the gene maps."

Slangsby twinkled at her, but she distrusted that twinkle. Marcia and Poots said nothing, and simply led her out into the aisle of the great barn. Cecelia looked up. Marcia's pigheadedness about Buccinator aside, she had excellent judgment elsewhere, and this barn proved it. Local wood, used as logs, so that even the most irate equine couldn't kick through the walls. Good insulation, too. Wide aisles, perfect ventilation for this climate, utilities laid safely underground—no exposed pipes or wiring—and kept immaculate by the workers Slangsby supervised. Tools properly hung out of traffic, the only barrow in sight in active use . . . and down the long aisle, one sleek head after another looking over the stall doors. The horses were under roof in the daytime to avoid the assaults of local insectlike parasites, who lived lives too short to learn that horse blood wouldn't nourish them. The bites—otherwise harmless—were painful and made horses nervous.

"The oldest live-bred Singularity daughter," Marcia said proudly. Cecelia had seen the mare before; her infallible memory for horses overlaid her memory of the four-year-old being shown in the ring with this matronly mare only a month from foaling. Star, crooked stripe, snip, all against a background of seal brown. Common coloring for Singularity offspring, because Marcia (like too many people) had a fancy for color. Predictably, she now said, "We sell the loud-colored ones." Buccinator's gorgeous copper color had been one of the things she didn't like about him, Cecelia knew. She also knew that basic coat color was the easiest thing to tweak in the equine genome; if Marcia had wanted all dark foals she could have had them. But other people wanted variety, and she produced brighter ones in order to increase her sales.

"Lovely," Cecelia murmured. She was, too, a good solid mare who had produced both ova and live foals. "I'm surprised you're still using her to produce live—isn't it a bit risky at her age?"

Marcia's face creased in a real grin. "I keep telling you genetic wizard types that if you breed live, you get real soundness, long-term soundness. Of course we've stripped her ova a few times, because it's so hard to transport the mature horses, but the proof of the value of live breeding is right there: an eighteen-year-old mare who can withstand pregnancy and deliver a live foal."

Cecelia kept her face straight with an effort. Given the right pelvic conformation and good legs, any mare could do that. And any mare could get in trouble in any foaling, too. She preferred to use nurse mares of larger breeds for any of her own bloodstock. She moved to the next stall, and the next. Marcia's idea of perfect conformation hadn't changed since her last visit. Sound, yes, but sacrificing elegance for it. They all looked a bit stubby to her, heavier in the neck and chunkier in the body than necessary.

"And this is our pride," Marcia said. They had passed under the dome at the crossing of the aisles, and were now in the stallion end of the barn. Marcia's pride was, of course, the closest thing to Singularity she had been able to produce. He certainly looked like his famous grandsire, Cecelia thought. Dark brown with the merest whisker of white on his brow, a powerful, well-muscled body, and the arrogance of any stallion who comes first in the barn hierarchy.

"Very much like," Cecelia said.

"He's double-line bred," Marcia said.

"What's his outcross line?" Cecelia asked. She thought she could guess, but waited.

"Consequential," Marcia said, and Cecelia congratulated herself. Consequential had passed a curious whorl on the neck to his progeny, and this stallion had it. And trust Marcia to talk about the stallion side of the outcross line.

"He's a real bargain," Marcia said, and named a price per straw of frozen semen that Cecelia didn't think was a bargain at all. Not for an inbred chunk with all his grandsire's faults and probably few of his virtues.

To check that, she asked, "What's his speed?"

Not to her surprise, Marcia's smile vanished again. "He's far too valuable to risk on the track, Cecelia. His breeding alone, his conformation, show his quality. We wouldn't take the chance of injury." Of proving him racing sound, of proving that his grandsire's unlikely speed and agility had come through along with a pretty brown coat and a thick neck. Cecelia couldn't tell for sure, but even from this angle she suspected that his hocks were not sufficient for his build.

"What's your price for Singularity straws?" Cecelia asked. "They must be getting rare now."

"Well, they are, of course. And we must reserve a certain supply for our own program." As if they didn't already have all that influence they needed. "But I could let you have fifty straws for forty thousand. Each, of course."

Cecelia bit back the "Nonsense!" that wanted to burst out. That was only the asking price, which no one dealing in horses ever paid unless they were novices, in which case it was the price of their education. "Umm," she said instead. It meant she wasn't stupid enough to take the asking price, but might bargain later.

"So you see what a bargain this one is," Marcia went on. "Sixty-two percent Singularity—"

Cecelia had run into this before, the ardent preserver of

ancient breeds convinced that concentrating bloodlines would somehow overcome the limitations of time and restore the glories of Terran genetics. Cecelia doubted they had been glories anyway (well, perhaps those pretty beasts with the odd number of vertebrae). From the remaining video chips, most of the breeds had been minor variations on a few themes—large and massive, tall and fast, short and hardy—with serious improvement written out of possibility by restrictive breed registries. Half a dozen breeds supposedly intended for racing, for instance, never raced each other and weren't allowed to interbreed . . . stupid.

"Perhaps I could see this fellow moving a bit?" Cecelia said.

Marcia's smile returned. "Of course. Slangsby, put him in the front ring."

Cecelia stepped back to watch. Disposition mattered, as far as she was concerned. Slangsby clipped a lead to the stallion's halter before he opened the stall door, and ran the chain over the nose and back through the mouth. So. Not a quiet one. With that restraint, however, the dark horse stepped demurely from his stall with an air of innocence that Cecelia didn't believe for a moment. He did not dance, which might have been considered unmannerly, but he walked as if on eggs, as if any moment he *might* dance. Marcia urged Cecelia on, but Cecelia hung back. She wanted to see those hocks close up.

"He can be a bit fresh, when he's been in the stall this long," Marcia said, now pulling Cecelia back. Cecelia ignored this; she was farther back than the longest-legged horse could strike. She closed her ears to Marcia's earnest twaddle, and watched the hocks closely. The stallion swaggered a bit; stallions did that. So the sway of the rump might be swagger, and there would be, from swagger alone, a slight sideways jut of the hock as the weight came over it. But here, as she'd expected, was the real problem. From footfall to footlift, the hock described a crooked circle as weight came onto that leg, and the leg pushed the weight forward. She had seen—had even owned—lanky horses whose hocks moved like that, and they'd been sound. But the chunky, muscley horses, those were the ones to watch; those were the ones who needed rock-solid hocks.

The joint narrowed too quickly, too, more trapezoidal than rectangular, flowing into the lower leg too smoothly. Cecelia liked a hock that resembled a box, flat on either side and cleanly marked off above and below. In action, with weight on, it should flex in one plane only, not wobble like this one. She knew she wouldn't buy a straw of this one's semen; she might as well tell Marcia now . . . but that wasn't how the game was played. She strolled on, and took one of the comfortable padded seats just outside the display ring.

Slangsby unlooped the chain, and clipped on a longe line instead of the short lead. The stallion moved out on the line, circled Slangsby at a mincing trot, and exploded suddenly in a flurry of hooves and tail, storming around in a gallop, then flinging himself in the air, bucking. Slangsby growled something at him, and he quieted to a tight canter, then to a trot, slightly more relaxed than before.

"So athletic," said Marcia. "So balanced." Cecelia said nothing, watching the hind legs swing forward, back, forward, back . . . never quite reaching under as far as she liked. Of course he was not under saddle; he might never have been taught. That kind of explosiveness, she knew, came from a preponderance of fast-twitch muscle fibers, something jumpers and event horses needed, along with the slow-twitch fibers that let them gallop miles without tiring. But she didn't want the rest of that genome, at least not the way it was.

She began to think what it would cost to fiddle the Singularity sperm along. She'd need top equine gene sculptors, and the best were in the Guerni Republic, where a healthy racing industry supported them. It might be simpler to go there in the first place, and not bother with Marcia's overmuscled stock, but the Guernesi concentrated on lighter-boned flat racers. Attempts to sculpt more bone into those had foundered on the difficulty of defining the ideal bone mass for each developing limb at each stage.

The rest of the afternoon, as she watched one horse after another, half her mind was wandering off to Rotterdam and the Guerni Republic. That brought up the last discussion she'd had with her doctors.

"You are physically a young woman again," they'd said. "Your body is in peak condition. But rejuvenation doesn't make your mind forget all it's learned. You are not in your early thirties: you are, in your experience, between eighty and ninety. You will find you want to use your new body in ways that satisfy your mature mind."

She had not imagined what that might mean. What was she to do with the abundant energy that now made her restless? The Wherrin Trials had shown that she could be competitive; she was sure she could regain the championship. She had swum easily against the strongest current the yacht's pool provided, refreshed and not tired by an hour's swim. Pedar's revelations of a Rejuvenant clique didn't attract her, except when younger people were being especially tiresome . . . but they were more tiresome now than when her aging body had left her with less energy to express her irritation.

She considered her family: would young Ronnie have been so feckless if his parents had not been Rejuvenants? Parents who knew they would live forever didn't want competition from their children . . . might be glad if the children were "too immature" at twenty or even thirty to be given responsibility. Were the Rejuvenants heading for a society in which the young would have no opportunity to develop mature judgment? The youngsters had done well enough when they had to—when they had the chance, like Brun, to demonstrate the maturity they should have.

"Would you like to try out some of his get?" asked Marcia. Cecelia yanked herself back to the present, where the chestnut stallion posed in the ring, showing off his muscles. The Singularity line, whatever its structural faults, had never been short of showy personality.

Would she like to ride one? She thought of Marcia's past, and her past, and the way she always felt on a horse. No contest. It was never any contest. She always wanted to ride a live horse, even a bad horse.

An hour later she felt that even the Singularity line had its virtues. True, they didn't have the extension she liked. True, they had trouble with lateral flexion of their stubby bodies. But they provided both springy comfort in collection, and explosive leaps over fences. Cecelia dismounted at last, feeling almost smug. She had seen, in the look on Slangsby's face, that he had not expected her to be that good. And Marcia, who had surely rejuved more than once, must not have expected it either—they both looked slightly stunned.

It might be worth it to have one just for fun—just for herself. Not to breed—she still didn't like the structure—but to ride. An embryo transfer to Rotterdam, brought out of one of the big old mares Meredith kept for the purpose. In a few years, she could play with it—hard to believe she had those years now, could look that far ahead.

It did change the decision points.

"Let's talk about this," she said to Marcia. She was very glad she'd taken care to see her bankers before coming out here; Marcia had made everyone on the circuit uncomfortable about money years ago, and that sort of stinginess didn't change.

Aboard the *Vigilance*, docked at Xavier Station

"Excuse me, Commander, but Captain Serrano asked if she could come aboard. She'd like to speak to you personally." It was past half, in the second shift, a time when attention blurred toward dinner. A time when, according to Koutsoudas and his instruments, Garrivay gathered with his conspirators for a daily conference. The guard at the access, crisply efficient in his spotless uniform, watched Heris and the others closely as he spoke into the intercom. A pause, during which Heris tried not to hold her breath visibly. He must want her to come; it would make things so much easier for him. A Serrano with an armed yacht was the only menace he faced; if the mouse walked into the cat's parlor, it saved the trouble of hunting it down. He had to be smart enough to figure that out. If only Koutsoudas's genius had included mind probes . . .

"Oh, very well." The reply was easily loud enough for her to hear. Then, in a more cordial tone. "Yes, yes—do bring her aboard, and any of her crew that came along. Delighted . . ."

Delighted. She let no hint of her own delight at setting foot on a cruiser deck again slip past her guard. She was the renegade, the outcast who hadn't dared come back in the Fleet. She was a coward who hadn't yet admitted it; she let herself shiver as Garrivay's security patted her down, as if it bothered her.

None of her weapons would show. Behind her, her crew submitted as well. She had worried some about Meharry, who had been a bit too eager to come along, but Meharry said nothing untoward. They were all in obviously civilian shipsuits with Cecelia's family name stenciled (a few hours before) on the chest. Heris had not known how Garrivay would react to this many crew—she had alternate plans for different possibilities—but they were led to his office in a clump.

"Ah . . . Captain . . . or may I call you Heris?" Garrivay, expansive in his own ship, eyed her up and down with the clear intent of discovering any lingering scrap of backbone. As she had hoped, he had not dismissed the other officers. She had suspected he would prefer to humiliate her before an audience.

Heris drooped as submissively as she could, giving a nervous laugh. She scarcely glanced at the other officers in the compartment. They would all have been junior to her, if she were still in; they were all junior to Garrivay. And they were all conspirators. She hoped Koutsoudas was right about that. She had enough innocent blood on her conscience.

"You're the commodore," she said. Would this be too much? But no, he accepted that as his due.

"Right," he said. "I am. You know, I really wish you had left here with your rich lady, your owner. I might have to confiscate that ship if there *is* an emergency."

"I know," Heris said, heaving a dramatic sigh. "She just wouldn't listen. She doesn't understand things; she doesn't believe it can happen to her." Koutsoudas had assured her that Garrivay could not have intercepted the messages between her and Cecelia supposedly discussing that possibility; she hoped not, because all the messages had been fakes. Cecelia had gone blissfully into that horse farm and had yet to emerge. The safest place she could be, right now. "I suppose you'd install your own crew?" she asked, aiming for wistfulness.

"Do *you* want the job?" he asked.

Heris shook her head, looking down as if ashamed. She was afraid she couldn't control the expression in her eyes. "No, I—you know I—had the chance to go back in Fleet."

"And got out while the going was good, eh? Well, probably wise. And your crew—ex-Fleet as well—I don't suppose any of them want a berth on a real fighting ship again?"

"No, sir," said Meharry. *Shut up*, Heris thought at her. *Don't ruin this.* "I got more'n enough scars, sir." Meharry at her best didn't sound entirely respectful, and at the moment she sounded downright sullen.

"I hope we won't have to impress you, then," Garrivay said, in a voice that enjoyed the threat. "If there is trouble, and we run short of . . . whatever your specialty was . . ." He waited, but Meharry didn't enlighten him. Heris stared at the carpet, waiting, feeling the others at her back. Garrivay chuckled suddenly, and she looked up, as he would have expected. "Don't look so worried, Heris. I'm not planning to run off with your owner's ship and your crew unless I have to. You'll never have to fight another battle. Now . . . what was it you wanted to talk to me about?"

"Well . . . Commodore . . ." He liked the title; she could see him swelling up like a dampened sponge. "It's partly my owner and partly the local government. You see, before you arrived, they kind of got to asking me things. . . ." She went off into a long, complicated tale she had thought up, something that kept offering Garrivay hints of intrigue and possibly profit, but entangled in enough detail that he had to listen carefully. She had rehearsed it repeatedly, adding even more complicated sections so that it took up enough time. It had an ending, if needed, but within the next anecdote or so Koutsoudas should—

"Sir—an urgent signal—" There it was; the prearranged distractor, one of Koutsoudas's elegant fakeries. A bobble on the ship's scans that might be incoming ships, something the bridge crew would have to report and Garrivay would have to acknowledge.

"Yes?" Garrivay turned away, reaching for his desk controls; his officers, for that instant, looked where he looked.

No one needed a signal. Heris threw herself forward and sideways, in a roll-and-kick combination that caught Garrivay on the angle of the jaw. His hands flew wide; before he could recover, she was on him, the edge of her hand smashing his larynx. Her other hand had reached the com button, preventing its automatic alarm at the sudden loss of contact. Garrivay, heaving as he tried to

suck air and got none, thrashed against his desk and fell
to the deck. From his earplug came the tinny squeak of
someone reporting the surprise Koutsoudas had created
for their sensors.

She looked up, to meet four triumphant grins. Too early
for those; they had just started. She leaned over and
removed Garrivay's earplug, inserting it in her own ear.

"—it's moving insystem at half insertion velocity, while
the other—" She listened, only half hearing what she
already knew, but aware of a little bubble of delight at
being once more connected to a real ship's command center.
Even if it wasn't her ship. Though it was—or would be—
if the rest of this worked.

Already the others were stripping the bodies of their
uniforms. Oblo looked up and waved something, a data
strip it looked like. Heris leaned again to Garrivay, now
unconscious, his body twitching with oxygen deprivation,
and unpinned his insignia. Her nose wrinkled involuntarily
at the unpleasant stench; she ignored the source and pinned
the insignia to her own uniform. Thank goodness she had
a uniform that could pass for Fleet in a pinch . . . because
this was a pinch indeed.

"I can wear this," Petris said doubtfully, nodding at the
uniform he'd removed from someone with major's rings.

"No," Heris said. "It won't really convince them, and
once they discover where the uniforms came from they'll
worry again. I'm the key: if they accept me, they'll accept
you." Otherwise, of course, they were all dead. In her ear,
the flow of information stopped. She hit the com button
twice, the usual signal of a busy captain that the message
had been received.

From Garrivay's inside pocket—no more twitches now—
Heris took the thin wand that gave access to captain's
command switches. From here out, it would get more
dangerous. Murder was one thing. Piracy, treason, and
mutiny were . . . she didn't think about it.

The wand slid into the desk slot easily. The hard part came next. To forestall just such coups as they had accomplished, the use of the captain's wand triggered a demand for an identity check.

"Serrano, Heris," Heris said, adding her identification numbers and rank, mentally crossing more fingers than she owned . . . *if* Koutsoudas was right, her aunt admiral might have managed to leave a back door in the Fleet database.

Lights flared on the captain's desk, and the computer demanded a reason why Serrano, Heris, Commander was using Garrivay, Dekan Sostratos, Commander's wand.

"Emergency," she said. Then, with a deep breath, took her aunt's name in vain. "On the orders of Admiral Vida Serrano."

The computer paused. "Authorization number?" A sticky one. The only number her aunt had shared with her recently was the Serrano encryption code on that datacube. Would aunt admiral have risked putting her family code into the database, hiding it in plain sight, as it were? Right now Heris believed her aunt admiral might have done anything. She found another mental finger to cross, and gave that number. After the second group, the computer blinked all the lights. "Authorization accepted." So . . . aunt admiral had had more in mind than an apology, had she? And had she known Heris would be in this sort of trouble? Koutsoudas's remark about "lighting rods" flashed through her mind. Interesting—infuriating—but she had no time to sort it out.

Now a touch on the desk opened the service functions. She picked up the command headset and settled it on her hair.

"You don't want the combat helmet?" Petris asked.

"No. If we can do this at all, we can do it this way. We cannot take the whole ship by force, if everyone's turned." She could, with the command wand, destroy it and everyone on it—and, in the process, the station to which they were docked. But she hoped very much that her string of good guesses would continue to hold. "They need to see my face. I'm legitimate, remember? The computer accepts me; my aunt is an admiral." On the desk, she keyed up the status displays. Personnel . . . there were fifteen more known traitors on this ship, and four on one of the patrol craft. Koutsoudas thought he knew which fifteen, and she located them . . . on duty, six . . . one on the bridge, and five elsewhere about the ship.

"You can't take the bridge alone," Petris said.

"No . . . but I can isolate the compartments." She touched the control panels. Now each was blocked from communication with the others, and if she could get control of the bridge crew, if they believed her, there was a chance of capturing the other traitors without a major fight in the ship.

The first thing was to establish her authority with even one legitimate onboard officer. Now on the bridge was a major Koutsoudas thought unlikely to be a traitor. Again, he had better be right. She selected his personal comcode from the officers list.

"Major Svatek, report to the captain's office."

"Yes, sir." He had a voice that gave nothing away; she felt no intuitive nudge of like or dislike. Heris nodded to her crew; they placed themselves on either side of the door and waited.

The major came in without really looking, and by the time he had registered the bodies on the floor and the stranger behind the captain's desk, Petris and Meharry had him covered.

"Sorry about this, Major," Heris said. He looked stunned, and then angry, but not particularly frightened. "It is necessary that you listen to what I have to say, and there was no safe way to do this on the bridge without imperiling the ship."

"Who . . . are you?" The expletives deleted by caution left a pause in that.

"I'm Commander Heris Serrano," she said. It was not an officer she had ever seen before, but he had to know that name. "I'm on special assignment."

"But—" The major's eyes shifted from her to Petris to the bodies and back to her. Recognition; that was good. For once Heris didn't mind having the family face. "But you were—I heard—"

Heris smiled. "You heard correctly. I resigned my commission and took employment as a civilian . . . in anticipation of recent crises."

"Oh." The blank look cleared slowly. "You mean it was all—all faked?"

"Well . . . not uncovering Lepescu's plot," Heris said cheerfully. Everyone knew about Lepescu, she was sure. "That wasn't faked at all."

"But—what are you doing *here*?" This time his glance at the bodies had been longer. His first anger was leaving him, and she saw a twitch of fear, quickly controlled.

"Right now, I'm taking command of this ship, as ordered."

"You—are?" The major's gears were trying to mesh, but achieved only useless spinning; Heris could almost hear the loose rattle. "As ordered?"

"You're aware that this system will shortly be under attack by the Benignity of the Compassionate Hand?" Giving it the full title added weight, Heris thought, to the claim.

"Uh . . . no . . . uh . . . Captain." Victory. The major didn't know it yet, perhaps, but he had accepted Heris in command.

"They scouted it, sent a fake raider in to check out the defenses—"

"That raider we heard about?"

"Yes. With a surveillance ship in the distance. This group was then dispatched . . . but not by the R.S.S. command."

"But—but what are you saying?"

"That your former captain, Dekan Garrivay, was a traitor, in the pay of the Benignity. That certain of his officers were also traitors, that the purpose of this mission was to strip Xavier of any defenses, including me—since I had killed the raider—and open it to the Benignity."

"But—but how do you—" Disbelief and avid curiosity warred in the major's expression.

"You may recall that I have an Aunt Vida . . . Admiral Vida, that is."

Comprehension swept across the major's face, and he sagged. An aunt admiral, a secret mission . . . it was all right. Behind the major, Petris relaxed a fraction. Heris didn't.

"Now," Heris said, "my people need uniforms; they've had to wear those miserable civilian things too long." She paused a moment, wondering if she dared promote her associates to officers. She needed all the loyal officers she could find . . . but instinct said that even the smallest additional lie could topple the major's fragile belief in her story. If he stopped to think, if he doubted, she would become a common murderer again, not a legitimate officer who had been operating under cover. She gave them their original ranks instead, and watched the major's response. He might not know it, but he could still be dead any moment. "And you'll need to get someone up to tape the scene for forensics, put the bodies on ice, and clean up this office afterwards. We strongly suspect that one or more are carrying discreet CH ID markings. And the following personnel must be located and put under guard." She handed him Koutsoudas's list. Making it all up as she went along, she realized, was a lot more fun.

"Yes, sir." A long pause. "Anything else, sir?"

"No," Heris said. "I'll be on the bridge, speaking to the crew."

"But you've got Cydin on your list, and she's on the bridge now," the major said.

"Thank you," Heris said, as if she hadn't known that. "Then I'll take Mr. Vissisuan with me—" Oblo was almost as well known in the Fleet as Koutsoudas. "Who's bridge officer at this time?"

"Lieutenant Milcini," Major Svatek said.

"And the M.P. watch commander?"

"Lieutenant Ginese—" Svatek looked at Arkady Ginese, startled. Ginese smiled.

"That's probably my Uncle Slava's oldest boy. I'd heard he'd been commissioned." Another thin layer added to the skin of belief; Heris could see Svatek processing this. Not only the famous Serrano name, but someone related to the ship's own security personnel.

"Mr. Ginese, you'll accompany me as well," Heris said. "Let's go."

✧ Chapter Fourteen

The corridors of Garrivay's ship—no, *her* ship—were as familiar as the shapes of her own fingers. Command Deck, dockside corridor, aft of the captain's office. A passing ensign saluted her insignia without appearing to notice anything; his eyes widened at her escort. She wished they'd been able to wait for uniforms, but the scanty tradition behind her acts emphasized the need for immediate action.

Ahead, the hatch leading to the bridge, just where she'd left it, as if she had walked back onto her own ship. This *was* her ship, she reminded herself. A marine pivot stood at ease by the hatch, snapping to attention at the sight of her insignia.

"Sir!" Then his expression wavered, as if he weren't sure.

"Pivot." She snapped a salute. "These personnel are with me." Before he reacted, they were past; she came through into her own kingdom, home at last.

She took the three steps forward, paused while the bridge officer caught sight of her.

"Sir—uh . . . Commander . . . ?"

"Commander Heris Serrano, special assignment." She pitched her voice to carry through the whole compartment. "As I've explained to Major Svatek, I have taken command of this vessel. You are Lieutenant Milcini, is that correct—?" She was aware of heads turning, the pressure of many startled looks. One of the officers on the bridge was Cydin. Heris didn't worry about that;

Ginese and Oblo would be watching for her. More important now was the reaction of the loyal crew. So far astonishment held them.

The lieutenant found his voice again. "Captain Garrivay—?"

"Commander Garrivay has been relieved." Heris held up the command wand. "The computer has accepted my authorization code."

"Liar!" There. Lieutenant Cydin, a rangy redhead who reminded her inexorably of Cecelia. "She's a traitor—don't listen to her! She was cashiered—she's not Fleet!"

Heads turned back and forth, uneasy. Lieutenant Milcini started to reach out but froze in a parody of indecision when Heris looked at him.

"Lieutenant Cydin, you are hereby charged with treason," Heris said steadily. "Evidence in possession of Fleet—" Koutsoudas, after all, was legitimately Fleet, even if presently on a yacht "—shows that you conspired with Commander Garrivay and others to yield Xavier to the Benignity of the Compassionate Hand."

"What!" Cydin's face went paper white.

"Recordings of conversations with Commander Garrivay . . ." Heris said. "You are hereby relieved of your duties and will be held in confinement until such time as a Board can be convened—" The familiar phrases rolled out of her mouth as if she herself had never felt their impact on her own life. Necessary, she knew; such formality, such familiarity with tradition, was another proof of her own legitimacy. "Mr. Ginese, Mr. Vissisuan—" She nodded, and they moved around her. Lieutenant Cydin looked around for support she did not get.

"No! I'm not a traitor—*she* is! Ask her what happened to our captain! It's all lies!" But around her was a subtle withdrawing. "Look at her—that's not a Fleet uniform! Those men—they're in civvie shipsuits!"

"*I* know her," someone said. Heris looked for the voice,

and found a face she vaguely remembered from several ships back. Her mental name file revolved.

"Petty-light Salverson," she said. "But you've had a promotion—congratulations, Chief."

"I never believed you'd been thrown out," Salverson said. She was a pleasant-faced brunette that Heris remembered best for a difficult emergency repair during combat. "So it was all special ops?"

"I'm not at liberty to say," Heris said; Salverson grinned, and those nearest her—people she would have known well—grinned too.

"You *fools*!" Cydin yelled. "She'll get you killed, all of you." Then, with a glance at Ginese and Oblo, who were almost to her side, she gave Heris a final, furious glare. "You won't win," she said. "You can't—even if you get the ship—" And she slumped where she stood. Those nearest tried to catch her, but failed; her head hit the decking with a resonant thump.

Heris felt a chill pang she had not felt when she killed Garrivay. Cydin seemed so young; she could have outlived her mistakes if she'd wanted to. She had no time for more regrets. "We'll need an autopsy," she said to Lieutenant Milcini. "Until all my people are back in uniform, we'd better have someone else convey the body to sickbay."

"Yes . . . Captain." She left him to arrange it; she had more pressing duties. He had forgotten, in his confusion, to transfer bridge command, but she could never forget that.

She moved to the command desk. "I have the bridge," she said. "Let me explain the situation briefly. I expect communications from the admiralty, and possible hostile action from the Benignity. This action may be imminent; unless we find details in Commander Garrivay's private notes, we must assume that it could come any time."

Silence, attentive now rather than confused. Confront a fighting vessel with an enemy and confusion yielded to training. She had counted on that reaction. Heris went on.

"Officers not involved in the treasonous plot to yield Xavier will be briefed as soon as the ships are secure. In the meantime, all scans will be fully manned all shifts; record in battle code from this hour—" The scan positions, after a last glance at her, erupted in a brief flurry of activity. Garrivay had had them shut down, probably to prevent the operators from noticing when the CH ships arrived.

"Captain—" A light on the command desk, a voice in her ear.

"Yes?"

"Lieutenant Ginese, watch commander. I have just been advised by Major Svatek to take certain persons into custody, and among them a Lieutenant Cydin who is on the bridge—"

"Was on the bridge. She killed herself rather than accept arrest."

"I see. May I ask the captain's authorization for actions taken in relieving Commander Garrivay of his duties?" Deftly put, Heris thought.

"Admiral Serrano," Heris said. "It was a special assignment."

"So I gathered." Like her own Arkady, this Ginese had a healthy lack of awe for officers. After a long moment, the honorific appeared. "Sir. Does the captain have other orders?"

"Secure the ship," Heris said. "No station liberty, no leaves, no offship communications without my express orders. That list is almost certainly incomplete, and as we'll be in combat shortly—" Not too shortly, she hoped, but it couldn't be long enough.

"Yes, sir. Those personnel on the list have been secured under guard, although—we can't maintain a suicide watch with all of them separately confined *and* do the rest of it. Would the captain clarify the priorities?"

"Ship first, of course. If they kill themselves, it's regrettable—the other could be fatal." He shouldn't need to be told that, but she realized he was still feeling his way, not quite sure she was trustworthy.

"Major Svatek said a relative of mine was with you—would that be Vladi?" Despite the casual tone, Heris knew this was a trick question. She had never heard of a Vladi Ginese.

"Arkady," Heris said. "Would you like to speak with him?"

"No—just checking. Sorry, sir. It's my—"

"Job, I know. Now if you'll excuse me, I have other duties myself." As have you, went unsaid but clearly understood. Heris unlocked the inship communications, and keyed for an all-stations announcement. If there were other traitors—or even highstrung overreactors—this would flush them out.

"Attention all personnel. This is Commander Heris Sunier Serrano, now acting captain of this vessel. We are in a state of emergency, expecting the arrival of a hostile force from the Benignity. Your executive officer, Major Svatek, has been informed of the nature of the emergency, and of the reasons for a change of command. Those of you who have served with me before know that I will give full explanations when there's time." A calculated risk, but surely there were others who had been with her before, who would explain to their anxious fellows what kind of commander Heris was. "Some of you will have heard that I resigned my commission and am no longer a Fleet officer; in fact I was on special assignment, and my authorization code is still active, as the ship's computer recognized. This is an unusual situation; I understand that many of you will be confused, but at the moment we have more pressing problems. The Benignity wants this system as a base for invasion; we're going to defend it."

From the expressions of the bridge crew, relief outweighed anxiety. Garrivay could not have been the sort of commander who inspired confidence.

"I want all division heads in my office in one hour," Heris went on. "I notice some discrepancies in the status lists that we'll have to address in order to complete our mission. In the meantime, I'll expect you all to bring all systems to readiness." Which made it sound as if she had an official mission. "Captain out."

She grinned at Lieutenant Milcini. "I'll post the hardcopy of my orders when I get them from *Sweet Delight*. Considering the secrecy, I couldn't bring them aboard with me at first." Certain phrases from the cube her aunt had sent her could, with the proper surrounding verbiage, be taken as orders. Oblo had produced a surprisingly realistic document.

"Yes, sir. Uh—you'll be taking over the captain's quarters?"

"Of course." Implicit in that was her transfer to the *Vigilance* as her primary vessel; the *Sweet Delight* was no longer hers in the same way. And who would captain the yacht? She might need it in the fight. No, first the very dangerous patrol ships.

She had the cruiser . . . maybe. If they captured the other traitors aboard before they could arrange a mutiny. If the other two craft didn't try to blow the cruiser.

"Who's our communications first, Lieutenant Milcini?" Heris asked.

"Lieutenant Granath, sir."

"Have Lieutenant Granath hail the *Sweet Delight*, civilian band four, and route the response to my set."

"Sir."

Moments later, Sirkin's voice answered for the yacht. "*Sweet Delight*, Nav First Sirkin."

"Sirkin, it's Captain Serrano. I've taken over here. How's the longscan look?"

"Captain, there's something far out, Kou—our scan tech says. Very faint, just a ripple."

"I'm having communications here hold an open line.

If there's a change, let me know." What she said and did not say fit the prearranged code; Koutsoudas would remove the block he'd put on communications out of the cruiser. Now for the patrol ships. *Paradox*'s captain had died with Garrivay in the captain's cabin; *Paradox*'s executive officer might or might not be loyal. He had not shown up on any of Koutsoudas's scans, but he had been with the traitor captain for two years. The more distant *Despite* had as its captain an officer definitely disloyal. Koutsoudas had recorded her during a conference aboard the cruiser. Heris expected that the crews of both ships were predominantly loyal; she had not forgotten Skoterin, but still believed traitors were rare. If the exec of *Paradox* accepted her . . . that left only *Despite*. Would that captain betray herself? The patrol craft could be lethal, especially if any distractions arose on the cruiser.

"Major Tinsi, I am Commander Heris Serrano, acting captain of the *Vigilance*. You are hereby confirmed as acting captain of the patrol craft *Paradox*."

"What?" The face onscreen matched the database holo of Major Tinsi. "What's—where's Captain Ardos? Who *are* you?"

"Commander Serrano," Heris repeated. "Heris Serrano. I've been on special assignment for the admiralty, investigating irregularities." Such a handy word, irregularities. She was a little shocked at how easily the lie now rolled off her tongue.

"But you're not—and where's Commodore Garrivay? What's going on over there?"

"Commander Garrivay has been relieved of his command," Heris said. "I'm sorry to say that he and your Captain Ardos were involved in these . . . er . . . irregularities." She held up a packet within pickup range. "We have recordings implicating both of them, and some other officers. We assume that officers not implicated are innocent—and that includes yourself, although the investigation will continue. May I take it that you are not in the pay of the Benignity?"

"Of course I'm not—what? The *Benignity*? Captain *Ardos*?" Captain Ardos, Heris reflected, must have been relieved to have so dense an executive officer. No wonder he had kept the man around for two years even though he couldn't confide in him. No better camouflage than honest stupidity, ready to swear he had seen, heard, and suspected nothing.

Heris waved the packet, and Tinsi shut up. "Apparently several officers on each ship were involved. I suggest you take immediate steps to secure your position, in case there are more traitors aboard. We expect hostile forces in this system shortly; you will prepare your ship for combat, Captain Tinsi."

"But I—but—"

"Or, if you feel yourself unequal to command, I can relieve you and assign another officer," Heris said. Tinsi stiffened as if she'd filled his spinal column with a steel rod.

"No, sir . . . Commander . . . Commodore . . ."

"Commander will do. Now. I have a list of possible traitors aboard *Paradox*. These are not confirmed, but you might want to take precautions." She transmitted the names in a burst of code. "You will maintain a shielded link to *Vigilance*, while I make contact with *Despite*."

"Captain—*Despite*'s moving." That was Koutsoudas, not waiting for Sirkin to transmit the call. "Pretty good delta vee, outbound toward the border."

At least it wasn't an attack on the station or her ships. Yet. "Weapons, bring us to readiness."

"Sir."

"*Paradox*, you are authorized to bring your weapons to full readiness." What was *Despite* doing out there? Not simply running away; that would be too easy. Going to feint a retreat and then come back? Going to meet someone? And had she any chance to stop them? "We need to transfer gear and personnel from the yacht *Sweet Delight* to this ship— see to it—" she said to Major Svatek, who had reappeared on the bridge just before she called *Paradox*.

"Yes, sir. How many personnel, sir?" A good question. She still wanted to crew the yacht, in case they needed it. But right now she wanted Koutsoudas back at the boards of a Fleet ship, with direct access to the onboard databases, and to her. If it cost her a chance at *Despite*, so be it.

"Two," she said. "The gear will be for myself and the personnel who came aboard with me—not much, a little less than standard officer duffel." Already packed, it lay in the access hatch.

"Any problem with them going through the station? Do you mind if the civs know about it?"

"No—that's fine." It would be much easier, both now and when she assigned a crew to the yacht.

"*Despite*, hold your station. Hold your station. This is Commander Serrano, acting captain of the *Vigilance* . . . hold your station or—"

"Or what?" The display flickered as the signal stretched with the other craft's acceleration and the comunit's logic struggled to reassemble it, but Heris could see the face clearly enough. Lt. Commander Kiansa Hearne, not that much different from the days when she and Heris had shared a compartment in the junior officers' warren aboard *Acclaim*. "I don't know what you've done, but you have no authority. You're a civilian now, Heris."

"No," said Heris. "Special assignment, Lt. Commander." She would not use the old name. Kia had been a difficult young woman, but not yet a traitor. Heris had left the *Acclaim* thinking she had made a friend, proud of herself for the effort she'd put into it. "Surely you don't think I was out here by accident."

"I . . . think you're bluffing."

"I think *you* are. We have recordings from Garrivay's office."

"Blast." Hearne's face sagged. "That bastard. I finally get a ship of my own, and the next thing I know—" That had been Kia's problem all along; she always had someone to blame for her failures.

"You've got a shipful of innocent crew," Heris said. "Turn command over to your exec, or another loyal officer, and I'll see what I can do—"

"I'm not stupid, Heris." Hearne scowled. "If you've got real evidence, I'm dead meat anyway. Under the circumstances, I think a strategic withdrawal is in my best interest. You'd have a tough time catching me— especially if you're crazy enough to stick around and try to stop the Benignity."

"Your crew—" Heris began.

"My crew will have to take care of themselves," Hearne said. "You understand that—*yours* did."

The old rage and grief broke over Heris like a wave; she fought her way out of it in seconds, but made no more effort to convince Hearne.

"Captain, we have a statement from one of the officers on the list." That was Oblo.

"Go ahead," Heris said.

"Seems he was recruited by a Benignity agent about four years ago, and hasn't done a thing for them since. Claims he didn't know about the plan to surrender this system, but after he heard the recording he changed his tune and said he was coerced."

"Well, it's evidence," Heris said. "I assume Lieutenant Ginese knows about this?"

"Yes, sir. And they've got uniforms for us now—"

"Good. You know what to do. Koutsoudas and your duffel will be aboard shortly. I'll be contacting the Xavierans now."

✧   ✧   ✧

The General Secretary and the Stationmaster were side by side in the screen, looking grumpy until they saw who it was, then relieved. That relief wouldn't last long, not with what she must tell them.

"I've taken command of the Fleet units operating here," Heris said. "The former commander was removed for treason."

"I wondered!" The General Secretary looked angry, ready to pound someone. "Well, you'll have our backing, such as it is. What can we do?"

"Sir, you need to prepare for assault. We have no idea now how many ships are coming—we'll tell you when we can— but delay is the best we can do. Remember what we talked about before. Get your people downside into the best shelters you can find—scattered far away from recognizable population centers, ready to live rough for some months. If you have deep caves, out in the mountains or something, that would be best." She hoped the horse farm Cecelia was on was far enough out; she reminded herself to find out.

"But our militia—" Heris remembered the proud troops in their colorful uniforms, marching to the music of that jaunty band. How could she save their pride without costing them their existence? "I can't recommend resistance; they'll have trained troops and plenty of them—but if you can hide out for a few months, Fleet should be back in here. Your militia will be best used keeping order on the way, and while you're in exile."

"We can't evacuate?"

"Where?" Heris paused, then went on. "You don't have enough hulls in the system to take everyone, or time to load them. You have only the one station, and they'll blow it. They'll install their own, rather than risk yours being boobytrapped. Get everyone out of the station, downside, and get away from your cities and towns. It'll still be nasty, but that will save the most lives."

This wasn't what they had wanted to hear, even though she had said much the same thing before Garrivay arrived. They tried to talk her into some other solutions. Heris held firm. She would do her best but she could not promise to save the planet from direct attack. And she would need control of every space-capable hull they had, once they'd evacuated the station.

"But you can't hope to fight with shuttles!" the station-master said. "They don't have shields worth speaking of."

"No—but we can sow some traps with them. Then we can extract the crews, onto one of the warships."

"And the shuttles?"

"They'll be lost, one way or another. But with any luck, they'll have made things tougher for the invaders."

The General Secretary agreed to have the empty upbound shuttles loaded with readily available explosives. Those waiting for evacuation were kept busy shifting incoming cargo from the shuttles. A few, who had experience with explosives, helped manufacture them into crude mines.

Then she thought of Sirkin and Brun. She had realized that Sirkin, intelligent and hardworking as she was, lacked precisely what Brun had—the flair or whatever it was that picked the right choice when things got hairy. She needed to get Sirkin to such safety as was available, which meant downside, and underground. She had no safe place to stash Brun. What would her father want, given the options? His assumption that Brun would be safer with her now seemed utter folly. She was taking ships into battle against great odds, and very likely the planet would be scorched. Brun, as usual, had her own opinions, and interrupted the transmission from *Sweet Delight*.

"Captain Serrano, please—give me a chance. 'Steban, just a minute—please let me come with you."

Lord Thornbuckle's daughter on a warship? Not likely. "Why?" she asked.

"I know I'm not Fleet, and I know I'd be in the way, but it's better than going downside. Surely there's something simple I could do, so that someone else could help fight."

"There may be, but you can do it onplanet. I want someone I trust with Lady Cecelia. You and Sirkin can keep an eye on her. It's going to be rough down there when the shooting starts." Particularly since Cecelia would be thinking more about horses than the war, she was sure.

"But—"

"I don't have time to argue, Brun. This is one time you'll just do what I say. Besides, you can represent the Grand Council to the General Secretary—assure him that Xavier won't be forgotten." She cut that connection, and found herself faced with a choice of five others. The stationmaster wanted to know what she would do about the small mining settlements on the second satellite of Blueyes, the smaller gas giant. She could do nothing but send them word of what was happening; she had no time to think of anything else. The General Secretary wanted to know if she could use elements of the local militia. (Yes, if they volunteered.) Experienced shuttle pilots? (Yes.) A local news program wanted to interview her. (No. The General Secretary's staff would handle news.) The station's own medical team—doctors, medics, nannies and all—volunteered to come along on one of the ships, because they were certified in space medicine. (Yes!) And what about the breakdown in the financial ansible? And . . .

Koutsoudas had come aboard with his kitbag of gadgets, and installed them while the other techs gave him startled looks.

"Some of you," Heris said, "may have met Commander Livadhi's senior scan tech, Esteban Koutsoudas. He's been assisting the admiralty in this investigation." By their reaction, they might have waited years for a chance to watch the legendary Koutsoudas in action. "By the way, someone find him a uniform—you would prefer a real uniform, wouldn't you, 'Steban?"

"Mmm? Oh—yes, Captain. Although right now I just want to get these things installed and running." Everyone chuckled; Heris grinned. Better and better. She noticed that Koutsoudas managed to keep a hand or his head between the watchers and what he was actually doing, most of the time. Then his scan lit, obviously sharper than the ones on either side.

"How'd you *do* that?" one of the youngest techs asked.

"Don't ask," Koutsoudas said. His fingers danced across the plain surfaces of his add-ons. Heris never had figured out how he operated them. His display changed color slightly, showing the departing *Despite* in a vivid arc of color that zoomed suddenly closer. Heris flinched, even though she knew it was Koutsoudas, and not the patrol craft. Along one side of the display, three sets of numbers scrolled past. "There—eighty-seven percent of her maximum acceleration, but she's got a bobble in the insystem drive. Sloppy . . . it's cutting their output. Weapons still cold. That's odd. Shields . . . there goes the pre-jump shield check."

"I never believed it," said someone at the margin of Weapons. "I heard about him but I didn't believe—"

"It's impossible," said someone else.

"Cut the chatter." That was the grizzled senior chief poised behind Livadhi's shoulder, absorbing what he could.

"Send a tightbeam," Koutsoudas said, and gave the vector. Showoff, Heris thought. Worth it, in what he could do for you, but a showoff all the same.

"There they are." Now his display zoomed to another vector, where three . . . five . . . seven . . . scarlet dots burned. "Tag 'em—" Beside each one, a code appeared.

"Range?" Heris asked. She leaned forward, as if she

could pry more information out of the display. Numbers flickered along both edges of the screen.

"They're in the cone," Koutsoudas said, answering her next question first. "They'll get whatever *Despite* sent— and the range is still affected by downjump turbulence. I won't have it to any precision for an hour, Captain."

"Three to four hours for me, Captain," said the scan-second promptly.

"But they're at the system edge," Koutsoudas said. "It's a cautious approach—very cautious. They won't spot us for another several hours at least, even with boosted long scan; they're blinded by their own downjump turbulence."

"What's *Despite* doing?"

"Running fast," Koutsoudas said, flicking back over that ship's departing signature. "Considering scan lag, I'll bet she's already gone into jump."

Cecelia arrived at the shuttleport in a foul temper. It had taken forever to get a groundcar out to Marcia's place, and she hadn't been about to take any favors from Marcia. Not after that insult—as if she had ever failed to pay her bills! So she had endured a long, bumpy, dusty trip in to the shuttleport. Traffic crowded the road going the other way. It must be some local holiday, with early closing. But once in town, clogged streets delayed them, and she was afraid the shuttleport would be just as bad. She had tried to call Heris, but Sirkin was uncharacteristically vague about where she was, only saying she wasn't on the yacht. Cecelia didn't care where she was, she just wanted to be sure they could leave when she reached the station. Marcia's last words rankled . . . "It is not our habit to haggle, Cecelia," said with injured innocence. Stupid people. Stupid breeders of inferior horses; she would get some Singularity genes from a gene catalog if she wanted, and be damned to them. She forced a smile at the ticketing clerk, glad to find that she wasn't at the tail of a long line.

"Any room on the up shuttle?"

The clerk looked surprised and worried both, but clerks often did. His problems were his problems; she had room in her mind for only one thing—leaving Xavier far, far behind. "Yes, ma'am, but—"

"Fine. First class if you have it, but anything will do." What she really wanted was a long shower, a cooling drink, and a good supper. Depending on how long she had to wait for the shuttle, she might eat here, although she didn't remember the shuttleport having anything but machine dispensers.

"But ma'am—you don't want to go up right now," the clerk said earnestly, as if speaking to a willful child.

Cecelia glared at him. "Yes, I *do* want to go up right now. I have a ship; we're leaving."

"Oh." He looked confused now. "You're leaving the system from the station?"

"Yes." She was in no mood for this nonsense. What business was it of his? "I'm Cecelia de Marktos, and my ship, the *Sweet Delight*, is at the station; we'll be leaving for Rotterdam as soon as I arrive."

"Oh. Well, in that case—let me see your ID, please." Cecelia stared around the terminal as she waited for the clerk to process her ID and credit cube. Beyond the windows, a shuttle streaked by, landing. She had timed it perfectly. She glanced at the clerk; he was talking busily into a handset. Checking her out? Fine. Let him. She was sick of this place.

The shuttle came into view again, taxiing to the terminal. A ground crew swarmed out to it. Cecelia peered down the corridor to the arrival lounge. Finally a door opened, and people started coming out, a hurrying stream of them. More and more . . . more than she had thought the usual shuttle held.

When they got closer, she realized they looked scared. Had the raider shown up again? Was that why Heris didn't answer? But the clerk tapped her on the arm.

"Lady Cecelia—here—first-class ticket up to the station, but I've been advised to tell you that you really should reconsider. I can't sell you a round trip; if you change your mind, you may not be able to come back down. There's an alert. This is the last shuttle flight; they're evacuating—"

"I'm not planning to stay there," she said, accepting the ticket. "When's departure?"

"As soon as they refuel and turn her around," the clerk said. "You may board right away. And I'm afraid you'll have to hand-carry your luggage."

"Not a problem." She hadn't brought much; she could carry it easily. She heaved her duffel onto her shoulder and started down the corridor. She noticed that no one else joined her.

In the first-class cabin, the crew were scurrying around picking up trash. The seats had been laid flat; she wondered if people had been crammed in side-by-side on them. One of the crew looked up, startled.

"What are you—you have a ticket? A ticket *up*? Are you crazy?"

"I'm going to meet my ship, which is departing," Cecelia said. "Don't worry about me." She unlatched a seat back and pulled it upright herself, then stowed her gear on the seat next to her. If she was to be the only passenger, she saw no reason to worry about regulations. Then she heard other footsteps coming, and started to move her duffel. But it wasn't passengers. Instead, a line of men in some kind of uniform formed down the aisle, and began passing canisters and boxes covered with warning labels hand to hand. Cecelia leaned out to look down the aisle and see where they were being put, and nearly got clonked in the head.

"Excuse us, ma'am . . . if you'll just keep out of the way," said the nearest. Cecelia sat back, wondering what the labels meant—she vaguely remembered seeing markings like that on the things Heris had installed in her yacht.

"If you could just move that," said someone else, and

handed her duffel over. She sat with it on her lap, and
began to wonder just what was going on. On the seat
where her duffel had been, one of the men placed a
heavily padded container labelled FUSES DANGER DO NOT
DROP and strapped it in as carefully as if it were human.
"Don't bump that," he said to Cecelia, with a smile. She
smiled back automatically, before she could wonder why
or ask anything. Someone yelled, outside, and the men
turned and began filing out. She heard the hatch thud
closed, and felt the familiar shift in air pressure as the
shuttle's circulation system came on. A crewman came
back from the front of the shuttle and smiled at her.

"All set? You might want to set your stuff on the floor.
It might be a bit rough. Last chance to leave, if you're
having second thoughts."

She was having third, fourth, and fifth thoughts, but
she still didn't want to get off the shuttle and go back to
Marcia and Poots. Or anywhere else on this benighted
planet. Surely, when she got to the station, Heris could
get her out of whatever problem was developing locally.
Besides, it would look damn silly to back out now.

"I'm fine," she said. "Thank you. I suppose it is
permissible to use the facilities?"

"Yes—but we aren't carrying any meals on this trip. If
you need water—"

"I know where the galley is," Cecelia said. "I can serve
myself—or you, if you want."

"Great. Stay down until we're well clear." She felt the
rumble-bump of the wheels on the runway even as he
turned away from her . . . whatever it was, they were in
an almighty hurry. The shuttle hesitated only briefly when
it turned at the end of the runway, then screamed into
the sky . . . she supposed, since the usual visual display
in the first-class cabin wasn't on, and the heat shields
covering the portholes wouldn't slide back until they were
out of the atmosphere.

Nothing happened on the trip; she used the facilities, found the ice water, and a bag of melting ice, offered the pilots water (which they refused) and foil-wrapped packets of cookies, which they accepted. She rummaged in the lockers, finding a whole box of the cookie packets jammed into a corner, and a card with *"Meet you at Willie's tomorrow night, 2310"* on it in swirly flourishes of green ink. In the top left-hand locker, a pile of coffee filters tumbled out, and she gave up the search for anything more interesting. She shoved the coffee filters back behind their door, and opened a cookie packet. They could call it "Special Deluxe Appetizing Biscuit" if they wanted, but it tasted like the residue of stale crumbs in the bottom of a tin. Cecelia decided she wasn't that hungry.

✧ Chapter Fifteen

A line of passengers crammed the corridor as she came out; most of them gaped at her. She tried to remember which was the shortest way around to *Sweet Delight*. Then she heard someone calling her.

"Lady Cecelia!" Brun, waving a frantic hand. Sirkin was with her.

"Brun—whatever are you doing there? Why aren't you on the yacht?"

"Don't you know about it?"

"What?"

"The invasion. The Benignity is coming. With a fleet or something. Captain Serrano doesn't think she can hold them off; they're evacuating this station and telling people planetside to go into shelter. Underground if possible."

Across her mind scrolled the broad acres of Marcia and Poots's studfarm, the great log barns, the handsome paddocks, the gleaming horses . . . admittedly horses with conformational faults, but still horses.

"You're serious?"

"Yes—Captain Serrano told Sirkin and me to go downside, find you, and take care of you. She's having a military team crew the yacht—"

"Where is *she*?"

"On the cruiser," said Brun. "Wait—I'll explain—but you have to get into this line. You have to come with us—downside—"

"I don't want to go back down there," Cecelia said, aware

261

even as she said it that it sounded foolish. "I've been there. I want to be on my ship."

"Come on," said Brun. "You can't do that—there's no crew, and when there is a crew it won't be people you know—come on, get in line with us."

Cecelia wavered. "Well . . ."

"Come on." Brun stepped back, making room, but as Cecelia started toward the gap, angry voices rose.

"Hey! No cutting in front—you got no right—"

Brun turned on them. "She's an old lady; she's my mother's friend—"

Another voice louder than the others. "A Rejuvenant! I'm not losing my chance to get home safe for any damned Rejuvenant!" People shoved forward, slamming into Brun and Sirkin, who could not help slamming into those ahead.

"Damn you!"

"Stop it!"

"No shoving there . . . keep order, keep order . . ." That was two harried-looking station militia. "What's this now?"

Voices erupted, accusing, explaining, demanding. Finally things were quiet enough for explanation.

"I'm sorry, ma'am, but we don't have even one space left on the down shuttles. One's filling now—hauling maximum mass—and the one you came in on will be the last down. You bought a one-way; you assured the clerk you were bound outsystem on your own ship—"

"That's right," said Cecelia. "But I can't just abandon these two—" She nodded at Brun and Sirkin. "They're friends' children—"

"Sorry, ma'am . . . the clerk did try to warn you. As it is we don't have shuttle capacity for everyone. Some's got to stay and risk it—"

"I'm staying," Brun said, swinging a long leg over the rope that kept them all in line.

"Brun, no!" Cecelia said. "If there's real danger, I want you safe."

"There's always danger," Brun said. "And Captain Serrano said to keep *you* safe. I can't do that from down there—" She jerked her head in the direction of the planet. The line had closed in behind her, without a word but with absolute determination.

"Brun—" Sirkin turned, started to move.

"No!" Brun and Cecelia spoke as one. "No," Brun said a moment later. "Not you."

"Yes, me." Sirkin too stepped over the rope. "I'm a navigator; I'm good for something in space, and nothing much onplanet. I know I don't have your kind of flair, Brun, but I can free someone else by doing my own work."

Over her head, Cecelia met Brun's eyes. Nice child, Cecelia thought, and if we get out of this alive I will find her a safe berth on some quiet commercial line. Surely I have that much influence. She smiled at the station militia.

"Then you now have two more places for those who thought they must stay," she said. "Do you need these tickets?"

"No, ma'am. Thank you." One of the militia jogged toward the head of the line, and the other nodded to them.

"Well," said Cecelia. "Come along, before the yacht vanishes into space and we're left up here wondering how to run a space station."

"It's a lot like a ship," Brun said. "I've been talking to the people who work here, and met this man who's in charge of—"

"Fine," said Cecelia. "Then if we're stuck we have a chance of survival, but in the meantime, let's catch a ship."

No one was aboard the *Sweet Delight*. Brun and Sirkin both knew the dockside access codes, and the hatches opened for them. Cecelia lugged her gear to her own suite, and activated her desk. A stack of messages had accumulated since the last time she'd retrieved them, including one from Commerce Bank & Trust which informed her that her balance was more than adequate to purchase all the Singularity straws she wanted. She unpacked her duffel, and decided to shower. Whatever emergency was coming, she might as well meet it clean, in comfortable clothes. She stuffed her dirty clothes in the wash hamper, and turned the shower to full pulse.

She was finally feeling clean, all the travel grime and irritation out of her system, when the lights blinked off and back on so fast that her new panic in darkness didn't have time to reach full strength. She elbowed the shower controls, from water pulse to radiant heat and blow dry. Her pulse slowed, as the lights stayed on, and the fan whirred steadily. She turned, running her fingers through her hair to let the warm air reach her scalp. Then she saw the shadow beyond the shower door, a moving shadow.

"What the hell—!" A male voice, a strange one. The door opened, yanked hard from outside, and Cecelia found herself face-to-face with a uniformed man armed with one of her own hunting rifles, the expensive ones Heris had bought for her back on Sirialis. At second glance he looked more like a boy dressed up to play soldier—a fresh-faced youth who couldn't have been over twenty. "Who are *you*?" he demanded.

"Kindly hand me my robe," Cecelia said, not bothering to hide what he'd already seen. It wasn't her problem anyway, even if he was turning an unnatural red around the collar. She felt wickedly glad that he was seeing her younger body, not the eighty-six-year-old version. When he didn't move to comply, she lifted her chin. "It's drafty— and my robe is right there, beside you on the warming rack."

"Uh . . . yes, ma'am." Without looking away, he reached out and snagged the robe, fingering the pockets quickly. Cecelia's brows rose, then she realized he thought she might have weapons concealed in it, and her brows rose higher.

Weapons? In a bathrobe? Her? He handed it over, and she shrugged into it, tied it around her waist.

"I'm coming out," she said, when he showed no inclination to move, and he stepped back, giving her room. Without haste, she picked up one of the towels on the warming rack and finished drying her feet, then took another and toweled the rest of the dampness out of her hair. She moved to the mirrors, and picked up the comb on the shelf. "I'm Cecelia de Marktos," she said into the mirror as she shaped her hair with the comb. "This was my yacht . . . it's technically Heris Serrano's now, but I've hired it. And who are you?"

"Pivot Major Osala . . . from the R.S.S. cruiser *Vigilance*. Ma'am."

"And what are you doing on my ship?" Her hair was fluffing into an untidy brush after the shower; it needed trimming. Her lips felt dry; station and ship air was so much drier than the humid surface of Xavier. She spread a protective gloss on her lips and glanced at the soldier in the mirror. He was looking at her as if she were something else—a monster of some sort, a freak.

"Commander Serrano said—is that the same person you called Heris Serrano?"

"I suppose," Cecelia said, turning to face him directly. "Heris Serrano, formerly an R.S.S. officer, and now my captain. She told you to come aboard? I suppose it's all right then."

"Commander Serrano . . . she's taken command of the *Vigilance*." He sounded unsure.

"She has? Good for her. Even though she did kill a raider with this yacht, if there's trouble coming, she'd much better have a cruiser to fight with."

"But ma'am . . . aren't you scared at all? Of . . . of *me*?" The confusion on his young face almost made her laugh. "I have a *weapon*—"

Cecelia snorted. She couldn't help herself, even if it

was cruel, but she suppressed the laughter that wanted to follow. "Young man . . . pivot major is it? . . . didn't Commander Serrano tell you about me?"

"Uh . . . no, ma'am. The ship was supposed to be empty, only we found the entry hatch open, and Jig Faroe went to the bridge with the rest of the crew except me and Hugh, we were supposed to look for stragglers."

"Well, young man, if you ask Commander Serrano, she will explain that I'm a very old lady who has been rejuvenated, and I've been face-to-face with more firearms than you might think. You can kill me, but you are unlikely to scare me."

"Oh . . . are you . . . are you an undercover, too? Like Commander Serrano was?"

What was this? Undercover? Heris? A luxuriant vine of suspicion began unfurling in her mind, extending tendrils in all directions . . . Bunny . . . that vicious weasel Lepescu . . . the coincidences . . . and hadn't Heris mentioned some relatives who were admirals? Could Heris possibly have been fooling her all along? While that ran through her mind, she simply stared at the young soldier, until he looked away. "If I were undercover, would I tell you?" she asked finally. "I don't know what your security clearance is."

"Uh . . . no, ma'am. I mean, you don't . . . you wouldn't . . . but I still have to tell them you're here."

"Of course you do," she said reasonably. "Tell Commander Serrano I'd like to speak with her at her earliest convenience. When I'm dressed." She headed for her bedroom, and the muzzle of his weapon wavered, then fell away. Idiot, she thought to herself. Suppose I *were* a spy or whatever he suspected. I could have an arsenal under my pillows.

She pulled open drawers, rummaging through the clothes she'd left in the ship when she went down. She felt something practical was called for, rather than grandladyish. The cream silk pullover, the brown twill slacks, the low boots with padded ankles. When she glanced in the mirror, the soldier had disappeared, no doubt to report her existence. Idiot, she thought again. Heris would have something to say to him about that.

Her desk chimed from the outer room, and she strode out to answer it. There was the young man, looking embarrassed, by the door to the corridor. Another stood with him. Cecelia gave them a distracted smile and touched her control panel.

"Cecelia, what are you doing on that yacht?" Heris, sounding impatient. Cecelia queried for video, but found that the signal carried no video.

"I got fed up with Marcia and Poots, and came back; I was going to ask you to take me to Rotterdam."

"And no one told you about the emergency?"

She didn't feel like explaining why she hadn't heard what she'd been told, not on an all-audio link. "I didn't know, until I arrived at the station, on the last up-shuttle, which was going to be overfull going down." A pause. Heris said nothing. "I found Brun and Sirkin," Cecelia added. "We're all safe." The next pause was eloquent; Cecelia could easily imagine Heris searching for a telling phrase.

"You're not *safe*," Heris said finally. "You're square in the midst of a military action. This system is under attack by the Benignity; their ships are in the outer system now, and I need that yacht and its weapons . . . not three useless civilians who were *supposed* to be down on the surface digging in."

Anger flared. "Civilians aren't *always* useless. If you can remember that far back, one of them saved your life on Sirialis."

"True. I'm sorry. It just . . . the question is, what now? I can't get you to safety onplanet . . . if that's safe."

"So quit worrying about it. Do you think I'm worried about dying?"

"I . . . you just got rejuved."

"So I did. It didn't eliminate my eighty-odd years of experience, or make me timid. If I die, I die . . . but in the meantime, why not let me help?"

A chuckle. She could imagine Heris's face. "Lady Cecelia, you are inimitable. Get yourself up to the bridge; someone will find you a place. Jig Faroe's in command. I'll let him know you're coming."

"Good hunting, Heris," Cecelia said. She felt a pleasant tingle of anticipation.

Even in more normal conditions of war, when Heris had had time to make plans and go over them with her crew, the last hours before combat always seemed to telescope, accelerating toward them in a way that the physicists said didn't make sense. This was far worse. A change of command so close to battle was tricky at best, when it resulted from a captain's sudden illness or other emergency. She had not had time to gain the crew's confidence; she had not had time to assess their competence, their readiness for combat.

The normal thing to do—the textbook thing to do— was get out fast and get help. She had no orders to defend Xavier. She was clearly outnumbered; the loyalty of her crews was questionable. Or, if she chose to stay, it would be prudent to send the yacht, with its civilians . . . it could reach a safe jump radius in time to get away, long before an attack could reach it, and go back to a Fleet sector headquarters and report.

If the Benignity invaders hadn't mined the nearest jump point insertions. They could have, and that could be the reason for the gap in the financial ansible's transmissions. Many communications nodes for ansible transmission were located near jump points, for ease of maintenance and repair. She had an uneasy feeling about the jump points.

I have complete confidence in your judgment. Her aunt

admiral had said that, her aunt who had not commented on her performance since the Academy. What did "complete confidence" mean in a situation like this? Would her aunt back whatever decision she made, or did her aunt really think she had some special ability to choose the best course of action?

She could not let any of these thoughts interfere with her concentration. The only plans she had were hasty improvisations: very well, that beat no plans at all. As far as her officers could tell, her plans came down from the admiralty. That the plans were in direct defiance of common sense wouldn't bother them overmuch—it wasn't their judgment on the line. If the message capsule she'd sent reached the Fleet relay ansible—if no one was suppressing such messages—someone would, eventually, consider her judgment, her decision to stay, her choice of tactics. With luck they might even get help before the Benignity blew them away.

"What we've got," she told her more senior officers, "is a very unorthodox force for defending an inhabited planet." They knew that, but they needed to hear the obvious from her, at least at the beginning. "One cruiser, one patrol craft, one armed yacht, one very ancient Desmoiselle-class escort, three atmospheric shuttles, one of them armed with phase cannon—inadequately mounted, but perhaps good for a single round, assuming a suicidal crew."

"Phase cannon in a *shuttle*?" Major Svatek looked as shocked as Heris had felt when she first heard.

"It's what they had," she said. "It's never been fired—of course. We've warned them. It would take weeks of refitting to strengthen the mounts, and we don't have that time. *Grogon* is supposedly hyper-capable, but I don't trust its FTL generator, and neither did my engineers when they inspected it. The yacht is, of course, and it's carrying substantial weaponry for its hull—" She pulled up the display and pointed it out. "But the tradeoff there was on shields—she has only her light-duty civilian screen shields. Nothing else in the system is hyper-capable; the mining colonies have little shuttles and one ore-carrier. It's a big hull, but it's underpowered. And no weapons."

"So—what's our plan?" That was Major Tinsi, on the tightbeam from *Paradox*.

"Harassment with deception," Heris said. "We won't have real surprise, because of Hearne on *Despite*, but she didn't know about everything. Unless we're extremely lucky, we won't destroy the incoming ships—or even deflect them permanently—but we probably can delay their attack on the planet itself, by making them unsure how many of us there are. Even if they never use the phase cannon, for instance, they'll light up someone's weapons scans. So will old *Grogon*." Something else nagged at her memory, and finally broke through. She called Koutsoudas into the conference line.

"Did Livadhi falsify his ID at the commercial level that time when he hailed us with the wrong name?"

"You saw through it," Koutsoudas said.

"Yes, but we had military scan, as you know. I didn't bother to check what a commercial scan would have shown. How did you do it, how long does it take, and could you have falsified your beacon to military scanning?"

"It's pretty simple," Koutsoudas said. "It's all in knowing how; it takes maybe an hour or two, that's all. Yeah, you could do it for both kinds of beacon transmissions . . . of course it *is* illegal." He said that in a pious tone that made Heris chuckle. "Captain Livadhi didn't want anyone in Fleet to mistake him."

"I'm sure," Heris said, with deliberate irony. "Could you do it for this ship?"

"Well . . . yes. Why?"

"Oblo has installed two different fake beacon IDs in the yacht. If we could patch something up for this ship, and *Paradox*, we could give the Benignity something to think about."

"We still have only two real warships—"

"But they don't know that. They know *Despite* said that, running away, which can't have been the plan. They were expecting Garrivay and friends to be here, welcoming them in. They probably had a name, possibly even a familiar contact. They drop out of FTL and find one of their expected allies fleeing, telling them not to worry there's only a single cruiser and patrol. Would *you* believe that, if you were a CH captain?"

"No . . ." Koutsoudas looked thoughtful. "I wouldn't. I'd think double-cross. The conspirators discovered . . . betrayal. Something like that, anyway."

"Right. Is this a hands-on patch, or can you explain to *Paradox* how to change their beacon too? I want both ships to be able to switch back and forth—"

"It's doable, but it doesn't change the basic scan— nothing's going to convince them that there's more ships, if the beacon data on a masspoint suddenly changes."

"Don't worry about that," Heris said. "Just get hold of Oblo, and the two of you give us some fake identities that would hold up to Fleet standards. I have an idea." She had more than one; ideas flickered through her mind almost too fast to see.

Off to one side, she imagined the Benignity formation commander—he would be one of their Elder Sons, equivalent to the R.S.S. admiral minor. Hearne's message would make him bunch his formation, counting on its weight of weapons and numerical superiority as long as he found what he expected: a cruiser smaller than any of his ships, a patrol ship, a lightly armed yacht, and a slow-moving, nearly toothless scow. But if the scan data didn't fit—or worse, if it was inconsistent, suggesting that Hearne had lied—he would hesitate, pause behind his screening barrage, and prepare for a more extended combat. He might even be unwise enough to detach a ship or so.

If each of her three ships could appear to be one or two other ships—and if she could use the Benignity's barrage as a screen for her own movements—

"We could fake some beacons, as well—launch them—" That was Tinsi, over on *Paradox*. Heris nodded; she hadn't expected him to show that much imagination.

"No mass readings," Koutsoudas said. "It won't fool them more than a few seconds—"

"If we could get mass?" Another glimmer of an idea. Xavier's system wasn't overly full of handy rocks the right size, but those shuttles, loaded with anything massive from the station, and with faked beacons, might distract the CH commander.

"You and Oblo get on it," Heris said to Koutsoudas. "We need it done before their scans clear from jump insert."

"Yes, sir."

Heris looked around at the others, and saw thoughtful looks, only the reasonable amount of tension. "Let's get going," she said.

When she reached the bridge, Koutsoudas called her over. He had the first reasonably detailed scans of the arriving force.

"They're sticking to normal tactics," Koutsoudas said. "Throwing out a screening barrage on jump exit . . . it'll have tags keyed to their IDs. Coming on in a clump—"

"When will they have scan return?" Heris asked.

"Normally—a solid twelve hours after jump exit, and that's with efficient boosts. They exited eight to nine hours ago, so that means we have three blind hours for certain. But with *Despite*'s signal, if they picked it up—"

"They'll have a lot more detail than the best scans would give them. Current ship IDs. But not everything." That was less comforting than it might have been.

"I'm getting some separation in that clump, though,"

Koutsoudas went on. "Looks like one or two may be trailing back a bit farther than normal."

"Jump-exit error?"

"Could be. I'll stay on it."

Sweet Delight

Cecelia strolled into the bridge compartment trailed by the two young soldiers. Sirkin sat at the navigation console, looking scared. Brun perched where Petris usually sat, looking excited. Cecelia could not tell who was in charge, and was annoyed with herself for not knowing what all the insignia and markings were.

Cecelia had had no direct experience with the military until she hired Heris. Now she watched as the young man with two comma-shaped bits of metal on his collar organized his crew and set about carrying out Heris's orders. He looked to be Ronnie's age, or perhaps a few years older—she couldn't tell—but he had a hard-edged quality unlike her nephew's. Not courage, exactly—Ronnie was brave—but a definition, a focus, as if he were carved out of a single hard material by a sharp tool. So were the rest. She had noticed that with Heris's old crew, but assumed it was the result of the ordeals they'd been through as a result of Lepescu. And they had been cordial to her, once they knew her. Even Oblo. Of course, she'd never seen them in anything but civilian shipsuits. These all wore R.S.S. gray, with sleeve and shoulder patches and marks that meant something to them and nothing to her. Most seemed very young, but the one sitting where she remembered Oblo had a grizzled fringe around the margin of his bald head.

"You're Lady Cecelia," the young man in charge said. "I'm Junior-Lieutenant Faroe. Jig Faroe is the more common way to say it. Commander Serrano says you offered to help out—"

Cecelia grinned at him. "I presented her with a dilemma, is what you and she both mean. There's bound to be something simple that you need done. Watching gauges or something."

His expression suggested that that had been a stupid idea. "I wish I knew her better—how she thinks. What she thinks you might do—"

"That I can help you with," Cecelia said briskly. "I've worked with her for a couple of years now—" She admitted to herself that the time she spent in an apparent coma wasn't exactly "working with" Heris, but the start of a war was no time for long explanations. And she certainly knew more about Heris's thought processes than this young man. One had only to see someone ride across country to know more about their character than any dozen psychological analyses, no matter what the experts said.

"Oh—you were part of her . . . uh . . . cover?" He looked both eager and embarrassed, someone who wanted desperately to ask what he knew he should not.

"I don't think I should discuss it," said Cecelia. Especially when she hadn't the faintest idea what Heris had actually said and done.

"Oh—no, sir—of course not. Sorry." He dithered visibly, in the way Cecelia found so amusing in the young, and finally blurted, "But feel free, ma'am, to . . . to advise me whenever you have any insight into Commander Serrano's wishes."

"I will," Cecelia said, sorting rapidly through the little she had heard or read about covert operations and Fleet procedures. If Heris had been fooling her, then what would this youngster think she was? All that came to mind was the explanation for the officer's misuse of "sir"—in the military, officers of both sexes were called sir. Which meant that for some reason he thought she was an officer. Odd: surely he would have some sort of list which proved she wasn't. But his mistake could be useful. "For one thing, I can tell you that Commander Serrano found Brigdis Sirkin a most accomplished navigator. She said often that Sirkin should've been Fleet."

"Yes, sir; she told us. Says Sirkin has special knowledge of this ship's capabilities."

"So does Brun," Cecelia added. Should she mention that Brun was Thornbuckle's daughter? Probably not. It wouldn't add anything to the mix at this point. "She's been working with Meharry, I believe it is, and Oblo."

The bald man turned to face her. "That civilian *kid* has been working with Methlin Meharry? And Ginese? And Oblo?"

What was that about? She had expected them to know Heris's name, but the others, as far as she knew, had been enlisted. Enlightenment came just before she made a fool of herself. Foxhunters knew foxhunters, and stud grooms knew stud grooms—of *course* Heris's top people would have their own fame.

"Meharry," said Cecelia, as if pondering. "Tallish woman, blonde, green eyes? Yes. Brun, didn't you tell me she'd . . . er . . . prodded you through some level of weapons certification?"

"Yes, Lady Cecelia," Brun said. Her eyes sparkled; whatever else happened, Brun was having a marvelous time.

"What level?" growled the bald man to Brun.

"Spec third," Brun said promptly. Cecelia had no idea what that meant.

"And what did Oblo have you doing?"

"Well . . . we only got up to second, on account of Captain Serrano asked me to spend more time with Arkady."

A short nod, and a glance at Jig Faroe, who was almost prancing from foot to foot.

The communications board lit, and the bald man touched the controls, then moved back to clear the pickups for the captain. Koutsoudas appeared on screen, with Oblo behind him. "Let me speak to Sirkin and Brun, please, Captain Faroe."

"Right away." He sidled along the arc of the bridge, making room for Sirkin and Brun to squeeze past, into range of the pickups.

"We need to enable the alternate beacon IDs," Oblo began. "Brun, you remember how I showed you the lockout sequences?"

"Yes—you—"

"You'll want them all in readiness; you'll be switching them at your captain's order. Is Cesar there?"

"Yo, Oblo!" That was the bald man, leaning toward the pickups now.

"She doesn't know how to set up that kind of switching, so give her a hand. Quick learner, and she does know the lockouts cold."

Cesar nodded. "Right. Priority?"

"Yesterday. Now—Sirkin—"

"Yes?"

Koutsoudas took over. "Brigdis, Serrano wants you as primary nav for the yacht, because you know the . . . uh . . . special capabilities for FTL insertions and exits. As well, do you remember that little packet I gave you to take downside?"

"Yes, I have it."

"Good. Set it beside your main nav board, right under the shift control. It is not—repeat NOT—to be activated by anyone but yourself, and that is Commander Serrano's direct order. Is that clear?" A chorus of sirs, of which Sirkin's was the weakest. Koutsoudas glared out of the screen. "It's keyed to you anyway, but just in case one of those others gets too curious, it can blow the entire navigation board if you upset it. Hands off." A long pause. "You do remember the activation code, don't you?"

"Yes, it's—"

"Don't repeat it—just use it when it's time."

Cecelia could see that this mysteriousness gave Brun and Sirkin more prestige with the military, but why? Then

Koutsoudas appeared to see her for the first time. "Oh! Sorry, sir—didn't recognize you for a moment." As if anyone else would be wearing a silk pullover shirt; as if anyone else could be mistaken for her, with that red hair and plain face. And he knew perfectly well she wasn't a "sir"—she was the civilian who hadn't even wanted him aboard. "Lady Cecelia . . . I believe Commander Serrano would like to speak to you."

Again? But Heris was there now, looking at her with an expression half-concerned and half-gleeful. Damn the woman, she was looking forward to this battle. "Lady Cecelia." She said the name in audible quotes, implying that it was a pseudonym. "Captain Faroe has been instructed to give you every consideration. You have my authorization for the necessary decisions."

What necessary decisions, Cecelia wanted to ask, but she could tell that this was not the time. If she was a Fleet officer who had been pretending to be a civilian, she should know that already.

"Thank you, Captain Serrano," she said with what she hoped was appropriate military formality. Then she ventured further. "I presume that our primary objective remains . . . ?"

"As it was," Heris said, with a look that refused any more inquiries. "When the time comes for you to jump out of the system, don't hesitate." Cecelia blinked. Was Heris telling them to run away and leave her stranded? Not a chance.

"Should that be necessary," Cecelia said, stressing the unlikelihood, "I'll have a word with your aunt."

"You do that," Heris said. "Now I need to speak with Captain Faroe.

"Let Sirkin show you the critical jump distances," Heris told Faroe. "We've put her into jump much closer than the usual: it's part of the nonstandard equipment aboard. You've got the information from Ginese and Meharry on weapons capability?"

"Yes, sir."

"Remember to change beacon IDs based on your determination of the situation, once the CH splits up. Give them as many different vectors as you can—"

"Yes, sir. I understand." Cecelia could tell that Heris wished she had her own hands on the controls. She herself wished she could see Heris on the bridge of the cruiser— it must, she thought, be a sight. But the woman couldn't ride two horses at once; she had to let go the reins of this one. She moved back into pickup range.

"We'll do fine, Captain Serrano. I have every confidence in Captain Faroe." For some reason, that made Heris look bug-eyed for a moment. Then she regained her calm.

"Well, then. I'll expect acknowledgment when the last orders go out." And the beam cut off.

"Do you have any idea what Heris is up to?" Brun whispered a few minutes later. Captain Faroe had insisted that they were off duty for the next six hours, and they'd gone back to Cecelia's suite to relax.

"Aside from fighting off an invading fleet, not a clue in this world." Cecelia rubbed her temples. "I'm so far behind I can't even hear the hounds. I didn't even know that an R.S.S. battle group was here, let alone that she'd taken command of it. I was down there touring breeding farms and getting into a row with Marcia and Poots—paid no attention to the news, except when the financial ansible went *pfft* and convinced Marcia that I'd gone broke. Idiot fools. I told her to check her own balances, and she had the gall to tell me she didn't need to, she knew her standing, and that's when I stormed out and came back."

Brun was trembling, but with suppressed giggles. "Lady Cecelia, you're incredible! Didn't they tell you at the shuttleport?"

"I suppose the man tried. He kept talking about no round-trip tickets, but of course I didn't *want* a round-trip ticket. I kept telling him I had a ship here, and would be leaving the system. Would you please explain?"

Brun laughed aloud. "Ronnie's so lucky to have an aunt like you. Well, briefly, our Captain Serrano discovered that the captain of the cruiser and some of the others were traitors, planning to help the Benignity take the Xavier system. And she and Petris figured out that they had to get command of the ships, so they got invited aboard—"

"How?"

"I don't know. But I know she took Petris, Methlin, Arkady, and Oblo with her, and the next thing we heard, she was in command. Koutsoudas told me, before he transferred to the cruiser, that the traitors were dead. The cruiser's command computer accepted her—"

"But she's not in Fleet anymore. How could she—?"

"I don't know, I said. She and her old crew had their heads together—sent Brig and me away, said we shouldn't be party to it, so we couldn't be blamed later. She meant us to go downside and take care of you—" Cecelia snorted and Brig grinned. "I know, that bit was silly. You don't need taking care of. But that's why we don't know what she did, exactly. I think I can find out—there's a couple of these new people that will let it slip if I hang out with them."

"I'm sure they will," Cecelia said. "And meantime I'll try to be inscrutable." Inscrutability came easier when she really did know nothing.

✧ Chapter Sixteen

Part of Heris's strategy needed no explanation. Cecelia could see for herself the advantage in having the yacht able to switch beacon IDs, and the importance of timing was obvious as well. She cut short Faroe's attempt to explain with a curt, "Yes, I can see that it's best to change when we're not in their scan. My question was, are they still clumped up behind their barrage screen?"

"It won't really screen our change," he said again.

Cecelia closed her eyes a moment and gave him a stare that had shriveled young men years before this one was born. He gulped and froze in place, as she intended. "I. Know. That." She had picked it up from the conversations, but he didn't have to know how new her understanding was. "What I'm interested in is whether *we* can tell where *they* are, and whether they're still clumped. When the prey scatters—"

"But—they're hunting *us*," he said. Cecelia felt sorry for Heris. If this was the best she could find to send back to the yacht, she must be working with a real handicap on the cruiser. She should have let one of her own have it.

"So they think," she said, and watched Faroe's face wrap itself around that concept. "I don't believe Commander Serrano looks at it that way." She paused again, waiting for his wits to waken. When she saw a glimmer of intelligence, she went on. "You see, in my experience, Commander Serrano considers *herself* the hunter."

"Oh."

"And it is our responsibility, as I see it, to . . . er . . . herd the prey into . . ." Into what? she wondered in midphrase. You herded domestic animals, not hunting prey. She shook her hand, as if it were obvious, and rushed on. "—Or lure them, confuse them—you see my point."

"But this is a defensive action," he said. He didn't sound convinced.

Cecelia gave him another, but less wounding, haughty look. Even aged civilian aunts knew better than that. "Come, Captain Faroe: what does the textbook say about defensive actions?"

He brightened. "Attack on defense . . ."

"Very well. Which makes us—" What *could* she use as an example. If Heris was the main pack, were they terriers? One terrier? Somehow the image of the yacht as a terrier digging into some vermin's hole simply didn't work. Then that ridiculous exhibit of Marcia's came to her. "Cowhorses," she said. He looked blank. Damn the boy, didn't he have any ability to switch metaphors in midstream? "Riding . . ." What was the term now? "Drag," she said. "Or flank, or something like that. We keep the stragglers from getting away." She risked a glance around the bridge and intercepted some dubious expressions from the rest of the crew, expressions quickly wiped to blank respect. That would have to change. She grinned at them all, until she got answering smiles, however weak. "I'm a scatty old woman," she said. "Don't let my gorgeous red hair fool you—I'm a Rejuvenant, and it's all fake. And sometimes I lose the words I want . . . the brain's stuffed too full of too many damn disciplines."

Cesar chuckled aloud. "It's all right, sir. It's just we never heard a spaceship compared to a cowhorse before . . . or the Benignity as cows."

"I spent the last fifty-eight days at bloodstock farms," Cecelia said. "Horses are my passion, and I've spent all that time with other horse fanciers. Came back up with

my head full of bloodlines and genetic analyses, instead
of technical data for ships." As if her head had ever been
full of technical data. But they didn't have to know.

"And you really think Commander Serrano is planning
to do more than just hold them off?" asked Cesar, with a
quick glance around.

"Yes. And so do you." That made Faroe straighten up.

"But Commander Garrivay said—"

"Commander Garrivay's dead. Heris is commanding.
It's a new hunt."

As the hours passed, Cecelia decided that only
inexperience kept Faroe from being a reasonably good
young officer. He kept tripping over his former captain's
negatives: "Captain Garrivay said no one could . . ." this
and "Captain Garrivay said never . . ." that. She had the
impression, from him and the others, that Garrivay had
wanted no more initiative in his officers than it took to
wipe themselves, and he'd have preferred to have them
do that on command. But with Cecelia behind him, Faroe
began to think of some things for himself. He would glance
at her fearfully each time; she discovered that a smile and
nod seemed to increase his intelligence by ten points.
Success breeds confidence; she knew that from riding.
She still wished Heris had sent Petris or Ginese to
command, but she realized that it wouldn't have worked.
The real military—the military she had always avoided,
and especially the military as molded by Garrivay's
command—had its own unbreakable rules, and Heris had
bent them as far as they would go.

And Faroe's judgment, when he actually got up his nerve
to make decisions, was sound. He accepted Sirkin's
expertise, and they made their FTL hop on her mark. The
first switch of beacon IDs went without a hitch, and then
they were tucked in behind Oreson's rings, Sirkin having
managed to drop the extra velocity of the FTL jump in

some clever way that let them crawl into cover with, as Faroe put it, just enough skirt trailing.

"Which satellite has the mining colony?" Cecelia asked.

"That one." Faroe pointed it out. "But they've got nothing useful."

"For now." The image of terriers still danced in her head. "Who knows . . . if we asked them, they might be able to help."

"I'm not sure I have the authority to talk to civilians at a time like this," Faroe said, looking worried again.

"I do," Cecelia said. What that authority was, she wasn't sure, but her instinct said it was time to form a pack.

Aboard the Benignity cruiser *Paganini*

Admiral Straosi glared at his subordinate. "What do you mean, *Zamfir* is out of action? There has been no action."

It could be the Chairman. It could be the Chairman's way of punishing him for that foolish jest in the Boardroom, to make sure a problem ship came along. Easy enough to do. Not easy to handle. He could hardly go back and complain. And he wondered if the Chairman had any other surprises for him.

"A drive problem," the younger man said. He looked nervous, as well he might. "A failure of synchronization in the FTL generator, with resultant surge damage on downshift."

A real problem, although it usually resulted from poor maintenance. In safe situations, the best solution was complete shutdown of both drives, with a cold start of the sublight drive, once the residual magnetics had diminished to a safe level, but that left the ship passive, unable to maneuver at all. Straosi had his doubts, though. He could not verify the problem from here, and he didn't trust the Chairman's great-nephew.

Admiral Straosi was glad to have a target for his temper.

"You are telling me that you did not adequately inspect your ship before starting off on this mission?"

A pause. "Sir, the admiral knows we were assigned to this mission only fourteen hours before launch—"

"The admiral also knows the entire fleet has been on alert—all ships to be ready to depart at one hour's notice. Had you slacked off, Captain?" Of course they had; everyone did, on extended high alert. But now, with the results of that slack endangering his mission, and his own life, he was not about to be lenient.

"Er . . . no, Admiral. It wasn't that, it was just—"

"Just that you somehow failed to notice a problem that any first-year fresh out of school could see . . . Captain. Let me put it this way—" That was ritual introduction of a mortal challenge. "Either you get your ship back into formation, or we leave you. I am not risking this mission for someone too stupid and lazy to do the job for which he was overpaid."

"The Benignity commands." That was the only possible answer. The admiral grunted, and watched the scans. *Zamfir* continued to lag . . . the lag widened. By the estimate of the senior engineer aboard the *Paganini*, the other cruiser's insystem drive had lost thirty percent of its power.

"If the R.S.S. ship was right, their cruiser might be able to take *Zamfir*," an aide murmured.

"If they want to waste their time attacking our stragglers, they have my blessing," the admiral said. "Let them trade salvos with *Zamfir*; Paulo might actually blow them away and regain my respect, and at least they'd be out of our way. Our objective is the Xavier system, to prepare it for the use of the entire fleet. We don't care what happens to *Zamfir*."

"And *Cusp*?" The admiral considered. The little killership now flanking *Zamfir* had been intended as rear guard and as messenger both. Had the damaged cruiser been where it should, *Cusp* would have been the tail of the formation.

"Bring *Cusp* to its normal position," he said. He was almost glad to leave *Zamfir* out there unprotected. Paulo's carelessness was going to cause trouble no matter what happened; he was the Chairman's great-nephew. He was supposed to come out of this a hero. Instead, he had already caused trouble. He stared at the scans, waiting for *Cusp* to close up. Nothing happened; the two ships dropped still farther behind.

"What is his problem?" the admiral asked. Then he remembered. The captain of *Cusp* was Paulo's brother-in-law. They had always been close. Well, fine. Let them both hang back, and maybe the Familias commander would think it was some new tactic, and engage them. Together they should be an easy match for an R.S.S. cruiser. Perhaps this would work out after all. Of course it was bad for discipline . . . but he could rescind the order. "I've changed my mind," he said. "Order *Cusp* to hold position, and engage the enemy at will. We have sufficient margin of superiority; we can afford to test new tactics."

Heris tried to think herself into the enemy's mind. Assuming that Hearne had told the truth as she saw it, the Benignity commander believed there were three hyper-capable ships near Xavier, and an obsolete defense escort with no FTL drive. A cruiser: the most dangerous, commanded by a Serrano, a name they should know. A patrol craft, whose new captain was far enough down the table of officers that he might not even be listed in the CH database—certainly there was no combat command listing for him. And an armed yacht, whose real capabilities Heris had screened from Garrivay's personnel. She had told Hearne that she expected a Benignity attack "in a few days, certainly within ten local days." In other words, the Benignity commander would expect them to be looking for trouble, but not necessarily on full alert yet, particularly not after a hostile takeover of the ships. Hearne would have transmitted her assessment of the situation, but her main concern had been to escape. She certainly hadn't stayed around to answer questions.

On the bridge, four clocks were running countdowns: Koutsoudas's estimate of when the CH ships could get reliable scan on them, Koutsoudas's estimate of when standard Fleet scans would have shown the CH jump point exit, the scan-delay display, and the realtime clock which her own crew would use for its timing of maneuvers and firing.

"She's jumped," Koutsoudas said, pointing at the yacht's icon. "You know, I thought Livadhi would pass out when you jumped her that close to Naverrn. What did you *do* to that hull?"

"Ask me no questions," Heris said. At some level below current processing, she was distantly aware of other gears ticking into alignment. Amazing how all those unauthorized and illegal changes to *Sweet Delight* now made sense, in light of her pretense to have been on undercover assignment. She was going to be really angry if it turned out her aunt admiral had diddled with her memory and she only *thought* she'd been forced to resign.

"I always knew Oblo was a genius," Koutsoudas went on. "Him and Ginese . . . and Kinvinnard . . ."

"And you. Don't be greedy. I envied Livadhi for years."

"It was mutual. Ah—she's back. Her . . . er . . . third incarnation, it is. The one from the Guernesi."

"Speaking of geniuses. I think Oblo would emigrate in a flash if they didn't have such stringent rules on personal weaponry." Heris watched the screen. The old *Grogon* now occupied the approximate volume of space where the yacht had been, and its beacon reported that it was the yacht. Although of different shapes, they had similar mass. Light-hours away, the yacht curved around the largest chunk of rock in this section of the "rockring"—the remains of a small planetoid that had come apart eons before. It still showed on *Vigilance's* scans, but from the angle of the CH flotilla, it should have appeared briefly, as if it had darted out to get a clean scan or tightbeam message, and then gone back into hiding.

Vigilance itself bored out at half the maximum insystem drive acceleration, as if in cautious pursuit of *Despite*.

"We would be cautious, because we would worry if *Despite* had an ally out there, something Garrivay didn't chart. He didn't even drop temporary mines, did he?"

"No, sir." That was her new Weapons First. "He said there was no need to cause a problem for incoming commercial traffic. It would cost too much to clear later."

"And no beacon leeches, either," said Communications. "That's standard, but we just thought he was in a snit to be sent out here away from Third Ward HQ, when all the excitement was going on."

"He didn't want any clever amateurs on Xavier to pick up a warning," Heris said, wondering what excitement that had been. Something else she didn't have time to pursue.

"They might have us," Koutsoudas said, meaning the enemy. "Another hour, and we have to assume they do." The Benignity flotilla, knowing exactly what to look for and where, would see them as soon as the limits of their technology made it possible. The FR vessels could be presumed to divide their attention in more directions. They might not notice the distant flotilla at first if they were looking elsewhere.

"How's our angle?"

"Well . . . it's close, sir. If they believe that we believe *Despite* is leading us straight to them, then we could miss a signal . . . for a while . . . but the normal cone would pick it up as a primary signal.

"And their insertion barrage?"

"There's nothing between us to cause detonations before

we run into it, and the drives should be off by now, realtime."

Time passed. Heris had walked most of the ship by now, letting the crew see her . . . dangerous but necessary. If they were going to fight well, they had to know who commanded them, one of the textbook rules that actually seemed to work in the real world. They were busy; she had told her officers to use whatever training drills they could to get the crew up to peak efficiency. That included rest and food; she herself had left the bridge for a hot meal and a short nap in the captain's quarters, with Ginese keeping watch outside. Now she was back on the bridge, restless as always in the last minutes before action.

"We should be noticing them now," Koutsoudas said. Heris glanced over, and his screen flared as something blew. The enemy icons rippled, their confidence-limit markers spreading out.

"Damn!" Koutsoudas hunched lower. "They blew some of their own barrage screen—they *really* want us to see them."

"The Benignity hates uncertainty," Heris said. "It must have been driving their commander crazy when we didn't seem to notice them."

The *Vigilance*'s screens flicked on at full power, as Heris had planned, and Weapons brought all boards hot. Heris said nothing; she had given the orders hours ago, and so far all was going as planned. They were far enough from Xavier now to jump safely; the cruiser popped in and out, a standard maneuver, slipping back out with a lower relative velocity—*not* a standard maneuver. The low-vee exit on a very short jump meant minimal blurring of scans on exit.

"Got 'em again." Now the scan lag, with Koutsoudas's special black boxes, was less than ten minutes. "Captain, they've brought the heavies with 'em."

"So we expected," said Heris. "Let me see the data." The CH ships had their beacons live; they were not pretending to be anything but what they were, an invading force, and they were in more danger from each other if they went blank. Heris recognized the classes, but not the individual ships, whose names meant little to her. She knew the composer class was usually named for composers—and she knew Paganini—but who was Dylan? Or Zamfir? Not that it mattered. The Benignity cruiser was a third again the mass of *Vigilance*, and thus could mount more weapons. Three cruisers meant impossible odds. Assault carriers held atmospheric shuttles, assault troops for groundside action if needed, and the components for an orbital station that would serve a larger fleet later. Two of these were more than adequate for assault on a planet with Xavier's population and defenses. And the final two ships, much smaller killer-escorts, had the maneuverability the others lacked, along with the firepower of an R.S.S. patrol ship. Which meant Heris's meagre force would have been outgunned even if *Despite* had stayed. Which meant staying was suicidal. The best she could hope to do was delay the invasion long enough for the R.S.S. to defend the jump points exiting this system. So much for "complete confidence" in her decisions.

She could still run. Legally, logically . . . but not as Heris Serrano.

"Those two we thought were lagging are farther behind," Koutsoudas said suddenly. "Not their usual formation."

"A new trick?" Someone across the bridge laughed. The Benignity weren't known for minor innovations like trailing a ship or so from a standard formation. When they changed, they changed radically, usually because new technology provided new opportunities.

"A precaution," Heris murmured. "What class?"

"One cruiser, one killer-escort. The cruiser's really dropping back. It must've come out of FTL with low relative velocity."

"Got to be a feint," Svatek said. "I wish we could eavesdrop."

"Admiral Straosi, the drive continues unstable. If the admiral wishes, it can be confirmed—" Straosi didn't want to hear this.

"What do you want to do about it?"

"We're still losing power. If it drops much more we can't support the weapons—" In other words, they would be slow, unarmed, helpless. Fat sheep in the path of wolves. Admiral Straosi allowed himself a moment of gloating: he hadn't wanted Paulo along, and this whole mess was, ultimately, the fault of the Chairman. But experience suggested that the Chairman would not be the one whose neck felt the noose, whose liver danced on the tip of a blade. At the least, he must conceal his gloating.

"Captain, I apologize for my earlier remarks." That would go on the records. "I am sure you would not have missed such a major problem in your drive. Have you considered sabotage?"

"I—yes, sir, I have."

"There are those who opposed this mission, Captain. I will make sure that no blame accrues to you for your ship's failure to participate in this action . . . and I'm sorry, Captain, but I cannot jeopardize the invasion for your ship alone."

"Of course not, sir." As he'd expected, Paulo didn't want to appear cowardly. Perhaps he wasn't.

"As one man of honor to another, may I suggest that you could do us great service by conserving power for your weaponry, even though that places your ship in greater danger. . . ." It was not a question, and not quite an order. They both would understand. *Zamfir* was doomed, but it might kill a Familias ship with its death.

"It would be my honor, Admiral Straosi. If the Admiral has specific suggestions—"

"I trust your judgment, Captain." And that was that.

Let the boy figure it out for himself, and if he killed that pesky Serrano, Straosi wouldn't mind a bit recommending him for a posthumous medal.

"We'll drop a few buckets of nails on their road," Heris said. She and the weapons crews had already discussed the fusing and arming options. They hadn't nearly the number of mines she really needed, but the more of the enemy, the greater the chance of a hit. She presumed the enemy would see them drop the clusters, and that would provoke some kind of maneuver. "And immediate course change, getting us the vector for jumps two, three, and five."

The trailing pair of enemy ships, cruiser and killer-escort, worried her. Why *were* they hanging back? If the rest of the Benignity formation reacted normally, flaring away from the mines, how would that final pair react? Too much to hope they were back there because they were scan blind or something, and would just sweep on majestically into the mine cluster.

That thought, however unlikely, brought a grin to her face. She had not anticipated how happy she would be, back on the bridge of an R.S.S. cruiser. It was ridiculous, under the circumstances: she had come back only to find herself in a worse tactical mess than any she'd experienced. She had less chance of surviving—let alone winning—this engagement than she had had with the Board of Inquiry. But that didn't sober her. This was where she belonged, and she felt fully alive, fully awake, for the first time since she'd left. Not that she regretted the experience of the past years, but—but this was home.

And *Vigilance* answered her joy with its own. Every hour she could sense the lift in crew morale; they believed in her, they accepted her. From their reactions alone, she learned things about Garrivay that erased the last doubts she'd had. A man might be a traitor to the Familias, and a good leader for his own people, but Garrivay had been a user, someone who abused power.

If they'd had time to prepare, even ten or fifteen days, she'd have had a reasonable chance, she was sure. Now—she didn't even bother to calculate it. Either luck—and whatever training Garrivay had done—would be with them, or it wouldn't. She intended to give luck all the help she could. While she wouldn't mind dying in action, it wasn't fair to the people of Xavier.

Space combat had a leisurely, surreal phase in which nothing seemed to happen . . . weapons had been launched, to find targets or not minutes to hours hence, and the enemy's weapons were on their way, with scan trying desperately to find and track them before maneuvering. No one used LOS, line-of-sight weapons, at this distance, despite their lightspeed advantage; what the best scans "saw" was far behind the enemy's location.

"They're starring," Koutsoudas said. "Avoiding our mines." That was the usual Benignity move; she'd expected it.

"Jump two," Heris said. She had laid out a series of microjumps, options ready to take depending on the enemy's reaction to the mines. This had been the most likely, the starburst dispersal . . . if she had kept on course, she'd have gone down the throat of the bell they made: easy meat. Instead, the course change and microjump popped them out—

"Targeting—" said Weapons First. "On target."

"Engage." —Popped them out in position to fire their forward LOS weapons at the flank of the massive assault carrier they'd chosen, as it clawed its way into a shallow curve away from its former course. Four light-seconds away, an easy solution for the computers. A roar punctuated with crashes burst from the speakers.

"Turn that down!" Heris had never quite believed the

theory that said humans needed to hear the fights they got into. Ground combat had been so noisy it drove men insane—so why had psychologists insisted on programming fake noises for combat in space? "Keep it below ten," she said. It couldn't be turned off completely, but it didn't have to rupture eardrums.

"Sir."

She had had a captain once who had reprogrammed the sounds to be musical . . . he had had other, stranger, hobbies, which eventually led to early retirement, but she had never quite forgotten the ascending major and minor scales he had chosen for outbound LOS weapons. If they hit their targets, the system then chimed the appropriate chord. It had enabled everyone, even the doubting Jig she had been then, to tell whether it was the port (major) or starboard (minor) weapons firing, and from which end of the ship. Forward batteries sounded like flutes, and the aft ones like bassoons, with the intermediate woodwinds ranged down the sides. She'd never attempted anything like it on her own ship.

"Jump six, then eight." On their new vector, a microjump that put them safely away from the probable response of the Benignity's cruisers. If she guessed right. Another immediate microjump following, that brought them out at an angle to another part of the starburst. Another quick targeting solution, another burst with LOS, then back into jumpspace, this time long enough to open a twenty-minute gap, while Koutsoudas and the other scan techs reran the scans of the targeting runs.

The first run confirmed the starburst, and the mass classes of the vessels involved. Seven of them, three heavy cruisers carrying half-again *Vigilance*'s weaponry, two assault carriers massing three times the cruisers, and two killer-escorts. One cruiser and one killer-escort lagging well behind. The second run scans confirmed a hit on the assault carrier, partly buffered by its screens.

"They do have good screen technology," Heris said, scowling at the scan data. They had hit with both of the cruiser's forward LOS, but one ablated against the screens. The second had penetrated, but hadn't breached the ship . . . the screens appeared to be weakened, perhaps down, and the infrared showed substantial heat, but no atmosphere.

The enemy's starburst had modified after the attack, with one side of the starburst rolling over—but slowly, with those massive ships—to regroup along the axis of the original attack. Also quite visible on the second scan was the trace of weapons that had narrowly missed *Vigilance* when she jumped after the attack.

"Damn good shooting," Ginese commented. "From one of the cruisers—their command cruiser probably. We weren't onscan a total of eight seconds, and they nearly got us. It would have been glancing, and the shields would have held, but . . . whoever it is over there is sharp."

"How long did it take us to get our shots off?"

"Six seconds." Long. On her old ship, they had drilled until they could pop out of a microjump and fire within four. No wonder they were almost fried.

"We'll do better," she said, with a confidence she didn't feel. She couldn't move her old crew into every critical position—she hadn't enough of them, and besides, she needed to get this crew working. In a long fight—and she had to hope this would be a long fight—shift after shift would have to fight with peak efficiency.

From twenty light-minutes away, she could not follow the *Paradox*'s attack in realtime, even though Koutsoudas bought her a little advantage with his boosted scans. Tinsi, having the advantage of the postscans of her own attack, had chosen to have another run at the possibly wounded assault carrier. But he took ten seconds to come out of jumpspace, locate his target, and shoot. The assault cruiser's shields failed, but he himself was under attack, and he scorched the Benignity ship without breaching it. He jumped just in time, and Heris wondered if he would follow up his attack or simply microjump his way to a safe jump point.

She had not been sure he would attack at all; he had reported having two serious fights aboard after taking command. Although he had seemed slow, even stupid, when she first talked to him, clearly he had plenty of command ability. His ship not only obeyed orders, but had survived a live engagement.

In any case, it was time for *Vigilance* to re-enter the fray. Another pair of microjumps brought them in behind the laggards. This time Heris chose ballistic weapons, half of them heat-targeting, and the other half fitted with the "kill me, target you" guidance systems that converted scrambling countermeasures into secondary guidance. They might hit the trailing pair; even if they missed, their overrun might bring them up on the other CH ships. *Vigilance* launched all its weapons within six seconds, and was safely back into microjump without being touched.

"There's *Paradox*," said Koutsoudas, as soon as they'd jumped back again; he was replaying the scan of their attack. The patrol ship had come across the bottom of the CH formation, this time firing within three seconds of their jump exit. CH response didn't come close.

"Of course, they'll start microjumping soon," Heris said. "They're going to be highly peeved with us." She glanced at the clocks. "Take us over to Blueyes now." Blueyes was the second largest gas giant in the system, with its own set of rings and satellites to hide in. It was a considerable distance away, but if she could lure them into pursuing her over there, all the better for Xavier. The jump lasted just long enough for Koutsoudas to switch the beacon ID— the ship that went into jump at point A was not, apparently, the same one that emerged from jump at B.

Redlining the insystem drive to get a tight swing around

the gas giant—and then out on a new vector, a longish run on insystem drive to let the enemy get a good look at them while their own scans scooped data.

The CH ships had regrouped, snugging in again and boosting toward Xavier itself. All but the laggards . . . which had vanished, leaving behind roiled traces that indicated either badly tuned microjumps or explosions.

"A lot of infrared," Koutsoudas said. "Lots and lots of infrared, and interesting spectra—not quite what I'd expect if they blew, but definitely not normal jump insertion."

The scans looked messier, cluttered with the probable courses of ballistic weapons that had not hit their targets and the extended lines of LOS weapons. As dangerous as enemy fire, in an extended battle, were the hundreds of armed missiles heading off in all directions. As the ships maneuvered, especially with microjumps, they could find themselves in the midst of these hazards, being blown away by their own or enemy weapons. Long microjumps even offered the possibility for inept commanders to shoot themselves down with their own LOS beams.

"If they've got a new way of foxing our scans, that might explain why they were hanging back," Heris said.

"Dammit," Ginese said, watching the main clump continue steadily towards Xavier, "you'd think they'd have the guts to chase us—"

"Too smart," Heris said. "They know we're outgunned. Well, no one said this would be easy. Is that another one lagging?" The icon indicated that it was the other killer-escort.

"They've slowed," Koutsoudas said. "Gives them more maneuverability."

"And more options for microjumps," Heris said. "Wait—I see only four now."

"Their killership is missing . . . no . . . there it is, sneaking over to—oh, shit."

Over to the yacht's hiding place, and it would be coming

in on their blind side. Its commander probably didn't know the yacht was there, Heris thought. He hoped to conceal his ship in the rings, to catch them on the flank. But instead of ambushing a fox, he was going to scare a rabbit out of the brush.

It was already too late to help; their scan data's lag meant that whatever was going to happen, had. Heris said nothing, waiting for the disaster she expected.

When the flare came, it wasn't the yacht.

"They laid their own mines," Ginese said, in a tone that matched her own surprise. "*Faroe* thought of that—"

"Kill," Koutsoudas said, unnecessarily. That size flare had to be a kill, and the spectra matched the reference patterns. "Detonated their onboard stuff—I hope the yacht wasn't too close."

Heris felt a little jolt of satisfaction. She had picked the right junior officer to captain the yacht after all—and whatever effect Lady Cecelia had had on him, he'd managed to kill a bigger, more powerful ship. And the enemy's advantage was eroding . . . from seven ships, any of them a match for hers, the Benignity commander was down to four, one with severely damaged shields.

Assuming the two that had vanished weren't hiding cleverly somewhere. Instinct told her no, that they had either been destroyed, or had fled, damaged, into FTL. Not smart. Ships that entered FTL with major damage rarely emerged on the other end.

If only she'd been able to lay a proper array of mines around Xavier, she'd have a chance to win outright, with all her own ships intact. The sparse ring the shuttles had spread in equatorial orbit would only annoy the ships— might injure the assault carrier whose shields were down, but no more.

Still, they'd done better than she'd expected. In the long hours that remained of the inward traverse, they would have several more chances for the quick, darting attacks that gave her ships the best chance. Especially since the CH formation no longer had killerships to duel with them.

"We can't let them alone long enough to repair their shields," she said. "I want to change shifts now—" Two standard hours early. "We need the freshest reflexes we have." She herself had been up and running too long. She didn't even want to think how long it had been since she assembled the small group that had taken over the *Vigilance*. "I'm taking four hours, myself. You have your orders, Svatek."

✧ Chapter Seventeen

When Heris woke, she saw that the CH group had not wavered from its course; they had drawn back into a tight cluster where shields could reinforce each other, with the damaged assault carrier in the middle, and they could shrug off the fast, brief attacks. *Paradox* had missed sixty percent of its shots; Heris sent them a tightbeam ordering them to jump a safe distance away and rest for six hours. Faroe, on the yacht, offered to come help harry the enemy. Heris decided against it; the yacht's weak shields and relatively light armament meant that it could be little help, but easy prey. If it bumped into any of the stray weapons now cluttering the scene, it would have no chance. Instead, the yacht could flit in microjumps, reappearing with different beacon IDs, distracting the CH crews from the real attacks, tempting them to waste shots on it. That was dangerous enough. And, in the end, the yacht should run as fast as possible to spill its scan records at the nearest Fleet base. She warned Faroe that one or more nearby jump points might be mined.

For the next six hours, Heris sent *Vigilance* in and out of FTL, harrying the CH group. With every run, the mess on scan worsened, until it was almost impossible to find a safe place to shoot from. Although her ship escaped damage, it inflicted nothing beyond temporary ablation of the enemy shields, and the CH group did not maneuver at all in response to the attacks. Typical of the CH approach: they expected to bull their way through to their goal. If she'd had their mass and firepower, she'd have done the same.

✧   ✧   ✧

"Return no more fire," Admiral Straosi said. "They're trying to make us waste it—"

"We have plenty," one of his subordinates said.

"If that traitor told the truth, and there are no more Familias ships to fight. We cannot count on that." He admired the discipline of the enemy ships; they had wasted little of their capacity. Even the misses were close enough to give everyone a scare. His crews were exhausted; they were not used to such sustained fighting, and the loss of *Zamfir* and *Cusp* had shaken them. And then *Snare* . . . he still had no idea what had happened to *Snare*. It could have been as simple as miscalculating the location of ring components, but if that tiny little ship—yacht, the traitor had called it—was capable of blowing a killer-escort, then he had to be wary of it. At least he had not been fooled by the beacon changes, after the first few times.

"If we don't return fire, they'll just come in closer and closer until our shields fail."

"To come that close, they'll have to be in realspace longer. *Then* we return fire." Then we blow them away, he thought with satisfaction. "They are gnats . . . mosquitoes . . . annoying, but not really dangerous. When they get greedy and sit still, we swat them." They were dangerous, and he knew it, but even so he had no other options. Xavier was his target; he could not waste time chasing a Serrano around the system.

He did hope that Serrano hadn't managed to find a way to lay mine-drifts out here somewhere. Or around that miserable planet.

"So—do we close in now?" asked Svatek after they'd made two attack runs with no return fire.

"No." Heris munched on a sandwich. "He's just conserving his weapons—he's not helpless. He must wonder if we've got more ships coming."

"If only *Despite*—" Heris shook her head at him, and he said no more. They had all debated the chance that *Despite*'s crew might mutiny and come back to help them—assuming that most of the crew, like the crews of *Vigilance* and *Paradox*, were loyal. But the hours had passed, with no sign of return.

"If our packet made it out, someone should be getting a poke about now," Heris said. "That still means hours—more likely days—before other ships could arrive." If some traitor at the other end didn't suppress it. If a battle group or wave was ready to set off when the message arrived. She wondered again about her aunt. How much had she guessed of the enemy's intention? Was there a worse problem somewhere else, that she committed so little resources to this likely target?

"At best—we have to hold them off the planet for—"

"Hours and hours," Heris said. "Forever, basically. We don't know how far behind this group their main invasion force is." Far behind, she hoped. Benignity policy usually required an attack force to report back before the supporting force arrived.

They continued their darting attacks, run after run, as much to keep the Benignity crews tired as anything else. And the enemy closed on Xavier, braking in perfect formation.

Xavier Station died in a burst of coherent radiation that fried its way through the station and on into the planet's atmosphere, where its degrading beam wreaked havoc on communications and finally on the surface. The station reactors, as they blew, sent pulses of EMC that destroyed surface-based computers. "I wonder how many were left aboard." Heris glanced at the speaker, one of the enlisted working the engineering boards.

"Supposedly they were all evacuated," she said. "I hope the General Secretary got people into shelters downside. With any luck, everyone was off the station. . . ." But she knew a few wouldn't have been—the last shuttles had been overloaded, according to Cecelia, with near riots as they left.

But planets are large, and spaceships, however large, are small in comparison. It takes time to scorch a planet so that it can be garrisoned shortly afterward—easier to flame it, but that makes it hard to install the kind of military base the Benignity was planning. Heris had counted on that, on their need to be careful, precise. Now that it was five to three—the injured assault carrier's weapons weren't functioning, and the weapons it carried for installation would be stowed away—she might just pull it off.

The CH ships took up equatorial orbits, spacing themselves around the planet where their scans and weapons could reach the entire surface, the two cruisers higher and the two assault carriers slightly lower. The assault carriers would soon crack their bays and start disgorging drop shuttles and equipment drones. The damaged one wouldn't even wait for the cruisers to turn the attacks.

"Damn—I thought we made it clear where to lay the mines," Ginese said, when the data on the orbits sharpened. "Those assault carriers are low enough—or almost—"

"Maybe they went for the lowest orbits—to catch the drop shuttles on the way down. They don't have diddly for shielding—"

"Mmm. And they don't have to stick to equatorial transits, either. Idiots. If they'd done what we told them—"

"Captain, there's a big ship behind us—"

"*Behind* us?" An icy breath ran down her spine.

"It's—it's that ore carrier." Miners. They'd had a big hull, she remembered.

"Weapons?"

"Nothing." It seemed to wallow, even on the screens, a huge hull massing considerably more than anything but the assault carriers. Neither weapons nor screens colored its display.

"What—do they think they're doing?" Heris asked the silence.

"Helping us?"

"With no weapons? Ha. At least, if it has no weapons, it can't shoot us." What had made the miners think they could fight with a bare hull, however large? And why now? Heris forced herself to ignore that enigma and went back to the battle at hand.

So far they'd been lucky. The destruction of the killer-escorts had removed the only enemy hulls that could match them in maneuvering at speed. Now, if they were to save Xavier's population, she had to bring her ships out of hiding and engage in a slugfest. Not her kind of fight, but she saw no alternative. At least, the CH ships were also limited in their options, committed to orbital positions and unable to combine their fire as effectively.

With near-perfect precision, *Vigilance* and *Paradox* exited from microjumps in the positions Heris had selected: within a tenth of a light-second of their targets. Heris had chosen to take on one of the CH cruisers; *Paradox* would hit the weakened assault carrier; and Faroe, on the yacht, would seem to be a new menace to the other cruiser.

The computers fired before even Koutsoudas could have reacted. By the time the scans had steadied, they picked up the results of that salvo, even as Heris emptied another into the nearest cruiser, and sent a raft of ballistics at the ships to either side of her. Her target had suffered shield damage, and the hull flared, hot but unbroken.

"Ouch," said Petris, as their own shields shimmered and the status lights went yellow. The cruiser had returned fire before their second salvo, and now poured a stream of LOS and ballistics both at them. Shield saturation rose steadily, then levelled off. Their scans wavered, unable to see through the blinding fury outside even at close range.

"Faroe fired something," Koutsoudas said. "I can't see if it hit—and he's jumped again." That was good news.

"Both flanks engaged," said Ginese. One of those was the undamaged assault carrier, now clawing its way up from its lower orbit.

Then one entire board turned red, and the alarms snarled. "Portside aft, the missile—" CRUMP. A blow she felt from heel to head, as *Vigilance* bucked to the explosion of her own missile battery. Before Heris could say anything, Helm rolled *Vigilance* on its long axis, so that unbreached shields faced the cruiser that had raked them.

"Good job, Major," Heris said. Around her, she heard the proper responses, as medical, engineering, damage control, environmental, all answered the alarms. Her concern was that damaged flank, now turned to the less-armed but still dangerous assault carrier.

She kept her eye on Weapons, but her crew needed no prodding; they were throwing everything they had at the enemy. The weapons boards shifted color constantly, as discharge and recharge alternated in the LOS circuits, as crews below reloaded missile tubes.

"Captain—portside battery's breached—casualties—" So it was as bad as that.

"Compartment reports!" That was Milcini, doing much better than she'd expected.

The reports matched the displays Heris could see. Several LOS beams at once had degraded their shields, and then fried a hole in the hull and the warheads of missiles in storage. These had blown, ripping a larger hole in their flank. Lost with it were a third of the portside maneuvering pods. Lost, too, were the crews of the batteries on either side of the storage compartment, and a still uncertain number of casualties in neighboring compartments.

Only Koutsoudas's boosted scan still penetrated their own screens and the maelstrom of debris and weaponry beyond them. He hunched over his board, transferring position and ship ID data to Weapons, shunting other data to other stations. He stiffened.

"We got the *Dylan*," Koutsoudas said. Its trace on his screen fuzzed, then split into many smaller ones; its icon changed from red to gray. "There's the reactor, that hot bit there." That hot bit, which would, on its present trajectory, fry in the atmosphere on its way down, shedding a spray of active isotopes. Couldn't be helped, and the nukes already launched were worse. Their scans blurred completely, as the last burst of *Dylan*'s attack hit their shields. Lights dimmed; the blowers changed speed. Then the lights came back up.

"Shields held," someone said, unnecessarily.

The scans cleared slowly. Heris ignored them for the moment to look at the inboard status screens. The breach hadn't progressed, and hadn't compromised major systems. The lockoffs held, and would if not damaged further. Slowly, from the spacesuited medics and repair crew working their way aft, Heris learned more. The hole in the hull couldn't be repaired now—perhaps not at all—but somehow some of the stored missiles had *not* exploded. The force of the explosion had gone outward through the hull breach, and the heat flash in the compartment hadn't been enough to overcome the failsafes on those racked inboard. Some had broken loose, and were probably, the petty chief said, out there ready to blow up if the CH would only be so kind as to hit them. Thirty-eight were still racked, and—if they could get airlocks rigged to the nearest cross-corridor—could be transferred to the surviving batteries.

Engineering reported that the ablated shields could be reset when they'd rerouted some damaged cable. Fifteen to twenty minutes . . . if they had fifteen minutes. Heris forbore to hurry them; it would take as long as it took. She checked again with sickbay: most of the casualties were dead, as expected, but there were eighteen listed as serious, and another five as moderate, out of duty for at least twenty-four hours.

Three to two now. If her two ships had been undamaged,

if they had had plenty of weapons left—but *Paradox*, though undamaged, had run out of missiles, and its LOS beams were discharged. In another five or six hours—hours they didn't have—it could support her with beam weapons. Now, though—an undamaged cruiser a third again the size of hers stalked her. Encumbered as it was with a crippled assault carrier it must shelter, how would it choose to fight? The other assault carrier still had more firepower than *Vigilance*, but it was far less maneuverable.

"There's something jumping in," Koutsoudas reported. "Something big—lots—DAMN!"

Heris said nothing. She couldn't help whatever it was, and snapping at 'Steban wouldn't get her the data any faster.

"And skip-jumping. They know exactly what they're coming into." Which meant the Benignity, probably. She had small hope that her own message, sent on the station's equipment, had gotten through.

"It's *Despite*," Koutsoudas said. He didn't sound as if he believed it. Heris certainly didn't. Hearne changed her mind? Hearne led the Benignity fleet in herself? With Hearne, it could be either. Koutsoudas leaned over his screen as if that would help. "The distant ones—it'll be hours before I can get an ID, unless they skip their way into closer range."

"And here's the other cruiser," said another scan tech. "*Paganini*, their admiral's flagship."

"Well," said Heris, "I suppose it's time to face that music." A moment of blank silence, then a groan from half the bridge crew; she grinned at them.

Benignity cruiser *Paganini*

"That patrol craft has quit attacking," the captain pointed out. Admiral Straosi grunted. That patrol craft had almost hulled an assault carrier by itself, and that should not have been possible. If only the damn things weren't so maneuverable.

"What about the others?"

"There's a big cargo vessel moving very slowly in from the gas giant—it could even be an ore-hauler with no communications capacity, possibly unmanned. It's no threat. The cruiser's damaged; *Dylan* and *Augustus* have it bracketed and it won't last long—"

"Sir—" A scan tech, his face paper white. "It's *Dylan*—it's gone!"

"Nonsense."

"It is—and that damnable Serrano is still there."

Straosi's blood seemed to take fire. The bitch had ruined his attack, and his career. The Benignity would have not only his neck, but his family's fortune. "Enough!" he roared. "First we kill that patrol—we show her! Then her. All ships—" The assault carriers could keep her busy while he blew the patrol ship, and then—then all three of them would blast that stupid, stubborn woman right out of this world.

R.S.S. patrol craft *Despite*

Jig Esmay Suiza had survived the battle for control of *Despite*, and after Major Dovir finally died, she ranked all the others—the small band of ensigns and junior lieutenants who had been the nucleus of the loyalists. Now she faced the grizzled, balding senior NCO, Master Chief Vesec, who had just called her "Captain" and asked for orders.

She managed not to say, "Me?" and instead said, "Dovir's dead, then?"

"Yes, Captain Suiza." There had been a time when she dreamed of hearing that . . . of coming aboard her first command, of being congratulated. Now she stared back, her mind foggy with fatigue. Vesec stood in front of her, a stocky man her father's age, with her father's air of impatience with youthful indecision. She was captain. She had to know what to do. She wanted to burst into tears. She didn't.

"Position?" she heard herself ask, in a voice steadier than it had been five minutes before.

"Three minutes from FTL exit through jump point Balrog." That didn't give her much time.

"Balrog has a Fleet relay," she said.

"Yes, sir. Also there's usually a manned station." A wave of relief washed over her. Help. Someone senior who would tell her what to do.

"We'll drop a packet," she said.

"If the captain permits—" he said.

"Yes?"

"It might be wise to take precautions. Sometimes when the Benignity attacks, they've mined nearby jump points."

She hadn't thought of that. She hadn't known about that. "And what would Captain—what's a good way of being careful?" Graceless, but the sense got across. He rewarded her with a careful smile.

"Low relative vee insertion. Shields hot as we come out. Wait for scans to recover."

"Very well," she said. "Then make it so."

"Yes, sir." A ghost of a twinkle as he turned away. She saw covert glances from others on the bridge. Peli, only six months junior, who had proved more than once he was better at things than she was. He stared at her, then his lips moved. She read them easily. Oh—yes. The captain's formal announcement of command. She moved over to the command position and picked up the command wand Dovir had given her after he was shot. She couldn't sit— the command chair still stank of blood and guts—and she had to lean down to insert it in the slot.

"Attention all posts." They had had to memorize this, back in the Academy, and she remembered saying it to the mirror, to her roomies, to the shower wall. "This is Lieutenant Junior Grade Esmay Suiza, assuming command of the patrol craft *Despite*, upon the deaths of all officers senior in the chain of command." She had never commanded anything bigger than a training shuttle, and now—she wouldn't think of it. The computer requested her serial number; she gave it automatically. Then it was over, and she was formally and finally in command. Her vision wavered.

Peli came closer. "Captain," he said formally. The challenge she usually saw in his eyes was missing. "Captain, we're not going back, are we?"

"Back?" She hadn't thought that far; it had been Dovir's decision to run for help, to call in Fleet. Now it was hers; she shook her head. "We're coming out of jump to make our report, Peli. What we do next depends on what we find."

Jump exit brought a ripple of light to the blanked scan screens. Gradually, the ripples steadied, and became points of light, icons tagged with ID numbers, colored lines defining traffic lanes in the Balrog system. Debris sparkled in a ragged shell around the jump point.

"Debris," Master Chief Vesec confirmed her guess. "One thing about it, whoever got blown took most of the mines with him." Esmay felt cold. That could have been their ship, coming out of jump with high vee, fleeing trouble.

"The Fleet picket?" she asked. None of the icons showed a Fleet ID; she could see that for herself. All were far away, days or weeks of travel at normal insystem velocities, and all were civilian.

"We'll hope not," Vesec said.

"Launch that packet," Esmay said, as steadily as she could. "Estimate time to a Fleet node with live pickup."

"Three or four days, sir." Add to that the response time, and it meant that those two ships back at Xavier would be sparkling debris in someone else's scan by the time help arrived. The juniors had discussed that, in the hours before someone appeared to offer them a place in the mutiny.

She didn't want to go back. She had no combat experience. She knew nothing about commanding this size ship on a routine voyage, let alone in combat. She could get them all killed without helping Serrano at all. The smart thing to do was go on, take the jump sequences as fast as possible, back to the central zones, and find an admiral with a battle group ready to go.

She had been a very green ensign, shy, afraid that everyone could see through her shiny insignia and new uniform to the fear—and she had stumbled and dropped her duffel right at the feet of a couple of senior officers waiting to enter the lift. One of them had laughed, and said, "They get younger every year." The other had picked up her scattered datacubes, and said, "Ah—your specialty's scan technology? Good—we've got an excellent Chief. You'll like him."

She had never forgotten that face. She had gotten in a disgraceful (so her commander said) fight with another Jig when Heris Serrano left the Fleet, defending her. And she had seen that face again, trying to talk Hearne into turning around . . . Dovir had played the tape for any doubters among the mutineers.

"We're going back," she said. Vesec looked startled, but didn't argue. "I want the fastest possible transit back into Xavier. They can't wait." She still didn't want to go back, any more than she'd wanted to be part of a mutiny, to have Dovir's blood and organs splashed into her face, to have this command. But it was her ship now, and she would do what she had to.

"Prepare for battle," she said, when they were back in jumpspace. No one argued. No one bothered her at all. She still had no idea how she was going to fight, but she would.

Aboard the R.S.S. *Vigilance*

"They're after *Paradox*," Koutsoudas said.

"And she's out of darts," Heris said. "Dammit, Tinsi, get her out of there!" But the patrol ship was too close to the planet to risk jump, and at these distances its maneuvering advantage disappeared. Scan showed acceleration, but the need to keep the screens on full combat strength held it well below maximum. Then the rising curve took *Paradox* out of their line of sight, behind the planet. She would have to go closer to *Paganini* before she could pull away. If she could.

Vigilance couldn't help. Their flank screens were still down, though the engineers kept saying, "Just another minute or two," and the damaged assault carrier lobbed enough missiles at them to keep them busy, shifting so that those which broke through met solid shields.

"It's not Hearne, on *Despite*," Koutsoudas said a few minutes later. "Someone named Suiza."

A moment later, someone said, "By the crew list, that's a Jig. What'd they have, a mutiny?"

"Must have." Heris had other things to worry about than who had killed whom on *Despite*. "But why are they here *now*?"

"They're coming almighty fast," Koutsoudas said. Their scan icon had the bright blue edge meaning a relative vee in major fractions of lightspeed. "Came out fast, and haven't slowed. Their scans will be useless."

"They're running on maps," Heris said. "Can they slow that thing by Xavier, or are they going to blow by?"

"Wait—there it is—they are braking—by timelag, that's two hours back—" The scan fragmented, as the incoming ship's relativistic motion skewed all the data. When it steadied again, *Despite* was only hours away. Now the audio broke up, until finally Heris could hear a very young voice announcing their arrival.

"Regular Space Service patrol craft *Despite*, Esmay Suiza commanding . . . in advance of a Familias Regnant force—" She probably hoped that would scare off the Benignity ships; Heris knew it wouldn't. They had lost too much; they would fight to the death now, having no alternative.

"At least her weapons are hot," Ginese said, as the newcomer lit up the scan screens like fireworks.

"No Jig can fight an admiral of the Compassionate Hand on his own flagship," Oblo said. "He's no fool. . . ."

Despite had arrived with too much relative velocity, and now she swung wide of Xavier, still trying to brake. "Fire now!" Ginese pleaded. "Dammit—microjump into position—do something—" But *Despite* rolled on.

A moment later, just as *Paradox* came back into line of sight, clawing its way up, its shields flared.

"Damn," Heris said. "He's going to lose them—" Now they could see the enemy cruiser, in the textbook position for killing smaller, faster ships. Its greater firepower had full weight now; the shields flared again and again, each time a little more. Heris wanted to close her eyes, but forced herself to watch. Toward the end, Tinsi must have realized his position was hopeless. Suddenly *Paradox* accelerated, full power—

"He cut the shields," breathed Ginese. "He's going to ram—"

"He's too far away." Koutsoudas was right; the Benignity commander hadn't let *Paradox* get close enough for that. Instead, a final round of fire poured into the unprotected ship, and *Paradox* blew. The enemy cruiser's shields sparkled briefly as it fended off debris. One thousand, eight hundred, twenty-three, Heris thought . . . no one was going to survive that blast.

"Well." Koutsoudas looked up a moment, and rubbed his eyes. "Dammit—if that idiot on *Despite* had done something—anything—to distract that admiral . . ."

"Later," Heris said. If they had a later. Even with *Despite*, the odds were no better than before, and she could not count on an inexperienced captain. Three to one, she faced—and here came the cruiser, and the other assault carrier.

"Shields are up," said an engineering rating.

"Good," said Heris. It didn't make that much difference. They'd lost over half their remaining missiles; they were outgunned and too close to the planet to go into jump. But shields would help—at least delay the end.

The end came first to one of the assault carriers, the one with damaged shields. Heris, concentrating on the enemy cruiser, had no idea why the carrier suddenly burst and spewed its load of vehicles and personnel and heavy equipment into space. No one did, until afterward, when the sole survivor of the shuttle that had used its phase cannon told them. At the time, she assumed that *Despite* had gotten off a lucky shot.

The captain of the other assault carrier reacted by taking his ship down—trying to cut beneath *Vigilance* and perhaps also release his load. He paid for this mistake when he hit a drift of mines so crudely made that they neither showed on his sensors nor responded to countermeasures intended to make mines blow prematurely. Individually, or clustered at any distance, they could not have damaged the ship, but enough of them in direct contact, lodged in the many crevices a deep-space ship offered, blew a sizeable hole in the hull. The carrier immediately launched its drop shuttles, only to have most of them blown by other orbiting mines on the way down.

Heris had no leisure to enjoy his plight, for the remaining cruiser attacked with all its force. *Vigilance* faced the same problems as *Paradox*; its shields bled power from the drive, and kept them from using their superior speed and maneuverability. Through the maelstrom that combat made of their scans, no one could find *Despite*.

"If she'd only come up his rear," Ginese said. "She couldn't blow him, but she could distract him—take a little of the heat off us—"

Then the *Paganini* blew, a burst of debris and radiation that completely blanked their screens. "Ouch," said Koutsoudas. Heris said nothing. She didn't quite believe it. She would have pinched herself if a dozen people hadn't been staring at her, their faces full of her own disbelief.

When the scans cleared at last, *Despite* hung steady, a light-second away, with a very nervous-looking young Jig on a tightbeam link to *Vigilance*.

The extra signals Koutsoudas had noted when *Despite* first blew into the system belonged to Regular Space Service ships: cruisers, patrols, escorts, battle platforms, and the supply and service ships needed to keep them going—tankers, minelayers, minesweepers, troop carriers.

"The question is," Heris said, "whether they're with us or against us." She felt drained; what she saw in the faces of her crew was the same exhaustion. "Considering the last multiple arrivals—"

"More likely they're answering your signals." Koutsoudas fiddled with his scans, and grunted as if surprised. "Well, Captain—it's family, whether that pleases you or not. That's the *Harrier*, Admiral Vida Serrano's flagship. Signalling admiral aboard, too."

"At us, or in general?"

"In general. They won't have us on scan yet." Even after so long, even with exhaustion dragging the flesh below his eyes into dark pockets, he still had that smug tone about his scans. And deserved to.

"Fine," Heris said. "Then continue our present broadcast, and I want this shift bridge crew to go down for six hours."

"We're as rested as the others," Ginese protested.

"Which is not rested at all. I want my mainshift crew rested first, then the others in rotation. Tabs for all. Oh—and add a timetag to that broadcast, with the end-of-battle-all-secured code. That way they won't have conniptions if they come roaring in and find out I'm asleep." They would anyway, but she would tell the next shift to wake her, once she'd gotten this gaggle off to their racks.

The second shift, called back, looked no worse than the

ones they relieved. Heris waited to be sure the young major understood what to do, then headed for her quarters. She had to be awake and alert for the coming confrontation with her aunt. She remembered to put in a call to *Despite*, telling them to get some rest, then fell into dreamless sleep.

She woke feeling entirely too rested, and a glance at the chronometer told her why. Nine solid hours? She would rip the hide off someone, just as soon as she quit yawning. A shower woke her the rest of the way and she came back into the compartment wishing she had a clean uniform. The one she had worn for days looked almost as bad as it smelled.

In that brief interval, someone had made her bunk. Someone had also laid out a clean uniform. She could see where other insignia had been hastily removed, and the right number of rings sewn on. She tried it on; although it was a bit loose and slightly longer than she preferred, it would do. As she fastened the collar, the com chimed. She grinned. Of course they knew.

"Yes?"

"Captain, if that uniform fits, we can have a complete set ready in a few hours." She didn't recognize the voice; it wasn't any of her former crew.

"Thank you," she said. "It's fine. Whom may I thank for the loan of it?"

"Lieutenant Harrell is pleased to be of service, sir."

"I'm most grateful," Heris said. She noted the name on her personal pad, and headed for the bridge. The familiar uniform felt so comforting—it was going to be hard to take strips off a crew that took such good care of her.

The bridge officer, Milcini again, looked guilty when she glared at him. "He said to let you sleep," he said. "I thought it was your orders, sir."

"He who?" Heris asked.

"Me, sir." Major Svatek, bleary-eyed and haggard. "I

know what you said, but we haven't had any urgent messages, and the incoming group hasn't changed course. It's continuing to decelerate. The senior surgeon recommended that all shifts take a full eight hours—"

"You haven't," Heris pointed out. "Does this mean second shift's just going off?"

"No, sir. If the captain recalls, second and third had been on a four-hour rollover standby, while first was on that last long watch. First went out, and after four hours I sent second down, and brought in third. First had eight hours off, six in full assisted sleep; second's been down for five hours, and third's just gone down. In another three hours, second will have had its eight hours, and by the time they're off—"

"Makes sense," Heris said. It wasn't what she'd ordered, but it was what she would have ordered if she'd been thinking clearly. "Good decision. Now—why are *you* still on the bridge?"

He grinned. "Because, Captain, I'm the one whose neck you could wring if you wanted to."

"Better decision." She had to admire that. "Now—take yourself off to bed and don't come back until you've slept it out. At least eight hours. And this time, obey orders." She put no sting in that last.

"Yes, sir." A pause, then, "If I could make a suggestion, Captain?"

"Of course."

"The galleys are back in operation. I'm sure they'd be glad to send something up."

Heris felt her mouth curling into a grin. "What are you, my medical advisor? No—never mind—you're right. I presume first shift ate on the way up?"

"Yes, sir."

"Good. Go on now—don't hover." He smiled and left the bridge. Heris looked around, checking each position. Everything seemed normal, as normal as it could be with a hole in the side of the ship and a civilian very illegally in command of it. She checked the status of the casualties in sickbay, the progress of repairs, and realized that Svatek was right. She needed food.

"I'm going to my office," she said to Milcini. "You have the bridge."

◇ Chapter Eighteen

In her office, she looked around a moment. She had hardly seen it since it had been Garrivay's, since she had killed him. Nothing showed in its surfaces, no stains on the rug, no scrapes on the furniture. She sent for a meal—anything hot—and began working through the message stack. *Despite* reported some garbled transmissions from the planet's surface. They had also carried out the orbital damage survey. The Benignity commander, intending to put down his own troops, had used less toxic weapons than he might have. Although the two small cities had been flattened, and wildfires burned across the grasslands and forests near them, the rest of the planet wasn't damaged. It would remain liveable. Heris thought of the pretty little city she had ridden through, with its white stone buildings now blasted to rubble, its colorful gardens blackened . . . it could have been worse, but that didn't make it good.

She ate the food when it came without noticing what it was. One group of miners wanted to know if it was safe to go back to their domed colony. Another claimed salvage rights on the destroyed killer-escort and asked permission to start cutting it up. She suspected it had already started doing so. Those in the ore-carrier, without any explanation of what they'd been doing, announced that they were going back.

Heris called the bridge, and asked for tightbeams to both *Despite* and *Sweet Delight*. The young captain of *Despite* wanted to explain the mutiny, but Heris cut her

318

off. "That's for a Board of Inquiry," she said. "Right now I need to know what you've picked up from the planet."

"We have no estimate of the number of survivors," Suiza said. "We've picked up two transmitters, but one may be an automatic distress beacon. It's repeating the same message over and over. The other seems to be trying to contact the first, not us."

"Ah. They probably don't know who won up here, and they're trying to collect their forces on the ground. A good sign, though it may be tricky for our people to land if they're going to be mistaken for hostiles."

A light blinked on her console. "Excuse me, Captain," she said; the youngster started, as if she were surprised at the formality. "I'll get back to you," she promised. This time it was Jig Faroe on *Sweet Delight*.

"Come on back," she said, only then remembering that she'd told him to keep his distance until called. "We'll need to get those civilians off the yacht, or you off the yacht, I'm not sure which."

"Yes, sir." He seemed much older than the other Jig— but then he hadn't been through a mutiny, and the command of a yacht was well within his ability. Heris still had to find out how Suiza had ended up in command, and how she'd destroyed a Benignity heavy cruiser. "Uh— a couple of them aren't aboard."

"Aren't aboard? What do you mean?"

"Well . . . Lady Cecelia said it was a good idea. Brun's acting as our liaison with the miners."

"Oh. Well, make sure someone brings her in." Another blinking light. This one must be the admiral's call. "Be sure we know your ETA," she said, and clicked off.

"Captain—tightbeam from the admiral—"

"Coming." Heris left for the bridge, very glad of the clean uniform. She nodded to Milcini and sat in the command chair. She hadn't actually sat down in it before; she'd been too busy running a warship in combat, when she always thought better on her feet. Now she put on its headset and enabled the screen. There on the display was her Aunt Vida, admirals' stars winking on her shoulders.

"Captain . . . Serrano." That pause could be signal stretch, an artifact of their relative positions and velocities, but it felt like something else.

"Sir," Heris said. She was aware of a grim satisfaction in the steadiness of her voice. Defiance tempted her, the urge to say something reckless. She fought it down, along with the questions she could ask only in private.

"Situation?" That was regulation enough; it might mean any of several things, including the straightforward need for information.

"No present hostilities," she said, back in the groove of training and habit. "Xavier system was attacked by a Benignity force, which destroyed its orbital station and did major damage to both population centers. Damage estimates for the planet and its population are incomplete; we have not established communication with survivors. There are at least two functional transmitters. The population did have some warning, and the local government tried to evacuate to wilderness areas."

"And Commander Garrivay?"

"Is dead. May I have the admiral's permission to send an encrypted sidebar packet?"

"Go ahead." Heris had prepared an account of her actions, and the background to them; now she handed this to a communications tech, with instructions.

"Status of Regular Space Service vessels?" her aunt went on.

"*Paradox* was lost in combat, no survivors known. *Vigilance* has structural damage to an aft missile bay from a blowout. Engineering advises that it would not be safe to attempt FTL at this time. *Despite* is jump-capable, and essentially undamaged, but extremely short-crewed."

"How dirty is the system?" In other words, how many

loose missiles with proximity fuses were wandering around on the last heading they'd followed.

"Still dirty," Heris said. "And we laid orbital mines around Xavier, nonstandard ones improvised with local explosives. None of those are fissionables, but they're potent."

"Very well. Hold your position until further orders. We'll send the sweepers ahead; we're laying additional mines in the jump-exit corridors and closing this system to commercial traffic until the new station is up and operating." A long pause, then, "Good job, Captain Serrano. Please inform your command of the admiralty's satisfaction."

"Thank you, sir." Heris could not believe it was ending like this. Of course there were reasons an admiral wouldn't get into all the issues even on a tightbeam transmission, but she had expected something, some demand for explanation . . . something.

"Well," she said to her bridge crew. "Admiral Serrano thinks we did a good job." A chuckle went around the bridge. "I think we already knew that. Now let's get things in order for the admiral's inspection, because if I know anything about admirals, she'll be aboard as soon as *Harrier*'s in orbit."

Brun woke slowly, in fits and starts. It was dark. It was cold. She couldn't quite remember where she was, and when she reached for covers, she discovered that she was quite naked. The movement itself set up competing fluctuations in her head and belly. She gagged, gulped, and came all the way awake in a sudden terror that slicked her cold skin with sweat.

After uncountable moments of heart-pounding fear, Brun wrestled her panic to a dead stop. She wasn't dead. She hung on to that with mental fingernails. In twenty minutes, maybe, or two hours, or a day, she might be dead . . . but not now. So now was the time she had to figure something out.

You wanted adventure, she reminded herself. You could have been sitting in a nice, warm, safe room surrounded by every luxury, but . . . no, no time to think that, either. Only time for the realities, the most basic of basics.

Air. She was breathing, so she must have air of a sort. She didn't even feel breathless, though her heart was pounding . . . that was probably fear. She wouldn't let herself call it panic. She felt around her . . . finding nothing, at first, in the darkness. Nearly zero gravity, she thought. And air, and not freezing, or she'd be dead. Her stomach wanted to crawl out her mouth, but she told it no. She'd already gagged once; her belly was empty. Dry heaves would only waste energy, she told herself, and hoped that she hadn't already compromised the ventilation system with vomit.

Still, even if she had air now, she might not always. She had to get somewhere and find out where she was and how long she had. She tried to remember what she'd been taught about zero gravity maneuvers. If you were stuck in the middle of a compartment, someone had said (who? was her memory going too?), you could put yourself into a spin and hope to bump into something. A slow spin, or you'd throw up. And how to spin? She twisted, experimentally, and then drew up her legs while extending her arms.

Something brushed her leg. She grabbed for it, automatically; her hand found nothing, but nausea grabbed her, proving that she'd tumbled. She flung out arms and legs both, to slow the rotation, and felt something brush her left elbow. Maddening—she couldn't tell what it was. Slowly, she tried to reach across with her right hand. Whatever it was slid along her arm; she was moving again. On her shoulder, down her back . . . it was hard not to grab, but she waited . . . something linear, like a rope or length of tubing. Smooth, not rough. Cool.

Her head hit a surface, hard; she saw sparkles in the

darkness for a moment, then her vision settled. Cautiously, she moved her hand up, found the surface, knobbly with switches. Some were rocker switches, smooth curves of plastic. Others were little metal toggles. A few were round, flat buttons with incised lettering—she could feel that, but not what the letters were. A control panel, but on what? She tried to remember what she'd seen before everything went wrong.

The image that came to her was grinning faces, mouths open, singing. A party. It had been a party, loud and happy— the rest of the memory burst over her. The ore-hauler, stuffed like an egg carton with the little four-person pods: the miners had their own plans for dealing with Benignity invaders. Faroe had been horrified—he knew they couldn't survive a fight with the big ships. She had offered to go talk to them; he'd agreed. Then, against Faroe's expectation (though she had never doubted it) Heris Serrano had defeated the Benignity ships. And Fleet had arrived: they were safe. The resulting celebration involved mysterious liquids far more potent than the fine wines and liquors her father served, even more potent than the illicit brews at school. The last she remembered was sinking peacefully into a bunk while a group of miners sang the forty-second verse of "Down by the Bottom of the Shaft." Or perhaps the twenty-first verse the second time around. It had a fairly repetitious form, minor variations on the same few innuendoes, and she hadn't exactly been paying close attention.

Which meant she was probably in one of the personnel pods, which meant she had seen the control panels before. She didn't want to push any of the flat buttons. They were all critical; one of them, she remembered, was the airlock main control.

She had drifted closer to the control panel; her knee bumped something with an edge (the desks below or the storage shelf above? It didn't really matter) and she felt cautiously around with her foot until she was sure she had the foot hooked under that edge. She felt carefully with both hands until she had the little metal tip of a toggle pinched in either hand. Now she was anchored, if she didn't lose her grip. Her feet defined "down" for the moment. She let the other foot wave slowly until her toes found the same edge and crawled under it. Both feet hooked in . . . now she could release one hand and feel around in a more organized way.

Out to the right . . . the switches ended in a smooth cool surface. That made sense with her memories. Carefully, forcing herself not to rush and break loose, she moved her right hand back, caught hold of the toggle, and slid her left hand across the switches there.

Should she push this switch? Any switch? Panic shook her again, as if some great beast had its jaws around her chest. Think. What would happen if she didn't? She'd be here, naked in the dark, until she died, and she would have no idea when that might be. Was that what she wanted? No.

The first switch she pushed produced no detectable change. Nor did the second. She hesitated before pushing another. If the electrical system was off, none of the switches would do anything. But if the electrical system was off, the air wouldn't be circulating, and that tiny draft on the small of her back suggested that it was, though perhaps on a standby system.

Where had the electrical system controls been? On the left-hand side of the consoles . . . if she was right-side up. Now she could think of that, and how to tell. Below the consoles a kneehole space accommodated the person working them; above was the storage shelf with netting. Her toes wiggled down, and found themselves snagged in something tangled. Netting, she hoped. That meant— her mind struggled. It was surprisingly hard to think upside down in the dark . . . the lower left console would now be . . . up *here*. She felt over it, slowly. The main lighting control should be about halfway up—perhaps this big rocker switch? She pushed it.

Light stabbed at her; she squinted. She was indeed upside down; her stomach lurched, and she fought back the nausea. It wasn't really upside down, not in zero G, just *relatively* upside down. That thought didn't help. Move slowly, Ginese had told her repeatedly. Now, as she tried to turn her head and look across the tiny compartment, one foot came unhooked and she lost her grip on the toggle. Don't panic, Ginese always said. Just drift, if you have to . . . she drifted, held by her right toes clenched on the shelf's retracted netting. Light was definitely better. She could put up a hand to fend off the stool that tumbled slowly before her (was that what she'd kicked before?) and she could see that what she'd first felt was indeed a length of tubing, perhaps two or three meters of it. She had no idea what it was for.

After a long struggle, she finally twisted and coiled herself into an "upright" position, with her feet under the consoles. With a firm grip on the edge, she rested and tried to think more clearly. She was, as she'd thought, naked. She saw no sign of a spacesuit, but across the compartment were personnel lockers. Perhaps in there she could find something. Meanwhile . . . with the lights on, she could identify most of the switches. She pushed DISPLAYS ON and the smooth screens to either side of the consoles lit up. For a moment they blurred into fuzzy rainbows as tears rose, but she blinked hard. She could cry later, if she had to. For now, first things first. Air: she had air, more than a hundred hours at present usage. She had electrical power keeping the internal temperature high enough for survival—calories, in that limited sense. Water? She found none listed, but that didn't mean much; she might find juice in one of the lockers.

Slowly, carefully, she worked her way around checking

the lockers. Two plastic flasks with zero G nipples full of clear liquid—the first she tried gave her a fiery drop of the same stuff drunk at the party. She grimaced and pinched the nipple shut. The other was water, pleasantly cool. The next locker was half full of concentrate bars, sticky-taped to the racks. Better and better: food as well as water. Brun alternated sips of water with bites of concentrate.

She still didn't know why she was in a pod in zero G. Was it someone's idea of a joke? A political move, an attempt to use her as a pawn in play against her father, or Heris?

"I don't think so," muttered Brun. She felt much better even without clothes on, now that a bar of concentrate was doing its work in her belly. She looked at the exterior scans again. The miners had explained their reference system; she could locate Xavier, Oreson, Blueyes, Zadoc. Rock-blips were supposed to be one color, and ship-blips another, which meant—if she was right about it—that there were a lot of ships out there. One of them would be the *Sweet Delight*, and one would be *Vigilance*, with Koutsoudas on scan. Somebody should be able to see the pod—if they bothered to look, with the battle over. And there were lots of little blips going by, some of them marked by the scans as thermally active. Thermally active rocks? Brun frowned. Weren't thermally active rocks found in volcanoes? She'd never heard of volcanoes on anything smaller than a planet.

Ahead, a drift of blips slid across the screen, thickening. She was moving too fast, she realized, relative to those rocks. Pods were tough, but not that tough. It took her a few moments to locate the thruster controls, and confirm the full fuel tanks. Then she began maneuvering, using short bursts, as she remembered someone telling her, trying to work away from the thickest clumps of blips.

❖　　　❖　　　❖

"She's *what!*" Heris struggled to keep her voice under control. Faroe looked miserable enough, and he wasn't the one who'd done it.

"She volunteered to go talk to the miners aboard the ore-hauler, to convince them to go back into hiding. I was going to pick her up before our final jump out. When we—you—won, I sent word . . . and apparently they had this party."

Heris could imagine. An ore-hauler full of drunken miners who had just learned that they weren't going to commit suicide by attacking warships with pods . . . they'd have been crazy to start with, and the party hadn't helped.

"—And apparently she passed out, and someone threw up on her, and they cleaned her up and put her in a pod to sleep it off, only someone hit the jettison control by mistake hours later—"

And now Brun was out there in a little personnel pod, unconscious or sicker than sin if she was awake, in space thoroughly contaminated with spent weapons from days of fighting.

"Why didn't they go after her?" Heris asked.

"They *said* that whoever hit the jettison control was so drunk he didn't realize he'd done it—they only realized the pod was gone when they went to give her some clean clothes."

Great. She was not only unconscious, but naked. Heris could imagine explaining this to Lord Thornbuckle: sorry, sir, but I let your daughter experience war in the company of drunken miners and they dumped her into a pod, unconscious and naked, and shoved her out into the debris of battle. . . . No. Not a good plan. Something had to be done. "Do they have any kind of location on the pod?" she asked.

"No, sir." Faroe looked miserable, as well he might. "I've had our scan techs on it since I heard, of course, but there's so much—"

"Captain, you won't believe this." It was Koutsoudas, from across the bridge. Heris looked up. "Some idiot rockjumper is trying to collect weaponry with a personnel pod." He pointed to an icon that darted into a drift and then back out. "At least he's got some sense, but—"

" 'Steban, put a lock on that pod. Can you do a retro analysis—could that have come from the ore-hauler four or five hours ago?"

"It only turned its beacon on a few minutes ago, but let's see if I can get any kind of trace on the recordings. Hmm. Yes, it could've. Why?"

"Because it's Brun," Heris said. Only Brun could be that lucky, although her luck could run out any moment. "You're going to have to guide *Sweet Delight* to it for a pickup. Faroe, are you getting this?"

"Yes . . ." He sounded less confident than she felt. He hadn't been around Brun that long. "It's pretty thick stuff to take the yacht in. . . ."

"You're right." Heris thought a moment. "What we need is in the incoming formations. If we can help her stay alive that long . . . I need a tightbeam to the *Harrier*," she said.

Brun had forgotten everything but the scans that told her where the rocks were thickest. She had once thought it must be fun to pilot a pod like this in the rings of a gas giant; now she understood the look she'd gotten when she said so to the miners. And although she'd read that rocks usually drifted along together, all moving about the same vector and velocity, these rocks didn't act that way at all. She was constantly having to dodge rocks coming in at different angles, different speeds. She was almost glad she hadn't found any clothes, since she was dripping with sweat.

When the control panel suddenly spoke to her, in a scratchy simulation of a voice she knew, she didn't notice until it repeated her name the third or fourth time. "Brun! Brun! Can you hear us? Brun!"

Communications. Now where was that switch? She groped around until she found it and another little screen lit up to say that her transmitter had full power. "I hear you, but I'm busy," she said, flicking the starboard thruster on again. One thing about it, she was getting better at this all the time.

"Brun, is that you?"

"Yes, it's Brun. There's a lot of rocks out here." Then curiosity got past her concentration. "Who is this?" she asked.

"Koutsoudas," she heard. "Brun, you need to let me give you some guidance; someone's going to pick you up."

"Why can't you just give me a vector over to *Sweet Delight*?"

"Won't work," Koutsoudas said. "And I doubt you've the fuel for it." Brun glanced at the fuel display and was shocked at how much she'd already used. She'd been trying to do short adjustments but— "Give me a tenth-second burp starboard," Koutsoudas said, before she could think about it. "Now port." Something slid by in the scan, long and narrow with a thermally active tip.

"I don't understand all these thermally active rocks," she said to Koutsoudas. "I thought volcanoes had to be on planets."

"They aren't rocks," he said. While she was thinking about that, he gave her more directions. Now the scan blips thinned out.

"But they're not ships . . ." Brun said. She could see the ships clearly. These things were a lot closer.

"No," Koutsoudas said. "They're weapons."

"You mean—someone was shooting at me? Why?"

"No, you were crossing drifts of misses—missiles that didn't hit their target. You're almost out of it now—"

Brun realized she was shaking. It was stupid; she was almost out of it now.

"Is there a suit aboard?" Koutsoudas asked. "You've got ten minutes before your next drift, if you can find a suit—"

She found an EVA suit, a drab utilitarian model nothing like her custom suit. Its owner had been shorter; Brun felt the pressure all along her spinal column once she'd struggled into it. But the locks did fasten, and the internal gauges did turn green. It was fully charged with air, water, and power. Best of all, the suit boots had gripper feet; she now had a solid *down*.

She worked her way back to the control panel and discovered that it was just possible to handle the switches in gloves. She plugged in the suit com to the pod's com, and told Koutsoudas she was suited.

"Just in case," he said, in the same calm voice he'd used all along. "Now—what's your fuel situation?"

"Down to ten percent." And she didn't know what ten percent was, in terms of use. She didn't even know how long she'd been using it.

"Then give me one-half second, thrusters seven and four." She could see the fuel display sag at that, and she said so.

"Not much longer," Koutsoudas said.

When the blow came, it took her by surprise, and slammed her against the adjacent lockers. The suit's padding protected her, but the boots came unstuck from the deck, and she tumbled. Another blow to the pod sent her tumbling in another direction. The pod rang with noise: clangs, scrapes, piercing squeals. Finally it was still. Brun put out a cautious foot and it stuck. She could hear nothing; the end of the communication cable waved around, making it clear that she'd come unplugged. She moved slowly back to the control panel, and plugged it in. A patient voice was calling her, not Koutsoudas but someone else.

"Brun—Brun—Brun—"

"I'm here," she said. "Just shaken up."

"Good," the voice said. "You're now locked onto the R.S.S. minesweeper *Bulldog*, en route to the *Harrier*. Remain in your spacesuit; do not attempt to leave your vessel until docking is complete and you have received notification." And that was the end of that; her comlink cut off and would not reopen.

It seemed like a long time later that a gentler series of bumps woke her from a nap. The comlink hissed gently, live again, then another voice spoke to her.

"Brun?"

"Yes," she said, feeling grumpy. "I'm here." Where else would she be?

"Your pod is aboard our ship—it's the R.S.S. *Julian Child*—"

"I thought I was going to something called *Harrier*," Brun said.

A chuckle. "Oh, you are. But *Harrier* has no facilities for docking like this, and the admiral thought it would be safer to transport you by shuttle, not make you swim tubes."

"Oh. Thanks." Admiral. What admiral? Where was Heris? Where, for that matter, was Lady Cecelia?

"We understand you're in a vacuum-capable suit . . . if you'll open your hatch—it's the left-hand flat button—"

"That says exterior hatch, caution. Yes, I know."

"That will put you in our number six docking bay. It's not aired up—if you have any concerns about your suit air, please tell me now. There's an airlock to ship-normal air about six meters to your left, as you exit, and suited personnel will be there to help you."

Outside the pod, Brun saw a vast cargo bay open to space; craft she had no name for were parked along the sides, and her pod filled the open middle. Beyond the lip of the bay, she could see the hull of another ship, a shape so odd she wasn't at first sure it *was* a ship. She stared until someone touched her suited arm, took the dangling cable of her comunit, and plugged it into his own suit.

"It's a minesweeper," she heard. "Odd beast, isn't it? Nothing else could go in after you."

Then they guided her to the airlock, and on into the ship, where she had a chance to change into a gray Fleet shipsuit before her shuttle flight left for the *Harrier*.

"Some party," the admiral said, without preamble, when Brun had arrived in her office.

"I—don't remember most of it," Brun said. The admiral looked familiar, though she didn't think she'd met admirals before. Not this one, anyway.

"My niece tells me you once wanted to run away and join the service," the admiral said. Niece. Aunt. Brun looked at the admiral again. Graying hair, but the same evenly chiseled dark features, the same compact body, the same confidence.

"You're Heris's aunt," she blurted.

"Yes. And you're Lord Thornbuckle's daughter. Tell me—are you cured of your desire for adventure?"

Brun thought a moment, even though she didn't need to think. "Not really," she said. "I mean, I'm still alive."

The admiral nodded, as if she'd expected that answer. "Do you now understand why my niece and her crew insisted that you learn all those boring bits you complained about?"

Brun laughed, which startled the admiral, then she smiled too. "I always understood," Brun said. "I didn't realize the complaining bothered them. Doesn't everyone gripe?"

Admiral Serrano—she supposed they had the same surname as well as the same genes—tipped her head as if to inspect Brun more closely. "You are a remarkable young woman," she said. "My niece thought so, and you just proved it again. Will you eat with me?"

Brun had no idea what meal might show up, but her

stomach was ready for any of them. Any two or three of them. "Thank you," she said, hoping that the admiral would ignore the far less mannerly answer her stomach gave at the thought of food. "I'd be honored."

"She's safe aboard the *Harrier*," Koutsoudas said. "If that's safe . . . they won't let me talk to her."

"I don't think my aunt eats girls for breakfast," Heris said. "Not even that one. Who, I'm sure, is cheerful and bright-eyed and ready to tell an admiral everything she thinks she knows about everything she's heard."

Heris put in a call to *Sweet Delight*, to reassure Cecelia that Brun had survived. Cecelia, relieved of that anxiety, had a long string of other topics to discuss. Heris really didn't care, at that moment, about the fate of the breeding farms she'd visited, the status of the financial ansible, or what might happen to the miners who had thrown the party. She would have been far more annoyed with Cecelia, if the conversation had not included an inquiry about each of the former *Sweet Delight* crew. Cecelia might have her batty side, but she did care about people. She even cared about the present crew, especially Jig Faroe, whom she praised until Heris finally cut her off. She could almost feel his embarrassment through the intervening thousands of kilometers of vacuum.

"You know," Ginese said, without looking around, "it's going to be very interesting when your aunt and Lady Cecelia get together."

Heris had not thought of that. "Oh . . . my," she said. Those of the bridge crew who had been on *Sweet Delight* had the same expression she felt on her own face.

✧ Chapter Nineteen

Castle Rock, Rockhouse System

"Patchcock? What are they doing on Patchcock?" Kevil Mahoney dropped the faceted paperweight and stared at Lord Thornbuckle.

"I haven't the faintest idea." Bunny stared out the window at a day that suddenly seemed less sunny. "It probably has something to do with the technical data on the rejuvenation drugs that they sent us . . . but it'll take me hours to wade through that. And in the meantime—Patchcock! Of all places in the universe."

"It's not a good sign," Kevil said. "Things have gone wrong with this from the beginning. D'you suppose Kemtre had this sort of feeling—that everything was suddenly coated with grease and slipping away in all directions?"

"I don't know, but *I* do. First the financial ansibles in the distant sectors go offline for a few days, and then some crazy admiral demands authorization to take a whole wave on a live-fire maneuver out to the frontier, 'just in case there's trouble. . . .' "

"And you gave it," Kevil reminded him.

"Well . . . they were already gone by the time it actually crossed my desk. And they claimed it involved Heris Serrano, that she was in some kind of trouble—"

"It's probably George's fault," Kevil said. When Bunny looked confused, he said, "Not that, the Patchcock thing. Whatever you don't want George to see, he sees. Whatever you hope he doesn't know, he knows. Some evil instinct

334

told him that there was one place we didn't want our children to go, and he headed for it like a bee to its hive."

"From the Guerni Republic?"

"I know, it's unlikely. But so is George. I wish he'd realize what his talents are, and use them profitably. He—" Kevil broke off as Bunny's desk chimed at them.

"Yes?" Bunny glared at the desk; he'd told Poisson that he didn't want to be interrupted.

"A Marta Katerina Saenz, milord. Says she's going to talk to you."

"I'm—" But the door was opening already.

Raffa's Aunt Marta had the dark, leathery face of someone who spent most of her days outside. On her, the coloring and features that made Raffa look like a Gypsy princess had matured into those of a wisewoman. She wore clothes that layered improbable color combinations to give an overall effect of archaic flamboyance. Bunny had never met her before, since she preferred to live in the mountains of her own planet, but he had no doubt who she was.

"Where is my niece?" she asked.

"You are naturally concerned," Kevil began.

She gave him a look that stopped the words in his mouth. Bunny felt his own mouth going dry. "Don't try your honey tongue on me, Kevil Mahoney," she said. "You've the charm of a horse dealer, but I'm not buying. You sent Raffaele off somewhere, and now you've lost her. Isn't that so?"

"She's not exactly lost," Bunny said, wondering why his collar suddenly felt so tight. He had aunts of his own, formidable aunts, whom he had learned to work with or around, as needs must. But this— "They're on Patchcock," he blurted, surprising himself. He had not meant to tell her.

"They . . ." she said, meditatively. "I presume Ronald Carruthers is one of 'them.'"

"And my son George is the other. She should be safe enough—"

Her dark eyebrows rose alarmingly to the iron-gray hair above. "Did you not hear me before? Your son George, indeed. I've heard about your George." Then, before Kevil could answer, she waved a hand. "I'm sorry. That was uncalled for. Your son's not a bad young man, and what I heard is years old by now. Just that he had a clever tongue in his head, inherited no doubt from you."

"Quite," Kevil said. Bunny glanced at him, glad to see the flush receding from his neck. Kevil's profession required him to keep his temper, but no man was at his calmest with his son under fire.

"So—you sent Raffaele somewhere with Ronald and George—"

"Not precisely," Bunny said. When cornered by an aunt of this caliber, the best plan was complete disclosure. "We sent Ronnie and George to—on a—to do something for us. And they didn't report in—"

"I'm not surprised," she said, this time with no softening. "And you sent Raffaele to rescue them? I suppose it made sense from your viewpoint."

"Not exactly rescue. We wouldn't—I mean, we assumed they'd just gotten . . . er . . . sidetracked, as it were."

"And because Raffaele loved Ronald, she would seek him out as the stag seeks the doe—though it's backwards in this case—and put them back on track?"

It sounded ridiculous, put like that, and he had realized how ridiculous weeks before. "Something like that," he said, in a tone of voice that admitted the foolishness. She didn't pursue that, but came back to the current problem.

"So now she's on Patchcock, with Ronald and George, and—what's wrong now?"

Kevil spoke up, his famous voice completely under control, its power blunted. "They didn't know that Ottala Morreline disappeared there months ago, after disguising herself as a worker and infiltrating a workers' organization. We are fairly sure she was found out, and killed. We hadn't told them, because we didn't have any idea they would suddenly hare off to Patchcock from the Guerni Republic— it's hardly on the direct route."

"Raffaele," her aunt said, "always had a nose like a bloodhound. Give her a sniff of intrigue, and she would follow it through any amount of boring coverup."

"Really?" Bunny asked. "I hadn't known that."

"She's not your niece. And I'm not sure she knows it herself. But it's one reason I asked her to start going through my files, to test my hypothesis. And sure enough, she discovered one little fiddle after another—spooked the accountants concerned, and delighted me. So if she headed for Patchcock from the Guerni Republic, then whatever you sent them there for is connected to Patchcock."

"But it couldn't be—unless—"

"You might as well explain," Aunt Marta said, "because I'm not leaving until you do." She looked about as moveable as a block of granite, and while technically they could call Security to haul her away, neither of them was willing to get in that much trouble.

"Let's see," Kevil said. "We have now involved five or six major families—"

"At least," said Aunt Marta. "Don't stop now." She sounded dangerously cheerful.

Bunny shrugged. "All right. It's the rejuvenation drugs. And others. Lorenza—" He paused to be sure she knew which Lorenza; she nodded. "—Lorenza had been dealing illegal neuroactive drugs through the upper crust, and we suspect she might have been involved in tampering with rejuvenation drugs. When we looked into it, our supplies are supposed to be manufactured in the Guerni Republic. But they're shipped on a route that could allow the Compassionate Hand—whom we know Lorenza was working for—to get access to some or all of them."

"Not healthy," Aunt Marta commented. "I'm glad I manufacture my own."

"You *what*?"

"Well, not personally. But if you think I'm going to put things into my body that have been manufactured by people who might be my enemies, think again. You know I have pharmaceuticals—"

"Yes, but you can't—but no one in the Familias is licensed—"

"By the Familias. Don't be stuffy, Bunny. We're over near the border; I have a valid license from Guerni, and we manufacture a small supply. Enough for me and my people, and a small . . . er . . . export."

"You smuggle," Kevil said flatly. Her eyes went wide.

"Me? Smuggle? Surely you jest. I do international trade with the Guernesi, who the last time I heard weren't enemies."

Kevil opened his mouth and shut it again. Bunny would have been amused if he hadn't been worried—he had never seen Kevil at a loss for words. Perhaps he didn't have an aunt of his own, and wasn't familiar with their unique abilities.

"I wish we'd known that," Bunny said, hoping to regain control of the situation. It wouldn't work, but he could try it. "We needed reference samples—that's why we sent Ronnie and George. We could have simply asked you."

"Assuming that my starting materials haven't been adulterated. If I remember correctly, the starting materials come from several sources. Come to think of it, quite a bit used to come from Patchcock, before that unfortunate incident."

"The Patchcock Incursion," Bunny said, just to make sure they were talking about the same thing.

"Yes. Once the Morrelines took over, exports dropped; I assume the damage to the infrastructure limited production. And perhaps they found other markets; I don't think I've seen quotes on their production when we've been in the market for materials."

"That's odd," Bunny and Kevil said at the same time, and looked at each other. Raffa's aunt looked thoughtful.

"You're right. It's been years—they should have everything back up to speed. The Morrelines have been gaining in the Index." She blinked, and a slow grin spread across her face. "I wouldn't be surprised if that's what Raffa found out—where the materials are going."

"If they were going to the Guerni Republic, why would she care?" Kevil drummed his fingers on the desk. "And besides, raw materials are raw materials. They may have found something else to make with the same starting material, something more profitable."

"Than rejuvenating drugs? You jest." Marta pursed her lips. "I hate to tell you this, if you don't already know, but the profit margin is . . . ample. Quality control is a bitch—you have to have really good chemists keeping an eye on it, because the lazy ones keep thinking they've found a shortcut. The Guernesi warned me about that—there's an alternate synthesis that looks good but is much more sensitive to minor variations in processing. I've had a research team on it for twenty years now, and we haven't found a way to improve the Guernesi process."

"So . . . you can't think of anything more profitable to do with the substrate?"

"Not unless they've discovered an alchemical stone that lets them transmute it to whatever's highest at market. No—if it's being produced in the quantities it was, the only thing more profitable than selling to me and to the Guernesi would be vertical integration. Produce it themselves."

"And Raffa could have figured that out." It was not quite a question; Marta nodded.

"If not in detail, enough to follow the lead. Especially if the samples you provided gave the Guernesi any clue—isotopic analysis or something like that."

"Are you a chemist?" Bunny asked bluntly. One did not

usually inquire the formal training of Family Chairholders, who were presumed to be broadly educated. But Marta seemed more comfortable with this than he had ever been with the food chemistry that underlay part of his family's fortune.

She grinned. "As a matter of fact, yes. It was a way of avoiding something my parents wanted me to do, so I completed a doctorate. Then I did post-doc work at Sherwood Labs—not that it would interest you, the details. In the long run, it was more fun to be a rich dabbler with time for other interests than a full-bore researcher, though I may spend a rejuv or so going back to it someday."

"It's all very interesting," Kevil said, "but we've got three young people headed into far more trouble than they anticipate, and I don't see any way to warn them—or help them."

"I shall go, of course," Marta said. "It is, after all, my niece. And I understand the chemical side. But I shall need assistance."

"Yes. Of course." Bunny looked at Kevil, who looked back. Neither of them could leave.

"You won't want to involve Fleet directly," Marta said. "Not after what happened last time. But don't you have a tame Fleet veteran—that woman Cecelia de Marktos hired? Raffa told me about her, how she helped with that mess on your planet—"

Bunny choked at the thought of anyone considering Heris Serrano "tame." Still, it was a better idea than the nothing he'd had. If only Brun weren't with her . . . he really didn't want Brun on Patchcock, along with her old cronies. Rejuvenation would fix the gray hairs, but not the fatal heart attack he felt coming on.

"I suppose—yes. Possible. She's a long way off, but we can signal—" If something else hadn't happened to the ansibles, which had only been back up for a day; messages were backed up and only emergency traffic could get through with its usual speed.

"I will make my own way to Patchcock," Marta said. "Rather than wait—it may take me longer anyway. You will contact this person?"

"Yes," Bunny said, not letting himself think of the difficulties. "Yes, I will. And I'm—" He couldn't think of the right word. Sorry to have dragged her niece into this? Sorry she found out before he got it fixed? Sorry that Kemtre had let this whole mess get started? "I'm glad you came," he found himself saying, and meaning, to his own surprise.

"Secrecy," Marta said, "is usually a bad idea." Then she swept out, with a flourish of her cape.

"That," said Kevil after a pause, "is a very dangerous woman. But did you ever see such bones?"

"Not my type," Bunny said, with more caution than honesty. He opened his mouth to say more, but Poisson came in with an expression that meant trouble.

"It's Fleet," he said. Bunny froze inside, thinking *mutiny*, but the next words relieved him. "They've successfully fought a Benignity incursion—"

"Where?"

"Xavier. It's a fairly isolated system out—"

"I know where it is," Bunny said. "What happened?"

Poisson gave a crisp precis of the action as reported through Fleet channels. "All enemy ships destroyed, and a substantial reinforcement of Regular Space Service in place. And apparently there's a personal message to you— from the admiral."

Bunny took the cube with its encrypted recording, fitted it into the desk, and inserted the earplug. "Lord Thornbuckle," a woman's voice said. "This is Admiral Vida Serrano. I'm glad to be able to tell you that your daughter Brun is alive and well. So is Lady Cecelia de Marktos, whom I understand is a friend of yours. We need to confer at your earliest convenience. The Rockhouse Major Base Commandant can arrange a secure ansible link. Thank you." Bunny pulled the plug from his ear and stared at Poisson.

"Had you heard this?"

"No, milord. It's encrypted."

"It's—I need to speak to the Rockhouse Major base commander; please set up a tightlink for me."

"At once," Poisson said, and went out. Kevil raised his brows.

"Well?"

"Apparently Brun was in the middle of a battle for Xavier—which means that Cecelia and Heris Serrano were, too. And the admiral wants to speak to me . . . says we must talk. Brun's on her ship, I gather. I don't like that at all."

Xavier System, aboard the *Vigilance*

"You have to do something," Cecelia said. Heris had run out of things to say in answer; she just looked at Cecelia and waited. "You have to," Cecelia went on. "Surely you care!"

"Of course I care," Heris said. "But surely you see my problem. I can't just leave—"

"Why not? You're not in the military anymore. You're a civilian; you assured me all that talk about a secret mission was just something you made up in an emergency. You can just walk away, take my—your—yacht, and go find out what's wrong."

"Lady Cecelia, it's not that simple. I am . . . not free to go."

"You mean you don't want to. It's more fun to play soldier—"

Heris's temper snapped. "I was not playing, Lady Cecelia; people *died*, in battle and as a direct result of my actions. Whatever you think about the military, you personally and everyone you know on Xavier would be dead without us. If you want to talk playing, how about a grown woman so fixated on horses that she can't tell a game from war?" The moment the words were out she would have snatched them back, but entropy prevailed. Cecelia glared, speechless . . . but only, Heris was sure, for a moment.

"If I could interrupt." That was a voice more used to command than either of theirs. Heris glanced up and saw her aunt, Admiral Serrano, in the doorway. She started to stand, but the admiral waved her down. "At ease, Captain. I have things to say to both of you." Cecelia had whirled, still angry and ready to attack, but Vida Serrano seemed not to notice as she came in and took the other chair across Heris's desk. "Lady Cecelia," she began, "I am glad to finally meet the person my niece so respected."

Cecelia's expression stiffened even more. "Not much respect, if you ask me."

"As a matter of fact, I'm not asking. I'm commenting on an observation anyone might make. Now—I understand you've had an upsetting communication from a relative on Patchcock. I was unaware that your family had interests there."

"We don't," Cecelia said. Her face flushed unbecomingly as her anger shifted focus. "I have no idea what Ronnie is doing there, or why Raffa is with him—they had both agreed to her parents' request that they avoid each other for a while. But I don't see what business it is of yours."

Admiral Serrano ran one hand over her short silver hair. "As the commander of this battle group, I have a natural interest in anyone trying to suborn one of my commanders—"

"Suborn!" said Cecelia.

"Commanders!" said Heris. Admiral Serrano's lips twitched.

"The two of you are a well-matched pair. Lady Cecelia:

by whatever means she obtained it, Captain Serrano now commands an R.S.S. cruiser. She commanded it in battle, against an enemy of the Familias trying to invade. Now that I'm here, and since I outrank her, I am in command—and she is one of my subordinates."

"I see that," Cecelia said irritably, "but she's not really military anymore. She's a civilian. She assured me—"

Admiral Serrano tilted her head slightly. Heris felt a pang of sympathy for Cecelia . . . everyone in the Fleet knew what that head tilt meant, the final pause before the prey was impaled. "Lady Cecelia, you tell me: if you put a cow's horns on a horse and hung a placard with COW on it, would that make the horse into a cow?"

"Of course not!"

"Very good." Admiral Serrano might have been praising a slow student in some class. "Captain Serrano was bred and trained as a military commander. She functioned as a military commander for twenty-odd years. Do you really think a couple of years running your yacht could change what she is?"

"But I *like* her," Cecelia said. "And I don't—"

"Like the military. Sorry about that. It's always happening, you know—people who think they know what we're like, and then actually meet one of us and discover we're human."

"You're patronizing me," Cecelia said. "I'm not as young as I look."

Admiral Serrano laughed. "I know that. Regulations forbid us to wear them, but . . . I was one of the first multiple Rejuvenants in the Familias. I would have three rings. A volunteer to study the effects, in fact. I would bet our birthdays aren't that far apart."

"You look older," Cecelia said.

"Admirals must have a certain maturity of presence," Admiral Serrano said. "I chose to combine other therapies with my rejuvenations, so that I look old enough to scare

young cadets, and can still outrun most field-grade officers."
Admiral Serrano waited to see if Cecelia would comment,
but she didn't. The admiral went on. "You should know
that I, too, have had communications about Patchcock.
Lord Thornbuckle is concerned about the situation there.
He wanted Captain Serrano to take the yacht and find
out what's happening to the young people."

"That's what I said—she should go, and—"

"Lady Cecelia, I can't leave without—"

The admiral raised her hand, a teacher to unruly children,
and they both fell silent.

"You want her to go to Patchcock and she won't; she
correctly considers herself under orders . . . there's a
solution, you know."

Heris realized what her aunt meant a long moment
before Cecelia did. Cecelia looked up, startled. "You
mean . . . you?"

Admiral Serrano shrugged. "I can order her—" She
turned to Heris, "And you had better go, if I do."

"If? Why if? Why not just do it?" Cecelia looked ready
to leap out of her seat. Admiral Serrano turned to Heris.

"Captain—what would your orders be, if you were the
admiral?"

"I wouldn't send R.S.S. warships to Patchcock," Heris
said promptly. "It's likely to make things worse."

"So?"

"So . . . if I could insert a small, nonthreatening civilian
ship, with some specialists to . . . find out what's happened,
rescue personnel if necessary—" If they weren't already
dead.

"Good choices. I was going to relieve you as captain of
the *Vigilance* anyway—you don't need to waste your time
shepherding her to a repair dock. *Despite* is too big for
this job, and too small for anything else. You're not officially
on the List, even if you are . . . mmm . . . tucked away in
a corner of the database. I don't have to notify anyone at

Personnel about your transfer. Whom do you want on that yacht?"

"You want me to go on *Sweet Delight*?"

"It's the right ship—small, fast, civilian, and full of specialists—or it will be when you select the right crew for this. Covert, remember."

"Yes . . . sir." Was this really an order? Would she really have the authority to pull out the crew she wanted?

"Actually this will simplify things for me," the admiral went on. "I have some loose ends to tidy before you come back in the Regs—assuming that's what you want—?" She looked at Heris, and nodded before Heris could get the words out. "Yes—I thought so. It's almost time—this little chore will fit in nicely."

"I'm coming," Cecelia said, with a touch of defiance, as if she expected to be refused.

"Of course," the admiral said. "It's your ship and your nephew. Now about that girl—"

"She stays," Lady Cecelia and Heris said together. The admiral raised her brows.

"That's what her father said. What's your reason?"

"She's stretched her luck well past its elastic limit," Heris said. "And she's too valuable as a hostage. She'll be happy enough here if you let her soak up practical matters from your specialists."

"She already is," Admiral Serrano said. "When her father wanted to speak to her, she was down in Environmental, learning to tear down a scrubber and fascinating the Chief at the same time. This afternoon, she was deep in the hull specifications for minesweepers. I hope I'll still be in command of this wave when you've finished on Patchcock." She didn't sound worried. Heris suspected that she'd enjoy Brun as much as the young woman would enjoy a few weeks aboard the flagship.

"Well, then," Cecelia said. "If that's decided, I'll go back to *Sweet Delight*. . . . I expect you two have a lot to talk about." She nodded to Admiral Serrano; Heris called someone to escort her back to the other ship.

"We do need to talk," Admiral Serrano said. "But this isn't the best time. I'll see you after Patchcock."

"There'll have to be a Board," Heris murmured. The thought—the word—sent shivers down her spine.

"Of course." Her aunt looked at her. "It worries you? It shouldn't. There's ample evidence—just in what you've sent me so far, and in what Suiza sent from *Despite*—to support your actions. Not even counting the battle itself. You're in no danger, Heris, not this time. You've done well." She paused, then went on. "You're coming home, Heris. Back where you belong, back with those who love you."

But did they? She could not doubt her aunt, not faced with the warmth in those eyes. But others . . . she would have to know why they had ignored her before. She kept herself busy the rest of that day, visiting the sickbay, arranging the change of command, choosing the crew to go with her in the yacht.

She was choosing the crew for Patchcock—the same familiar faces: Oblo, Meharry, Ginese, Koutsoudas, Petris. Petris. She looked at him with no less affection than before, yet it was different. How many days had it been . . . and she hadn't missed that part, not really.

When all the transfers had been done, when she was back on the familiar (but *tiny!*) bridge of *Sweet Delight*, with the familiar crew around her and Lady Cecelia simmering in her suite like a kettle on the hearth, she realized that the trip to Patchcock would not be peaceful for one person at least.

"I've missed you," he said, slipping into bed beside her. He was warm and smooth, the shape her hands had wanted without knowing it. And yet—even before Xavier, neither of them had taken up the many opportunities. She thought she knew what it meant for her; what did it mean for him?

"I'm just not comfortable aboard ship," Heris said. She rolled her head sideways, facing what must be faced, but Petris merely looked thoughtful.

"I'm not either, if you want the truth of it. I love you; I loved you for years, and getting to be with you was wonderful. But—it doesn't feel right aboard ship, and it's not just the memory of those damnable cockroaches." Heris began to chuckle helplessly, and in a moment his mouth quirked. "Really. I swear."

"I know." Her chuckles subsided. "But we do have a dilemma, especially if you feel the same way. I love you; I want to be around you. And I love being in space—"

"Me, too," Petris said.

"But not in bed in space." She frowned, hardly realizing it until his finger began smoothing her forehead.

"We are grown-ups," Petris said. "We can take our pleasures serially instead of binging. It's fine with me if we put this part of our life aside when we're aboard. For one thing, we won't be waiting for some crisis to interrupt."

"Thank you," Heris said. She sighed.

"I almost wish—" Petris stopped that with a sudden lurch. "Sorry. Nothing."

"Wish what?" Heris pushed herself up on one elbow to look at him. The sight of his brows, pulled together in a knot of concentration, almost undid the previous agreement.

"Nothing we can change. Not about you, is what I mean."

"Petris!"

"It's just—we don't have anything to *do*. This little ship is a beauty, and it was fun fitting her out with some decent equipment and weaponry, but—we don't get to do anything with it. *Vigilance*, now—while I was scared out of my skull shift-and-shift, I felt needed. Competent."

"I know." Heris rolled all the way over and buried her

chin in the mat of black hair on his chest. "And that's why I'm going back in, Petris. And I want you to come back too."

"I thought so." He took a deep breath that lifted her head to an uncomfortable angle. "Then we can't—"

"Yes. We can. We're not going to waste what we do have. Either you'll end up with a commission from all this, or we'll simply use common sense—confine it to times we aren't aboard."

"Is that an order, ma'am?" he asked.

"Sir," she corrected, and set about undoing the pact they had just made.

Later, before they were quite asleep, Petris said, "Lady Cecelia would have made a good admiral."

"Mmm. I'm not sure. She might have been booted out down the line; she's got a difficult streak."

"And you don't?" He tickled her extensively, but nothing came of it then but giggles. Finally Heris batted his hand away.

"I admit it; I'm difficult too. But my difficultness is the kind Fleet recognizes and knows how to deal with. And so's yours. And we will work it out—for all of us—and that's a promise."

"Fine with me," Petris said. "I trust you." She lay awake longer than he, stricken again by the weight of all those who trusted her.

✧ Chapter Twenty

Patchcock System

"I don't like it, letting Raffa go off by herself like this,"
Ronnie said. He slapped at a tickfly, and hit it, which left
an itchy wet spot on his arm and a mess on his hand.

"She'll be all right," George said. "She's inside, isn't she?
Not out here being eaten up by these . . . *things*." He
flapped the gray-green cloth hanging down from his hat
and swung his arms in a sort of uncoordinated dance. He
had draped himself in the recommended insect-proof veil
for their trek along the shore, only to discover that tickflies
could crawl up the arms . . . and once inside the veil, they
couldn't get back out. Even satiated with blood, they still
whined around inside the veil with annoying persistence.

Ronnie looked seaward, where sullen waves lifted murky
brown backs; they rolled sluggishly landward and slapped
the crumbling shore with spiteful warm hands. Far out, a
line of dirty white might mark the reefs he'd seen mentioned
in the tourist brochure. Landward, the low boxy shapes
of Twoville's monotonous architecture cast uninteresting
shadows as square as the buildings. He hadn't seen the
hotel, but in the transient workers' hostel, the cramped
room smelled of disinfectant and the ventilation fans
squeaked monotonously.

"It's not exactly . . . exotic," he said. "Not even the planet
itself."

"No." George kicked at a mound of crumbly stuff, and
jumped back as a horde of many-legged, shiny-backed

things ran out. He backed up a couple of steps. "Look at that—what d'you suppose . . ."

"Stingtails," said a voice. They both looked up, to find a tall, lean individual with a slouch hat and long, white, perfectly pointed moustaches grinning at them in a way that emphasized their ignorance. "If I were you," the man said, "I'd move farther away. Stingtails know the scent of their nest on the critter that kicked it—" George, who had been fascinated by the fast-moving swarm, backed up again and watched as the swarm continued to move toward him. When he shifted sideways, the front end followed his path, but the swarm kinked in the middle as some of the followers caught the scent and cut the corner.

"Dammit!" George backed away faster. "Now what?"

"Hop," the man advised. "Big hops. When you're twenty meters away, they'll lose track."

George hopped, looking ridiculous with his veil bouncing up and down; Ronnie jogged along, keeping wide of the swarm just in case, and the stranger strolled at ease, hands in his pockets. When they halted again, George breathless and disheveled, Ronnie took a longer look at the stranger.

Despite the old battered hat, with odd decorations stuck in its band (a tiny horseshoe? a fish-hook with feathers? a long, curling quill from some exotic bird? a blue rosette?), the man was otherwise tidily, even foppishly, dressed in crisp khaki slacks and shirt, the pleats pressed to a knife edge. A tiny pink flower in his buttonhole, a perfectly folded white handkerchief peeking from one pleated pocket. Stout low boots of fawn leather. And those moustaches . . . which matched bushy white eyebrows over bright blue eyes.

"You boys must have let Marshall at the station tell you what to buy," he said. Ronnie would have been annoyed, but he was already hot, sweaty, and bug-bitten. "I can smell the Fly-B-Gone from here . . . but of course it doesn't repel tickflies. Marshall got it by mistake three years ago, and none of us will buy it—he has to foist it off on tourists."

Another pause; Ronnie slapped at his neck, and missed that tickfly. "Not that we get many tourists," the old man said. "Certainly not your sort."

"And what is our sort?" asked George, whose grumpiness always found voice.

"Rich young idiots," the man said. "More money than sense. I mean, we'd heard the Royals were disbanding, letting loose a plague of your sort, but I thought Patchcock was too far away and too boring to attract any. . . ." His friendly smile mitigated, but did not negate, the sting of that. "And that veil will only trap the tickflies inside," he said to George. "Besides making you hotter."

George tore off the veil and glared. "I know that. I was just about to take it off, when—"

"When you kicked a stingtail nest. And now you're angry with me. I understand." Ronnie had the odd feeling that he did. In fact, he liked the old fellow, and he hoped George wouldn't say anything too rude.

"I'm Ronnie Carruthers," he said, putting his hand out. "And this is George Mahoney."

The old man looked at his hand, and Ronnie realized it was smeared with blood and tickfly juice. "Sorry," he said, pulling it back to wipe on his slacks.

"No offense," the man said. "I'm Hubert de Vries Michaelson. Retired neurosynthetic chemist. Let me tell you what I already know, before you tell me something else. Truth between gentlemen, y'know."

"Ah . . . yes." Ronnie slapped another tickfly, and swiped his damp hand surreptitiously on his shirt.

"I wouldn't do that, by the way. Won't come out in the wash." Hubert grinned, showing a row of very white, very strong teeth. "Now—Ronald Vortigern Carruthers and George Starbuck Mahoney. Arrived yesterday, in company of a pretty young girl named Raffaele Forrester-Saenz. Right so far?"

"Yes, but—"

"You'd travelled together from the Guerni Republic, specifically from the planet Music. Kept to yourselves, but the girl let it be known that she and you, Mr. Carruthers, were travelling together in blatant disregard of her family's wishes." The old man peered at him, blue eyes suddenly frosty. "I hope that was a cover story."

Ronnie felt his ears going hot. "Well, sir . . . not exactly. That is, we didn't start to—it just happened that we—and anyway, it wasn't like that—"

"I see." The blue glare didn't give a millimeter. "Going to marry the girl, are you?"

Ronnie's spine straightened before he realized it. "Of course!" Then, more calmly, he tried to explain. "We didn't start out together. George and I were on—we had something to do in the Guerni Republic." That sounded weak; he rushed on to the part he could tell strangers. "When Raffa showed up alone—"

"You decided she needed an escort—protection?"

"More or less," said Ronnie. He was not about to explain to this old fellow that the protection had gone the other way. The bright blue eyes blinked, then Hubert grinned. "Well, well. Young blood. Still runs hot, I see. In that case, young man, you've made a serious mistake."

"What?"

"Letting her go unchaperoned here, of all places."

Ronnie looked around, but saw no particular menace. Besides, Raffa was safely inside.

"You should have registered with her," Hubert said. "The people at the hotel think she's alone."

That had been the idea. Ronnie fumbled for an explanation and came up with partial truth. "The fact is, sir, that hotel—it's the only one fit for her, but—but I couldn't quite—"

"Ah. Funds low, eh? What is it, boy, gambling or chemicals? Give it up, boy. Girl like that is worth it."

"It's not that," Ronnie said, feeling that his ears must

be glowing now. "It's . . . it's family." He didn't want to drag Aunt Cecelia into this, and anyway it wouldn't make sense to anyone outside.

"It's his aunt," George said. George never suffered from this sort of embarrassment. "His aunt's suing his parents, and that's why Raffa's parents wanted her to drop him— because his aunt's in the mood to put his parents in the poorhouse, and Ronnie along with them."

"Never mind, George," Ronnie said. "It's not quite right, anyway—Aunt Cecelia isn't vindictive, not really."

"Cecelia . . ." Hubert said.

"Cecelia de Marktos," George said. Helpful, that was George. Ronnie wanted to smack him. "Rides horses. Red hair."

"Ah." Hubert looked Ronnie up and down again. "*That* Cecelia?"

"You know her?"

"Never met her. Never heard of her. Now I know." He shook his head. "You have a problem, boy. Your young lady may be in serious trouble."

Now Ronnie felt cold. "What? Why do you think that?"

"Because Patchcock in general, and Twoville in particular, are not that friendly to strangers. Especially strangers with a mission." He gave them that toothy grin again. "And no one is going to believe you sneaked off to Patchcock to enjoy the beautiful scenery together."

"I've got to get back." Ronnie turned, and took a long stride without looking. This time it was his boot that smashed into a stingtail mound.

"Look out!" Hubert and George yelled together; Ronnie jumped back from the angry writhing swarm of stingtails that poured out of the hole.

"Not so fast," Hubert said, grabbing his arm. "Here— this way—walk through these—" He led Ronnie a few meters farther from the shore, onto matted rust-brown vegetation that crunched underfoot and released a sharp, garlicky scent. "Now settle down—getting yourself eaten up by stingtails isn't going to help your young lady."

"Eaten up?" George asked. He looked back at the mound, now covered with stingtails.

"Of course. Didn't Marshall tell you? They swarm on you, and start stinging—somewhere between fifty and a hundred stings paralyzes the average human. Unfortunately, it doesn't numb the rest of the stings . . . we lost quite a few settlers at first, people who thought stingtails were no worse than ordinary ants. Luckily, they can't follow a scent across stinkfoil."

"And you didn't tell me!" George glared. "You had me hopping down the shore like an idiot—"

"It worked," Hubert said. "Got your attention, too. Now. Enough flabbery-dabbery. Your young lady."

"She was taking a tour today," Ronnie said. "Her Aunt Marta, you see, sent her here—"

The old man's expression so clearly said *Pull the other one; it's got bells on* that he didn't have to open his mouth.

"I know she was taking a tour. The operative question is, did she come back?" Ronnie felt a sinking inside; he could easily imagine his heart having turned to iron, slowly plunging through his guts to the center of the planet.

"We're supposed to meet tonight," he said. "At someplace called Black Andy's, for dinner."

The blue eyes rolled up. "Oh, dear. Black Andy's is it? Not wise, not wise at all. Let me tell you what to do. You go back to your digs, get cleaned up. Go by her hotel and see if she's back. If she is, stay with her—eat there— and you'll hear from me tomorrow. If she's not, give me a call—" He fished out an immaculate business card, and handed it over with a flourish. "And do be careful on the way back. No more stingtails."

"Can't we just walk on the . . . er . . . stinkfoil?" asked George.

"Not advisable; it's a bit corrosive—if you'll look at your

bootsoles—" George lifted a foot and winced at the lines etched in the sole. "It would probably eat through before you reached town. If you're careful along the shore, you shouldn't have too much trouble. I can't go with you— wouldn't be advisable at all, you see." Ronnie didn't see, exactly, but he was ready to run the whole distance back to their lodgings, if only it would help Raffa.

"Thank you, sir," he said. "We'll—we'll be in touch."

By the time they got back to their lodgings, they were both hot, sweaty, and reeking of stinkfoil. The one-armed man at the desk glared at them. "Tourists!" he said. "Didn't have no more sense than to go dancing on stinkfoil—you'll smell up the whole place." He got up and shuffled around the desk. "Might as well throw the boots away; you'll never get the smell out."

"But—"

"We don't like that stink in here—" Two large, beefy individuals had come out of the door to the right, and another from the door to the left. "We don't really like *your* stink in here."

A half hour later, Ronnie and George limped barefoot back to their room, where someone had been kind enough to ransack their luggage and sprinkle it with cloying perfume.

"I don't think they're friendly," George said. Their assailants had done no real damage, beyond bundling them into a smelly blanket, wrapping it with sticky repair tape, and then manhandling them downstairs into a storage closet. It had been locked, once they worked their way out of the blanket and tape, but it was a flimsy lock.

"I wish I knew if Raffa's back," Ronnie said. The room's comunit would be no help; he could see the severed cable from here.

"We'll have to go find out," George said. He pawed

through the piles of clothes on the floor. "I hope they left us some shoes."

They had left shoes, filled with something that looked and smelled like rancid cottage cheese. "Not friendly at all," George went on, in a tone of voice that made Ronnie forget all about Raffa for a moment. He remembered that tone, and the smile that went with it.

"George—" he started.

"No," George said. "These were my best pair of Millington-Cranz split-lizard, custom-dyed . . . how petty of them. Truly, truly petty."

"George, you aren't—"

"I have some sense," George said. Ronnie doubted it, in that tone of voice. "Priorities, Ronnie. Great minds always keep their priorities straight. First things first, and all that."

"Yes?" Ronnie hoped to encourage that trend, providing they could agree on the priorities.

"Raffa first; as a gentleman, I fully agree that her safety must come first."

"Good. Then suppose we clean up, and—"

"Just how do you suggest we clean up?" George's expression suggested that Ronnie had just lost his senses. "Are you planning to go down that hall, and into those showers, assuming that ordinary decency prevails and you will come back clean and all at peace with the world? While nothing happens to your belongings here?"

"Well . . ." Ronnie had thought, in the brief intervals available while struggling with three very strong men, with the blanket and tape, with the locked door, that a nice hot shower would be next on his list. Followed by clean clothes. Followed by Raffa. He realized now that George had a point—someone, if not the same men, might be lurking in the halls, or in the showers. The clothes on the floor weren't clean anymore. "I guess I thought we could be ready—"

"No." George shook out a cream silk shirt, sniffed it,

and shuddered. "No, we'll simply have to wear these things, producing an olfactory melange that should certainly confuse any stingtails we meet, and hope that Raffa doesn't pretend she never saw us before."

Glumly, Ronnie agreed. He found a green knit shirt slightly less fragrant than the rest, poured the odoriferous slimy goo out of his own brown shoes, and watched as George put the gritty stained towels to use wiping out his.

"I think," George said, holding one up for inspection, "that it may be salvageable. Good shoes are tougher than they thought. Here—" He tossed the remaining dry towel to Ronnie.

On their way out, the desk clerk said, "Have fun, boys," without looking up. George waited until he was outside to mutter.

"Schoolboys. That's what it is, really. They didn't steal anything; they didn't take our money or papers. Taking revenge on good clothes just because we have them . . . like those ticks in the fourth-floor end dormitory—"

Ronnie was seized with an unnatural desire to be fair. "We did put cake batter in their things first, George."

"Not in their *good* things. In their sports clothes. I have never in my life desecrated a pair of Millington-Cranz shoes, and I cannot imagine sinking so low." He stalked on, in silence, through the hot dusk that ended a Patchcock day. Ronnie, aware of an unpleasant dampness between his toes, followed him gingerly.

The hotel's doorman looked them up and down, sniffing ostentatiously. George stared straight ahead; Ronnie gave Raffa's name and smiled. The doorman pointed to the public comunit in the upper lobby.

"What a hole," George said, as they made their way around the open shaft.

"Yes . . . just a moment." Ronnie called the desk, who

transferred his call to Raffa's room. It bleeped repeatedly, and just when he was sure she had been kidnapped by vicious thugs who would stake her out over a stingtail nest, the receiver clicked.

"Hello?"

"Raffa! It's Ronnie!"

"Oh—I was in the shower." His mind drifted into a fantasy of Raffa in the shower—of himself in the shower— of both of them—until recalled by her impatient "Ronnie!"

"Yes, sorry. We had a few problems, and I was wondering—could we come down?"

"Here?" She sounded almost as prim as her mother. "I mean—why? We weren't going to be seen together—"

"It's too late, Raffa." He took a deep breath and told her about Hubert, and the men at the transient barracks, as fast as he could. "And we need to use a shower, and get some clean clothes. . . ."

"I suppose," she said. "Or—wait—I'll come up. If you're that raggedy, they might not let you come down."

He and George leaned their elbows on the railing of the open shaft, watching the waterfall and ignoring the disapproving glare of the doorman that periodically scorched their backs. Raffa was safe. That's what mattered.

Raffa emerged from the lift looking clean, cool, and confident. She handed them each a plastic strip. "Here. You can't go back there—not to stay, anyway—so I went ahead and got rooms for you here. I'd be delighted to have you in mine, but there's not enough space. I've got things spread all over."

"Angelic Raffaele," George said. "Are you sure it's Ronnie you want to marry?"

"Absolutely," said Raffa. She gave Ronnie a look. "Don't worry. I don't mind about the smell."

She led them to the lift, smiling brilliantly at the doorman, whose dour expression finally shifted. He shrugged, hands out, and gave the boys a friendly nod. "My mistake, sirs."

"You're on ten," Raffa said. "Adjoining singles—I thought you might prefer that, in case—" In case of what, she didn't say. It meant two showers, anyway. And, in this hotel, modern clothes-freshers. By the time Ronnie had showered, his clothes held no trace of the flowery perfume. His shoes still reeked faintly, but at least they were completely dry.

Dinner, in the hotel's dining room, completed his cure, he thought. Raffa in the cherry-colored backless dress with the full sleeves, the waterfall cascading behind her . . . good food . . . he could live with that. He was not sure he could live with George, who was giving his own version of their day. Finally even Raffa had had enough.

"All right, George. I understand—you had a horrible day and found out nothing useful except that there's a retired neurosynthetic chemist who wants to meet us. Let me tell you about mine." She described a tour of a pharmaceutical plant, a vast production line where gleaming robots ground and mixed chemicals, where the resulting paste, forced into molds, popped out as pills, to be coated with colored liquid that dried hard and shiny. Thence through pill counters, into boxes, past inspectors . . . boring, Ronnie thought. It made his feet ache to think of it.

"But the funniest thing—when I said Aunt Marta was interested in investing here because someone had died in the Morreline family, he turned absolutely white."

"Who?" Ronnie asked.

"My guide. And hustled me back to the corporate offices. You'd think I'd just insulted the CEO or something. I just made it up, really; someone's always dying in big families."

"Ottala!" George said. "It's Ottala who died." The shock hit Ronnie with the same unpleasant thump of reality as the bullies' fists. That made sense of a lot of things.

The disadvantage of a good hotel is that there is no way for guests to sneak out unobserved. Someone is always on duty by the public exits. And Twoville offered no nightlife of the sort to attract three wealthy young tourists . . . not after that afternoon. Raffa had suggested a walk along the shore, but Ronnie explained about stingtails and tickflies. They ended up in Raffa's suite by default; she had a sitting room.

"But if Ottala was killed here—if she was in one of the factories—"

"We're not here to solve Ottala's murder," George said. He paced around the room, peering at everything, before settling into a chair. "Dear heavens, what an ugly lamp! We're here to find out about the rejuvenation drugs—"

"Aren't you forgetting Ottala's Aunt Venezia?" Raffa asked. "She would want us to find out about Ottala's murder."

"Not if it included getting killed," George said, then added hastily, "and even if it did, I personally don't want to get killed finding out. I want to go back to civilization, which this isn't, and let Patchcock stew in its own mess." His shoes, unlike Ronnie's, had peeled in the automated shoe cleaner. The only footwear in the hotel gift shop were sandals, iridescent lime-green straps over black soles.

"It can't all be the same villains," Raffa said. "The Morrelines making Ottala's aunt do those hideous pots so that she won't have time to interfere in the business is one thing. But they wouldn't have killed Ottala. Whoever killed Ottala had another reason."

"They hated her because she was rich," George said gloomily, staring at his ruined shoes.

"It had to be more than that," Raffa said. "We're all rich, and no one's killed us yet."

"Not for want of trying," George said. "Look at the past few years: we all got shot at on Sirialis. Someone shot Sarah, thinking she was Brun. Ronnie and I were kidnapped by the clones."

"That wasn't because we were rich," Ronnie said. "It

was because we knew something someone didn't want us to know—they thought we were dangerous."

"So you think Ottala knew something she wasn't supposed to know? And if we can find out—" Raffa kicked off her shoes and curled her legs under her.

"What if she found out her family were making rejuvenation drugs illegally—would they kill her then?"

"What if she found out someone was adulterating the drugs—maybe not her family, maybe someone else?"

"But why?" Raffa bounced a little, on the couch. "What could anyone gain by adulterating rejuvenation drugs?"

Ronnie thought about it. "Well . . . if people don't like the whole process—if they think it's wrong—then they might do something to make it not work . . . or something." He had no idea how that might be done.

"If I were an ordinary person," George said, in the tone of one who knows he will never be ordinary, "I would resent rejuvenation. There are all these rich people, who are going to live forever, and then there's me—the ordinary person making pills, say—who's never going to get anywhere. It used to be that even rich people died, sometimes inconveniently, and fortunes shifted around—there were opportunities—but now—"

"Even rich people could resent it," Ronnie said. "Take my father . . . he's rejuved only once, but he will again, I'm sure. They want me to be grown up and responsible, but not enough to challenge him. I could be eighty or ninety myself before I have a chance to run a business. Even older."

"And we're always making snide remarks about free-birthers, but if people died off soon enough, there wouldn't be any worry about overpopulation. Not even on ships." George nodded, as if he'd said something profound, then his gaze sharpened. "Free-birthers!"

"What?"

"Logical group to oppose rejuvenation technology. Raffa, where's the work force from? Originally?"

"They're Finnvardians, mostly. Why?"

George sat up abruptly and reached for the comunit. "Let me check the database. I'll bet you they're free-birthers, and now they're having to make rejuvenation drugs, and—" His voice dropped as he scanned the reference files. "Drat. We need a better database."

"You need to mind your own business." That was the leader of four men in hotel livery, who appeared in the doorway to Raffa's bedroom. Another disadvantage of a good hotel is that anyone in the right uniform can go anywhere without being noticed. All were tall, pale-skinned, blue-eyed. "However, since you didn't, I'm afraid you're going to have an unfortunate accident." He had a weapon; Ronnie stared at the black bore of it with the sick certainty that he was going to die. George had paused with his hand poised over the comunit keypad; Raffa simply sat there, looking like Raffa.

"It won't work," George said. "Someone will investigate."

"A major industrial accident? Of course they will. But not your deaths individually. The failure of a field generator explains so much."

Now Raffa moved, a convulsive twitch and a frantic glance at the p-suit hanging from its hook behind the door. The leader laughed, pure glee at her fear. Ronnie wanted to smash his face.

"Not a chance, rich girl. You and your gallant lovers will all die together, just like in a storytape."

"You killed Ottala," Raffa said. Calmly, Ronnie noticed, as if she were commenting on someone's garden. You raise roses, don't you? You killed Ottala, didn't you?

"With great pleasure," the leader said. "Would you like to know how?" His voice promised horrors; he longed to tell them.

"Not really," Raffa said. "I'm sure it wasn't a failure of the field generator."

"I think you should know," the leader said, with a nasty

whine in his voice. Ronnie prayed to unnamed gods for a miracle. Raffa should not have to die hearing horrors.

"*You're* not Finnvardian," George said suddenly. Everyone's attention shifted to him. He was looking at the comunit screen, and he read it aloud. " 'Finnvardians, dolicephalic, males generally between 1.8 and 2 meters in height, skin color index M1X1, eye color index blue/gray. Religious objections to contraception, plastic surgery for other than reconstruction after trauma'—but *you've* had plastic surgery, and you're wearing contact lenses." Now that George had said it, Ronnie could see that the leader's eyes were a different blue, darker, intense.

"Nonsense," the leader said. But two of his followers looked at him with obvious suspicion. "Not all of any human stock have blue eyes; they're recessive."

"The reference says, 'Alone of human stocks, the severely inbred Finnvardians have eliminated dark eyes; the light blue or gray eye color has been stable for seventy generations, with the usual medical sequelae. Finnvardians therefore prefer to work and live underground, away from ultraviolet radiation that hastens blindness.' Your eyes are dark," George pointed out. "Your colored lenses make them dark blue, not Finnvardian blue. Furthermore, a Finnvardian should know that all Finnvardians have light blue eyes."

"Is this true, Sikar?" asked one of the others. "You are one of us, aren't you?" All three were looking at him now, light blue eyes narrowed, lips tight. The leader's forehead gleamed in the light.

"Of course I'm one of you," he said. "Who else can speak your obscure language—?" He stopped short, and flushed.

There was a short, uncomfortable silence. Ronnie wondered which deity he now owed for that miracle. If it was a miracle.

"*Your* language," said the man to the leader's right, thoughtfully. He glanced around the leader to one of the others. "Sounds good to me," he said. The man on the left nodded, his hand slipping into a pocket of his uniform.

"No!" the leader said. "Take care of them first—then we'll talk—"

"Talk is talk," the man on his right said. And then he said something Ronnie couldn't understand, Finnvardian apparently, and flung himself on the leader, who shot him. The shot didn't make much noise, but the man yelled. Raffa rolled over the back of the couch, out of sight of the struggle. Another shot rang out. The struggling figures staggered across the room, screaming incomprehensible insults. Ronnie dodged the row, found Raffa behind the couch, and began to crawl cautiously toward the outer door. Maybe they would forget—

"Stop!" yelled someone. He stopped. Someone—perhaps *that* someone—had a weapon.

"No you don't," George said from the other side of the room; Ronnie looked up just in time to see the entire comunit, screen and all, hurtling toward the man with the gun, who shot it. A tremendous crash followed, spraying the whole room with broken glass and plastic. Water gushed from the ceiling, where something had hit a sprinkler control. Ronnie leapt up just in time to catch a blow to his head, but he was already in motion, and his head connected with someone's stomach. That person grunted, and slid down; Ronnie stepped firmly where it would do the most good, ignoring the shriek of pain, and fended off another man's assault with a bit of unarmed combat he'd learned in the Royals. George, he saw, was doing his best to bludgeon one of the attackers with the desk the comunit had been on.

Raffa took care of the last one, with the lamp off the end table. "I didn't think a little more mess would matter," she said. "And it *was* an ugly lamp." And then she was in Ronnie's arms, sobbing a little. He picked her up and carried her into the hall before she could cut her bare feet on the broken glass.

In the distance, he could hear alarms clanging and angry voices. George limped out into the hall, water dripping from his hair.

"He really isn't a Finnvardian," George said. "I have his lenses—look." There on his palm were two contact lenses, bright blue.

"Is he dead?" asked Ronnie. "What about the weapon?"

"He's dead," said George. "One of the others stabbed him. I think it was a ceremonial Finnvardian gelding knife. His weapon's right here—" He pulled it from his trousers pocket.

"Hold it right there!" From the end of the hall, two men in uniform pointed guns at them. "Drop that weapon! Get on the floor! Move!"

"But—but *they* did it," George said.

"DROP THAT GUN! NOW!" George dropped the gun, shrugging at Ronnie. "GET ON THE FLOOR. FACEDOWN. NOW."

"You don't understand," Ronnie said. "There are . . . spies or something in our room—in Raffa's room. They attacked us. They did something to the field generator, and—"

"GET DOWN NOW!"

Raffa slipped out of his arms. "We might as well," she said. "They aren't going to listen until we do."

In the event, they didn't listen at all. Two dead men, in hotel uniforms, and two unconscious men in hotel uniforms . . . and the guests involved were rich young tourists from the inner worlds?

"How much did you offer them to have sex with you?" the policeman said, leaning over Ronnie.

✧ Chapter Twenty-one

Patchcock Station

"Cecelia—so glad to see you!" The tall dark woman in swirling reds and purples reminded Heris of someone— she couldn't think who.

"Marta! It's been years!" Cecelia turned to Heris. "Raffaele's aunt . . . Marta Saenz. So—they called you, too?"

"Not exactly." Marta made a face. "Raffa sent me a message saying she was going to Patchcock with Ronnie and George, to follow up a mission for Bunny. I landed on Bunny, because as far as I'm concerned he had no business risking Raffa on any harebrained missions—and frankly, my dear, he was already scared out of his wits, because of Ottala—you did know about Ottala?"

"Yes."

"And so I said I'd come here, but I wanted help, and he said he'd get your Captain Serrano—whom I presume is you?" She turned to Heris.

"Yes," said Heris, not quite sure how to address Raffa's Aunt Marta. She was clearly someone of importance, if she could pressure Lord Thornbuckle to ask favors of her aunt admiral, but did she use a title?

"I just got off the commercial flight a few hours ago, and saw that your yacht was listed as incoming, so I waited—I haven't tried to call yet. I thought I'd see what Captain Serrano advised." Her glance at Heris combined deference and command.

"No harm in calling, I wouldn't think," Heris said carefully. Two aunts! Three, if you counted aunt admiral. She felt outnumbered and very much outgunned.

"I'll do it," Marta said. They followed her to a row of combooths, and waited while she made her call. Heris wondered again if she should have brought along some of her crew, and reminded herself again that she and Cecelia had booked the last two seats on the next down shuttle. When Marta opened the door of the booth, her face had a dangerous expression that erased all musings from Heris's mind.

"You won't believe this," she began. "They're under arrest."

"What?"

"For murder and attempted sexual assault."

"Ronnie? George? Raffa?"

"According to the hotel security chief, they tried to get four hotel employees to engage in—and I quote—'unnatural and lascivious acts against their will.' Then tried to beat them into submission, and then shot two of them. George, apparently, had the gun."

"George is Kevil Mahoney's son," Cecelia said. "If he *had* shot someone, he wouldn't be caught holding the weapon."

"We'll see about this," Marta said grimly. "They're not holding my niece—"

"Or my nephew—"

"Or George," said Heris, purely for symmetry. If George had had an aunt, she would have said it.

The waiting lounge for the down shuttle was decorated with the ugliest ceramics Heris had ever seen. It filled slowly, though it didn't seem to hold a full shuttle load. Perhaps they had small shuttles here, or perhaps there was a heavy cargo load. Cecelia and Marta paced back and forth; Heris sat and watched them. The time for scheduled departure came and went. People began to grumble. Grumbles mounted as time passed.

"We always have to wait if *they're* coming," she heard. "It's got to be family—it's always family."

Heris kept an eye out along the corridor, and soon spotted the likeliest candidate, a short, bunchy, gray-haired woman swathed in layers of uneven soft colors. Behind her, a harried-looking man trundled a dolly loaded with boxes and soft luggage. Sure enough, when she entered the lounge, the signal light came on for boarding. Heris picked up her own duffel, and caught Cecelia's eye.

But Cecelia and Marta were staring at the newcomer. They pounced before she could move past the others, in the lane cleared for her by flight attendants.

"Venezia!"

She turned, her wrinkled face lighting up. "Cecelia! Marta! How lovely to see you—I didn't know you were coming."

"Why did you—"

"Your idiot police—" Their voices had collided; they both stopped, and into the brief silence Heris spoke.

"Let's get aboard first." She grabbed Cecelia's elbow and pushed. Cecelia snorted, but let herself be guided into the clear lane behind Venezia; Marta closed in behind Heris.

The shuttle was full only because Venezia had reserved an entire section. Cecelia and Marta followed her into it as by right, settling into the wide padded seats; Heris noticed that the attendants didn't challenge them. She wished she could call the yacht and slip a couple of her crew into the seats she and Cecelia would have used, but she could not delay the shuttle now.

The shuttle had not cleared the station before Cecelia attacked again. "Venezia, my nephew is down there on your planet being accused of murder that he didn't do—"

"And my niece," Marta said. "Locked up in your filthy police station—"

"What do you know about this?" demanded Cecelia.

"Yes, what?" Marta glared.

Venezia shivered, as if she were a leaf dancing in stormwinds. "I—I don't know anything. I just got here from Guerni. When I asked Raffa to come here and investigate, I had no idea—"

"*You* asked her!" Venezia flinched from that tone as if Marta had hit her.

"I just—it seemed—nobody would tell me anything about Ottala, and I thought maybe she'd done something foolish, like a girl might do, and Raffa being young, maybe she'd figure it out—"

"You sent her into danger—my niece—!"

"And my nephew," Cecelia said, with no less heat.

"I didn't know it was dangerous," Venezia pleaded. "I thought—I thought Ottala had just run away. Perhaps fallen in love with an unsuitable young man, the way Raffaele did—"

"Ronnie," said Cecelia stiffly, "is not unsuitable."

"Raffa," said Marta, "did not run away."

"And I still want to know what happened to Ottala," Venezia said. Silence fell; Marta and Cecelia looked at each other, then at Heris, then at Venezia. "You know, don't you?" she asked.

"Not for sure," Heris said. "But—what is known is that she infiltrated a workers' organization, after having skinsculpting to match her appearance to the Finnvardian workers on Patchcock. Then she disappeared. If she were discovered—"

"Then she's dead." Venezia's chin quivered.

"And the same people could have killed Raffa," Marta said. "And the others."

"Only now they're in jail," Cecelia said, "for crimes they certainly did not commit. And it wouldn't have happened if it hadn't been for you."

The rest of the trip to the surface passed in very uncomfortable silence.

❖   ❖   ❖

"I want to see my nephew," Cecelia said.

"I want to see my niece," Marta said.

"I want to see whoever's in charge," Venezia said. Heris said nothing. The three older women had charged off the shuttle like a commando team, every action coordinated for maximum efficiency. Venezia made the three necessary calls—to the police, the hotel, and the local corporate headquarters. Marta arranged ground transportation. Cecelia gathered everyone's luggage and dealt with local customs. Heris wondered how they'd worked that out when they hadn't said a word after that first confrontation. She was supposed to be the military expert, but she felt like a young ensign on a first live-fire maneuver.

The groundcar driver, after a look at Venezia's ID, had driven as if they not only owned the road but had proprietary rights to a sizable volume of space above and on either side of it. The three older women stared at each other in grim silence; Heris, after looking out the window to see two battered trucks diving for the nearest ditch, looked at the back of the driver's neck.

When they arrived in the scruffy little town, and pulled up at the police station, Venezia led the group inside. Now they were lined up in front of a long gray desk.

The uniformed officer behind the desk blinked. The mirage didn't go away. Three angry women—three *old* angry women, the young-looking one wore a Rejuvenant ring—loomed over him like harpies on a cliff. Behind them was a younger but no less formidable woman, who had the unmistakable carriage of a military officer.

"And your name, ma'am?" the man said, trying to stick to ordinary rules.

"I am Lady Cecelia de Marktos, and my nephew is Ronald Vortigern Carruthers." She leaned over as he reached for one of the pencils in a particularly gruesome pottery jar that leaned drunkenly to one side. As he began to write out the names laboriously in longhand, she growled, "Use your computer, idiot, and hurry up."

"What's the problem out here?" That was the captain, languid and unshaven after a night of interrogating the most infuriating prisoners he'd seen in years. "Let's not have any rowdy behavior, ladies, please." Then he blinked at Venezia. "Uh—sorry, Madame Glendower-Morreline— we weren't expecting you."

"You should have been," Venezia said. "I sent a message from the orbital station, and the shuttleport."

"It's here somewhere, sir," the first policeman said, waving his hand at a desk littered with scraps of paper. "The computer's down again."

The captain muttered a curse, in deference to ladies, and then scowled at them. "Your relatives murdered two hotel employees, and beat up two others. They discharged firearms in a public hostelry; they destroyed hotel property; they falsified records—"

"They did not!" Cecelia said.

"And they're being held without bail, pending charges, which will be filed as soon as we have all the data."

"I found madam's message, sir," the desk officer said.

"Forget that. She's here now." The captain wavered, aware of his disheveled appearance and the weight of wealth before him. "Look—as a special favor, I'll let you speak to your relatives—one at a time, in the interview room, with an officer present. But that's all." A disgruntled silence fell. Finally Cecelia and Marta nodded.

"I didn't do it, Aunt Cecelia. None of us did." Ronnie looked exhausted, but not guilty. Cecelia had seen him guilty.

"I know, dear, but what did happen?"

"I told them—"

"Yes, but they haven't let us see the transcripts yet. I need to know."

Ronnie went over it again. "And I'm sure they weren't really hotel employees—the uniforms didn't really fit— but the important thing is the leader wasn't Finnvardian, and George proved it, and the others jumped him."

"Who has the contact lenses?"

"The police, I suppose. George had them, but they took them away from him."

"They've got it all wrong, Aunt Marta." Raffa's hair hung in lank strings, and the cherry-colored dress had been torn somewhere along the line. "Ronnie and George didn't do it." She gave Marta her view of things. "And if you could possibly bring me some clothes—"

"I'm going to bring you a way out of here," Marta said, "or rip this place up by its foundations."

Raffa turned even paler. "I forgot! They said something about sabotaging the field generator, the one that holds back the sea—"

"I'll tell them. Don't worry, Raffa."

But the captain shrugged off her mention of the field generator. "It's a red herring," he said. "No amateur could sabotage a field generator." Marta glared at him, recognized invincible ignorance, and made a strategic withdrawal to the hotel.

Their descent on the hotel was almost as startling as their descent on the police station. The doorman . . . the hotel manager . . . the concierge . . . all bowed and scraped and fawned and disclaimed all intent to cause trouble for them or any member of their illustrious families. Only . . . there was this matter of shots being fired, and bodies on the floor. . . .

"Were they your employees?" Cecelia asked, when the gush of apologies and explanations ended.

"The dead men? Well, no. They were in our uniform, so at first we thought, of course, that they were, but they weren't. Perhaps they wore the uniforms to provide some . . . er . . . excitement. The police said—"

"My niece," Marta said with icy emphasis, "does not get sexual kicks from playing with men in hotel uniforms."

"No—of course not, madam." The manager attempted, unsuccessfully, to find an expression which made it clear that he had not thought any such thing.

"Nor does my nephew," Cecelia said. "He is, after all, engaged to her niece."

"Yes, madam. Of course, madam."

"And since they weren't your employees, isn't it possible that they wore those uniforms to gain access to Raffa's rooms without being detected—that they did in fact initiate the attack?"

"I suppose so, madam." This with a dubious look, and an exchange of glances from manager to concierge and back. "But that is a matter for the police to decide. And there is still the damage to hotel property. Valuable communications equipment—lamp—sprinkler system—"

"Insurance," said Cecelia and Marta together.

"Never mind that," Venezia said. "*We* own the hotel." She had been glaring at the masks on the walls and the vases holding floral displays, muttering something about "execrable decorations" since she arrived; Heris wondered why she cared so much about bad pottery, but perhaps she felt responsible for all the details of a family property. She fixed the manager with a steely eye. "It will not be a billing item."

"No, madam."

"Excuse me, ladies." Heris looked around and saw an elderly man who held his hat in his hand. Bright blue eyes peered out from under bushy white eyebrows; his white moustache had been waxed to perfect points. He wore a fresh pink rosebud in the lapel of his gray suit, and his shiny black shoes were covered with white— spats, she finally remembered, was the right word for them. Cecelia, Marta, and Venezia were momentarily speechless.

"I understand the young people have had a spot of trouble. I tried to warn them yesterday—the young men, I mean."

"You talked to Ronnie and George?" Cecelia asked.

"Yes—I'm Hubert de Vries Michaelson, by the way, and from his description you must be his Aunt Cecelia."

"Yes—"

"I'm retired—formerly a neurosynthetic chemist here. Never quite made enough to retire offworld—"

"Can you recommend an attorney, Mr. Michaelson?" Cecelia asked.

"No . . . but I can help you, if you'll let me. I believe I have evidence that may convince the police someone else is involved."

"What concerns me most is this field generator Raffa mentioned," Marta said. "Apparently one of the men said something about arranging a failure. The police wouldn't listen—"

The hotel manager broke in. "They said *what*? About the field generator?"

"Raffa said one of the men claimed it would fail—that their deaths would be blamed on its failure."

"It would destroy this entire structure," the hotel manager said. "And most of Twoville within days or weeks, as the seawater infiltrated." He looked frightened enough. "Should I evacuate now, or—?"

"Of course with one of them dead, and the others injured, maybe there's no danger," Cecelia said. Heris looked at her and wondered if she should get into this discussion. If they were talking about a Tiegman field generator, "danger" was too mild a word for the risk of collapse. Had the threat been serious, or just an attempt to panic the youngsters?

"I think someone had better interview the survivors—

I presume they're under medical care?" Marta looked around as if expecting them to be rolled out in their beds, for inspection.

"They're at the clinic," the hotel manager said.

But the survivors had disappeared from the local clinic, to the annoyance of the nursing staff. Their annoyance paled beside that of the aunts, who had walked from the hotel to the clinic at a pace that made Heris breathless.

"They *what*?" demanded the aunts, almost in concert.

"Have you notified the police?" Hubert asked. He had joined their parade, where he formed a decorative accent.

"No. They weren't charged with anything—" That was the nursing supervisor, who had begun with a complaint about the missing patients, as if that were Venezia's fault.

"They will be," Cecelia and Marta said together. "Call the police *now*." The nursing supervisor looked stubborn a moment, but then reached for the com.

"The field generator," Heris said, bringing up the topic which had not left her mind. "If they're loose, and well enough, they could still sabotage it. Who's in charge of the Tiegman maintenance? Where's the power supply?" She wished she had her Fleet uniform, her Fleet authority, and most of all her own expert people who would know how to recognize a problem if they saw it. The thought of someone playing games with a Tiegman field made her feel queasy. She knew a way to knock out a Tiegman field generator with only a few kilograms of explosive, placed accurately for the field configuration. Granted that the calculations were difficult for anything but a spherical field, they were still at the mercy of the saboteur's incompetence. She wasn't at all sure Cecelia and the other older women understood how bad it could be if the field blew.

"Ah—there I can help you out," Hubert said. "I've played cards with the Chief Engineer out at the control station every week for years." He beamed at Heris, and she wanted to smack him. He was no substitute for Petris or Oblo.

"If you'll excuse me, ladies," Hubert said. "I think a word with the Chief Engineer is necessary at this point. Perhaps he can be persuaded to take precautions—at least be ready to divert all power to the field—"

"Go ahead," said Venezia, dismissing him with a wave. "Take care of it. We're going back to the police." She marched out. Heris wondered if she ought to go with the dapper little man—how reliable could someone in spats be?—but Cecelia beckoned to her.

"I know it's dangerous," Cecelia murmured to Heris. "I saw your expression. But we can't do anything about it, and if this field-whatever doesn't kill us, Venezia can do something about the worse problem which made this threat possible." That made sense, though Heris wasn't happy to be left out of the action.

By the time they made it back to the police station, both the hotel manager and the clinic had reported. In addition, a perspiring manager from the local corporate headquarters, bearing a bunch of flowers for Venezia. They began a low-voiced conversation while the others approached the front desk. The captain, still bleary-eyed but now depilated and in a clean shirt, glowered at them. "You're complicating a very simple case," he said. "I understand family feeling, but even the best families have bad apples—"

Heris could have told him this was the wrong approach.

"It *would* be a simple case, if you would listen to your prisoners," Marta said.

"When my niece Ottala disappeared," Venezia put in, looking away from the manager, "you found nothing."

"There was nothing to find; there was no evidence." Heris doubted that he had ever looked for any; the rapidity with which the young people had run into trouble argued for a superfluity of evidence somewhere nearby.

"I asked that girl Raffa to come here, to find out what happened to Ottala. I thought a girl could find a girl better than some man. And she did find out what happened, and it nearly happened to her, and now you're ignoring it." Venezia, who had seemed the most insignificant of the older ladies, now had the intensity Heris associated with weapons-grade lasers. Quite unlike the incandescent flash that was Cecelia's anger, Venezia's steady rancor seemed ready to cut its way through any obstacle.

"Just because someone is not Finnvardian, and not really a hotel employee, does not make them a spy or a murderer. Wearing contact lenses is not a crime—"

Stupid captain, Heris thought. He should back down now, before she cleaves him along a flaw he doesn't recognize.

"Ah, so you *now* agree that one of the men was not Finnvardian," Marta said, taking over from Venezia. Heris had to admire the tactic, and the way in which they passed the turn without any prior planning. "Do you know what he was?" The captain looked down. "Well?"

"He appears to have been a citizen of the Benignity of the Compassionate Hand," the captain said, with understandable reluctance.

"A Benignity agent? Here?"

"I have no evidence that he was an *agent*. Merely a citizen—"

"A registered alien?"

"Well . . . no. He had been working in the factory for about three years—"

"Illegally," Heris murmured; heads turned to look at her and she smiled. "I would consider that a Benignity citizen in disguise, not registered as an alien, and working in a critical industry for three years, was almost certainly an agent."

"Everyone thought he was Finnvardian," the captain muttered.

"Apparently," Heris said.

"But he was murdered," the captain said.

"By Finnvardians who discovered that he wasn't. Who thought, perhaps, he was leading them astray."

"George Mahoney had a gun in his hand—"

"And did that man die of gunshot wounds?"

"Well . . . no. He was stabbed. But there's no evidence that the other individuals under arrest could not have stabbed him."

"And I might have sung grand opera while hanging upside down in zero G," Heris said, to no one in particular. "But I didn't, despite the lack of evidence exonerating me."

"What about the ones who ran away from the clinic," Cecelia said. "Doesn't that convince you they're guilty?"

"Of pretending to be hotel employees, yes. But that's hardly a major crime."

"And the field generator?" Marta brought that up; Heris had been about to ask.

"Hasn't failed yet. Won't fail. Can't fail. It's—" The lights dimmed, flared again, and went out. In the darkness, Heris heard curses and cries, and between them the utter silence that meant no ventilation fans were turning, no compressors working, nothing electrical functioning at all. After too long a wait, dim orange emergency lights came on, and the reflective arrows painted on the floor to indicate the way out glowed against the dimness.

"Possible," Heris said.

"It's not—it's something else—" But the captain was clearly shaken. Sirens began to hoot outside. The company manager stammered apologies, shook himself loose from Venezia, and bolted for the door.

"Let's go," Heris said to Cecelia.

"I'm not leaving without Ronnie," Cecelia said. "No matter what."

"Sir, we've got to evacuate the lower levels—" that was someone from the back; Heris couldn't see the face.

"Very well," the captain said. "Go on now—we'll be

bringing them all outside, just be patient." But Cecelia and Marta and Venezia—and Heris—stood their ground until the prisoners came up, until they were sure that Raffa and Ronnie and George were safely above ground.

Outside, in the hot afternoon, the streets were full of sullen frightened people, more and more of them pouring out the entrances to all the buildings. Heris noticed a lot of pale, light-eyed Finnvardians. The police, after a despairing look at the aunts, gave up any pretense of guarding their young prisoners, and began moderately effective crowd-control efforts. At least they kept people moving away from the shore, away from the police station and hotel. Ronnie and George leaned against the wall, and Raffa leaned against Ronnie; the aunts pursed their lips but said nothing.

"Are all the factories underground?" Heris asked Venezia.

"I suppose," Venezia said. "I know some of them are. I never really—that is, my brothers were in charge, you see, after Papa died. They never wanted to talk to me about business. And of course if you *do* have underground facilities, Finnvardians are an efficient work force."

"I hope that nice little man in the suit didn't get hurt," Cecelia said.

"I hope that nice little man in the suit wasn't a mad bomber," muttered Heris. The rosebud and spats had done nothing to reassure her. The main field hadn't blown, or they'd all be dead, but something had gone very wrong. A misplaced charge could cause sudden loss of power, then field fluctuation and restabilization in another configuration. She could easily imagine Michaelson in the role of inept saboteur or not-quite-rescuer.

Suddenly the floor trembled. Heris eyed the nearby wall. "Out in the street," she said. "Now!" They all scuttled into the middle of the street, as the shaking worsened and bits of plaster fell off the walls. Luckily, Heris thought, these were all one-story buildings. Then a bouncing lurch sent them all to their knees, and the trembling died away, a fading rumble in the distance.

"Field's back on," Heris said as she clambered up, dusting herself off.

"Why did it shake?" asked Cecelia, pale but determined to be calm.

"Reconfiguration," Heris said. "My guess would be that the saboteur miscalculated the placement of the charge. With power, the field's inertia would damp the fluctuations—that's why the lights went out; the field bled power off the supply net—but it didn't find enough power to regain its former geometry. So it collapsed towards a sphere. What that means to the structures, we won't know until we look."

"Is it—safe now?" asked Marta.

"If someone doesn't tweak it again. We're lucky. If it had blown completely, we wouldn't be here to worry about it."

"I don't want to be here at all," Raffa said shakily.

"We'll go home soon," Marta said.

"No. I don't want to go home. I want to go with Ronnie."

Marta's brows went up, but whatever she might have said was interrupted by a blast from loudspeakers as electrical power returned.

"—Disperse! Go to your quarters! Danger is over; the Tiegman field has been restored. Shift Two, report to your supervisors in Level One. All Shift Two, report—"

"Let's see about the hotel," Cecelia said. "If it's not full of water, maybe we can get something cool to drink."

No one interfered as they made their way back to the hotel entrance. Heris noticed that the local manager trailed along behind, the now-disheveled bouquet still in hand. Venezia ignored him. The doorman, shaken but willing, opened the door. Inside, the lights were on, and the waterfall still plunged over the lip of the central well. The hotel manager scurried to meet them. "Ladies—

gentlemen—I'm sorry but our facilities are not back to full operation yet—"

"I want to sit down," Cecelia said firmly. "On something soft. In a cool, shady place. With something to drink— and I really don't care what, as long as it's cool and wet."

"The same," Marta said.

The hovering manager tried again to present his bouquet to Venezia, and she turned on him. "I will be in your office in one hour," she said. "And I will then expect a complete disclosure of your role in this fiasco."

Heris wondered which fiasco Venezia meant. From the look on the manager's face, he might have had more than one to conceal. Venezia finished her first tall glass, called for another, and then spoke to them all.

"You don't have to come with me—I expect it will be a long, tedious afternoon—"

"I wouldn't miss it," Marta said. "If you'll allow a rival into your files, that is—"

"Where I'm thinking of, that's no problem. Cecelia, will you join us, or would you rather babysit the youngsters?" Heris blinked. She still had trouble connecting the dumpy little woman she had first seen with this regal personage who seemed to know exactly what she was doing.

"Let Heris go," Cecelia said. "She can represent the government, if necessary. And it'll be good experience for her."

Great. Something Cecelia didn't want to do, and thought Heris would learn from. Tedious, Venezia had said. Files. Heris groaned inwardly; she could see it now. She was going to spend a hot, miserable afternoon cooped up in an office going through boring files that she knew nothing about.

In the event, Heris found the afternoon far from tedious. When they arrived at the corporate offices, Venezia brushed past the little receiving line the manager had put together, and stormed through the reception area so fast that Heris got only a glimpse of elegant charcoal-gray carpet and oyster-gray leather upholstery, a serene vision marred only by the unfortunate puce pottery statuette displayed on a stand.

The serenity of the front office vanished behind the first glass partition, where *kicked anthill* better fit the level and pattern of activity. Actual filing cabinets stuffed with papers, which scurrying minions shifted from drawer to drawer, with frantic looks when they recognized intruders. Other workers hunched over deskcomps, fingers flickering as they did something . . . Heris could not tell what, at the speed with which Venezia led them along. Where was she going? How did she know where to go? Behind her, the manager bleated occasional cautions, apologies, pleas, but Venezia ignored him. Marta followed Venezia, and Heris followed Marta, and the manager crowded Heris but lacked the force to push past her.

Along a hall, up a flight of stairs, along another hall. Clearly, this was executive territory, still carpeted, with offices opening off the passage and a larger one at the end. That would be the manager's office, Heris was sure; as they neared it, she could read the engraved nameplate.

The manager's office, when they arrived, had been cleared for Venezia, fresh flowers in a hot turquoise and green pot in the middle of the desk. Venezia snorted, and went straight to his assistant's office next door. There, piled in a heap on a side table, was everything that must have been on the manager's desk, including a family portrait. Here Venezia paused, and here the hapless manager caught up.

"Please, madam . . . my office is the best we have; it will suit you, I'm sure." He waved toward the door.

"Later," Venezia said. She prowled the room, eyeing the side table of files, cubes, loose papers. The manager's assistant broke out in a fine sheen, as if someone had sprayed him with oil. His gaze flickered back and forth between her and the screen of his deskcomp. He reached out a trembling hand.

"No!" Venezia said. She had not seemed to be watching the assistant, but her command stopped his hand in midair. "No—get up now, and go out."

"Out—?"

Venezia glared at him; he ducked his head and hunched aside, almost stumbling out of his chair. She moved into his chair herself.

"I'm going to assume that the enabling codes specified in the Morreline Codex are still active," Venezia said, without looking at the manager. Heris, watching him, saw a flush rise up his face, followed by pallor.

"Uh . . . yes, madam, but there are . . . other . . ."

"Give them to me." Heris had heard admirals in battle with less command presence. Stuttering, protesting, the manager finally gave Venezia the codes.

"But it will all be so confusing, madam," he said. "And I have prepared a precis—"

"Good," Venezia said. "If I become confused, I can look at it." She glanced at Marta. "You're the biochemist—what do you want to look at?"

"You're going to give me open access to your technical files?"

"I don't have time to worry about it," Venezia said. "It's an emergency; you're the only independent expert—tell you what, I'll hire you, put you on retainer, and then you'll have to give me a loyalty bond. What's your consultant rate?"

"You always were smarter than you looked," Marta said, and named a figure that Heris compared to a large fraction of her own yearly salary. "Contract accepted. I'll need comp access."

Venezia looked at the manager, who had faded to a depressing shade of gray. "In here, madam," he said softly, and Marta followed him into his own office.

Venezia glanced at Heris. "How are you with personnel files, Captain Serrano?"

Heris wondered what she meant. How was she with personnel files doing what? Her face must have been as blank as her mind, because Venezia sighed heavily. "Export/ import ratios?" That made more sense, but Venezia shook her head. "No. Just be ready to keep the interruptions away, if you would." Heris felt silly, demoted from partner to door watch. She said nothing, looking around the room instead. An ordinary office room, large and cluttered. More actual paper than she'd seen in years, including bulky metal files to keep it in. Cube files as well, cube readers, wall display units, schedules with colored lines all over them.

Venezia, when she looked back at her, was hunched over the deskcomp, murmuring something Heris couldn't follow. Heris could just see the flicker of rapidly changing screens, lines of text and blocks of numbers scrolling past much faster than she would have cared to read. Did this old woman really know what she was doing? Cecelia was sharp enough— at least about horses, and her own investments—but Venezia had not yet impressed Heris with her intelligence. She had seemed far more scatterbrained than Cecelia or Marta; she had kept muttering about pottery. What *was* she reading so fast?

"Aha," Venezia said in the midst of this musing. "He's sharpened the blade for his own throat this time!"

"What?" asked Heris.

Venezia glanced up at her. "It's a mistake to assume that people with artistic hobbies can't think," she said. Heris blinked; this was exactly the sort of statement she would have expected from Venezia eight hours before. "Or won't notice," Venezia went on, stabbing at the controls. She had bright patches of color on her cheeks, and Heris realized she was in a considerable rage.

Was it better to say nothing, or show an interest? Heris had opted for saying nothing when Venezia spoke again.

"My brothers," she said. "Did you have brothers, my dear?"

"Only one, and he died," Heris said. She had never really known him; she had been only five when he died, and he had been adult.

"Friends tell me they can be human," Venezia said. "But I always doubted it. My brothers—well, most of it doesn't matter now, except as background for not trusting them. But they've overreached themselves this time, and I'm not going to back down." She pushed back her chair and went to the door of the other office. "Marta—anything critical?"

Heris craned her neck to look. Raffa's aunt didn't glance up from the deskcomp she was using, but she answered. "Only if you want your product to meet contract specs. This is very strange, Venezia. Some of the problem is just your biochemists trying for a cheap way around a difficult synthesis, but some of it is . . . could almost be . . . deliberate sabotage. I'm not sure how these changes will function biologically."

"Product liability problems?"

"Unquestionably. You'll have to track the shipments to see how bad it is. And retainer or not, there's no way I can keep quiet about some of this."

"I don't want you to. We're going to have to close this facility down anyway, at least for some time."

"What will your brothers say? Can you convince them?"

The grin on Venezia's face reminded Heris of her aunt admiral on the trail of a feckless ship's captain. "I can do more than convince them, Marta. I can destroy them." Her grin widened. "I have the shares."

"I'm impressed," Marta said. "Then why did you let them get into this mess?"

"I was busy elsewhere." Venezia shifted from foot to foot. "I know that's no excuse, really. It's my money. My responsibility. I should have been keeping track of them, but Oscar . . . he's so difficult. It was easier to stay away. You're going to say I should have known."

"No need," Marta said, still not looking up. "You already know that. What can I do to help?"

"Be sure you bring along any evidence you'll need; I'll try to secure these files, but you can see how it is . . . these people will try to protect themselves."

Heris thought of something she could do. "If it would help—" she began tentatively. Both the older women turned to look at her.

"Yes?"

"If they think I'm an official Fleet representative, perhaps that will make them think twice about destroying things. Or, if it would help, I've got a really good scan tech who could probably put military-grade encryptions on them. And someone who could watch the door while he does it."

"Perfect," Venezia said. "How long before you can get your people down here?"

"I don't know the shuttle schedule," Heris said. She refrained from telling Venezia that it was her presence on the other shuttle that had kept them aloft. "It shouldn't take long for the little equipment he'll need."

"There will be a shuttle," Venezia said. "I'll order one." Heris was only mildly surprised at the efficiency with which Venezia ordered a shuttle, arranged a secure comlink for Heris to the *Sweet Delight*, and arranged ground transportation for Heris's personnel when they landed. Some officers didn't look as formidable as they were; Venezia must be that sort. And Bunny, she remembered, had had that uncanny ability to change gears from foolish, horse-besotted idle rich, to the very effective Lord Thornbuckle. She wondered what it would feel like to do that. And was it something that came with money and power, or with age? Or all of the above? If age was part of it, the increasing number of

Rejuvenants were going to affect society even more than she'd thought.

Marta and Venezia continued to unearth more problems, and discuss them—a discussion that went far beyond Heris's comprehension—until Koutsoudas, Oblo, and Meharry showed up. Heris explained what Venezia wanted.

"No problem, Captain," Oblo said. He looked around the offices. "Just how much trouble do we expect?"

"Not much, really. The damage is done; it's just a matter of protecting the evidence. And they know I represent Fleet. Unofficially, of course."

"Of course." Meharry grinned. She had brought some of the lethal weaponry Heris had bought on the first voyage, and the lightweight body armor under her shipsuit was obvious to the instructed eye. So was the military bearing of all three. Koutsoudas, busy at the computer terminal, had attached some of his pet boxes.

"I've secured the database," he said, in far less time than even Heris expected. "It'll snag and log any attempts to delete or alter anything, and lock the guilty terminal."

"And I'll just go around and put out a few scanners," Oblo said. He waggled the duffel he carried.

"Good," Heris said. The two older women looked pleased, and she let herself enjoy it. At least she didn't feel like a useless idiot next to them . . . although she was beginning to suspect they might not need even this help.

"I'm thinking of dinner," Venezia said, turning to lead the way back out of the building. "Did we ever have anything for lunch?"

All the way back to the hotel, Venezia and Marta discussed the culinary possibilities of the local cuisine, as if all they cared about was food.

✧ Chapter Twenty-two

They were all relaxing after a leisurely dinner, waiting for dessert to be served, when a deferential waiter brought Venezia a comunit and plugged it in for her. "A call, madam. From madam's brothers."

Venezia scowled. "Good. I have something to say to them."

But she didn't get the first word. Heris could hear the angry, "Venezia, you stupid cow, what are you trying to do!" from where she sat. Venezia did not click on the privacy screen. The angry male voice ranted on. "You're ruining us! It's all your fault!"

"No." Venezia grinned, an unpleasant grin full of teeth. "I am not the problem, Oscar. You are. I know about Ottala. I know about the drugs—"

"Venezia, no! Not on an open line!"

"I have called an emergency stockholders' meeting—" Heris wondered when she had had time to do that. "And you can either resign now or be thrown out."

"Venezia, you don't understand." Now the angry voice had turned conciliatory, pleading. "It's your artistic temperament; I understand that. Someone's upset you—"

"*You* have upset me." Venezia snorted. "Artistic temperament, my left little toe! Do you think I haven't seen what you did with those ceramics you said you appreciated so much? I even found one on the desk in the *police* station!" She cut off an apology. "Never mind. *I* haven't made a pot in years. I bought them wholesale in the Guerni Republic, just to keep you boys off my back so I could do what *I* wanted to do, and you never even noticed that I kept picking uglier and uglier ones, hoping you'd quit asking—" She ran out of breath, and panted a moment, her cheeks flushed.

"You just don't understand, Venezia . . . it was for your own good—"

"Ottala's death was not for my own good! She would never have been killed if you hadn't been involved in this mess with rejuvenation—if you hadn't ignored the workers' complaints—"

"Workers always complain!"

"You were forcing Finnvardians to manufacture rejuvenation drugs, and you tried to coerce them to use contraceptives," Venezia said. "Didn't you bother to find out anything about Finnvardians?"

"They're tough, hard workers, and they like living underground," her brother said.

"They're also fanatic about free birth and plastic surgery," Venezia said. "You remember when you wanted my investment in the expansion, I asked you then if you understood what a Finnvardian work force meant, and you said 'Never mind, Venezia, let us boys handle it.' I should have known better," she said bitterly. She looked as if she might cry.

Marta reached for the comunit, identified herself, and went on. "Lord Thornbuckle is personally interested in these matters," she said. "The supply of contaminated, adulterated, and illegal rejuvenation chemicals concerns the highest level of government. I think Venezia's right—resignation's your best option."

"But—but she's never managed any—"

"She has the shares, doesn't she? Besides, it's not a secret monopoly anymore. Your profit margin just collapsed. You'll be lucky if you're not held personally responsible for damages under the product liability laws."

Cecelia went next. "And if there's any evidence of

pharmaceuticals from here getting into the hands of that conniving Minister's sister—Lorenza—you know whom I mean—then I personally will sue you for the damages she did me."

Heris decided to join the party. "And while Fleet chose not to act openly, in recognition of the difficulties remaining since the Patchcock Incursion, I should tell you that I have a brief from my admiral to report on the situation here and determine if it poses a threat to the security of the Familias."

"But—but you're just a lot of stupid old ladies!" Oscar blurted.

"Wrong, Oscar," Venezia said, calm again. She looked at each of her allies and winked. "We're a lot of rich, powerful, *smart* old ladies. And as you know, I've never had any rejuv procedure—so I can take the Ramhoff-Inikin and repeat it as often as I like." She paused, but Oscar said nothing, at least nothing Heris could hear. "I'll always be there, Oscar," Venezia went on. "Older, richer, stronger, smarter. Live with it." She cut the connection and grinned at the others. Marta and Cecelia nodded.

"To aunts," Heris said, raising her glass. "Including mine."

Hubert de Vries Michaelson reappeared, this time in a formal black dinner jacket, with one arm in a black silk sling, just as the waiter brought their desserts. Graciously, they invited him to join them, and he eased himself into a chair, careful of his arm.

As Heris expected, he was glad to explain his role. He had tried to warn management of the danger of manufacturing Rejuvenant drugs with Finnvardian workers, he said—and he had argued against the cost-cutting synthesis that sometimes degraded the product—but he'd been forcibly retired, with not enough money in his account to go offplanet. So he had worked alone, gathering evidence as he could.

"It's a wonder they didn't just kill you," Heris said. She thought the black silk sling was a bit overdone. He couldn't be badly hurt—if he was hurt at all—and he didn't need that kind of fancy dress anymore.

"They would have," Hubert admitted, "if I hadn't made such a ridiculous figure. That's why I dressed so formally all the time." His shoulders shifted, emphasizing the well-cut dinner jacket. Heris had to admit it suited him. He twinkled at them, and went on. "They couldn't believe anyone with creases and rosebuds and spats and so on would be a menace. They let me alone, mostly, though I couldn't get access to open communication." His smile widened to a cheerful grin. "I was *very* glad to see you ladies . . . I'm not getting any younger, you know, and I was afraid my evidence would be lost when I died."

"And of course they wouldn't let you have rejuvenation." Venezia looked angry, her plump cheeks flushed again.

He shook his head. "Of course not. Although with what I knew about the production shortcuts here, I'm not sure I'd have wanted it. Now the field generator—I just wish I'd been faster. The Chief Engineer didn't want to believe me, and I couldn't get him to go look—"

"But the field didn't collapse." Heris was not sure how far to pursue this. She still did not know—and wanted to know—if the charge had been improperly calculated, or if Michaelson really had saved them all. Did he even know?

"No." Hubert paused to sip from his glass. "We were lucky, I suspect. Anyway, after the Chief Engineer threw me out of his office, I hung around the control room—I know a lot of the workers there—and was ready to throw the switch diverting all power to the field generator when the explosion came."

"And your arm?" Heris asked. Someone had to.

"I tripped," Hubert said cheerfully. "I'm not as spry as I was, you know. Someone tried to pull me away from the controls; I fell over a chair, couldn't catch myself—

and there it was. A simple fracture. A couple of hours in the regen tank, and all that's left is the soreness. They wanted to keep me overnight in the clinic, but I wanted to find you ladies—" Again that roguish twinkle.

"That's very gallant of you." Cecelia, Heris noticed, had a speculative look in her eyes. So did Marta and Venezia. They needed no help, she realized, in seeing Hubert for what he was: a minor player who wished very much to have a starring role on the strength of one decisive action.

"I was hoping we could celebrate together," he said, giving each of them a bright-blue-eyed smile.

"I think the company owes you a rejuvenation, Mr. Michaelson," Venezia said earnestly. "And I will have someone review your retirement folder; a senior scientist should certainly have had enough in his account to travel offplanet. Of course we are all grateful that you were able to do something about the field generator and prevent worse trouble. Unfortunately, while we certainly have cause for celebration, and I personally appreciate your help, we've all been traveling a long time, and would really rather go to bed."

"Oh." To his credit, his cheerful face did not lose its bright expression. "Well, in that case, I thank you for your interest, madam, and hope you have a very restful night." He bowed slightly and walked off, jaunty as ever. Heris found herself unexpectedly sympathetic, now that she was sure her gaggle of aunts was safe. He had been helpful, courteous, brave . . . she hoped he would find someone to celebrate with. With that twinkle, he probably would.

Morning brought more changes. A message had arrived from the police station that all charges against the young people had been dropped. Heris noticed pale bare patches on the wall where the ugliest pottery decorations had hung, and passed one hotel employee hastily tacking up a framed picture of flowers over another. The young people, with the resilience of youth, were attacking a huge breakfast in the hotel dining room when Heris got there; they waved her over.

"Wait till you hear," George said. "Ronnie and Raffa are going to elope."

"Not exactly elope," Raffa said. "But we are going to marry." Ronnie swallowed an entire muffin in one mouthful, and grinned at Heris.

"Aunt Cecelia has decided to drop her suit against my parents." He reached for another muffin. "She says if you are going back in Fleet, and can put up with your aunt the admiral, she can put up with Mother."

"And we're leaving this godforsaken hole," George said. He alone looked gloomy. "I suppose I have to go home—"

Cecelia chose that moment to arrive at the table. "We're *all* going home," she said. "Heris, we have to straighten out the yacht's title—"

"It's yours," Heris said. "It always was, and it still is—"

"Because I'm thinking of selling it." That stopped conversation for a moment as everyone stared at her.

Heris finally said, "Sell it? Why?"

"Because I don't really like living on it. Yes, it's nice to be able to travel when and where I want, but most of the time I want to be on a planet. With horses." She stared at the wall a moment, and turned to Heris. "And to tell you the truth, Heris Serrano, I don't want to travel on that yacht with any other captain but you—and I don't want you anyplace but where you belong. In Fleet." Heris could think of nothing to say. The moment lengthened uncomfortably, until George knocked over the sugar.

They were days from Patchcock, well on their way to Rockhouse Major, when Heris thought of an adequate answer. She looked across Cecelia's study and saw her employer frowning over a hardcopy of equine genetics studies.

"There's another way to travel freely, you know," she said.

"Hmm? Oh—don't worry about it."

"Seriously. You could use a smaller, faster hull than this. It wouldn't be as luxurious, but it would be too small to allow for many—even any—guests."

"I couldn't get stuck with Ronnie," Cecelia said, the beginnings of a grin quirking her mouth. "Although I have to admit that had good consequences as well as bad . . . and I realize I made some of Venezia's mistakes, letting myself be alienated from my family." So it was more than dropping the lawsuit. Cecelia was going home with more than her body healed, this time.

"Yes, but rescuing one nephew is enough," Heris said. She ticked off the other advantages on her fingers. "Faster—less time in transit—so you wouldn't miss the amenities. If you learned to pilot it yourself—"

"What!" Shock in the tone, but Cecelia's eyes sparkled.

"Would you rather ride or be driven?" Heris asked. "You're more than bright; you've gained enough time in your rejuvenation—as we now understand it—that the time taken to qualify for a civilian license would hardly dent what's left. I think you'd enjoy it; your psychological profile certainly fits." She watched as Cecelia's face ran its gamut from surprise to anticipation. "Your own ship under your own control—of course you'd need crew, a few, because it's not safe to solo at the distances you travel. But a small crew, and you yourself in charge—" That would be the real lure; Cecelia's lack of political ambition sprang from no contempt for power itself.

"How long would it take?" Cecelia asked. Ah. She would talk herself into it. Heris relaxed.

"Depends if you go full-time or part," Heris said. "Brun has all the current standards—she's planning to qualify too. As you Rejuvenants are discovering, there are no limits to learning new skills."

Cecelia had a faint flush on her cheeks, more excitement than anything else, Heris thought.

"I can't seem to get used to it—the idea that we could keep living for centuries . . . forever—"

"Maybe you can't. Maybe there are limits. But you will certainly have time to learn to pilot your own craft, if you want."

"I'd like that," Cecelia said. "I really would. And you?"

"Me? I go back in Fleet, of course—and, while you've been very courteous in not asking, that includes my former crew. Petris as well. We have . . . an understanding."

"Good," Cecelia said. "I'd hate to have you lose what you gained, there. And your family?"

That brought a knot to her stomach. "My family . . . well. My aunt the admiral said we'd talk. I'll do what I have to."

"It will be better than that," Cecelia said. She looked as if she wanted to say more, but Heris was in no mood to listen to auntly platitudes from someone who had taken her own family to court. Perhaps Cecelia recognized that; instead of going on, she asked about Sirkin's plans.

"There's someone you should talk to," Lord Thornbuckle said. He opened the door, and Heris managed by the slightest margin to keep her jaw from hitting the floor. She had not expected to meet her aunt *here*. Lord Thornbuckle nodded at Admiral Serrano, and went out, closing the door behind him.

"Good to see you again, Heris."

"Sir." Formality always worked; Heris fled into it as into a thicket.

"We're off duty, both of us. You can call me Aunt Vida, or Aunt Admiral . . . but not sir."

"Yes, sir—Aunt. Vida."

"Better." Vida took one of the big leather chairs and leaned back comfortably. "You did a remarkable job in Xavier, as you well know."

"Thank you." Heris eyed her aunt, wondering what was coming.

"And on Patchcock."

"That wasn't really my doing, sir—Aunt. Lady Cecelia and the others—"

"Nonetheless. I'm very pleased with your performance. You have more than justified my confidence."

"Thank you." Heris decided there was no use not asking the question that had burned in her mind for all the time since Xavier. "You *did* put that keyhole into the database—"

"Of course." Vida grinned. "If you were smart enough to figure it out, you were smart enough to need it."

That didn't compute, in Heris's mind, but she had no time to think it over.

"I want to talk to you about the family." Vida wasn't smiling now. Heris shifted uneasily in her chair. The old anger and confusion rose like a foul tide.

"I don't," she said shortly. "If they wanted to contact me, they could have easily enough. They haven't."

Vida shook her head. "Heris, your parents made a mistake. They didn't come to your assistance instantly. I do not know their reasons; I have not asked. The only person who really needs to know is you."

"I don't—"

"Perhaps not. If you can accept that they made the wrong decision, without rancor, then you don't need to know. But if not you, then no one. You are still angry; you are still hurt. You should ask them."

"It doesn't matter," Heris said. She had no intention of asking them. She didn't care what their reasons had been. The lump in her throat grew to choking size. She tried not to look at Vida's face, or anything else.

Her aunt sighed. "If you're going to be terminally angry with anyone, be angry with me."

"Why? You're the only one who ever contacted me, who ever bothered—"

"On my orders." A flat statement, no possibility of error. Heris stared at her, seeing nothing in that face she could understand.

"What?"

"On my orders, once you had resigned." Vida paused, and gave Heris another long stare from those remarkable eyes. "You know, that surprised us all. Your resignation, coming so fast."

"Surely Admiral Sorkangh told you—"

"Afterwards, yes. Not at the time of the Board. I would not have expected that—I would have expected you to fight back—"

Rage exploded in her head like ships in combat, vast flowering shapes of colored light. "By *myself*? With no one from the family coming to my aid? With Sorkangh against me? You weren't *there*—no one was there for me—" The fury came out of her mouth, the debris of her hopes, her career. When she ran down, shaking with rage and sorrow, her aunt sat as quietly as before.

"Heris, you're still suffering, but you aren't yet seeing clearly . . . you did not *ask* any of us. Most of us didn't know until afterwards—I didn't—and you did not ask anyone directly for help. Did you?"

She had not. She had not thought she had to. She had expected them to come to her side without being asked.

"No . . . I didn't." Had that been wrong? She had never wanted to depend on the family connection, overuse it.

"No. And of course we taught you that, early on. That was our fault, perhaps. We wanted all you youngsters to be competent in your own right, not to lean on the family name. All: not just you, Heris."

"But—"

"But you still think someone should have come. I think so, myself. Your parents could have reacted faster. As I said, I don't know why they didn't."

"If I had asked, would they have come?" Heris asked.

"I don't know that, either. Until this mess, I had no reason to suspect them of being any less committed to you than you to them. Had you?"

"No . . . we hadn't seen much of each other for some years, what with assignments, but I thought everything was fine." Heris struggled for calm, getting her voice back under control.

"You're aware that Lord Thornbuckle has some antagonism to our family?"

"Yes—he mentioned it on Sirialis, and I never did find out more."

"Did you ask?" This was becoming monotonous.

"No," Heris said.

"Ah. You know, Heris, someone who wants senior command should cultivate a lively curiosity. Technical competence, even tactical competence, isn't enough. Strategy depends on intelligence, and that depends on asking the right questions."

Heris grimaced. "I felt—uneasy. I didn't want to seem—" Her voice trailed away; she couldn't define now how she'd felt that far back.

"Disloyal?" Her aunt did not smile. "You were angry, bitter, hurt, and yet you didn't want an outsider to think you were disloyal to the family?"

"I suppose."

"You always were an idealist . . . it's one of the things I liked about you. Well, it's time you knew where all that came from." Vida took a long swallow from the drink at her side. "This gets complicated. Every family has its black sheep, or at least its less competent members. Serranos are no exception. One entire branch left the military—flunked out of the Academy, one after another—and went into business. I suppose the best way to put it is that they conducted their business affairs with the same flair as the rest of us conduct wars."

"I never knew that."

"No—like most families, we don't advertise our black sheep. Sometimes we can't even agree on who they are. But I suspect it's this branch which taught Lord Thornbuckle to distrust the name. At any rate, back to your parents—"

"It's still not right."

Now the famous tilt of the head. "Are you telling me you never made mistakes?"

"No—of course I did, but—"

"No personal mistakes, nothing that would look bad if everyone knew—" Sarcasm, when she least deserved it.

Heris glared at her aunt, hoping to shock her. "I have a lover—he was enlisted, one of my crew that was hunted by Lepescu—and when we found each other again, we—"

"Good for you," Vida said. "The burden of perfection ruins more people than you'd think. He's with the yacht?"

"Yes. Of course we haven't—"

"Of course." Vida grimaced. "Heris, I'd hoped you'd learned how to be human—how to forgive yourself for being human. Do you love him?"

"Yes . . . I do . . . but not . . ." It was going to sound crass, but she found herself unwilling to lie to this aunt, so much like Cecelia in some ways, so much like herself in others. "But not more than Fleet," she finished.

"Ah. Yes. A Serrano problem, not unique to you. When you talk to your parents again, perhaps you'll notice how little time *they've* had together in the past fifty years. One solution, it seems to me, is to encourage your friend to take a commission."

"A commission?" She had said that to Petris, but she hadn't thought it would really be possible.

"Yes, you idiot. Did it not occur to you that there's a lot of good cess to spread around after your defense of Xavier? Commissioning a civilian—even a civilian who used to be enlisted—will cause no difficulty." Vida grinned. "And I for one want to meet this paragon who overcame your resistance."

✧   ✧   ✧

Her aunt had insisted that she must make the contact. Would they answer? And if they did, what would they say? She hoped to find that they were outsystem somewhere, a safe distance. Instead, the directory listed them not only insystem, but on the base itself. Aunt Vida's meddling, no doubt. Heris left her message in both stacks, and waited. Tried not to query her own stack every five minutes.

Finally she made herself go to lunch, then to the tailor's, for a new set of uniforms. When she came back, her desk's telltale blinked. Someone had left messages. Her heart thundered; she could hear nothing past the pulse in her ears. A long breath. She touched the controls. And there it was: a formal request for a personal meeting. Her breath caught in her throat. She couldn't. She had to.

"Heris." Her mother and father stood side by side, formally, their faces as wary as hers must be.

"Come in," she said. She couldn't bring herself to call them by name.

"Thank you for seeing us." That was her mother, as usual the spokesperson.

"I . . . talked to Aunt Vida."

A quick look passed between them, the kind of sidelong glance Heris remembered so well. Her father spoke at last. "Heris, I won't try to explain—"

She wanted to say something, but couldn't. The silence stretched, until she felt that her bones were drawn out thin as wires.

"I will," her mother said finally. "I'm not a born Serrano; I don't have to play this game." Her mother, the bronze eldest of a bronze clan, the Sunier-Lucchesi, whose roots went as far back in Fleet as any. "We heard it; we didn't believe it; we expected you to come and tell us what you wanted us to do."

"So it's my fault?" Heris managed to say it calmly.

"No," her mother said. "It is not your fault. It was our fault, for listening to the wrong advice, and for not realizing that you would not come. And saying we're sorry doesn't change it. If you want to stay angry, you can."

"That's true," said Heris. But she didn't feel angry; she felt tired. "What do you mean, wrong advice?"

"Admiral Sorkangh. He called your father, and said you were determined to work your own way out of it—that if you needed help, you'd call. We didn't know until afterwards that he'd turned."

"And then you listened to Aunt Vida, who said let me alone?"

Her father grimaced. "No, then I tried to figure out some way of killing Sorkangh without getting caught, or hurting anyone else. I told him—never mind what I told him; it's on both our records now. And I called in every family member I could find. Your Aunt Vida came up with a plan—I didn't like it, but she pointed out that I had made a royal mess already."

Heris could almost smile. She could imagine her Aunt Vida making them all squirm. She was glad.

"Did she tell you about it?" her mother asked.

"She told me that she'd ordered everyone to avoid contact once I'd resigned my commission."

"Did she tell you why?"

"No—but I guessed some of it. A Serrano she believed loyal, in a perfect position to strain blackmailers and enemy agents out of the stream . . ."

"Something like that. When you got Lepescu, she felt she'd proved her point. I didn't." Her mother grimaced. "I thought that should be the end of it; you'd earned it. But your Aunt Vida—"

Heris felt tired. "I wish—" She couldn't finish; she didn't know what she wished, except that none of this had happened.

"I'm sorry," her mother said again. "But I hope you'll forgive us, in time. If not now."

If not now, when? A family saying intended to spur reluctant youngsters to try the difficult, to achieve the impossible. Forgiveness was impossible, looked at one way—the pain was still pain, the loss was still loss. In another way . . . it had been too long already. She could tell that they had suffered too; she was not alone in that.

"I missed you," Heris said, and reached out for them. "I missed you so much—"

Vida Serrano, in uniform, behind her own desk, was back to being the admiral, full of advice for younger officers.

"If you get your mind straightened out—if you learn to ask the right questions—you'll be an admiral yourself, in a few years. As for now—you did well enough with *Vigilance* and *Paradox*. We'll see what you can do with a real battle group. I'll expect you to be ready to ship out as soon as you get *Vigilance* back out of the yards."

A battle group. *Vigilance?* A real—? She looked at her aunt, and Vida grinned, a wicked grin of delight at her niece's surprise. "You've earned that much; I can't get you a star yet, but if you handle the group the way I expect, it'll come. You'll be going straight into trouble, of course—"

"What about personnel?"

"Your lover?"

"All of them," Heris said, persisting.

"I thought I'd give you Arash Livadhi as second in command," her aunt said, ignoring her question. "That should make an interesting combination, you and Arash."

"He's senior." Heris had her doubts about Arash, even now.

"He was. You're getting a promotion, remember?"

What was the right question? Did you trust me? Did you care? Heris fumbled around in her memories of the past few years, trying to untangle what she burned to know from what her aunt would consider strategic thinking.

"How did I get that first job, with Lady Cecelia?"

"Good girl." Vida's grin widened, pure approval this time. "That took a bit of pressure on the employment agency. I wanted you to have flexibility, a ship with decent legs, a wealthy employer with an irregular schedule. Lady Cecelia was the first one to meet those qualifications."

"Did you know her?"

"Not really. We'd met years back at a function she probably doesn't remember. That didn't matter. The other things did. And, since you're now on the right track, I won't make you drag the rest out piecemeal. Yes, it was more than blind good luck or your talented scavenger's native ability that put certain items in his way when you needed them—those military grade scans, that weapons-control upgrade. You'd earned that when you got Lepescu. I made sure Livadhi got the assignment to carry the prince, rather than Sorkangh's grandson. And yes, Koutsoudas was planted on you—and a good thing, too. Not that we didn't need to get him away from the trouble he'd brewed before it cost us his life and Livadhi's ship. You don't know yet how ticklish things were in Fleet after the abdication. Or how many holes I had to try to plug with too few resources."

"You're going to explain?" Heris said, doing her best not to let sarcasm edge her voice.

Vida smiled, and ignored the question. "As for the yacht, you can tell Lady Cecelia that the Fleet would be delighted to purchase it from her at a good price—we can always use ships like that on covert ops, and I really admire the beacon switch your technicians put in her."

"Uh . . . yes, sir." Admiral Vida Serrano was back to being entirely admiral.

"Welcome home," the admiral said, with just enough softening. "Welcome home and good hunting."

❖   ❖   ❖

"No, I'm not 'trying to copy that Thornbuckle girl' as` you put it." Raffa stared her mother down. "I don't have her flair. I don't even want her flair. But I do want my own life, and that life is with Ronnie Carruthers."

"I suppose you'll do it whatever I say," her mother said.

"Yes." Raffa waited while her mother worked it all out. "Where are you going?"

"We're going to migrate over to the Polandre Group and take up an investor's claim."

"But Raffa—dear—you don't have to do that. It's all right about Ronnie; now that his parents and his aunt aren't feuding—"

"We want to do that. It's nothing to do with his parents or his aunt—we want our own lives, and we can have it out on the new lands." She hoped she didn't sound bitter; she wasn't bitter. Not really. But she wanted her children to have a chance to advance, without a layer of Rejuvenants over their heads, smothering them. She thought of the specs she'd seen, and found herself grinning. "It's not like it used to be," she said to her mother. "Pioneers these days have it much easier." Never mind that she and Ronnie had already decided to spend most of their money on a bigger grant, and fewer amenities. By the time her parents found out—if they ever did—she and Ronnie would have it all straightened out.

Her mother gave her a long, straight look. "You must have more of your Aunt Marta in you than I thought. Well, just be sure to keep a little back for escape if things go haywire. Your father and I didn't stay on Buriel—"

"*You* pioneered?"

"Not exactly. We tried to go out and run a subsidiary by ourselves—"

"And you think *I* take after Aunt Marta!" Raffa laughed. "Mother, you're a fraud."

"I don't want you to make our mistakes," her mother said, primly.

"We'll make our own," Raffa said.

"Keep a little back," her mother said. "But—I hope you never need it." She sounded almost wistful. "You will let us give you a good wedding, won't you?"

"As long as it's in the sculpture garden," Raffa said. "And I get to choose my own dress."

George stared moodily at the ceiling. It wasn't fair. Ronnie and Raffa running off to play pioneer over in the Polandres. Brun being mysterious and busy and having no time for old friends. Captain Serrano suddenly restored to her former rank and commanding a battle group, with no interest in helping a former Royal Aero-Space Service officer transfer his commission to the regs. The clones off wherever they were. Nobody to play with.

"Moping?" George jumped; he hadn't heard his father come in.

"I feel left out," he said, and wished he hadn't. His father had that knack of extracting what you least wanted to say, fatal for many a witness.

His father came around and looked at him; he realized that his father looked older and more worn than he had seen him before. "Time to grow up, George. They have."

"It was fun," George said. He didn't like the petulance in his own voice.

"Yes. But it's over. If you want to enjoy the rest of your life, you'll have to find another way." That famous voice, which could sting like acid in a cut, or croon like a lover, spoke to him without sarcasm or contempt or anything but plain reason. He could have defended himself better against the sting or the croon.

"I don't know what to do," George said. "I'm not like Ronnie—I don't have Raffa, and Brun isn't the girl I grew up with anymore."

"You're not that boy, either, though you don't seem to know it yet. George, tell me—why didn't the clones kill you?"

George snorted. "I think I talked them to death, nearly, and it confused their circuits."

"And back on Sirialis—you influenced the men who captured you—"

"Not well enough. I got shot in the gut anyway." He shivered; whatever the experts said about the impossibility of remembering pain, he would never forget his.

"Well, then—what do you really like to do?"

"Talk," George said promptly, surprising himself. Then, more slowly, "Talk, and . . . and make people do things. Just by talking at them. Sometimes it backfires."

"Yes," his father said. "Sometimes it does, but when it works . . . you know you've just described my career."

"Law?! I wouldn't be any good at that!"

"Because you're lazy, self-indulgent, and sometimes drive people crazy?"

"That's not how I'd have put it, but yes."

"George, you've defined yourself in relation to Ronnie and Buttons and their friends for years. Rich, idle, spoiled, all that. But you're not, really. That's why they find you odious. Not because you are idle and spoiled, but because you pretend to be, and they scent it like hounds scent blood. For instance—suppose you tell me about Varioster Limited versus Transgene."

George scowled, and hesitated. It had popped into his head, but he didn't like where his father was headed. He gave a precis of the case, then said, "The only reason I know about it is that you left the brief out one time when I was trying to find your signature pad so I could get a signed excuse for class."

His father grinned. "George, most kids who want to forge a signature simply use a copy algorithm in their notepads. They don't wade through thousand-page briefs, and remember them well enough to give a cogent precis twelve years later."

"Was it that far back?" It surprised him; he'd thought it was only seven or eight, and said so.

"Not quite," his father said. "So you remember that as well, do you?" Tricked again. At least it had been by an expert. "You might not find it as boring as you think, George. After all, you've been sneaking looks at my work for years—has it been that bad?"

"Well . . . no." But law school would be. He could just imagine day after day with a cube reader.

"The thing is," his father said, "when you're in law, everyone assumes the odiousness comes from that. And you can save most of it for the courtroom."

"Law school . . ." he muttered.

"Law school is where I met your mother," his father said. "It's not all cube readers."

The ginger-haired girl he vaguely remembered from that Hunt Ball grinned at him from across the room when he went in to take the placement exam. She had certainly grown up, he thought. He had enjoyed that evening, but he hadn't seen her since he'd left Sirialis. Now—she winked at him and he winked back. *She'd* never called him odious. He looked at the exam, and realized it was full of things he actually knew something about.

Brigdis Sirkin reported to the crew lounge of the great liner, hoping her luck had changed. Lady Cecelia had found her this berth. She had said goodbye to Brun and Meharry and the rest the day before, over in the Regular Space Service section of Rockhouse Major. Now she was committed to a civilian life. She had few regrets.

"Brigdis Sirkin?" That was the third mate, checking crew aboard. "Welcome aboard! We've heard about you; we're all glad to have you on our ship."

Here they found her exotic. Her adventures convinced them she was extraordinary, someone of exceptional courage and wit. As the weeks passed, Sirkin relaxed, finding new friends and a lot less tension. She found it hard to define the difference; the crew were all highly competent, and the standard of courtesy was as high. But the great ship had polish without an edge, like a ceremonial, a work of art and not a weapon. She liked that. She was glad to have known Meharry and Brun and the others, glad to know what protected her and her crewmates . . . but even more glad that she was no longer trying to live up to that standard.

The curtained alcove gave them privacy; the cooks gave them the best food for light-years around. They ate slowly, taking the time to savor every nuance of flavor. Their table conversation lingered on the antics of favorite relatives: nieces and nephews, for the most part. The waiter, carrying away the remains of the fish course, commented to the kitchen worker who received the tray, "It's so nice to see real quality. Ladies who appreciate good food, who take the time to be courteous to the staff. Just sitting there talking about their families without a care in the world. Reminds me of my own auntie." Later, when they were giggling over something he didn't understand, he reported again. "Perhaps a bit tipsy—all that champagne, you know—but they're rather sweet, if you know what I mean. Perfectly harmless."

The End